Chapwell

M A Turner

Copyright © 2022 M A Turner All rights reserved

The characters and events portrayed in this book are mostly fictitious. Some characters are based on people I have known and been inspired by in my life. Some are genuine historical characters as befits the tale. Any similarity to real persons, living or dead, is not intended to cause grief by the author.

No part of this book may be reproduced, or stored in a retrieval system, or transmitted in any form or by any means, electronic, mechanical, photocopying, recording, or otherwise, without express written permission of the publisher.

maturner.co.uk

Cover design by: pro_ebookcovers
Formatting by Marissa Lete: marissalete.com

I dedicate this book to my English Teacher Philip Turner, who I found inspirational when I was at school back in the early 70's. Had I known then what I know now, things may have been different. I learnt that he also wrote books and led a very interesting life. He wrote under the name Stephen Chance. Oh, and he was a really nice person and tremendous teacher. I shall never forget him.

Chapwell

Chapter One: The Girl in the Chair; present day 1
Chapter Two: Twenty Years ago 7
Chapter Three: 10 Years ago 18
Chapter Four: 5 Years ago 34
Chapter Five: 6 Months ago 45
Chapter Six: Present day, Emily 63
Chapter Seven: Present day, Emily and Jane 79
Chapter Eight: David 100
Chapter Nine: Sandra 112
Chapter Ten: Threat 129
Chapter Eleven: Dead 151
Chapter Twelve: DNA 174
Chapter Thirteen: Missing 200
Chapter Fourteen: Found 214
Chapter Fifteen: Rescue 239
Chapter Sixteen: A new life? 255
Chapter Seventeen: Dragon 277
Chapter Eighteen: Dad 308
Chapter Nineteen: London 318
Chapter Twenty: The Tower 330
Chapter Twenty-One: The Lady Margaret 341

Chapter One

The Girl in the Chair; present day

Jane didn't know what had awoken her, she was dreaming quite contentedly, wandering through the garden, full of colourful flowers, the sun shining warmly on her shoulders. The calming sound of the bees gave the fantasy a feeling of total peace. If she could have seen herself sleeping, she would notice the tranquil smile on her own face. But her eyes were wide open now, her ears alert, searching for a sound. A sound, the sound that had woken her, but there was only silence. The gentle cushioned tick of the grandfather clock in the hallway downstairs assured her that she had not suddenly been afflicted with deafness. There was not even a creak from the old house. It was the sort of silence that appears to emit its own sound. What was it that woke her she thought? It was almost dark, almost, but not quite. The moon was full but low, a sliver of its light sneaking past the far edge of the heavy curtain creating a band of light, but not light, a glimmer, by the door opposite the bed. The bed was old, very old, she knew that, it had been there when she was a child. Her Aunt's bed, and who's before that even she didn't know. But it was soft and warm. She had been comforted by it in the past, saved from the ravages of a thunderstorm, embraced by her aunt. Still, she could hear nothing.

The room was silent, nothing to tell her why she was wide awake. But she knew that something had disturbed her sleep.

An owl hooted in the trees outside making her jump, the sound amplified by the concentrated silence. Perhaps that was it? She had slept through a lot worse, foxes playing, cats fighting, so an owl hooting was not the cause. She concentrated her eyes and, yes, there by the door, there was something, the moonlight not quite bright enough to see clearly, cast a pale glow down the wall by the door. She could see a bright pinprick of light on the door handle and the key in the lock, but there, next to the door was the chair, the outline of which was obscured. A faint shadow. A shadow so faint that she strained her eyes, squinting to see it through the darkness. Someone was sitting on the chair, a small person. The outline seemed to become clearer the more she concentrated, a head and shoulders, a dark outline against the wallpaper, no other feature visible, just the outline. Now she was scared. A flicker of fright pinched her heart and shot to her head making her eyes grow wide, her body shocked by a sudden heat, her skin prickled, her breathing stopped. She slowly, slowly moved to sit upright, not taking her eyes from the chair. The outline becoming smudged by the fright but again, it clears to become, yes, a person, there was a person sitting in the chair. She fancies she can see long wavy hair on the shoulders of a girl, yes, it's a girl. The image building in her mind, arms resting on the girl's lap, her hands crossed. It is definitely a girl. "Hello?" Jane asks in a faint, slightly hoarse whisper. Nothing, nothing changes, no movement, no sound, just the shadow of the girl in the chair. Her face is dark, no features can be seen, almost as if there is no face, just the outline of her head and shoulders, hair flowing down over them. Jane sits staring at this shadowed shape. She is absolutely convinced that there is someone sitting on the chair, but there can't be, can there? She lives here alone, she knows she is alone but she knows she can see a girl sat there, indeed she can feel that there is a girl sat there, a feeling of warmth, of trust and comfort, she begins to relax and studies the shape more closely. The girl would be about the same height as her and about the same build, maybe slightly smaller but still she cannot see a face but there is a face, she knows there is a face and she knows it is kind and friendly, pretty and unblemished but perhaps a little sad. Eyes that could melt butter. But still, she cannot see a face only a dark void outlined by the wavy shadow of her hair. Jane reached slowly across towards the nightstand with one hand, towards the light switch that will end the mystery, end the fright. But she hesitates. Does she want to end this illusion? This dream? She continues to stare at the girl's outline hoping that she will get a response. Again, she asks "hello?", expecting an answer, this time a little clearer, a little brighter, but still nothing. No movement, no sound. "I am going to turn on the light" she said, "I want to see you. I want to talk to you. Can you hear me? Can you see me?" Still nothing. Her hand moves closer to the light switch, creeping across the nightstand hesitantly, poised above it. She looks towards the shadow, willing the girl to speak, to move, to do something, to just show her that she is there. Her finger touches the switch, the girls hand lifts from her lap, just slightly, just enough, just 'don't'. But it's too late the switch has made, the light flashes on. The gold glow from the small bulb is enough to light the room, just enough to illuminate the chair, the empty chair. There is no girl, no shadow, nothing. Jane quickly turns the light off but her eyes have been blinded by the small lamp, the room is now totally dark. She sits still, upright, her hand remains by the light switch, waiting. Waiting for her eyes to adjust to the darkness, waiting for the moonlight to illuminate the chair. Slowly, slowly her eyes become accustomed to the darkness and, yes, the moonlight is stealing back into the room, she can see the sliver by the curtain, the band of light down the wall appears, moving the darkness away from the chair. But the chair is empty, no shadow, no flowing hair. No girl. Still, she doesn't move, willing things to go back as they were, for the girl to reappear. Nothing. The shadow of the chair is clearly visible against the wall, a sharp outline no longer softened by the wavy hair.

 Jane felt grief. She felt that a connection had been made. She had seen a girl sat on the chair, she had seen her hand move, a small hand, a small gesture but a movement that could not be denied. The owl hooted. Again, Jane jumped, she shook her head, her hands moved through her hair. She pulled the quilt up and rested against the pillow. "What just happened" she thought. "Was that a ghost? What was it? I saw a girl, I felt a girl, I can still feel her, a girl sat on the chair? I saw her hand move, she moved her hand, I think she tried to stop me turning on the light". Again, she looked towards the door, her eyes becoming more accustomed to the darkness but there was nothing, just the door, the sharp pinprick of light on the handle, the outline of the key, and the chair, the empty chair. But then, softly, she could smell a hint of lavender, fresh lavender. The smell became stronger and unmistakable, pleasant, relaxing, all around her. She loved the smell of lavender and deliberately disturbed it if she was in the garden just to release the fragrance.

She lay there thinking, enjoying the fragrance, still looking at the chair, willing the girl to reappear, but tiredness took over and she fell into a long, settled and solid sleep, no dreams, no awakenings, just undisturbed, lavender induced sleep.

Jane awoke, a Blackbird and a Thrush competing to bring the morning to her attention in a most pleasant way, right outside the window. The sun now knifing past the edge of the curtain slashing a sharp line down the wall by the door, right through the chair as if to cut it in half. The chair is empty, its stark outline vivid, but quickly she remembered the events of the night. No, it was not a dream. A dream is something that she sometimes remembered but she knew not to be true. A dream does not involve things she knew, they diverged, divided and confused. Dreams were sometimes bad, sometimes she wished she could go back to them as they were delightful but they were dreams. The girl, the girl on the chair was real, she could feel the girl, she never felt the people in her dreams like that. She could feel the girl as if she were still there, still in the house. She could feel her, stronger than anything she had felt before. She could still see her hair, the face that she could not see but could see, the slightly sad eyes, the unblemished skin and the dark wavy hair. She could even smell the lavender fragrance from the night before. She slowly drew back the quilt and got out of bed walking towards the window, feeling the soft oak under her feet, eyes on the chair. She grabbed the join of the curtains, hesitated and looked back at the chair, then threw the curtains open, the sun exploded into the room lighting the entire space, the bed, the nightstand, the dresser and the wardrobes, the oak floor polished to a deep conker colour with the dainty patterned rugs and the door, the solid oak door with its black doorknob and heavy brass key in the lock, its massive hinges showing it to be strong and reliable. And, the chair, the small occasional chair that would be more at home in the church than in this heavy room. It stood there barely touching the floor; its soft cushioned seat slightly indented from years of use. She walked over to it, stood over it, stared at it expecting to see something, something that would show her that she had not imagined the whole episode. The light in the room had invaded her head, dulling the sense of the girl, it was daylight. Ghosts, spectres, witches all vanish with the invasion of the sun. But still Jane knew, she knew that there had been a girl sat on the chair. She knelt slowly before it, inspecting it, examining the legs, the back and the cushioned seat, the indent. Was that made by a gentle, body as it had sat there looking at her in the darkness or was it just the indent from years of use. The stained and tanned wood of the chair showed its age, worn in places, darkened from many hands, the odd chip, smoothed by time. She touched the seat, smoothing her hand across the fabric almost expecting to feel the warmth left by the girl. But there, there on the floor just under the chair between the legs and the wall. A hair, just one. A dark hair, long and wavy, lay starkly upon the oak boards. Jane went to pick it up, reaching under the legs but stopped. She thought about the origin of the hair. Where had it come from? She knew in her mind where she would love it to have come from but it could have been from anywhere. It was not from Aunt Beryl though. Aunt Beryl's hair was a delightful silver, it shimmered in the sun; her hair had always been that colour. Jane had never known it to be any different. And, what would it be doing here, under the chair? It could have been someone from the solicitors or just a casual visitor. No, no, no. Jane was just trying to convince herself that it had come from anywhere but the girl. The girl from last night. The girl she knew had been sat there. She again, reached under the chair and gently, so gently picked up the hair with her forefinger and thumb, gently so as not to damage it, gently so as to preserve it. She brought it closer, it hung in front of her eyes, so dark and with those slight curves in it, curves that exactly matched those of the girl on the chair. There was no doubt in her mind that this hair came from that small head and was until recently framing that unseen face in the shadow.

    Jane looked closer under the chair, inspecting the floor for any other evidence but the boards shone back, clean and polished. She slowly stood and walked over to the dresser. sliding open the drawer in the base of the mirror she gently lowered the hair into it, watching it curve into the base of the drawer to lie still. Closing it, she turned back towards the window, seeing the morning as it was, streaming through the mullioned window with its paned leaded glass, dust motes hovering in the shafts of light as they pierced the room into the corners. Jane felt that she was different now, different from the woman who had entered the room the previous night. She had a new feeling in her heart. A warm feeling, a feeling of friendship and love, trust and companionship. Something she never thought she would feel again. She smiled to herself and walked over to the bed, picking up her dressing gown, she slid it on. Standing in front of the window, placing her hands on the sill she looked out over the garden, the well-tended garden with its pretty flower borders, tidy lawns surrounded by shrubs and trees. The sun, wakening the daisies, warming the faint dew on the grass, was bright and clear, its warmth felt through the glass and reddening her face making her squint. She looked down to her hands and there, right between them was a small bunch of freshly picked lavender. She picked it up and brought it to her nose, inhaling the strong fragrance that she loved so much. She knew that she had not put it there, she had not even cut any from the garden as yet, but there it was, a freshly picked bunch of lavender, in her hand. She placed it back on the windowsill, turned and opened the door to start her day, glancing down at the chair as she passed, a smile warming her face.

Chapter Two

Twenty Years ago

The car drew up to the gate, Jane was peering through the passenger door window, straining against the seatbelt, her heart fluttering with excitement as she knew she was going to enjoy her holiday. In fact, she enjoyed every holiday here at Chapwell House. It meant peace and love and fun and a comfy bed and delicious food. Well, everything was always just perfect here.

As the car stopped, Jane saw Aunt Beryl standing at the small wooden gate, open and welcoming, a perfectly trimmed hedge either side stretched along the road marking the frontage of this magical place, a narrow grass verge spotted with daisies demarking the house from the road. Jane opened the door and leapt from the car, running to a smiling Aunt Beryl, arms wide, the comfort of a hug gave her a feeling of relief and warmth.

"Hello chicken" said Beryl "My, you have grown so much, how old are you now?" Aunt Beryl knew exactly how old Jane was but Jane would always want to tell her how much more grown up she was.

"I'm Eight and three quarters" came the reply.

"My goodness said Beryl, you'll be all grown up before we know it. Now, let's get your bags out of the car and we'll go and have a cup of tea and a—"

"A scone?" asked Jane, face beaming, before Beryl could complete the sentence.

Yes, chicken, a scone, freshly baked just now and still warm"

"Oh, yes!" Exclaimed Jane punching the air. "And do we have jam?"

"Yes chicken," smiled Beryl "there is always Jam, and before you ask, it's the raspberry jam I made from last year's crop. Now, come on, you go inside and take the small bag with you. I'll be in just now but I need to speak to your mother."

Jane picked up her small bag, the bag containing her books, her wash bag and all those small bits and pieces that made her life complete. She skipped down the path, paved with large flag stones lined with colourful flower beds stopping briefly to look up at the house, wide with two large mullioned windows either side of the front door. Two equally large windows on the second floor sat to each side of the landing window. The old red brick deep and warm. The gabled rooves towering above with stout chimneys at each end. She never got bored with looking at the house. It was large and majestic, old and mysterious, warm and welcoming. She turned and looked back at Beryl, a huge smile on her face. Beryl smiled back at her and gently pointed towards the open front door. Jane continued along the path swinging the small bag and through the stout dark oak door. She always thought of the front door as the magical entrance to a different world. A world of the old. Clocks, paintings, lights on the walls and wood panelling everywhere. She stood in the hallway, her feet feeling the cool uneven floor, the huge flag stones, worn smooth and rounded by years of use. A clear path of wear reflecting the light coming from the kitchen door at the end. The staircase to the right stood tall, wide and solid turning towards the upper gallery landing. The banister so big she could not get her two hands around it. The Large oak acorn carved many years ago sat atop the bottom newel post. She could not help caressing it, she loved the intricate carving of the acorn cup, the smooth skin of the nut, even to the small pip on the top which was so worn it had nearly disappeared. She looked around again. Nothing had changed, the grandfather clock stood upright and commanding, it's gentle tick matching the swinging pendulum which made her think that time went slower here than anywhere else. The stair carpet runner was the same as always, worn in the centre, the rods holding it firmly in place. She smiled to herself, accepting that the house and everything in it was exactly as it had always been, nothing had changed. She trotted up the wide stairs to her room. Turning the large iron knob, she opened the heavy oak door which creaked gently. Standing on the threshold she looked inside, peering around the door as if she was expecting something to have changed. But, no, it was just as she had left it. Neat and tidy, clean and bright, comfortable and warm. She knew that Aunt Beryl had made it up, washed the bed linen, vacuumed the floor, polished the windows and made it just the way she liked it. She finally walked in slowly, placing her bag on the chair by the window glancing out into the summer garden resplendent with colourful flowers. Opening her bag, she started the unpacking process. Her book on the nightstand, her washbag on the deep, wide window sill. Her slippers placed carefully by the bed, her brush and comb on the dressing table. She drew out the stool, sat in front of the dressing table mirror and looked at herself. She felt as if she were a Princess with her own room, her very own room that was always hers, always here and always welcoming. The sun streamed in, lighting her face, making her smile. Her heart fluttered slightly as she anticipated the days ahead, excited, wondering what she would learn this time. She always learnt something new. It might be a new plant in the garden or a new biscuit recipe. She was content and happy as she looked around her room with its solid oak floor, tarnished by years of use, polished to a cool shine with pretty rugs adding colour. Her wardrobe, big enough to contain a complete adventure. She sighed and secretly thanked Chapwell for being there for her.

Beryl watched Jane as she made her way down the path, saw her stop and take in the house. This pleased her. She loved Chapwell House, always had, they both loved the house. But then it would be very difficult not to love it. It was everything a home should be. It provided warmth and security from its hundreds of years standing, outliving most things around it, except, perhaps the massive oak tree in the garden. It had history, history that went back beyond anyone's lifetime. It remained strong as if to go on forever.

As Jane vanished into the house, Beryl turned to Jane's Mother who was still stood by the open door of the car. "Would you like—"

"No Beryl" came the curt interruption "No, I must get off, I have so much to do. I'll collect her in a fortnight."

"Okay" said Beryl, looking down at her feet, her hands clasped tightly in front of her. She rubbed them together in an attempt to relieve the hint of anger that threatened to grow inside her. "I'll see you in a few weeks then?" No response. Jane's Mother just climbed back into the car, started the engine and drove off. Not a wave, a goodbye, a thank you or any kind of acknowledgment. Beryl stood, her eyes followed the car as it sped down the lane, far too fast for her liking as it disappeared around the corner, a cloud of dust the only evidence of its presence. She watched for a moment more, seeing the dust settling, frowned, bent to pick up the larger bag and turned towards the house, feeling somewhat disheartened but then happy that Jane was here to stay which always gave her pleasure, a smile returning.

Beryl went through the front door, shutting it behind her with a solid thump. Stopping at the bottom of the stairs she placed the bag down and called to Jane, her hand atop the acorn. "I'm just putting the kettle on and we'll have tea. Don't be long now."

"Just coming" came the excited reply, "just coming". Jane, her unpacking now complete, went to the window again, looking out across the garden, the trees and the fields beyond. All tended very tidily but she knew that there would be work to do in the garden with her aunt. There was always something to do in the garden regardless of what day it was or what season. Jane loved the garden, it had everything. Trees and the biggest was the oak tree. It was majestic and strong, stout and wide and so very old. There were quiet wild corners where the squirrels could be seen, the Blackbirds would be in there scuffing the ground looking for worms. There was always something to see. The distraction was endless but broken by another shout from downstairs. Tea was ready.

She raced down the stairs, turned the corner and walked into the kitchen. "I can hear when you run down the stairs. You be careful. We wouldn't want a broken arm, leg or neck, now would we." said Beryl with a slightly stern look on her face enhancing the pleasant wrinkles around her eyes, the same wrinkles that appeared when she smiled which was nearly always. The table was laid up with an elegant, crisp, white, table cloth, a place setting with plates, knives, spoons and in the centre a plate of freshly baked scones beside a jar of the very best raspberry jam and tub of clotted cream.

The tea was poured into decorative bone china cups and saucers. The proper way to do it. They didn't always have cups and saucers, just when it was scones and jam. Any other time and it would be a mug and the tea, well it just didn't taste quite the same from a mug.

Not a word was spoken between the two of them for the entire process of consuming the scones. Looks were passed between them. An understanding smile can mean so much when you are enjoying an experience as much as tea and scones.

"Oh, Aunt Beryl, they were delicious, just like always. They are the best." said Jane.

"Glad you liked them" came the reply. "Once you've finished your tea, we'll get your big bag upstairs and unpack that as well. Then we can go and have a wander around the garden so that you can see how it is."

"Okay", said Jane. "Where is Uncle John? Is he down at the shop?"

"Yes", said Beryl. "After we've had a wander around the garden, we can take a walk down to the village to see him if you want to, he'll like that."

"Yes" said Jane excitedly. "That's a plan."

Once the last of the tea was poured from the pot and drunk, the table was cleared and they went upstairs to Jane's room to unpack the big bag. Within minutes this was done and they were in the garden taking the tour. There were many borders and flower beds, all filled with the most colourful and scented plants and everywhere there was lavender, each border, each bed had a lavender bush in it and the path through the centre was lined with it. The buzzing from the bees and flies was a testament to how friendly the garden was for them. Butterflies flitted from flower to flower, bed to border and up into the sky, the bright blue sky, small fleecy clouds sailing along on the very slight breeze made for a perfect atmosphere. All this made Jane so happy, this was her happy place. No school, no having to make do with a small untidy garden to play in and not being constantly shouted at. Here she was relaxed and would spend her entire life here if she were able.

But it wasn't like that, she knew. Nevertheless, she would make the most of it while she was here, she had two weeks to enjoy it. All the things she loved doing she could do here. She could wander around the garden when she wanted. She could help her aunt with any work that needed doing. She could sit and read. They always played games in the evening, listening to a play on the radio, all three of them, until the news came on the television. Uncle John always watched the news and during the day there was always a radio on when Uncle John was home.

There was nothing complicated about this life, it was simple and happy, entertaining and relaxing. And the food, well the food was amazing. It was always cooked fresh and all hand made. Jane was learning the fundamentals of cooking whilst she stayed here and it was fascinating, plus you got to eat it when it was finished.

"So", asked Beryl turning to Jane, her hands on her hips. "What do you think of the garden then? Is it all okay? Have I looked after it?"

"Of course, it is." came the reply. "It is always so beautiful. All the colours of the flowers, the lavender and the bees and butterflies. I wish I could always stay here."

"Well," said Beryl "You know you can't, you have school and you must do well at school so that you can get a job and perhaps you too can have a house and garden like this".

"I know" said Jane, a frown wrinkling her face as she looked up at her aunt a slight squint in her eye.

"But don't forget," said Beryl "you can come here any time you like, you are always welcome as long as your mother agrees."

Beryl knew that Jane's Mother would always agree. Not that it was a problem, she knew that Jane's home life was not as good as it should be so it was always a pleasure to take Jane in for as long as she could. She knew that she could always educate Jane. Jane was receptive and pleasant, polite and well behaved, taking in all the basic behaviours needed for modern life. She just hoped it would all pay off and Jane could lead a happy life, one that was meant for her.

Once the garden tour was complete, they wandered down the quiet narrow lane to the village. Seeing the birds in the trees who appeared to be following them and chattering to them as they walked in the quiet sunshine. Beryl and John owned the paper shop which sold a lot of the basic things needed in life. Newspapers, tobacco, sweets and drinks, a few items of home-made foods, generally those made by the villagers and bought, generally by the villagers but it meant a small amount of business was generated and everyone got to sample the skills and labours of their neighbours.

Opening the door, the entrance bell jingled and within a few seconds Uncle John came from the back. On seeing Jane, a huge smile lit up his large, round, salt and pepper bearded face. He was a happy man, always happy. Everyone liked John and John like everyone. Always dressed in tweed, the state of the weather determined whether he wore both waistcoat and jacket or just waistcoat. Today was a waistcoat day. He came to the front of the shop and opened his arms, Jane walked to him and he picked her up, kissed her on the cheek and held her tight. "How's my little Jane then?" His beard smothering Jane's face. She leant back from the embrace and stated in no uncertain terms that she was eight and three quarters. "Oh!" said John "Not so little then? But you'll always be my little Jane, it doesn't matter how old you are."

They chatted enthusiastically about the garden and what wildlife had visited since her last stay. "Well," said John, "I'll be home at the usual time but here, take this jar of honey, it's from Mrs Philips so we can have it for breakfast tomorrow". Jane took the jar of honey carefully and waved goodbye, collected Aunt Beryl, who had stood quietly by the door listening to the two of them, a constant smile on her face. They slowly walked back up to Chapwell, all the while hand in hand listening to the birds and gently chatting about the village around them.

The afternoon was spent in the garden, a bit of weeding, dead heading and a check on the greenhouse ensuring all was well there. Once that was done it was evening duties in the kitchen, helping her aunt prepare dinner for them all, ready just in time for Uncle John to arrive where they sat quietly for their evening meal. The kitchen was large as befit the house, dominated by the table, centred in the room. It was a huge table littered with the signs of wear but kept clean and polished. The table was cleared and the washing up done. Jane helped her aunt and uncle, apart from the larger, heavier items which were left for uncle John. They spent the rest of the evening sat at the kitchen table playing cards and scrabble right up until Jane started nodding. "I think you're ready for your bed," said Beryl. Jane agreed, nodding her head, a long yawn escaping her. She had had a long and exciting day but welcomed the opportunity to go to her large and comfy bed, a short read and then to sleep.

Having kissed her aunt and Uncle goodnight she climbed the stairs to her room. Once the bedroom door was shut, she knew she would not be disturbed. No traffic, no-one shouting down the street and no neighbours arguing. She closed the heavy, dark red curtains and got herself ready for bed. Her ablutions done she climbed in and picked up her book. Two pages later she was fast asleep, the bedside light still on, the book resting on the bed cover.

Jane woke sharply, her eyes wide but it was just a fox in the field barking. The book had gone and the light was off. She turned and put the light back on, the book was right there on the nightstand. "I guess Aunt Beryl turned it off" she thought, not reading much into it at all. She returned the room to darkness, rolled over and resumed her slumber.

A knock on the door woke her in the morning. She could see the sunlight framing the window around the dark, heavy curtains.

"Breakfast will be ready in a minute," she heard Aunt Beryl say through the door.

"Okay" croaked Jane sleepily, sitting up and rubbing the night from her eyes. She slowly pushed back the covers, grabbed her washbag and carried out her morning ablutions, got dressed and went down for some longed-for toast and honey.

The table was laid and the teapot was just being placed in the centre as she came into the kitchen. Uncle John was sat at the head of the table as usual, the large carver giving him an air of respectability and strength. A large plate of fresh toast was brought over and placed by the teapot, they all selected a slice and started on the first meal of the day, the chink of knife on plate the only sound. The honey was delicious, sweet and aromatic, reminding Jane of all the bees in the garden. "Thank you for turning my light off last night Aunty, I must have fallen asleep reading."

"You are a one" responded Beryl. "But it wasn't me, you must have woken and done that yourself. We went to bed not that long after you and we saw the light under the door so we just assumed you were still reading." This mystified Jane as she was absolutely sure that she had not turned off the light nor placed her book back on the nightstand but she shrugged, accepting it was possible that she had done so without knowing.

Jane spent a delightful two weeks with her aunt and Uncle, though in truth they weren't actually her aunt and Uncle but merely family friends, the friendship, however went back years. Way too soon it was time to return to her life with her mother. Not that she really minded. She always looked forward to returning to school with her friends. It was a nice school and she enjoyed the learning experience. She always learnt a lot from Beryl and John during her holidays. Aunt Beryl knew a lot about history and John, a lot about the world in general and this gave her a greater insight into the world and what it was about. She particularly enjoyed the history, tales from long ago, including Chapwell. It was a very old house which had been built on the foundations of an older house. This she knew as her aunt had told her a lot about the history of the house, some of the people who had lived in it in the past and where the name Chapwell came from. It was the name of a family that occupied the house and land in the mid seventeenth century. This is Chapwell as it stands today, mellow and warm, settled and mature. A house that she loved so much and hoped would stand for centuries to come.

Sadly, for her, it was time to leave. Her Mother drew up in her car right outside the gate. Beryl and Jane brought out her bags to place in the boot of the car. Jane's Mother, Sandra did not even get out of the car, just flipped the lever to release the boot latch. The bags were placed in the car and Jane jumped in the back. Beryl closed the boot lid and moved around to the driver's door and tapped gently on the window. Slowly it lowered and Sandra looked up at Beryl scowling. "I was hoping to have a word Sandra" she said.

"There's nothing to say Beryl, the situation remains. Jane can come and stay any time she likes but that is it. You try this on every time I come, either to drop her off or pick her up. We have no need for pleasantries, it is as it is so we'll leave it like that shall we?" The look on Sandra's face was pure anger, tight lips and knitted eyebrows.

Beryl stood upright, folding her arms and looking around. "Very well," said Beryl. "Jane is welcome any time; you only need to call as you know. John and I always look forward to her coming and you know how much she loves it here."

"But that's the thing, isn't it? Jane has as much right here as you do, doesn't she?" Sandra's voice was now raised and bordering on shouting.

Beryl, not wanting to escalate the situation stepped back from the car. "Well, we'll leave it there then." said Beryl. "We'll wait to hear from you."

The window raised slowly as Sandra started the engine, put the car in gear and sped down the road, again leaving a cloud of dust. "I wish she wouldn't drive like that" Thought Beryl. Again, her eyes followed the car down the lane till it went out of view around the corner. She stood for a few seconds more and walked slowly back to the house. Closing the small wooden gate and latching it she bowed her head sorrowfully, leaning on it, she started to cry, her hand went up to cover her eyes, not from anyone in the vicinity but for herself. She hated the feeling she got when Jane had to leave, knowing what she was going back to. A life that really shouldn't be given to such a talented, polite and friendly young girl. Recovering her dignity, she turned back to follow the path to the house, closed the front door and went into the kitchen. She sat down where John was waiting with a fresh pot of tea.

"I know" he said, placing the teapot on the table and putting his arms around her. "I wish we could change things but Sandra is so stubborn and tied up. I could not come out there to see Jane going back to that, it breaks my heart. I would just get angry and I don't like being angry."

Beryl looked up at his quiet bushy face and smiled. "She's the only person I have known that makes you angry John. But I do know why. She just will not talk to us. There is so much we could do for her but she just refuses. As long as we can continue having Jane stay here, I'll be happy."

"Agreed," said John. "We'll just have to continue with this battle and hope that Jane does not suffer. We'll just have to make sure that there is always somewhere she can go, somewhere she can feel safe and loved. I'm not saying Sandra does not love her but I don't think the relationship is going to improve, particularly as Jane grows up. Questions may be asked. We'll just have to handle it the best we can."

They sat and drank their tea in silence up until The Archers came on the radio.

Chapter Three

10 Years ago

Jane was at work in the library as usual. She enjoyed the job as it allowed her to pursue her hobby. A hobby which a lot of her friends thought a bit strange but she really enjoyed delving into the history of the British Monarchy, particularly the reign of Henry VIII and Elizabeth I as these periods of rule changed the course of British culture and religion more than any other time. She spent many an afternoon whilst the rain pelted against the window, researching the detail of the reign of Henry VIII. She found the relationship between Henry and his closest aides the most fascinating. If it hadn't been documented it certainly would not have been believed but so many historians had carried out and documented so much research into this period of time it could be nothing less than fact. Some of which she found totally unbelievable. The biggest rush she got from this was to pick an individual event and try to imagine what would have happened if it had never taken place. For example, what if Anne Boleyn had actually given birth to a healthy baby boy? Elizabeth I would never have taken the throne. History from that point onwards would be so different. Britain would have been changed beyond imagination.

Today was one of those days. The library was quiet, the weather had kept people in their homes. The library in its current form could not compete with the internet, even though they had all the modern facilities for people to use and research. Mostly it came down to a handful of regulars on a handful of computer stations quietly sifting through the immense library in the cloud. Today was even quieter though, only two students working away in opposite corners of the room. But that was when she could be so productive in her own research. No distractions.

Jane never attended University; it was one of those things that she thought would not suit her. Not that she didn't want to learn but she felt that more could be achieved if she carried out her education to degree level using the Open University which would allow her to carry on working. Her hobby became her passion and the subject of her degree course in History. At least then she could justify the subject matter to herself as well as anyone else. She didn't have that many friends, a few from school but they did not have the same enthusiasm for the world around them like Jane. They preferred to be out partying, shopping and so many other things that young people tended to do. Jane liked to holiday in the countryside, mainly at Chapwell, but sometimes she would take herself off into the mountains and walk quietly among the majestic peaks and lakes knowing that her time amongst them was but a microsecond in the life of a mountain which made her feel quite humble. She preferred her own company in these adventures as she had never met anyone who appreciated the countryside like she did. She enjoyed taking it all in at the point in time that she was there. It was difficult to engorge herself with all around as there was so much, and she never knew if she would ever come back to take in the bits she may have missed. Photographs were okay but for her, there were the sounds, the smells and the little details that can only be seen on close inspection. The wren singling loudly from atop a large boulder, its voice amplified by the surrounding rocks and cliffs making it almost deafening and unbelievable from such a tiny bird. The small, insignificant flower that clings to the rocks, struggling to survive. These were the things that made the world around her special. She may spend most of her life on her own but it was worth it. Nothing could be better than experiencing the countryside with no distractions. Even if the weather was bad. Rain, snow and wind would not prevent her from taking in the environment to its full. This was how she sustained herself, the experiences were her food and drink. They kept her mental state totally stable. Nothing could happen that would disturb her, she was bulletproof. That was, until now.

Her phone buzzed across the desk under a pile of papers, shoving a pencil from its rest to fall onto the floor with a clatter. She grabbed the phone and hit the screen. New text message. It was from her mother. Very blunt and something that she couldn't initially grasp. Everything stopped momentarily. It just said "Your Uncle John has died" Nothing more, just that. She sat staring at it, trying to rationalise what it was she was looking at. Her mind went completely blank. She looked up, turned her head both ways almost expecting a change in the library but nothing, nothing had moved, the two individuals were still there, deep in their research. There was no sound, no movement. She looked back down at her phone. The message too, was still there. She was stunned, glancing around the desk as if there was something else that was responsible for it but there was nothing. She gently placed the phone down on the desk as if it were poison, the screen going blank. She touched it tentatively to awaken it, hoping that the message had gone, or, rather had not even come to her phone in the first place but, no, there it was, plain and simple, "Your Uncle John has died".

Her throat went dry, her mouth wide open, she couldn't breathe. She kept looking from the phone to random objects in the library, the shelves full of books, the main door, rain still pouring down the glass, blurred cars passing in the street outside. Her hands went quite damp, she tried to rub them dry on her jeans, her mouth still open, she put her hand to her forehead, her elbows on the desk and then they came. The tears, and with that came the first sob and then another, quiet. But the next was uncontrolled. The tears were now streaming, dropping like bombs onto the desk, her phone, her notes. She tried hard to retrieve the situation but it was impossible.

She cried, her face crumpled, she looked up at the ceiling, tears now flooding down her face. Her nose started to run, she wiped away the tears but needed a tissue to keep things under control. By this time the girl who was sat nearest to her in the library had looked up. She stood and calmly walked over to the main desk. "Are you okay?" she asked, leaning forwards to get closer to Jane.

"Yes, yes, no." came the sobbing reply. "Sorry" she blubbed, "I've just had some bad news."

"Here," said the girl, "let me get you some water as she walked over to the dispenser, a plastic cup filled, she returned and placed it in Jane's hand. Jane lifted the cup shakily and took a sip, and then another and then drank the entire contents down. This calmed her a little.

"Thank you" she said to the girl, attempting a smile. She took her tissue and wiped the tears, blew her nose and looked up at the pleasant face that was trying to console her. The brown hair, straight and quite short framed her face perfectly. No makeup made her look real and alive.

"Is there anything I can do?" asked the girl.

"No, no, it's okay" replied Jane "I'll be okay now, thank you."

"Are you sure? "

"Yes, I'll be fine, it was such a shock, that's all, I'll be fine." The girl smiled again then gently touched her hand. Her smile was one of those that would settle any argument, dispute, or like now, an uncomfortable situation.

"Okay, she said, but if you need anything just say, it won't be a problem."

"Thank you" said Jane, watching the girl briefly caress her hand softly, slowly release it and then walk back to her seat where she took one more look back, smiled and then returned to her studies.

She picked up her phone again to re-read the message, but contrary to what her hopes were, the message remained the same.

Jane immediately thought she should call her aunt, but with the situation as it was and her own state of mind, she postponed the idea, at least until she got back to her flat. She looked at the clock and it showed 16:45 so just another 15 minutes before she closed the library. She absently started to tidy her papers and books, put her pens and pencils away in their case, the same case she had carried right through school. One of those things that became a part of her, something that would be with her for ever, never to be discarded. Just one of those things that made her different. She became attached to simple objects that provided a service or function in her life. Things that were to all intents easily replaceable, but totally irreplaceable purely due to their history, even down to the fountain pen she carried in it, long emptied of ink but still there.

A glance at the clock now showed 16:55, time to lock up and return home. She stood and walked slowly over to the young chap in the corner, but he was already packing his papers away, being a regular visitor to the library, he knew the format. He placed the last items in his bag then presented the two books he was using to Jane. She took them with a smile and said goodbye as he quietly pushed his chair back under the desk and moved towards the door. As he passed the girl, she glanced up at him and they each raised a hand in quiet recognition.

Jane was making her way back to her desk as the girl was packing her stuff in her rucksack. She slung it over her shoulder, placed the chair back under the desk, grabbed the few books she had and came up to the desk. She put two in the returns box and placed the other two in front of Jane. "Can I book these two out please?" she asked.

"Yeah, no problem" said Jane, sniffing, quietly taking the two books and scanning the barcode to the girl's account.

"Are you feeling better?" inquired the girl, looking up at Jane's pale face.

"I would say yes" replied Jane "but that would be a lie. Thank you for asking anyway." The girl looked sad and seemed to show some kind of empathy. "It's just that I have had a message telling me that my uncle has just died."

"Oh, I'm so, so sorry." said the girl. "Was he close?" she asked.

"Very" replied Jane. "He was a favourite, a lovely man, full of character and love and I'll miss him terribly." With that the tears came again, the sobs burst from her mouth. The girl put her stuff down on the floor and walked around the desk. Jane turned to her and the girl held out her arms, took Jane close and hugged her tightly. They stood there for a few minutes, Janes sobs lessening in their vigour. She sniffed and moved away, took up her tissue and wiped away the tears. "I'm sorry." said Jane, her red eyes looking again into the face of this familiar and quiet girl.

"Don't be sorry." said the girl. "I understand, and there's nothing worse than facing this on your own. I guess you are alone?" she questioned.

"Yes" replied Jane. "I live alone. But I'll be okay. I have things to do and I'll phone my aunt. She is the one who is going to suffer terribly."

"You do that." said the girl as she picked up a piece of paper and a pen, writing her phone number on it. "Here's my mobile number, you know, just in case you are lost or just need somewhere to cry, talk or just sit quietly." she said, handing Jane the piece of paper.

"Thanks" said Jane, smiling. "Thank you so much." The girl turned and picked up her books and rucksack, walked to the door, opening it, she turned back.

"I mean it" she said "if you need a chat, just call me. I'll be there." Jane smiled back at the girl as she turned to go, the door closing slowly, leaving the library seemingly more silent and still than usual. She looked at the piece of paper the girl had placed in her hand. It just had a phone number and the girls name, Sarah. Jane carefully folded it and tucked it into her own phone case, absolutely sure she would use it at some point. She didn't have many friends, not people she considered true friends but Sarah seemed to be someone she could call on if the need arose.

Jane checked around the library, making sure all was well before setting the alarm and leaving herself. It was still raining but it wasn't far to her flat, which seemed not quite as welcoming as it was under normal circumstances. Her hunger gripped her as soon as she walked it and not wanting to go through the whole rigmarole of preparing what she considered proper food she dug out a ready meal from the freezer and zapped it. A glass of wine and a Chicken

Chasseur took the edge off the stomach pangs but didn't diminish the thought of losing Uncle John.

She dialled a number and waited for the call to connect. As soon as it was picked up, she said; "Mum, how could you do that?". The answer she got was as abrupt as the text message. She hung up, not wanting to exacerbate the situation. She thought to call Beryl but then considered the state she would be in and chose to call in the morning. It was Saturday tomorrow, so there would be no work and she could prepare herself for the call. She spent the evening watching a poor film on the tv, not really taking it in. A couple of glasses of wine brought the thought of her bed closer. By ten pm she had tucked herself up and had fallen asleep.

The morning came, the sun was shining which was a bonus, she couldn't face another rainy day, it would just make things look worse. Breakfasted and tidied she sat down and phoned Beryl. She was nearly in tears even before the call was answered.

"Hello Aunt Beryl" she said quietly, as soon as it was picked up. "I'm so, so sorry".

"I know chicken", came the reply, "I know, it was a shock but then not totally unexpected, you see, John hasn't been well for a while and his heart just gave up. We have had a while to prepare ourselves for it but to be honest, you just can't. He knew and I knew it would happen but you always just hope it won't be on that day but it was and we have to go on. He wouldn't have liked us moping around so we won't hey? How are you, anyway?"

"Sad, Aunt Beryl, very sad, I loved Uncle John so much and I'll miss him terribly. Would you like me to come over today, just to keep you company for a while?"

"I would like that" came the tremored reply, "I would like that a lot."

"Okay" said Jane, "I'll pack a bag and be over as soon as I can, I'll see you soon."

"I'll bake us a cake." said Beryl "It might distract me a bit." The call ended and Jane just couldn't keep the tears under control. She got up and blew her nose, went straight into the bedroom and packed a bag. Within an hour she was walking down the path to

Chapwell. The house was the same but even as she went through the gate, she sensed that there was a big piece missing.

Beryl was waiting at the open door, Jane dropped her bag and held Beryl tight, they both broke into tears, great shudders passing through the pair of them. Eventually, they parted and Beryl's tearful face smiled at Jane who she held by her shoulders. "Come on chicken, I'll put the kettle on and we'll have some cake, that'll cheer us up a bit."

Walking into the hall Jane could hear the clock, it's solid but gentle tick moving time along, seemingly oblivious to the events that had so recently been recorded by the hands as they moved inexorably around the face. The kitchen looked the same. For some reason she thought it would look different but it didn't, it just felt different. It smelt the same, fresh baked cake and a hint of herbs and polish. It seemed quiet but it was always quiet there apart from the firm but gentle voice of her Uncle John, discussing the latest news or encouraging the cricket when the commentary came from the radio. Never to be heard again. But then she thought, life must go on and there are hard things to accept but they must be accepted and with John, he would never want anyone to get upset or depressed, he would want everything to carry on and people to remain happy. "Here you are chicken" said Beryl as she presented Jane with a piece of chocolate cake and a mug of hot tea.

"Life's not quite going to be the same, is it?" asked Jane sipping her tea.

"No" came the reply, "it most certainly won't but we'll manage, won't we?" Beryl reached across the table and held Jane's hand. Looked at her, a sad smile on her face. "The house is still the same, the garden is the same, the amount of work is the same it'll just have a piece missing but we'll remember him always. Now, come on drink your tea and eat your cake and we'll have a wander in the garden."

Jane finished her cake and tea then took her plate and mug to the sink, gently placing them down. she looked out of the wide kitchen window with its deep sill. The garden, as always, was neat, blessed by the sun and colourful. The lawns were tidily trimmed and a lush green.

Beryl joined her and they both went through the door and along the lavender lined path to reach the main lawn and the bench seat that they had spent so many hours sitting and enjoying the garden and countryside around them. They sat in silence for a few minutes just taking in the colour, the birds and the fragrance of the flowers around them. Bees, flies and butterflies were busily flitting between plants, the quiet buzz calming the air.

"How are you going to manage the lawns Aunt?" asked Jane.

"To be honest chicken, Tom from the village has been cutting the lawns for a while now, John had to stop doing it as it was just too much for him. He did supervise though" said Beryl, a chuckle escaping her lips. "I'll manage just fine, Tom is a great help if I need him, but the gardening will carry on as it is, I'm quite content to do that myself. And you can always help if you want to, any time."

"I'd like that". Said Jane, "it would give me a break from the flat and work now and then. I was a bit annoyed with Mum though" she said.

"Why?" asked Beryl, turning towards Jane, an inquisitive look on her face.

"Well," replied Jane hesitantly, "The text she sent me about Uncle John was a bit abrupt, almost like she was gloating, and when I phoned her, she was the same. I had to put the phone down on her because I was getting a bit angry and I didn't want another row."

"What do you mean, Another row?"

"Mum and I have always rowed Aunt, ever since I can remember, I have never done anything right, leaving school and getting a job. But she was quite happy when I said I was moving out into my own flat and she is always happy for me to come here, couldn't wait to get rid of me it seemed. And she never came in to see you and Uncle John, just dropped me off and picked me up. Don't know what is up with her. I really only knew any different when I saw how other kids were treated and how their parents seemed to be close to them. I have never been like that, except when I come here. I've always felt different here and you're not even family. Not that, that has any bearing on anything but it's just that I have never felt that I had a normal home life like other kids. I don't know, it's a bit confusing and now Uncle John has gone there's a big bit missing and I don't think Mum even cares."

"Jane," said Beryl, turning in the seat to look directly at her. "Things have happened in the past that have made things the way they are." Beryl took Jane's hands and held them. "I know, things are not quite right and haven't been for a long time and there are reasons for it but this is not the right time to discover those things. Your Mum does love you in her own way, I know that much but she just doesn't know how to show it."

"Do you think she's jealous of me, Aunt?"

"I don't think jealously comes into it chicken, it's a kind of legacy that will never be forgotten nor forgiven. We just have to manage it the best we can.

"So, what happened?" Asked Jane. "In the past I mean, what could have happened to make her not be a normal Mother?"

"Like I said chicken, there will be a time and place for you to get the whole story, but not right now hey?"

"Does it have anything to do with Dad leaving her? I know I wasn't even born but I know he left and I've, well, I've never seen him. I don't even know who he is. Do you?"

"I do know him chicken, well, I knew him. I don't know where he is now and, yes, him leaving your Mum was a result of the problem."

"What problem?" asked Jane, slightly irritated.

"Jane, can we leave it there for now? I don't really want to drag all that up again. I know that you want and need to know but let's sort out the present for now. The past has gone and we'll explore it more in the future, when we're both ready. After all, I believe you are happy, you have a nice job that you enjoy and you've always got Chapwell as a refuge if anything happens, you are sad or you just need a little holiday. Your room is always ready. You don't even need to call to warn me you're coming. You can just turn up any time, you have a key so there we are." Beryl released Jane's hands placing her own in her lap. She turned to look out across the garden again.

Jane was of course, now intrigued but as with everything about Chapwell it could quickly dispel discomfort and restore peace.

Minutes passed while they watched the insects around the garden, took in the colours and scents, both silent, both now calm.

"Well." said Beryl "I suppose I need to arrange a funeral for John"

"I guess so." responded Jane, somewhat surprised at the lack of emotion. But then Beryl was a very pragmatic person.

"What do you think chicken? What would John like?"

Jane hesitated, but she knew now was not the time for emotion, this was a time for getting things done and done in the right way. "Simple", I would think, she said. "Uncle John would like a simple funeral with just the people who knew him and loved him and, if I knew Uncle John at all I would think he would like to be cremated, he respected the earth far too much to take up space in it." This made Beryl laugh.

"Couldn't have put it better myself" she said. "But if we only invite those who knew and loved him, we wouldn't get them all in the church"

"So be it" said Jane, "So be it, if the church isn't big enough then folk will need to stand outside. And I don't know how you feel about this but I don't think Uncle John would want us all in black, he didn't like that, I think he would like people to be comfortable and conspicuous."

"Absolutely" responded Beryl "He would love that, none of the mourning, drab things we normally see, just everyone out to say goodbye with a smile and a memory, eh?"

"That'll do fine," said Jane.

"Yes", said Beryl "That'll be just fine, see, we've sorted that in a few minutes, just like John would like. I'll speak with the vicar and the undertaker on Monday, till then we'll just carry on as we are."

"But what about the shop?" asked Jane. "What'll happen to that?"

"Don't worry chicken, it's all in hand. You see, John knew this would happen at some point, though it was a bit sooner that we both expected but there we are, we can't change that. The shop will be managed the same as it is now, only John won't be there. It'll carry on as it is, we have staff in there that run it quite well and the accountant looks after the finances. John made sure it would all be okay if he was ill. If it gets too much then I can easily sell the business, it's quite profitable and there will always be a buyer, so you don't need to worry about that either. Everything is in hand."

Silence descended on them again, just the buzz of the insects keeping them company under the warm sun and blue sky, flowers waving gently in the slight breeze.

The rest of the day was as it always was, except with the unhappy absence of John. A nice evening dinner, glass of wine, listening to the radio and playing cards. They were both quiet, both understanding that things could descend into tearful sobbing if either of them brought the subject up, both understanding the others reluctance to do so.

Sunday was spent mostly in the garden just enjoying themselves as best they could. The evening came and Jane packed her bag to leave. "I'll come and see you any time you like Aunt, if you just need a bit of company. I can come over straight from work if you need me or need some help with the arrangements, I'll take some time off if that would be easier. You've got my number and I'll give you the number at the library so you don't need to call Mum. I'm still so annoyed with her."

"Okay, chicken, but you can come any time you want to, just like I said and if I need you, I'll just call. And, no, I won't call your Mum. I don't think she is interested or affected by this and don't be surprised if she doesn't attend the funeral."

"No, okay." said Jane. They held each other tightly, neither wanting to let go, but let go they did and Jane was soon on her way home, sorry to leave Beryl on her own in that big, now empty house. As lovely as Chapwell was, her uncle was a massive part of it. He filled the house with his voice, his charm and charisma. She just hoped the house could stand to be without him.

The funeral was as most funerals are, tearful, quiet and sombre but it was a little more cheerful than most as the majority of folk who came were casually dressed, some even very colourful which she knew would have made Uncle John smile. Beryl was absolutely correct, in that there was not enough room in the church and truth be known the graveyard was pretty full as well. Virtually the entire village had turned up. To Jane this just confirmed to her how much everyone loved and respected her uncle.

The wake was similarly well attended, the village hall had been put at the disposal of Aunt Beryl but she hadn't had to lift a finger. Many villagers had spent a lot of time making sure it went as John would have liked it. Plenty of food with lashings of tea and cake, just like he would have organised himself.

Everyone paid their respects to Aunt Beryl, she constantly had someone in attendance and overall, it was a relatively jolly affair, again, just as John would have liked. Jane chatted with Christopher and Kate. John and Beryl's son and daughter. Christopher was a bank trader who lived and worked in New York. The spitting image of his father even down to the James Robertson Justice beard. If anyone ever asked what John looked like, this was a character whose image portrayed him best, and, now, here was his son looking just the same. It was as if John was right there, just 20 years younger. He had the same voice and deportment. Very English, very Chapwell. Kate was, and always had been cabin crew for a major airline. A job she obviously loved. She was smart and tidy and had an aura about her that you could see made folk in an aircraft feel safe and cared for. They both chatted to Jane as they had seen her at Chapwell on a few occasions, mainly for birthdays and Christmas festivities when they could both be there. Jane felt as if they treated her as a sister almost, she felt very comfortable in their company, never left out and always included in conversation. Particularly if it was about Chapwell, they all loved Chapwell.

It was whilst chatting to Kate that a cloud appeared, a family cloud that seemed to be a darkness that hovered on the horizon. "Have you seen David?" asked Kate quietly as she leaned towards Jane's ear.

"David?" queried Jane, slightly confused, looking up at Kate.

"Yes, David, my other brother."

Jane was now very confused. "I, well" she said "I didn't know you even had another brother; I only know Christopher. I've only ever known you and Christopher. Neither Uncle John nor Aunt Beryl ever told me they had another son."

"Oh, Okay," said Kate, a look of horror on her face. "Perhaps we should leave that there but suffice it to say, David is not a nice person. He was a bad child, a bad teenager and now he is a bad adult and there is no reason to believe that will ever change. Perhaps I shouldn't have mentioned it, though in all honesty I thought everyone knew who he was."

"Well, not me" said Jane, slightly irritated, "not me."

It wasn't until a lot later, back at Chapwell that the subject came up again. Truth be told it was Jane who brought it up. Christopher and Kate were staying at Chapwell which meant Jane would return to her flat, there only being two spare rooms. There was another room in the attic but it would have taken a bit of work to get it habitable again. The three of them and Beryl were sat around the kitchen table. The table that witnessed so many dramas, celebrations, happy occasions and downright sad ones. Jane could not keep it in any longer, she just could not stop fidgeting and had to have an answer. Kate seemed to know what was coming and gave Jane a warning look of disapproval. This, Jane ignored. Her tenacious manner came to the fore and demanded an answer.

"Aunt Beryl?" she asked.

"Yes chicken, what's the matter?"

"Who is David, and why have you never told me about him?"

Beryl's face turned to ice, any trace of pleasure instantly falling away. It was a face Jane had never seen before and gave her the feeling that she really should have kept her mouth shut. Before Beryl could answer, Christopher folded the paper he was reading and placed it neatly on the table. "How do you know about David" he asked calmly, his arms laying over the table mat, fingers entwined.

"I let it slip" said Kate sheepishly. "I'm sorry, it just came out, I just wasn't thinking".

"Okay," said Christopher. "I'll tell you what you need to know and nothing more, there is no point in you knowing all the gory details. Best you don't know for now. You will find out in time but this is not that time Jane, honestly you don't need nor want to know the whole story but it's like this." Jane sat back in her chair, folded her arms over her chest with an expectant look on her face. "David," continued Christopher "is what you would most definitely categorise as a black sheep and that's being unkind to sheep. As a child he was nasty to both of us." pointing at himself and Kate, "He is the oldest by a year and he wanted the pair of us to know it at all times. Mother could not control him and Dad had a difficult time with him. He got himself in all sorts of trouble at school and always, always tried to blame others, including me and Kate. Fortunately for us everyone knew the culprit for any misdemeanours that occurred in the village or at school. He was a compulsive liar and a danger to anyone and anything around him. He spent a lot of time in a young offender's institution and eventually, after a most hideous crime he was sent to prison. We know he is out now and living in Bristol, and, to be honest no-one here wants him back, brother, son, or not, he is not welcome. So, there you are, all you need to know right now, so please keep it like that, it'll only cause us all so much grief if that is all dragged up again. Please don't ask me again and under no circumstances ask Mother about it. Kate knows now not to mention it again so we'll just leave it there. Honestly, you are better off, so much better off, just not knowing."

Silence descended upon the kitchen. Jane didn't quite know what to do or say, the three of them were just staring at her. The look on Aunt Beryl's face had calmed, she looked almost sorry. Kate was still a bit shaken and guilty but it was done, now she knew.

"I'll put the kettle on" said Beryl, breaking the silence. We'll have a cup of tea and some cake, that'll cheer us up a bit."

From then on, the subject of David never came up. Jane felt that no-one wanted nor needed to talk about him. It was obviously something tragic, something that had badly affected the family and she knew to leave it there. When she left, she had a feeling of intrigue. There was a secret in Chapwell but one she knew needed to be kept a secret. At least for now.

Chapter Four

5 Years ago

It had been some months since Jane last visited Chapwell. Work was always a priority now, her Open University studies had come to fruition and she could consider herself a Historian, specialising in the Tudor monarchy. Her job at the library remained the same, though she now had more responsibilities and this meant she travelled around meeting other librarians, visiting other libraries and, of course, it meant she had access to more books and rarer books, some of which had restricted access but as she was now fully qualified her access to these books was justified and she took full advantage of this privilege. But she felt she just needed a break, a break from everything work-like.

She decided she would surprise her Aunt Beryl by just turning up. She could stay for a week if everything was okay as she had holiday to take and as it was the best time of year for the garden, she thought she would make the most of it and help Aunt Beryl at the same time, as late Spring is a busy time in any garden.

The journey to Chapwell didn't take long, which was one reason she loved it so much. A place of paradise was only minutes away from her flat. She drove down the lane, the last half mile was dead straight, from the village, right to the house, just past it, the road turned away but she was always intrigued by the footpath that continued the line of the road on into the distance. A footpath she had walked on many an occasion. It led over the fields and onto the hill in the distance where it became less distinct and less obvious. She knew that there had been archaeological digs on the hill and a Roman fort had been discovered, with evidence of iron age and bronze age settlements before that. A lot of history in a small area and a place she visited often just to take in the views all around and to sit in the history, to imagine the occupation over the years. Who had been there? What were they like? It really would be magical if she could go back in time if only to watch what was going on there. Just for a time, just to experience what life then was really like in comparison to, what are now, the accepted theories.

She pulled up outside the little gate and stepped out into the warming sunshine, the light clouds wandering across the landscape, wiping the blue sky clean. Birds were singing all around, Great Tits shouting 'teacher, teacher' from the hedges. A Wren loudly announcing its presence even if it could not be seen hiding in the undergrowth, the loud 'chick chick' telling Jane she was a bit too close. What a wonderful picture, it never failed to satisfy, relax and calm her. Having grabbed her bag, she closed the car door.

As she opened the garden gate, she could hear laughter from the rear of the house and a lot of chatter. She couldn't hear what was being said but it sounded rather jolly. The front door was open and the cool air of the hallway caught her as she entered, the smell of polish and wood all around with an overlay of lavender. This, she thought unusual as lavender wasn't flowering yet and she knew Aunt Beryl would never have air fresheners in the house. Perhaps she had made some pot pourri from last year's flowers? It smelt like the garden in the full sun and added to the relaxed atmosphere Jane always experienced when she came to Chapwell.

She dropped her bag at the bottom of the stairs and walked through to the kitchen, past the grandfather clock, its ubiquitous tick marking the time as she passed. On entering the kitchen, she could see that tea had been taken, but two china cups and two plates, crumbs on both? Wondering who had been entertained she could only assume it was the owner of the laughter she heard coming from the garden. She looked up and through the kitchen window, across the garden she could just see on the other side of one of the larger flower beds two heads. One, obviously Aunt Beryl, her silver hair shining in the sun. The other was dark, very dark with sharp braids cascading over the head. She strained to see exactly who it could be but just couldn't quite make them out. She wasn't aware of anyone else coming to the house in the past and couldn't quite fathom why Aunt Beryl had never told her about a new visitor, particularly one who seemed quite familiar with her aunt. She went to the back door and opened it fully, it's creak still as loud as ever. Standing in the doorway, she looked across the garden, expecting to see Aunt Beryl and her guest looking up at the house, alerted by the doors noise, but, no, just Aunt Beryl who was getting to her feet, a surprised look on her face that quickly brightened to a broad smile. Her hair not as tidy as it normally was, wisps of silver escaping the neat bun and waving in the sun. She had her gardening clothes on, a gloved hand gripping a fork. "Hello chicken" she shouted waving the fork in the air "what a lovely surprise". Dropping the fork and removing the gloves she hurriedly made her way towards the house. Confused, Jane stepped out of the doorway and tentatively walked down the flagged path, looking left and right, across the garden, down to the fields at the bottom expecting to see the other person, the owner of the dark hair but there was only Aunt Beryl coming up the path to meet her. "What's the matter chicken? You look like you've seen a ghost".

"I could have sworn I heard and saw someone with you Aunt, just now and I could hear someone laughing when I came through the gate."

"Oh, don't be silly, it was just the radio I expect, I often have it on in the garden and there's no-one else here as you can see" Beryl also looked around the garden, hands on her hips, a smile on her face twisting left and right.

"But there're two cups and plates on the kitchen table as well".

"Oh, that was me and Tom earlier, he came over to trim the lawn edges and we had a cup of tea and some cake. Your imagination is running away with you chicken. Come on in and I'll put the kettle on."

With that Beryl put her arm around Jane and guided her back through the kitchen door though she did turn her head to look down the garden almost as if she was expecting to see someone.

"Sit yourself down and I'll get some tea made" said Beryl as she washed her hands under the kitchen tap. "How are you? It's such a lovely surprise to see you. The weather has turned nice and the garden it coming into its own now."

"I'm fine" came the reply. "I've taken a week off work to come and see you. Would it be okay for me to stay for the whole week?"

"Of course, of course you can, you know you are always welcome and you can stay as long as you like."

"Thanks Aunt Beryl, I always look forward to coming here, you know that. It's so relaxing and I so miss the garden. I'll just take my bag upstairs while you're making tea, won't be a minute."

Jane collected her bag and trotted up the stairs, still a little bewildered. Opening the door to her room, she stood on the threshold like she always did, just to take in the comfort emanating from it. But it looked slightly different. The bed was made but not in the usual way. The cover was pulled right up to the headboard and not under the pillows. The window was open allowing the breeze and the birdsong to enter. Almost as if she was expected. She could smell lavender again, stronger here but there was no sign of its origin. Perhaps more fragrance from last year's flowering had been dropped around the room. She placed her bag on the small chair by the wardrobe and continued to look around, trying to find anything else that was not quite right. She had to admit to herself that it, indeed, didn't *feel* quite right. She couldn't explain it but it just wasn't the same as it normally was. She felt a very slight chill, a shiver passed through her, ever so slightly disturbing. It was difficult to describe to herself but there was a presence in the room, her senses where enhanced but there was still nothing to see or hear. Just a feeling. It seemed to pass but she remained wary, concerned and, perhaps, a little worried. She shook herself out of the paralysis and returned to the kitchen. Aunt Beryl just placing the teapot on the table, two fresh plates and a cake as centrepiece.

"Did you know the window was open in my room Aunt?"

"Oh, yes" came a hesitant reply. "I opened some of the windows up to let a breeze through as it was such a lovely day and upstairs could do with an airing".

"Also" said Jane "I can smell lavender everywhere for some reason and it's quite strong in my room. Not that I don't like it, it's lovely but I don't think I've ever smelt it at this time of year before, any ideas?"

Again, a hesitant reply came forward "Oh, that was just some lavender bags I made up last year, I left them around the house here and there and I expect the breeze in your room scattered the fragrance a bit."

Jane wasn't at all convinced as she held the mug of tea to her mouth, looking over the lip as a somewhat flustered Aunt Beryl.

"Here, have a piece of cake chicken." Said Beryl, slicing a large section of Victoria sponge from the half-eaten delight that was in the centre of the table. Aunt Beryl was probably the best cake baker Jane had ever known. Her cakes, regardless of recipe were always perfect. Luckily Jane had been taught by Beryl over the years and Jane's cakes, though not quite up to Beryl's standard were highly sought after by her friends and always made great gifts. As usual, silence came over the kitchen, both understanding the need for concentration when consuming these items of baking art.

With only crumbs left on her plate, Jane looked up at Beryl, a great smile showing the appreciation she had for her aunt's skills. "That was the best ever" she said.

"Oh", said Beryl. "Don't be silly, you say that every time. It's just a cake, same as all the other cakes I have baked."

"Yeah, but even better than ever, so soft and light, just the right amount of jam and fresh cream. Can I have another slice?" asked Jane sheepishly.

"You don't need to ask." said Beryl. "There's the cake, there's the knife, help yourself silly." They sat there opposite each other both seeming to ponder the situation. Beryl almost sensing that Jane thought she was hiding something from her and Jane sensing that Beryl had a little secret. Nothing serious but there was something there in her look that was not quite the same. Beryl was quite carefree but she was slightly reserved today. Almost as if Jane's arrival had disturbed something and she wasn't quite sure what.

Finishing her tea Jane stretched her arms, pushed her chair back and stood, looked around the kitchen and picked up her plate and mug. "Right, I'll go upstairs to change into my gardening togs and I'll be down to help you in the garden, I need a bit of horticultural therapy as I haven't touched a plant in months" she said, walking around to the sink. Placing the items on the worktop, she took another look out over the garden, almost expecting to see someone out there, someone with dark hair. But there was no-one. She could just see the weed trog by the flower bed right where Aunt Beryl had been working but nothing else.

"Right-oh chicken I'll carry on with what I was doing and I'll see you in a minute."

Jane trotted back upstairs to her room and went straight to the window to see Beryl walking down the path, looking left and right as if she was looking for something. She continued across the grass to the flower bed and knelt down on her mat, donning her gloves and picking up the discarded fork. She looked around the garden again before returning to her weeding.

Having changed, Jane wandered out of the kitchen door, along the path and across the grass to the flower bed. Looking down she saw another kneeling pad and fork adjacent to Aunt Beryl. "Are you sure there was no-one else here Aunt?" asked Jane, "only there's another pad and fork here, and, where's the radio? I thought you were listening to the radio."

Beryl looked across at Jane, that flustered look on her face again. "I, Um. I took the radio back in the kitchen and got you a pad and fork from the shed" came the stammered reply.

"Right" said Jane suspiciously but happy to accept the explanation in order to maintain decorum.

An hour weeding in the garden in the spring sunshine had them both chatting away in the more normal manner, laughing and giggling about stupid things, catching up on some of the entertainment they had each witnessed on the television recently. They talked about Uncle John and how things had changed. The shop now managed by one of the staff was doing well and the village had gotten used to life without him being there though, in truth, no-one could in reality get used to him not being there, not having his charm and character contributing to the quintessential village atmosphere. But then he would always be remembered and his presence would always be felt by everyone.

They finished the weeding and tidying of the various flower beds, and once the tools and rubbish had been removed, they walked around the garden, constantly commenting on the growth of the early plants and speculating on how the garden would look when it was all in flower and flourishing. Trying to imagine the summer colour with the bees and butterflies adding motion and sound to the colours, filling the summer air. They both constantly and surreptitiously glanced around the garden, not to experience the flora and fauna that was abundant but in order to check for the unknown, or, perhaps known presence that it seemed they both experienced. But as the tour came to an end at the kitchen door Jane had seen nothing else that raised her suspicions apart from the fact that Aunt Beryl was just not quite her normal self. She seemed somewhat disturbed, mildly flustered

"I've made a nice beef stew for our dinner; it's been in the oven for hours," said Beryl.

"Beef stew" commented Jane, "wow, I love your beef stew and I thought I could smell something cooking when I came in. You know, everything almost feels like you knew I was coming, you wouldn't normally cook a beef stew just for yourself, would you?"

"Well, I just fancied it, I haven't had one for ages and I can always put the rest in the freezer."

"What can I do then Aunt?"

"Go and get some potatoes in and you can peel them. We'll have them mashed with it. There're loads of veg in the stew so we don't need anything else.

CHAPWELL

This was what Jane loved most about a visit to Chapwell. A day in the garden and then an evening preparing food and then demolishing it with a nice glass of red wine. The rest of the evening they spent playing cards, chatting about nothing in particular with the radio on in the background providing them with some gentle music. Perfectly peaceful, de-stressed and content, Jane started to nod. "Okay" said Beryl, "Time we went to bed I think, I can't play on my own here, you're nodding like a donkey over there."

"Yep" said Jane dozily, her eyelids barely lifting. "It's this house you know Aunt, it has that effect on me, could be the stew and wine mind! Every time I come here; I feel totally relaxed. Nothing to worry about, nothing to hassle me, just total bliss. Just wish I could have it all the time. Do you feel the same?"

"Always have" came the reply. "I miss John of course but the house will always give me peace and tranquillity. That doesn't change. It's only the people in it that change it seems. Yes, it is different without John but I've got used to being here without him. I don't expect him to walk through the door anymore or hear him singing in the shower though to be honest that particular experience is one of those you think you hate but in fact you would do anything to hear it again."

This made Jane laugh, she too, had heard Uncle John singing in the shower, he always did it and they did all joke about the fact that he really couldn't sing but she too missed that sound, that occupation of the house. But time passes and the things you once felt, slowly, slowly diminish. Not to be forgotten but just not at the forefront of your thoughts.

Looking forward to a peaceful and rewarding night's sleep, Jane dragged herself up the stairs to her room. As she went in and switched on the light, she could see that, again, things weren't as she would expect them to be. The window was closed and the bed cover was under the pillows as it usually was. Thinking she had been mistaken and the excitement of being here had misled her, she dismissed this unusual occurrence with a preference to getting in that comfy bed for a fine snooze. But then, it could have been Aunt Beryl who had set things right when she came up to get changed from her gardening clothes. Whatever, it didn't really matter but Jane could not get that niggling little discomfort that had planted itself in her mind. "Tomorrow" she thought, "tomorrow will set my mind right." As she threw the quilt back to climb in, she could not help but be very aware of the lavender fragrance that wafted from the bed. She stopped briefly but, again, accepted that Aunt Beryl had, perhaps, been leaving lavender bags around, climbed in and brought the quilt up to her chin, feeling totally relaxed, swimming in the delightful aroma.

Just as she expected, she slept like the proverbial log, a gentle knock on the door waking her slowly, a stretch against the fresh linen, the slight but distinct smell of lavender gave her an instant pleasant feeling and the thought of a nice cup of tea on the other side of the door made her sit up.

"Come in Aunt, I'm awake" she said, the door opening the mug of tea leading the way as Aunt Beryl came in.

"Did you sleep well?" asked Beryl.

"No, absolutely terrible" replied Jane with a sleepy smirk on her face. "What do you think Aunt?" came the rhetorical question as she yawned.

"I have never had a bad night's sleep here, ever, even when the fox cubs were playing in the garden, do you remember that? Uncle John had to go out and shoo them off. They went, but, ten minutes later they were back as noisy as ever, but it was a joy just to lie here and listen to them." Beryl sat down on the bed and looked at Jane, a great smile warming her face. Jane looked back, her smile was a reflection of the happiness she felt, sat up in this bed with a hot mug of tea and her aunt smiling broadly at her. "What?" she asked enquiringly. "What's the matter?"

"Absolutely nothing" replied her aunt." a soft and caring expression painted her face. "Absolutely nothing. I am so lucky to have you Jane, you make my life complete and always have. Beryl gently stroked Jane's arm and smiled again, her eyes shining in the curtained sunlight that was pushing through the drapes.

"What shall we do today?" asked Jane.

"Well," said Beryl. "first, bacon and eggs for our breakfast and I'll do you some toast from the bread I made the other day. Then we need to start getting the vegetable patch ready, there is a lot to do there now as the greenhouse is bursting with young plants that need to be let loose in the big wide world."

Beryl got up and opened the curtains, the early sun flooding in through the delightful mullioned window almost making Jane squint. She stood, hands on hips just looking through the leaded glass, just like Jane did every time she went to the window. "I'll start getting the breakfast then chicken, don't rush, I won't get it cooking until you come down" she said turning towards Jane and then leaving the room, smiling as she went. Jane took this time to rest back into the pillow, sip the lovely tea and ponder the house around her. This was, always had been and always would be the finest place in the world. There could be nothing that could provide peace in the way that Chapwell did.

Refreshed and dressed, she went downstairs for breakfast, knowing full well that the day was going to be another blissful experience, which incidentally, it was.

As were the next few days and all too soon it was time for her to leave. Standing at the gate, her bags in the car she said "I have so enjoyed myself Aunt, I wish I could live here always but I can't. I have a flat and I work and I travel about a lot. Best I keep Chapwell as a special treat. If that's okay?" she added.

"Of course," said Beryl "You know you are always welcome. I shouldn't need to keep telling you." A long hug ended the week at Chapwell and Jane walked around to the driver's door of her car. She was just about to wave to her aunt when her eyes were distracted by movement in one of the upstairs windows of the house. She was sure she saw a dark braid of hair disappear behind the landing curtain which moved imperceptibly. She stared but the movement had stopped, it appeared as if nothing was there. Dismissing it she resumed her goodbye, waving at her aunt and getting in the car.

As she drove off, she couldn't help thinking of all the little incidents she had witnessed while she had been there but she had no choice but to render each as coincidence or imagination or, perhaps, just a small hint of Chapwell mystery.

Jane stayed at Chapwell House on a number of occasions over the next few years. On each visit, Jane tried to see if there was anything unusual in the house, anything that would vindicate herself of the thought that she had imagined someone else in the garden and house. But there was nothing. Aunt Beryl who was aging, needed more help in the garden, which, to Jane's surprise was always in immaculate condition. She could only make the assumption that Tom helped her, perhaps more than Beryl was letting on and wasn't just caring for the lawns but was helping with the other gardening as well. Jane even had the unforgivable thought that there was some kind of relationship developing there but she quickly wrote this off as inappropriate. That just would not happen.

Chapter Five

6 Months ago

There are few devastating experiences that can match the death of a loved one. Particularly one who had given Jane so much pleasure from a very early age. In fact, she could not remember any part of her life without Aunt Beryl. The phone call from Kate, in just a few seconds brought the entire world crashing down around her, giving her the terrible news.

Without even thinking she called Sarah, her friend. "Can you come over Sarah?" she asked, tears streaming down her face, barely able to speak, massive sobs shaking her to the core.

Within a few minutes Sarah was hammering on the flat door. "Jane, Jane, it's me, let me in." Opening the door, her tearful face, red with grief, presented itself to Sarah who, without words took hold of Jane and held her close. Tight enough to prevent Jane falling to the floor which she thought was about to happen. "Don't say anything, just hold her" she thought. She held on for a few minutes until the sobbing subsided slightly and Jane released herself, her face a picture of total misery, tears pouring down her cheeks and mouth. Sarah grabbed her handkerchief and gave it to Jane who promptly started mopping at the mess, still sobbing gently. Closing the door, Sarah put her arm round Jane and guided her towards the living room, sitting her down on one of the sofas. She removed her coat, not taking her eyes from Jane as she laid it over the arm and sat next to her. Putting her arm around her, Jane's head collapsed against her chest, her arm reaching around her neck.

"I'm sorry" blubbed Jane.

"Don't be," said Sarah, "that's what I'm here for."

Sarah held on for, what seemed ages, until Jane's crying subsided. "Better?" she asked.

"Yes, no" came the reply. "Oh, Sarah, it's Aunt Beryl, she's — she's died." The uncontrollable crying restarted and Sarah took her head to her chest again in an attempt at consolation. It took a good few minutes before Jane had her emotions even vaguely under control. Sarah left her to compose herself, handed her another tissue from the box on the table and looked her in the eyes.

"I'm so sorry Jane" she said "That must be so devastating. I cannot imagine what you are going through right now. Let me get you a glass of wine, perhaps that'll take the edge of it for now, eh?"

"Okay," came the snuffled reply.

A few gulps of rich wine later and the sobs had diminished to a gentle sniffing with occasional blows of her nose.

"What am I going to do?" asked Jane, her voice unsteady. "Aunt Beryl was my whole life, well, her and Chapwell. They were my whole life. What am I going to do without them? Chapwell was my refuge, my safe place. The place I spent growing up virtually."

"I know", said Sarah. Then hesitated. "Well, honestly, I don't know really. What I do know is that your aunt and the house meant everything to you but the house will still be there, won't it?"

"I don't know" replied Jane, looking up forlornly "I don't know what is going to happen. Christopher lives in the States and Kate is settled elsewhere. I guess they will inherit the house but what happens then?"

The sobbing started again so Sarah poured more wine for Jane. "Look" she said, I'm not working tomorrow so let me pop back home and get some things and I'll stay over here for the night. We can just sit and chat, work things out. I don't want you sat here all on your own."

"Okay, I'd like that," said Jane, "I really don't want to be alone tonight." That settled, Sarah put on her coat and left. Jane sat thinking, sobbing and sipping wine. She had just experienced one of the worst moments in her life. Everything she held dear, everything she kept as the best memories with the expectation of more to come had just be devasted by this news. Not only was she going to have to cope with the death of her best friend and confidante, she was going to have to come to terms with the loss of her safe place. The house, the garden, the comfort and love were all going to come to an end. She felt that her life had been brought to a very abrupt halt, hit the buffers, gone off the cliff. She felt that there was going to be nothing, a void without anything to fill it. She was thankful for the friendship she had with Sarah who had been there for her always, right from the death of Uncle John.

By the time Sarah returned, Jane had opened a second bottle of wine. She felt a little calmer now, the wine, obviously taking effect. Having dropped her bag in the bedroom, Sarah sat down beside Jane. "Feeling a little better?" she asked.

"Hmm, I guess" came the mumbled reply.

"Right," said Sarah "I think the first thing you need to do tomorrow is to have a chat with Kate, see if there is anything that needs to be done. It might help if you are involved in the short term. It might make things a little less terminal for you. You never know they might be keeping the house on and let you stay there, perhaps as a housekeeper or something, I mean, Kate might even take the house on herself and let you stay. She might just like to keep it in the family and keep it going. Christopher won't be there I know as he has his own life and work in the States but it doesn't instantly mean they are going to sell it."

Jane listened intently, just like she always did with Sarah, she always talked such sense and could always unravel a bad situation and lay it out into some sort of order.

"I mean" said Sarah, "let's face it, those two were brought up there, they spent their entire childhood there and love it as much as you do. I know they haven't spent any of their adult life there like you have but I'm sure they have as many if not more memories of the house than you do. To just get rid of it would not be constructive at all, and it's not like they need the money or anything. Perhaps they would rent it. Goodness, they could even rent it to you, how about that? You could even live there full-time. It's within easy commuting distance and I could still come and see you. See, even though things look totally bleak and your aunt's death is a tragedy I know but this might not be the end of things for you."

Jane was looking directly at Sarah the whole time, the sadness and redness in her face slowly dissipating, the last tears wiped away and even the signs of a small smile appeared.

"Do you know Sarah? She said "I now know why I chose you as a friend. You can find brightness in the darkest of situations, and I'm not just saying that because I've had a couple of glasses of wine either. You are a true friend. You have never demanded anything from me, never expected anything and never been judgemental, you are just the best friend I could have so thank you so much."

They looked at each other, smiled and embraced, holding each other for a good few minutes, happy in the knowledge that nothing could destroy the affection, trust and companionship they enjoyed with each other.

"Fancy a takeaway?" asked Sarah. "My treat, you can have your favourite Indian with those lovely Naan breads. I'm starving, to be honest, I haven't eaten yet." she said getting her phone from her pocket.

"Go on" said Jane "I must admit I'm a bit peckish as well."

They had their food and sat together watching a junk film on the TV, finished the wine and went to bed. Sarah had successfully brought things into perspective for Jane and had settled her down to thinking straight. It did not diminish the depth of the tragedy, she knew that but it had, at least removed some of the anguish and pain.

Sarah got up early and made tea, taking a mug of the hot liquid into Jane, who was woken by the door opening. She lifted her head from the pillow and rubbed her eyes, sitting up she saw Sarah with the tea and smiled. "See," she said yawning, "this is what a real friend does for you, wakes you with a nice cup of tea."

Sarah placed the mug on the nightstand and sat on the bed quietly looking at Jane. "How are you feeling? Did you sleep okay?"

"Yeah, I slept fine, the wine must have knocked me out. I wouldn't normally drink that much but it did the job." Have your tea and I'll make us breakfast. Boiled eggs? Soldiers?

Jane smiled as she picked up her mug. "You really are the best, boiled eggs and soldiers would be brilliant".

Perfect boiled eggs and buttery soldiers were one of Jane's favourites, and Sarah obviously had the knack of getting it just right. More tea, and breakfast was complete. "Right" said Sarah, "you go and have a shower, sort yourself out and I'll clear this lot away.

"Okay", said Jane "but I need to phone work to tell them I won't be in today."

"Don't worry about that, I'll give them a ring, you go and have a shower" With that, Jane stood up and went to the bathroom, leaving the clinking of plates and mugs in the kitchen.

When Jane came back in after getting dressed, Sarah was just finishing up, all done. Kitchen cleaned up; she was sat checking her phone. "Are you going to have a shower?" Jane asked

"In a minute" Sarah replied looking up "Just sorted some bits out. You know I don't mess about."

"Right, okay," said a bewildered Jane.

"And you don't have to worry about work, they were fine about it, said take as much time as you need. I spoke to Trevor? He said he knew how much Beryl meant to you so isn't expecting you back for a few days but he did ask if you could keep him up to date."

"Yes, thanks" said Jane "Trevor's great, a really nice chap, I'll text him later."

"I'll give Kate a ring, I'm sure she'll be up and about, being an early riser and all that." Jane went into the lounge and sat to make the call, they chatted for a good while, the inevitable tears started to flow and they shared their grief, both knowing how much Beryl meant to each of them.

A still tearful Jane walked into the kitchen, a sad expression on Sarah's face indicating the sorrow she felt for her.

"How did it go?" Sarah asked.

"As expected really." came the reply." Both Kate and Christopher are devastated. They are both going to the house to get things sorted out there. All the arrangements will be done from there and she's asked me to go over as well. Can you come with me Sarah? I don't feel like doing this on my own. I know I get on well with them both but they don't know me like you do and they'll like you there. They've never met you, have they?"

"No, they haven't" came the reply "And, yes I'll come with you, let me just phone work to extend my holiday a bit, I'm owed some time off. When are we going?"

"Kate's going over this afternoon so we can go this evening if that's okay with you?"

"Fine. No problem, let me just call work first and I'll nip home and pack a bit more in my bag or, easier if I stay here with you today, we can pack your bag, sort the flat out, go over to mine, sort my stuff out and go straight over to Chapwell. I've never been there before."

"God, no you haven't. This isn't going to be easy but you will see why I love it so much; I really wish you had met Aunt Beryl, thinking about it."

"Never mind." said Sarah, "She was your aunt and I feel I know her anyway; you are always talking about her."

The rest of the day was spent tidying the flat, packing Jane's bag and doing a little shopping for stuff to take with them. They went over to Sarah's house and sorted a few things there, packed Sarah's bag and were soon on their way to Chapwell.

Jane got out of the car, stood by the door, looking over the gate to the house and immediately burst into tears. Sarah, quickly came to her aid, putting her arm around her, comforting her. "Sorry" said Jane.

"Nothing to be sorry about Jane, this is going to be hard but I'm here to help you through it and if you want time on your own just say and I'll provide you with space but, equally, if you need me, just shout. I'll always be there."

"Thanks" said Jane, wiping the tears away. "Come on, let's find Kate."

Jane led the way through the gate and down the path to the front door. Opening it, she walked through, Sarah, close behind, looking around her as she went, taking in all that oak, the stone floor and amazing staircase. "Oh my God" she whispered, "This is fantastic, it's beautiful, wow, look at this clock."

"Now you can see what I meant," said Jane.

"Absolutely" came the reply as they entered the kitchen just as Kate was getting up from one of the chairs. Jane immediately went to her, no words just a huge hug and tears. "I'm so, so sorry." said Jane.

"I'm sorry too." said Kate "I know how much Mum meant to you, how much you meant to each other and of course the house as well, it means so much to all of us."

"Oh, sorry." said Jane releasing Kate and turning to Sarah. "Kate, this is Sarah, a really good friend of mine, Sarah, this is Kate" They shook hands gently.

"Jane has told me such a lot about you, your Mum and this house, I feel as if I know it and it is so nice. I first met Jane when your father died and we've been good friends ever since."

"She really is the best Kate, she really is" said Jane "I don't know what I'd have done without her, hope you don't mind me asking her to come along, I don't think I could cope without her here."

"Of course not," came the reply "She can stay with me in my room, it won't be a problem," said Jane.

"That'll be absolutely fine." said Kate. "Get yourselves sorted out and we'll have some food."

"We've brought stuff with us as well." said Jane. They got their luggage and carriers from the car, took the food into the kitchen and went upstairs with their bags. Jane opened the bedroom door and stood looking into the room. It presented itself as it always did, ready for her to stay.

"My god", exclaimed Sarah, peeping around Jane's shoulder "this is your bedroom? It's amazing, that bed's huge!"

"Good job, cos we're sharing it, hope you don't snore" said Jane chuckling. "You don't mind, do you?" Jane turned, a sudden concerned look on her face, "I didn't think, sorry, I can sleep on the floor" Sarah quickly interrupted.

"Don't worry Jane, I'm fine with it, as long as you don't snore that is." They looked at each other smiling, the friendship obvious as they worked around each other seamlessly unpacking their bags and loading drawers.

They went downstairs to the kitchen where Kate was preparing dinner for them. "What can we do?" asked Jane.

"You can lay the table" came the reply "you know where everything is. Just the three of us, Chris won't be here till tomorrow, he's getting an overnight flight but will be here sometime in the morning. Sarah, you can open some wine, glasses are in the dresser there and the bottle opener is in the drawer underneath."

Sarah could see that they were all going to get along just fine. She was with her best friend and could see that Kate was an expert at organising people whether they were on an aircraft or in the house. All very efficient and non-pretentious.

"Do you eat meat Sarah?" asked Kate turning from the range cooker.

"Yes, yes I do, there's very little I won't eat, just ask Jane."

"She's a food bin" exclaimed Jane jokingly. "I haven't come across anything she won't eat, and look at her, not an ounce of fat anywhere, a metabolic rate that could power a rocket." They all three laughed at this. Looking at each other as if they had all been friends for years.

"Excellent" said Kate, "we only need to start getting fussy when Chris gets here then, he's a pain when it comes to food, yet he lives in a country with the poorest diet imaginable".

They sat around the table in silence, eating their food. The level of conversation proportionate to the quality of the food.

"My," said Sarah, "you can seriously cook Kate, that was delicious, and I'm not just saying that, it was brilliant."

"Had a good teacher, didn't we Jane?" said Kate smiling across at Jane.

"And" said Jane "this cottage pie is a testament to Aunt Beryl, she taught you the same as me, this is as if she had made it."

"Well, I'm glad you enjoyed it. Drop more wine?" said Kate picking up the bottle and offering to her guests.

They cleared the table and washed up, the work shared equally between them in virtual silence, Jane just directing Sarah to the appropriate drawer or cupboard in order to stow the china and cutlery.

Task completed they sat back to the table and finished their wine. "Okay," said Kate "The Elephant in the room has to take a step forward and be noticed but I don't want to discuss too much until Chris is here as he might know something I don't. Suffice it to say, Jane, we know how much you love this house so we'll do whatever we can to ensure it stays that way. Personally, I have no idea what is going to happen. I don't know what is in the will and neither does Chris as far as I know."

"But" said Jane "This is nothing really to do with me, is it? I know I have spent a lot of time here over the years and, yes, I love it dearly. But it's your house, isn't it?"

"That's just the point," said Kate "We don't know, we don't know what is in the will, Mum might have left it to charity. You know what she was like with wildlife conservation. We'll need to wait till tomorrow at the earliest, see what Chris knows. He may not know anything. But before that we'll need to be arranging a funeral and I think that should be our priority right now. Well, at least tomorrow anyway. I'm really tired so I'm going to bed in a minute. You can stay up as long as you like. You know where everything is so If it's okay with you two, I'll just have a chocolate drink and go to my bed."

Jane immediately got up and grabbed some mugs from the dresser. "I'll make the chocolate Kate, Aunt Beryl taught me how to make the best, there's a bar of chocolate in the fridge. You're in for a treat Sarah." she said, looking across at her friend.

Kate took her mug up to her room with her, leaving Jane and Sarah umming and aahing over the deliciously rich chocolate drink. Sarah smiling at Jane. "I know this is a bad time but I'm beginning to realise exactly what it is you have had here over the years and I'm dead jealous. This is the sort of thing that spoils people but I can see that you and Kate have both experienced this life and have not taken it for granted, nor abused it, just loved it for what it is and appreciated it for what it has given you. I do hope it doesn't end, for all your sakes. It would be so sad to see it all disappear.

"I know" said Jane "We've been so lucky but as they say, 'all good things come to an end', we'll just have to see what happens."

The knock on the door startled Jane from her sleep, she groggily looked around, realising where she was and seeing Sarah fast asleep next to her brought her senses back. "Tea" came the muffled statement from the door.

"Come in" said Jane, sitting up, Sarah still fast asleep, barely visible under the quilt. The door opened and Kate walked in with a tray holding two mugs and a handful of Morning Coffee biscuits.

"Here you go." said Kate placing the mugs on the nightstand, arranging the biscuits beside them. "I know Dad always brought you biscuits in the morning so I thought I would do the same."

"Oh, thanks" said Jane, "I haven't had biscuits with my tea since, since, well, you know. A real treat. Thanks."

Jane nudged Sarah and got a grunt as a reply, another nudge and Sarah stirred, turning over to face Jane. "Oh" she said rubbing the night from her eyes "what time is it?"

"Tea time" came the reply. "Kate has brought us tea, and biscuits."

"Oh, right" said Sarah, sitting up and looking around, not quite sure yet of when or where she was.

"Awake now?" asked Jane.

"Yeah, I think so, slept like a log. Oh, hi Kate, thanks for the tea." The bewildered look on Sarah's face made Jane and Kate laugh.

"What?" exclaimed Sarah.

"Nothing" came both replies simultaneously. "I'll see you both downstairs when you're ready." said Kate turning to leave.

"Never had biscuits with my morning tea before." said Sarah "And certainly never had them brought to me."

"Another one of those special things that is unique to Chapwell." said Jane, sharing the biscuits equally. They sat there in silence nibbling the crisp squares.

"This house, it's like everything you could possibly dream of, isn't it? Asked Sarah.

"Yes." came the reply. "I don't know what might have happened to me if it wasn't for Chapwell, the house and the family."

"How do you mean, the house and the family."

"Oh," said Jane. "I probably failed to tell you that bit. The house is called Chapwell and the family name is Chapwell, and they both go back hundreds of years."

"Oh, wow!" exclaimed Sarah." I bet that's a rarity these days."

"It is rather unusual." said Jane. "There are very few family houses that retain the name of the family or vice versa. It is very well worth preserving, but this is a crucial time. We don't know what is going to happen as yet."

The smell of bacon floated up the stairs as Jane and Sarah left the bedroom. Entering the kitchen, they could see that Kate was preparing a simple breakfast. "Anything we can do? Asked Jane placing their mugs on the worktop.

"Pour the tea if you like." came the reply. "You can sit yourself down Sarah, the eggs are nearly ready."

The weather was looking good, the sun was shining brightly through the kitchen window giving a warm glow to the enormous kitchen table, the table where so many happy meals had been consumed, so many great games had been played and so many discussions had taken place. "I'll take you around the garden after breakfast Sarah." said Jane, "You'll see what I was on about all this time."

"Oh, I'd love that" replied Sarah.

Sarah was treated to a full tour of the garden which was absolutely immaculate in every respect, borders tended, no dead heads on the flowers, not a weed to be seen and the lawn trimmed to perfection, edges neat and sharp. "How on earth did your aunt manage all this?" asked Sarah.

"I don't know" came the bewildered reply "I really don't know." Looking around Jane could see that everything was as it always had been. So neat and tidy. She was confused as she knew how much it took to keep it all neat like this. Aunt Beryl must have spent every minute of every day tending it.

"How on Earth did Aunt Beryl keep the garden so neat" Jane asked Kate when they returned to the kitchen. Kate looked up from the newspaper she was reading, placing her glasses on the table.

"Really don't know Jane. Tom does the grass, I know that, but she must have spent all her time out there, even so, it's a lot to look after.

"There is one thing I remember." said Jane.

"What's that?" asked Kate."

"Well, a while ago I came to stay for a few days and things weren't quite right."

"How do you mean."

"Difficult to say really but when I came to the house, I was sure there was someone else in the garden with Aunt Beryl. I am not one hundred percent sure but there were other things not in their usual place. I just wondered if she had any other help. I'm pretty sure it was a woman, dark hair, plaited. That's as much as I saw and there were things in my bedroom that were not quite right. I don't know, perhaps I did imagine it. But I haven't forgotten it; it still niggles me."

"I certainly wasn't aware of anyone else." said Kate. "Mum never mentioned it."

They all turned towards the hallway as the front door opened, Christopher walking through it and along the flagstones, dropping his bag on the floor he just fell into Kates arms. Silence was the only expression that would suit. Jane and Sarah both turned and went back out to the garden, leaving the siblings to their personal grief. They went and sat on the bench looking out across the borders, taking in the flowers, the birds, bees and other insects making busy around the garden.

"Hello Jane" said Christopher as he walked up to them.

Jane stood up and gave him a hug, briefly, then introduced Sarah.

"Pleased to meet you, Sarah." he said.

"Pleased to meet you too" came the reply.

"I hope you don't mind Sarah being here Christopher?" asked Jane.

"No, of course not" came the reply, "Any friend of yours is a friend of ours, you know that, you are welcome, Sarah." he said, looking straight at Sarah bowing slightly, immediately making her feel comfortable.

"Come on, let's go in, I need tea" said Christopher guiding them both along the path before him.

They, all four sat at the table with tea prepared. "Okay." said Christopher, "Before we do anything else I think we just need to quickly see where we are with things. I know it is a difficult time, for all of us but we do need to be practical and I know full well if either, or both of our parents were watching us right now, they would just be telling to get on with it and get everything sorted so that's just what we'll do. And, from what I do know, everything should already be sorted, we all know what Dad was like and Mum would not disrupt that."

"Hang on." said Jane "Are you sure I should be here; and what about Sarah?"

"Jane, Jane" said Christopher "You know full well what you are and have been to this family. Mum and Dad loved you so much for who you are and what you brought to them and this house. Kate and I left home to start careers and families but you were always here, you replaced us as a companion to them both. As far as we are concerned, you are family and as Sarah is your best friend, there is nothing here that needs to be kept secret from any of us."

"Oh, okay" said Jane slightly taken aback and feeling a little embarrassed at how she didn't quite realise how much of a part of this family she appeared to be. The funeral would be arranged by Christopher and Kate according to the plan put in place by their father. There was not much Jane was required to do but she and Sarah spent the rest of the day in the garden, sat in the sun. Jane, thinking that this could possibly be the last time she would be staying here was making the most of it. Sarah sat quietly by her side holding her hand and taking in the beautiful garden. Fully understanding why Jane loved it so much, having spent most of her spare time in it over the past years.

The four of them stayed in the house for two more days, the dreadful feeling they were all experiencing diminished imperceptibly to a condition of acceptance. They all knew things were going to change, perhaps dramatically for them all. The single thing that kept them all together seemed to be losing its grip and they all felt a similar dismay with the possibility of it ending suddenly. The house had been in the family for generations and neither Christopher or Kate knew what the future would bring. Even though the heart of the house had been cruelly taken from them all, Chapwell was still here, unchanged. The oak still gleaming, the floors still hard and worn, the clock inexorably marking the passage of time as it had for years. They couldn't even speculate as to what the future would bring. Neither of them could afford to keep the house even if it had been passed onto them. They had their own lives to live and neither wanted to lose Chapwell but, then, neither could believe that it could possibly stay in the family without causing financial difficulty.

They all sat in the kitchen with tea and cake one final time before Kate, Jane and Sarah had to leave. Christopher said that he would stay at the house until all outstanding issues had been addressed, the funeral over and the future for themselves clearly defined, whatever the outcome.

Two weeks later, the funeral was over and things began to reset. Christopher returned to the US and Kate went home. Jane, however was left to keep an eye on the house, much to her surprise and delight. She could stay in the house for a few days and spend some time at her own flat. That way she kept up to date with everything in her life. She realised that a new life was in front of her now. It may or may not include Chapwell, and she was slowly coming to terms with the fact that the house may disappear from her life. So, she spent as much spare time in the week and every weekend there. She wanted to keep the garden tidy and cared for but each time she arrived; the garden was as it should be. The house was always clean and neat, everything in its place which was certainly baffling. Only

Tom came to keep the grass tended but that did not account for the flower beds being kept weed free, dead heads removed from the flowers. There were even new plants appearing here and there.

She had a call from Kate. The Will was to be read and Jane was required to attend. She did not know why but accepted that perhaps there were a few items within the house that Beryl had decided to leave to her.

She met Kate in town and they both went around to the Solicitors at the required time. Christopher had flown over from the States the day before and met them there. Jeremiah and Jeremiah, Jane saw on the highly polished brass plaque which showed the signs of wear that could only be acquired by years and years of polishing. The building was powerful and official, obviously old. The sort of building seen in Dickensian novels, even the name seemed to have been dragged straight from one of his tales.

They were brought into a high-ceilinged room adorned with dark mahogany panelling, paintings of past owners and partners hung around the walls. The gentleman behind the desk, on their entrance stood, his smart three-piece suit adding to the general aura of the room.

He introduced himself as Jeremy Green. "Please, please sit, I have tea and coffee here if anyone would like." He served the refreshments carefully to delicate cups and saucers. "As you know, Christopher and Kate, I have been the solicitors for your parents my entire life. All the time I have been working here and, in fact the company of Jeramiah and Jeremiah have been attending to the needs of the Chapwell family and estate for over three hundred years. This is new to you, Jane but by the end of this meeting you will realise that you too become part of this history." Jane suddenly felt quite out of place, the building, the room and Jeremy built the situation almost to a fantasy, the Dickensian feel, enhanced by the elegant and polite words from the gentleman in front of them. "Now," he said "I will read the document through in exactly the order in which it was given to me. Your father, sorry Jane, John, presented this document to me during his last year with us and your mother, Beryl has kept it up to date with events as they dictated the situation to her. Before I start, I will say, and you may not know this but John had a hobby which proved to be quite lucrative. Many years ago, he began investing on the stock markets and, from what I have seen, became quite successful. His main objective being that he needed to ensure that there was sufficient money available to maintain Chapwell House and to keep it within the family." Jane was relieved to hear this as it meant the house was not going to be sold, her tentative grip on her sanctuary was becoming firmer. "So," said Jeremy, "The document is quite simple but it does come with the odd caveat. Nothing that should worry anyone and all the while it protects Chapwell House. Christopher, you have been left fifty percent of your father's money, being a total of five hundred thousand pounds." The three of them looked at each other, totally stunned. Even Christopher and Kate where unaware of their father's prowess with the stock markets. "Kate, you have been left the other fifty percent of your father's money, again being five hundred thousand pounds." Again, the three of them looked at each other, totally flabbergasted and speechless. "What is going to happen to the house?" queried Christopher. "That is the next thing in the will." said Jeremy. "The house and its contents have been left to Jane Campbell here." he said with a smile, looking directly at Jane. Her face was a picture of total shock and disbelief. She sat, mouth agape, unable to speak, she looked at Christopher and Kate in turn. A smile greeted her from each of them. "That is not all." said Jeremy. "There is a caveat." Mystified, the three of them looked at Jeremy expecting, what, they didn't quite know. "Jane has been left the house and also a fund, which is to be maintained as a trust in order to care for Chapwell House. The sum of one million pounds will be placed at her disposal in order to maintain the house. The trustees will be myself, Christopher and Kate. Jane can use the money to maintain an income for herself, again, with the agreement of the trustees. The primary objective being the care of the house and estate. There, Jane, you are now officially the caretaker of Chapwell house. And, having been John and Beryl's solicitor for many years I am very happy with this result." He slowly and deliberately closed the file on his desk, he laid his hands on the brown card as if protecting it from any outside influence.

The reading only took around half an hour but by the time it was over Jane's life had changed completely and forever.

Jane was totally stunned and as they descended the steps having left the solicitors office, she turned to Kate and asked "Are you angry Kate?"

Kate stopped and looked at Jane, took her arm and with a huge smile said "No. No, of course I'm not angry, why would I be angry, things just could not be better." With this she took Jane in her arms and hugged her tight. "This is just perfect" she said. "Both Christopher and I sort of knew the house was not going to be left to us, and to be honest, neither of us really wanted that responsibility. We had told Mum a while ago when she brought it up that she needs to make sure the house was looked after and that it shouldn't involve Christopher or myself, so there you go. The right outcome has presented itself. The house stays in the family so to speak and we all know it will be looked after."

"But Kate" said Jane "I'm not family. I'm not a Chapwell am I?"

"Well, if we're going to be pedantic, I'm not a Chapwell either am I?" said Kate with a broad knowing grin. "Look", she said laughing, "Let's just go and have a coffee and a cake and perhaps you'll stop trembling".

Christopher was very quiet as they stepped onto the pavement. "Are you okay with what you heard Christopher?" asked Jane timidly.

Christopher looked down at Jane and just smiled. "I could not be happier." he said. "I am so relieved that the house is being protected and cared for, staying in the family for us all to continue to enjoy. Come on," he said, putting his hand on Jane's shoulder, "let's go and have cake."

Within six months the legal transactions were complete. Jane kept her little flat but rented it free of charge to Sarah, who was absolutely delighted. Jane understood how difficult things could be when you were young and alone and as Sarah had been such a good friend and confidante, she knew it would make them both happy. It meant their friendship could continue and develop even more, as Jane knew, like herself, how much Sarah loved Chapwell.

Chapter Six

Present day, Emily

Jane was still a little bewildered over last night's events though, surprising herself, she felt totally comfortable with it and being honest, slightly excited. She knew what she had seen and while she was showering thought about how she could move things on if at all possible. She was totally intrigued and memories of past events came back to her. There was something about Chapwell House that was not quite normal though, she didn't feel in the slightest threatened by anything she had experienced whether now or in the past.

She was now feeling very sensitive to changes to anything in the house. It was a house she was very familiar with; she had grown up with it. She knew, or at least thought she knew every nook and cranny that the house had, having spent her childhood roaming around, imagining she was in a castle and being the Princess within that castle. But she considered further investigation would do no harm. Kate and Christopher had removed their personal stuff from the house and it had been either taken away or stored in the massive attic. She still could not quite believe what had happened over the last 12 months, how her life had changed completely. She now owned a large, very old house that had absorbed so much history, so many secrets to be discovered, so many places to explore. She could not quite decide where to start. The attic, huge and dusty but easy to access or the cellar, or cellars in reality as there seemed to be quite a labyrinth down there as she remembered.

Eventually, after having toast and honey for breakfast, washed down with tea she decided on the attic as that, she felt, would be the simplest place to start. The first thing to note about the attic was that it was huge. It was split into the four different areas of the house, the two largest areas over the front and two smaller areas over the rear two wings of the house but over the years access had been made easier by the addition of a small staircase from the rear upper hallway and it had been floorboarded for many years. One area had been adapted as a small guest bedroom with a wonderful view from the dormer window over the surrounding countryside. As a Historian Jane had quite a knowledge of houses of this age and noted architectural features that were original, had been added since the house was built or modified during its life. The timber framing of the roof space was basically Tudor. Large Oak trusses supporting the heavy roof tiles. She even found carved initials on some of the large timbers and other markings. These she knew were the markings of the carpenter who made the individual piece. The initials could have been from anyone who worked or lived in the house. Even though there were lights in the attic they could not cover the entire space so she went to get a torch from the kitchen. "Might as well have a cup of tea while I'm here." she thought. Filling the kettle, she looked out of the window across the garden and noticed how it was not up to its normal standard whereas it had mysteriously been kept up to scratch in previous months which she could only assume was due to the absence of Beryl's green fingers. Tom, she knew was still coming to mow the grass, which she continued having him do as it gave him some work and relieved her of the task. But the flower beds were now looking somewhat neglected, a few weeds and dead heads making it look a little sad. Knowing this and as the weather was fine, she decided to get out there once the attic exploration was finished.

Tea finished, torch in hand, she returned to the attic. Starting in the furthest corner she found very little that she was not expecting. Apart from, that is, the architectural beauty of the building's skeleton. Everything she could see was totally man made. Carved from oak trees by hand and crafted to fit the house. Each part fixed to the next just using pegs and dowels. Not a nail or screw to be seen. Even the modern electrical wiring had been carefully hidden so as not to detract from the look of the stunning wooden structure. Feeling disappointed at not finding any treasure, she decided to spend the rest of the day in the garden as she felt as if she was letting the place down allowing the garden to degrade.

Walking into the kitchen she felt something strange in herself, a slight tingling sensation, goosebumps raised on her arms and her hair felt charged with electricity. She stopped abruptly in the doorway, a chill running down her back. She could feel her face flush, her heart pounding suddenly. All without obvious explanation but still she stood, awaiting the event, whatever it could be. But, nothing, nothing discernible anyway. But, then, where was her mug? She knew full well that she had placed it upon the work surface right by the sink. But it was gone. Flustered, she walked over to the dishwasher and opened the door, thinking, perhaps she may have put it in there and there it was, placed on the rack with her plate and knife from breakfast. She knew, she absolutely knew that she hadn't put it in the dishwasher as she was going to use it again. No point in washing up a mug when she was going to have another cup of tea later. She removed the mug and looked closely at it but there, just about detectable, the unmistakeable smell of lavender. Where, oh, where did that come from. Bizarrely she put the mug to her nose and the handle had a definite lavender smell, just as if it had been touched with essence, or coated in oil. A smell she loved but how had it got on the mug? She hadn't been near any lavender, flowers or oils or essence or any kind of fragrance. She looked around the kitchen almost embarrassed, as if she expected to see someone watching her. She felt that tingle again, it got stronger the more she looked. There was no one there, no one. She was imagining things. She placed the mug back on the worktop, by the sink, after all, she was going to use it again once she had tidied the garden a bit. She breathed in and blew out, her hair lifted as her breath passed it. "Don't be stupid" she said aloud "Get a grip woman." But even as she said it, she felt the shiver wash over her. She could not dismiss it out of hand, after last night, she knew there was something about this house that was different. What it was she didn't know but she always remembered the day she came to the house and surprised Aunt Beryl when she was in the garden. She experienced the same lavender fragrance on that day as well. And, there was the sprig of lavender on the windowsill this morning. What was it about lavender? She loved it but she knew she hadn't touched any since she had arrived yesterday.

Eventually she got herself together and went into the garden, collected tools from the garden shed and started on the flower beds. The sun was out and the birds were singing happily. There was a tractor at work somewhere over the fields. Sheep were bleating and a distant dog barked its presence. She had been working for about an hour, bent over the beds digging up the weeds and cutting any dead growth on the shrubs and plants, when she leaned back to stretch. Flipping her hair over her head, she looked up at the house. "My God" she thought looking at her old bedroom window. "Damn, what?" She was sure someone had ducked behind the curtain. It must have been. The curtain moved. She saw it move. She dropped the fork and jumped up, her back complaining at the sudden movement and raced along the path and through the kitchen door. Without taking off her boots she guiltily leapt up the stairs to enter the room. The door was open, she walked in expecting to see the guilty party behind the curtain, but nothing, no one. The curtain moved, just a bit but it moved. Jane quickly stomped across the room and grabbed the curtain but, there was nothing there, just the gentle breeze through the open window and that slight lavender fragrance wafting across her face. She looked around the room, confused, running her hand through her tousled hair. Under the bed, they must be under the bed, she thought. Diving down on her knees she looked. Nothing, just the slightly dusty oak floorboards. She opened the wardrobe, moved the clothes from side to side, thinking how it would be impossible for anyone to actually hide in there. Resigned to the fact that her mind, again, was playing up, she returned to the kitchen to make tea.

Her mug, where was her damn mug? "This is getting crazy" she thought exasperated. There it was, back in the dish washer. She put the kettle on and got a clean mug from the cupboard. She knew full well she had put it back on the worktop, she just knew it. Aloud she started talking to herself, "Well, if this is how it is going to be then, ok, I'll comply." she raised her arms in a sign of surrender and twisted from side to side as if to show whatever malevolent force was in control here that she was complicit.

She made her tea and went back out into the garden sitting on the bench to just watch and listen to the sound of peace. A family of swifts screamed overhead, speeding around the rooves and chimneys. Her eyes followed them with a smile. She kept thinking of each of the incidents she had experienced so far, recounting each in an attempt to explain. The key thing was last night. The appearance of the girl in the chair. She had absolutely no doubt that what happened during the night was real. After all, there was the strand of hair in the drawer. That was solid evidence but how could she explain it in simple terms. "It's got to be a ghost" she thought, "but that's just mad." She just could not come up with a rational explanation for all the things that happened, and, not just what had happened recently but over the many years she had been coming here. All the time, particularly in the last year, Aunt Beryl would explain them away as something she had done herself, or just her imagination. Jane now realised that Aunt Beryl had been making up excuses, every time. But why, she thought. Why would Aunt Beryl make up excuses for something that she could not explain in logical terms. What was she hiding?

It was 2am. Jane could see the time illuminated on her alarm clock that glowed very gently in the dark. Like last night she didn't know what had woken her but her eyes were wide open, her ears straining for the slightest noise. Nothing, but there was light. The light of the moon was again sneaking past the curtain, lighting the same narrow band down the wall by the door. Just like last night,

Jane thought, but now she knew what she should expect. And, yes, there in the chair was the outline of a girl, the hair the same, wavy and long. Jane sat up and adjusted her pillows to prop herself upright. She folded her arms in front of her, almost impatient, waiting for something to happen. She continued to stare, concentrating on the figure in front of her, sat there as still as a doll on the chair.

Then, a whisper, a voice from somewhere else it seemed, slightly echoed as if in a large room. "Hello Jane" it said.

Stunned, Jane realised her mouth was wide open and dry. She licked her lips and attempted an answer. "Hello" she said.

"Oh, good" came the reply. "You can hear me okay, that's a start anyway." The voice was still a quiet echo but could be heard easily.

"Who are you?" croaked Jane, her voice still not quite there yet.

"Emily" came the answer. "I'm Emily, Emily Chapwell."

This shocked Jane. She felt a shiver run right through her. A trickle of sweat ran down her back. "Ok" said Jane grabbing control of her emotions. "You're going to tell me now, that you're a ghost, aren't you?"

"If that's the way you see me then I suppose I am then."

"This is mad" thought Jane out loud.

"No" said Emily, "Not mad at all, in my world it is quite normal, and lucky for you, I can stretch across into your world as well."

"How do you mean?"

"Well, normally a person dies and they well, die, go, finished, the end. But for a few of us, well, in actual fact quite a lot really, we don't actually end or however you describe it. We are dead, yes but not gone, well not completely anyway. See, when a person dies there is a part of them that moves on. Their spirit, soul or whatever you want to call it moves on. It just goes to the next living thing that needs one. Sometimes though, this 'soul' let's call it, cannot find another life to go to, or it is somehow stopped or disrupted in its travel. It can go anywhere, to any potential life whether it be an ant or an elephant or on rare occasions a human. You think there are a lot of humans on the planet but let me tell you now, there are way more other lives on the planet and the chances that you hit a human are so small it is almost but not quite impossible. There, does that explain things a bit?"

"I guess" came the reply. "Does that mean that you are completely stuck as a ghost then?"

"As far as I know." said Emily. "No-one I know can explain anything different and every ghost I know is still a ghost and some of them have been ghosts for a very, very long time. Oh, and it doesn't only apply to humans, any living thing that dies but misses the train as it were remains in the form they were in when they die."

Jane was now totally engrossed in the conversation and was fascinated by this new experience. "Where do we go from here then Emily? Do I have to wait till the middle of the night to see you or can I switch the light on?"

"NO, NO, don't turn on the light, I'm not strong enough yet."

"How do you mean, not strong enough?"

"Well, I need to have someone to attach to."

"And that's me I guess?" said Jane.

"Only if you want it."

"What are the pros and cons then?"

"Not much to it really, pros are I get to be your friend and companion, I get to be able to be like you, almost."

"Almost?" enquired Jane.

"Yes, almost. You will be able to communicate with me and see me at all times generally. You would be my lifeboat, my energy, you would supply me with the strength I need to stay solid."

"And what will it cost me?" asked Jane

"Nothing" came the reply "You will not notice anything, because I will use the power and energy you have but you don't use anymore. A power that living things have that most, particularly humans have not used for millennia."

"And how does this come about" Jane enquired.

"I just need to touch you. It's as simple as that, well sort of. I need to refuel now and then but if you are like Beryl then it will be easy."

"Aunt Beryl?" Said Jane slightly louder than intended.

"Yes, Beryl," said Emily. "We have been friends and companions for a long time. Well, since John died really. Beryl was so brokenhearted I had to do something. I needed someone; I always do but Beryl was totally distraught. She was absolutely devastated so I did what I have done to you. I watched her for a long time and then I presented myself to her. She thought it was just her imagination initially, a bit like the 'imaginary friend' people have. But I'll tell you now, mostly they are definitely not imaginary. They are like me. A lost soul just needing to come back and be someone's friend."

"So," Jane said hesitantly "all those weird things I have seen have been you? And what was that with the mug and the dishwasher then?" she asked, her voice noticeably rising in volume

"Yes, the mug was me, all of the things you could not explain were me. The mug, well that was just annoying. A pet hate of mine, and Beryl for that matter. We both hated stuff being left out, so I put it away, sorry about that. I really miss her, in fact when she died, I was hoping upon hope that she wouldn't move on and we could be friends forever. Imagine that, all three of us would be together."

"So, how long have you been watching me then?" asked Jane.

"All your life" came the simple reply "Ever since you first came to stay as a little girl. I wanted to be your companion then but it just wouldn't have been right. I was going to wait till you were about my age but then John died and I had Beryl which worked out well for a few years. We had so much fun together and I hope, well, I know that Beryl enjoyed her last few years. You see, I was with her when she died and I couldn't do a thing about it apart from reassuring her that things past death are really ok. She might not come back as a person but then she wouldn't remember anything anyway. She rather liked the idea of being a butterfly or her favourite was to be a dragonfly, she loved dragonflies."

"How do we go about this, well, this procedure?" asked Jane.

"Like I said" replied Emily "I just need to touch you. Are you ready for that?"

"Yes, yes, I think so." said Jane, secretly excited at this unusual request. She thought, if it was good enough for her aunt, then it wouldn't do any harm. Emily stood and Jane could see her dark outline move gently across the room towards her and stand over the bed next to her. She could see no features. Just the outline of a young woman with long wavy hair. She could see Emily's hand reach across the bed towards her and, hesitantly Jane reached her hand out to meet it. Slowly they came together and they met. It wasn't a touch. More a soft feeling, like a feather being placed into her hand and then inside her hand, spreading up her arm to her torso filling her chest with a gentle wash. Up to her neck and down her legs a slight tingling and then into her head where she felt a wave gently wash over her mind, cleaning it, wiping it of all worry and concern. She reached further her whole arm now dissolving into Emily's. She could hear Emily breathing, groaning and she started to move, quietly at first and then more frantic. Jane could feel everything inside her tighten. This scared her, she didn't understand, she was frightened.

"Don't worry Jane," said Emily in a strained but more solid voice. "This is how it happens. You will get used to it." Jane could now feel her whole body engulfed by a pleasant feeling, a rich, warm sensation growing inside her, filling her whole body. She felt as if she was actually glowing in the dark, stars were popping from her skin, the bright pinpricks of light exploding into the room and filling it with light. She looked up at Emily whose back was arched, her head pointing to the ceiling. She could see her clearly now. The light in the room was intensifying, getting brighter. The stars started revolving around the room centring on the two of them, faster and faster until suddenly there was a blinding flash. The stars exploded outwards from the two women and disappeared through the walls, floor and ceiling. Darkness followed, total darkness. Jane could not see a thing but she could still feel Emily's hand in hers. Firm but soft and so full of life now. Warm and tingling. Emily released Jane's hand allowing it to slip away and drop back to the covers.

Silence deafened her now and darkness blinded her. She could see and hear nothing. Until, yes, a breath. She could hear the soft, gentle breathing beside her. The moonlight was just becoming apparent now. Jane could discern a shadow in front of the window. The outline got stronger, more distinct and she saw Emily move. Her head came forward, she trembled slightly and lurched towards the bed. Holding her arms out to prevent herself from falling, Emily placed both hands on the bed. Jane felt the pressure on the covers and raised her hand. She touched Emily's head; the smooth soft hair was like water as it passed between her fingers. "Are you ok?" she asked.

Emily's breathing was erratic and stuttering. "Yes" came the quiet, choked reply. Jane waited, gently stroking Emily's hair. She raised her head and Jane touched her face, soft and warm. Smooth and so alive. Emily's breathing quietened, steadied and slowly she stood. "Ok, Jane. You can turn the light on now".

Jane hesitated but reached over towards the bedside light switch. "Are you sure? You're not going to vanish like you did last night, are you?"

"No. You'll be fine. I'm ok now, all done, back to life as it were." she replied giggling. Jane pressed the switch and the lamp came to life, filling the room with a low, gold glow enveloping them both. They immediately looked at each other. Right into each other eyes. Almost daring the other to speak. Jane cracked first.

"Wow!" she exclaimed. "You're a fine-looking woman if you don't mind me saying. Your hair is amazing. So dark and soft. You need to tell me your secret."

"Be dead" came the giggled reply "But make sure that when you die you've just washed it." They both laughed at this little joke.

"Hang on." said Jane. "What are you wearing may I ask?"

"Pyjamas." came the nonchalant reply.

"Yes, but they're my pyjamas."

"Ah, yes, sorry. I borrowed them. You don't mind, do you?"

"Well, it is a bit of a shock. No, I don't mind but it is a bit bizarre seeing your own pyjamas being worn by a ghost."

Emily looked herself up and down and then returned her gaze to Jane. "Seriously Jane. Thank you. Thank you so much. You won't regret this. If we can have half as much fun as Beryl and I, we'll be a riot together. And just wait till I show you what the full benefits are for you." Emily released a massive yawn. Jane followed. "I am so, so tired," said Emily. "I bet you are too now."

"Come to think of it, I feel like I've not slept for a week." said Jane. Emily strode around the bed and jumped in next to Jane, turned away from her and fell immediately asleep. Jane, somewhat astonished and realising nothing else was going to happen tonight, together with feeling desperately tired, took a last look at Emily wondering what the future was going to bring, switched off the light and lie back trying to think about what had just happened but the sheer effort of coming to terms with it enveloped her and she also succumbed to a deep and dreamless sleep.

Jane awoke to the sun's warmth powering through the window, penetrating the join in the curtains and lighting the room. She turned her head to see a pile of dark waves of hair bounding over the pillow and cascading down the duvet. A gentle snoring coming from the body next to her. She looked at the clock. 09:30. "Blimey, I was tired" she stated, stretching. She turned back to look at Emily next to her, not quite believing what had happened during the night. She gently nudged the body through the covers. Nothing, not a movement, the snoring continued. A harder shake and a whisper. "Emily, Emily, wake up." Now there was a slight movement, a disturbance in the snoring cadence. Emily turned onto her back her face obscured by the dark hair flowing over her face. Hands came up from under the covers and washed the waves away to reveal the face Jane had seen last night. Eyes slowly opened to reveal deep, dark irises that looked at Jane. A smile appeared brightening the face in front of her like a flower blooming at high speed.

"Oh, my God" came the voice. "I slept like the dead." Jane laughed, putting her hand to her mouth. "You can't say things like that"

"Can" said Emily, "Can cos I am." They both laughed together. They scrutinised each other briefly and it was obvious that they were going to be great friends and as Emily had said, great companions as well. They looked very similar and could easily be mistaken for sisters. Both had dark wavy hair that streamed down their backs. Their eyes were equally dark and they were almost identical in height.

"Stay there Emily, I'm going to make tea. Do you drink?" asked Jane, a confused look on her face.

"Of course, I do and tea would be lovely, just a drop of milk please.

"Fair enough" said Jane, climbing out of bed and grabbing her dressing gown.

They both sat upright in the large double bed, sipping the hot tea looking straight ahead, nibbling at the biscuits Jane had brought. "What" said Jane just as Emily said "Why".

"Sorry, you go first Jane, I expect you have a few questions. After all, you don't actually know me but I know you very well. All your life in fact so fire away."

Jane continued, "What I was going to ask was, what happened to you? You are so young, well, we're about the same age, I think. I'm 28 now."

"Yes, I'm about the same age I suppose, at least when I died, I was 27. But as I died before the First World War then I'm a bit older. But as you can see, I don't age. I've been like this all the time. Even my hair doesn't grow so I can't cut it."

"Oh, don't cut it Emily. Never get it cut. It's beautiful hair. Most women would kill—" They both laughed at this. "Oh yeah, ok, but yes, a lot of women would do anything for hair like that. Now, here's the thing. I'm sure I saw you in the garden with Aunt Beryl one day when I turned up out of the blue and your hair was plaited?"

"Ah, yes," said Emily "I remember that day. You scared us both to death, well that is you scared Beryl to death, I'm already dead so you can't actually do that but, we had to do a bit of panicking because we were being very casual and complacent that day, certainly weren't expecting you to turn up. I'm surprised you didn't rumble our little game."

"How could I 'rumble your little game' of being a ghost? I don't or didn't even believe in ghosts. I'm a Historian and deal in facts so I was just very confused but now I know and it all makes sense, well at least I think it makes sense. But you haven't told me how you died. That is if you want to tell me."

"I don't have a problem telling you, no problem at all. And it was simple and stupid, rushing from my or as it is now, your room, well your old room, I slipped on the rug at the top of the stairs, went straight down head first and clouted my head really hard on the urn that was at the bottom. Saw stars for a second and gone, dead as a Dodo. I didn't even know whether it hurt or not."

"So, what happened then?" asked Jane "Did you like float out of your body or something or did you see a light? What happened?"

Emily placed her mug on the nightstand, brushing crumbs from the quilt and turned back to Jane. "To be honest Jane, I don't exactly know what happened in the next few seconds or minutes. The first thing I remember was standing at the top of the stairs, again looking down at myself sprawled across the floor, my mother, bless her, trying to revive me but I knew right there and then that I was dead. I sat on the top step and looked at myself. Checked my hands and arms, legs and feet but couldn't find anything wrong. It was a bit confusing really as I wasn't one hundred percent sure of what had actually happened. I stood up to walk down the stairs and happened to notice the big mirror on the landing so I took a look at myself to see if my head was bleeding or anything but guess what?"

"Go on, what?" asked Jane somewhat impatiently.

"Nothing"

"Eh?" said Jane, "what do you mean, nothing?"

"Nothing in the mirror, I was looking at nothing, well I could see the reflection of the landing, the carpet, the walls and the doors but no me. I checked myself again, looking down and I was fine as far as I could see. My dress moved if I moved. I could touch myself, walk and turn around but there was no reflection."

"Wow!" exclaimed Jane. "I bet that was a bit of a shock"

"Tell me about it" said Emily "Worse was to come though. You can imagine how confused I was. I shouted at my mother who was, by now, crying hysterically. No reaction, I shouted again but still nothing. So, I went down the stairs with the idea that I would comfort her and tell her that things were ok."

"And?" said Jane interrupting.

"What do you think? I went to lay my hand on her shoulder and it just went straight through her. I knelt beside her and tried to touch her again but my hand just passed straight through her again, didn't even feel it. I even touched myself, well my dead body and that was the same, my hand went straight through to the floorboards. Mother was getting frantic, crying terribly but there was nothing I could do. I just sat on the bottom step and watched it all happen. Father came in just then and then there were two of them going at it. The doctor was called but I think they both knew it would be useless as they could both see that I was stone dead. Not breathing. No heartbeat and blood pouring from a wound on my head. I even touched my head. My new one that is, but there was no wound which I thought a bit strange. I have learned since that your body returns in its last solid state with no defects."

Jane was mesmerised, to the point that she was nearly spilling her tea. She flinched and woke up, quickly drinking her tea and placing the mug on the nightstand, a look of bewilderment on her face. "I'm trying to figure out what was going through your mind at that point." she said "But it's impossible. What could you possibly think at a time like that? I mean. You're dead but sort of alive. Or, I guess you think you're alive, not having come to terms with the fact that you are actually a ghost. Wow, that would make your brain hurt."

"Long story short" said Emily "It took me a good few months to get used to the fact that I was a ghost. I had to watch the whole thing slowly unfold and happen. The grief in the house, which, by the way, I could do nothing about. I was grieving myself in a way. Grieving for my parents who had just lost their daughter and this, just after my brother Frederick had been killed in the war. The Boer war that is. I died in 1903, he died in 1902, just before the end of the war. There was only my other brother left now. John, and he survived the First World War thank goodness and it was down to him really that you are here now."

"How's that then?" asked Jane.

"Because he was the last Chapwell at that time. He married and they had children so the blood line continued. Christopher and David are Chapwell's though I know you've heard about David, nasty person. He was a horrible child, hideous, evil doesn't even begin to describe him and happily he's gone. And don't ask about him because I know his name should not even be whispered in this house so I don't particularly want to talk about that right now."

"Ok" said Jane "We can leave that. I know everyone else has denounced him and I have no desire to bring any of it back up if it's going to cause grief."

"Good" said Emily "That's settled. No mentioning David."

"Jane?" asked Emily.

"Yes" came the reply.

"Can we have breakfast? I'll cook. I know that there is bacon in the fridge and eggs in the cupboard and I'll do some fried bread". Jane stared across at her new companion in disbelief and could just see total excitement and delight on Emily's face.

"Help me here Emily. Why are you so up for cooking breakfast?"

"Because my dear Jane. I have not eaten for a few months and I am feeling exceptionally hungry."

"I'm confused" said Jane, bewildered. "Explain how a ghost can be hungry. Or even eat for that matter."

"As you can see Jane. Thanks to you I am now whole again. In one piece, well, nearly anyway. Ok, so I won't starve to death if I don't eat or drink and I can, and have, lasted for years without. So, you can imagine how I might feel right now eh?"

"I guess," said Jane. "So, you are to all intents and purposed a human being now?"

"Yes, sort of" replied Emily hesitantly. "As far as you are concerned, I'm like anyone else. But to others. I don't exist. They cannot see me, hear me, touch me, unless I want them to. Only you can and that's because we are bonded. Like me and your aunt were. There are a few anomalies but we'll get to those at some point. Just settle for the fact that I am your imaginary friend. You'll get used to it. Meanwhile, can we please, please have breakfast? You can shower first if you like and I'll get things ready in the kitchen."

It wasn't long before they were both sat opposite each other at the big old kitchen table consuming a massive breakfast of eggs, bacon, sausage, black pudding, fried bread, mushrooms, tomatoes and a lot of tea. "Told you I was hungry." said Emily stuffing more bacon into her already full mouth "And if you can't handle what's on your plate, hand it over. I'll destroy it. Something you might find interesting. This table is the same table that I sat at as a child and I believe it was here way before that as well." This was said all the time while Emily was waving her fork around, pointing at various objects. "Same goes for the clock in the hallway. That's always been here as well."

"Emily?" said Jane quite sharply.

"What?" asked Emily, looking up, surprised, eyes wide. Another forkful about to be dispatched.

"Can you finish your breakfast first? Sorry but it's one of my pet hates. People who talk while they are eating" said Jane sheepishly.

"Oh, sorry." said Emily apologetically putting the fork down and placing her hand in front of her mouth. Breakfast was finished in silence.

More tea was made and they sat just staring at each other, both leaning on the table. "What?" asked Jane, a smile growing on her face.

"I like you," said Emily with a smile "we're going to get along just fine, I think. You have grown to look an awful lot like me. Don't forget I know you quite well so I do know what you like and some of what you don't like. So, for me, some things will be relatively easy. Oh, and sorry about the talking while eating thing. I wasn't aware of that one. But in all fairness, I was so, so hungry. "Reciprocally, you know very little about me but we'll get that sorted as we go along." Emily stood and took their now empty mugs, obligingly placing them in the dishwasher, closing the door and looking over her shoulder at Jane.

"Yes, yes." said Jane sarcastically. "I've got that one now." They both laughed. As Jane stood up Emily came across to her and hugged her tight. Jane, slightly surprised at this slowly put her arms around Emily and felt the warmth and affection pouring out of her new friend.

"I still can't thank you enough Jane, for what you've done for me. I won't let you down. Honestly."

Chapter Seven

Present day, Emily and Jane

Jane wasn't quite sure what to make of the affection that seemed to be long standing, emanating from Emily, even though she had only really met her a few hours ago. It was comforting and she felt a link between herself and Beryl through Emily. This, she thought, very welcome and deep down inside she just knew that she was going to enjoy this newly made friendship. "What had you planned for today?" asked Emily nonchalantly.

"Nothing in particular" came the answer. "I am still trying to get to grips with what has happened to me and how my life has so suddenly changed, and changed dramatically. I mean, not so very long ago I was living in my little flat and had a quiet little job, which I enjoyed. I had a few friends and one special friend, Sarah."

"I like Sarah too" interrupted Emily.

"How do you—ah of course, I brought Sarah here didn't I? so you'll have met her so to speak."

"Yes, I know, it does seem a little sinister, but I have been in this house all the time you have been coming here. Right from when you were a little girl. Hey, I tell you what. Instead of standing here, let's go and sit in the garden. The birds can sing to us and the flowers can assault our noses and the sun can warm our faces."

They walked out into the garden, into the sunshine and the fragrant air to sit down on the bench seat. Jane jumped up and ran off towards the garden shed. "I'll get us some cushions" she shouted over her shoulder as she disappeared around the corner.

Now more comfortable, they continued their conversation. Jane looked across the garden, placed her hands in her lap and turned to look at Emily. "I have, as you probably know, always loved being here. Mum never told me why she jumped at the chance for me to stay here and I never really pursued it as I didn't want to jeopardise what I had here. I didn't have a lot of fun at home with my Mum. She blamed me for my father leaving us, even though, from what I can gather, he left before I was even born and I still don't know who he is. Mum would not entertain any conversation about my father and Aunt Beryl always told me that it was really down to my Mum to tell me about that episode. Even though I think she knew what had happened." Emily was totally enthralled by what she was hearing.

"So, you don't even know who your father is?"

"Nope, I just got shouted at even if I mentioned it so it was never brought up. I was happy at school and could entertain myself at home, reading and such like. I spent a lot of time in the library and of course this all turned out quite ironic really, becoming a librarian and now a historian. And now look at me. I have a lovely home; one I have loved all my life and I have enough money to enable me to be what I always wanted to be. A historian. I can pursue what was my hobby to my heart's content."

"And I can help you." said Emily.

"How?" asked Jane.

"Well, apart from the fact that I was living in this house in 1876 from when I was born, I have always been able to get information from the others."

"What do you mean 'the others?" asked Jane.

"The other ghosts, silly," laughed Emily. "There are loads of them. All of the people over the years, hundreds of years who, like me, had a spirit, soul or whatever you want to call it, that had no home when they died."

"What" exclaimed Jane. "So, you can talk to other ghosts?"

"Absolutely" replied Emily with a look of astonishment on her face. "Let me show you."

"Show me what?"

"Show you the others, well some of them anyway. Take my hand Jane and don't let go, not until I say so as it'll probably make you sick if you let go too soon. It's going to be a bit weird for you but normal for me. Ready?"

"Okay" said Jane with a look of trepidation on her face. She gently held Emily's hand. Emily immediately tightened the grip.

"Don't worry I just want to keep you from letting go" said Emily as the light around them seemed to fade as if a dark cloud had shrouded the sun. Jane felt the spark inside her again, the shiver that ran right through her body, totally filling her with warmth and that slight tingling sensation. She felt lighter as if she could float up from the bench into the air. The air itself seemed to still and solidify around them. She could see the garden, the flowers and trees but they all seemed slightly faded as if looking through a vaguely frosted window. "Nearly there," said Emily "Hang on. Really, don't let go." Suddenly the fading stopped and the air cleared and brightened perceptibly. The garden came into focus, perhaps even sharper than before. Sounds grew clearer and the smells more pronounced. Everything was in high definition. Jane could feel everything around her. She felt as if she were totally part of the world around her. She filled a void in the aether that was made for her and everything around her felt as if it was touching her, the sounds, smells, she could even taste the air. All her senses were enhanced. She looked at Emily slowly. Emily was sat with a knowing smile on her face. "Are you okay?" she asked looking deeply into Jane's eyes.

"Yes, yes, I think so" replied Jane "What exactly just happened?"

"You are now in my world."

"What? As in I'm a ghost?"

"Not quite" came the reply, "but not far off. The only difference between you and me right now is that you can return to your living state, whereas I cannot. As long as you keep hold of me, this is the world you can be in."

"But, why is everything so different?" asked Jane, looking around her. "Well, not different as such but so much clearer, everything is sharp and clean. I can sense everything around me. I can hear that butterfly over there. It's as if I can zoom in on it with my ears. I can almost hear it breathing. If they breath that is." She continued to look around her intently inspecting each object with a new vision.

"Amazing, isn't it?" said Emily "I'll never forget the first time I experienced it just after I died. Once I got used to the idea that I was actually dead and I was a ghost I suddenly realised that everything was, like you say, different but not, just so much clearer and sharper. There's no rush, take it in, get used to it, it's marvellous and I treat it as a gift to those who are trapped in this world rather than moving onto the next. Sort of compensation, I guess. Now, there are things you will see now that you couldn't see before. There are other ghosts like I said. But not only of people. There are ghosts of every type of living thing. They are all here for the same reason, their soul has not moved to the next body. They, too, are trapped here, so you will see all sorts of things wandering around. Look over there by the oak tree, see?" Emily pointed over towards the big tree, where, at its base was a dog, Jane could see quite clearly that it was a black Labrador. It was just laid there quite content, its muzzle resting on its outstretched paws, eyes closed, asleep. "He's a lovely, friendly dog but he doesn't move far from the tree. He'll always be in the garden somewhere. His master died right under that tree so I've been told, and the dog stayed there on the spot until he too died. His soul had nowhere to go so he's been here ever since."

"There seem to be more bees and butterflies around." said Jane.

"Same thing applies" said Emily "These are the lost ones but they, like the rest of us seem happy with their lot. It seems like a modern thing. The increase in the number of ghosts looks like it's due to the modern world. Beryl and I had extensive talks about the world and how there are so many extinctions and reductions in animals, insects and the like. You see, there are only a finite number of spirits on the planet. This means that—."

Jane interrupted "There are fewer new beings to move to, fewer births means that there are fewer beings to occupy."

"Exactly" agreed Emily. "I don't know how far it will go but the biggest increase is obviously in the population of the smaller beings, insects and such. There are definitely far more now that there were when I died that's for sure. Nothing we can do about it but it does make 'my' world a bit busier" she exclaimed. "Anyway, you need to experience what else you can see and do in my world I think."

"How do you mean?" asked Jane.

"Well," said Emily "what do you think we ghosts can do?"

"Appear and disappear?" questioned Jane.

"Goes without saying came the reply, but I'll just give you a run down on what we can do and some of the things you, maybe thought we could do but actually can't."

"What about walking through walls?" asked Jane somewhat sarcastically.

"Nope, that's not on the list, though it is fair to say we can pass through walls but it's not like walking through it more like getting from one side to the other, and here's the bit you'll like. You can do it too."

"What!" came the surprised response from Jane. "How?"

"Just hang on to me." said Emily standing up and pulling Jane with her towards the kitchen door. The pair were stood just in front of the door as Emily promptly closed it with a thump. "Door closed, yes?" she asked.

"It certainly looks that way." said Jane.

"Right, we'll just pass from one side to the other but don't let go of me for goodness' sake, will you?" Emily slowly moved towards the door pulling the slightly hesitant Jane with her. Emily slowly disappeared into the door with her arm outstretched behind her, gently pulling Jane towards her. Jane watched as first her hand and then her forearm vanished into the door. She stepped forwards closing her eyes expecting her face to collide with the oak planks but the next thing she knew she was on the other side. "Well, how was that?" asked Emily.

"Weird" said Jane, a confused look about her. She turned and looked back at the door and reached out her free hand to touched the wooden surface and her fingers felt the smooth oak, she stroked the door and turned back to Emily. "How come then, I can't put my hand back through the door?"

"Simple," came the reply, "because I control what happens. I mean, imagine if that function was always available. You wouldn't be able to move around very easily. I mean, if we were stood over the cellar, we would just fall through. The whole thing is selective. I control what object I, or in this case, we, pass through."

"Amazing" said Jane a look of total astonishment on her face. "I can't believe I have just passed through a door. Just incredible."

"Okay," said Emily, "check this one out then, come and stand in front of the mirror on the landing." They walked up the stairs hand in hand. As they reached the top and turned around, Jane looked towards the mirror fully expecting to see the two of them reflected in the glass, stood there, hands clasped. She took a sharp intake of breath and nearly choked with what she saw, or what she actually didn't see. There was nothing there, just the reflection of the landing and the picture on the wall opposite. "I'm going to let you go now Jane, it may feel a bit weird but I'll go slowly to try and make it more comfortable. You'll get used to the feeling eventually." Emily carefully released her grip on Jane's hand, letting her fingers slide gently away until just their fingertips were touching. "Ready?" she said.

"Okay" replied Jane. Emily moved her finger so that it was no longer touching Jane's but there was still a slight pull and a sparkling sensation between them and a barely visible thread of blue light joined their fingers, until Emily lowered her arm. Jane, looking in the mirror saw a hazy outline appear, a shimmer and the reflection faded until she could see her own outline slowly making itself visible. She then felt a thud within her as if she had been inflated. Her reflection was now solid and she could see herself completely. "That was so weird." she said, turning to Emily who was no longer there by her side. "Emily, Emily, where are you? I can't see you" she said twisting around, trying to see where her companion had gone.

"I'm right here Jane" came a voice from nowhere. Jane looked towards the point where the voice seemed to be coming from and saw the same shimmering effect that she saw in the mirror as Emily slowly appeared in front of her. Jane touched Emily on the shoulder just to confirm that she was now solid. She turned to the mirror, confused now because where Emily's reflection should have been there was nothing, even though Jane was actually touching her, Emily was not visible in the mirror. But then, she noticed the same shimmer in the air and the outline of Emily slowly made itself apparent, until, the reflection too was solid.

"What just happened?" asked Jane pointing at the mirror and then at Emily. She turned back towards the mirror and again to Emily as if to just confirm that both Emily and her reflection were still there. She looked directly at Emily, touching her face carefully, feeling that it was smooth and soft, her hair over her shoulder. Emily smiled and just pointed at the mirror. Jane turned and the reflection was gone. She turned back to Emily who was still there and Emily, again, pointed at the mirror. Again, Jane turned back to see the reflection appearing and disappearing randomly.

"This is a handy function." said Emily. "Being able to appear and disappear at will."

"I bet." said Jane, eyes wide. "So, did you and Aunt Beryl do all this stuff?"

"No" came the reply, "Beryl tried some of the things but didn't get along with it very well, made her quite sick really so we just didn't carry on with that. She just needed a companion, someone to talk to and share her life. And, for me, that was great as I was able to be my solid self rather than a wispy ghostly thing."

"So, you need a living person in order to remain solid?"

"Yes, like I said before and this is why I'm so grateful to you. A ghost needs a living human to remain in this state. Otherwise, I just exist in the aether, which is no fun at all really as I can't interact with others. When I first came to you in the bedroom, I touched your hand just enough to enable you to see me. See, after Beryl died my ability to appear solid lost its energy and I went back to being a normal ghost." Jane laughed uncontrollably at this. "What's so funny Jane?" asked Emily scowling. Her hands on her hips.

"Oh, sorry Emily." said Jane her hand over her mouth eyes ablaze with humour. "It's just you said 'normal ghost'." she laughed again. "Is there anything normal about a ghost?"

"To me there is." Emily's voice quite stern.

"But look at it from my point of view." said Jane "A while ago I didn't even believe in ghosts. But here I am right now not only talking to one but actually acting like one. Appearing and disappearing, passing through doors and just having you stood there. Who would believe me?"

"Right, yes, I guess so. Anyway, enough of this frivolity lets go and have some lunch and I'll tell you what else we can do now we are joined."

The pair discovered that they could carry out simple tasks in total harmony. Making some lunch was trivial as they seemed to know what each other was thinking and acted accordingly. Within a few minutes the table was prepared and sandwiches made. The ubiquitous cake adorned the centre of the cloth. Sitting opposite each other they devoured the spread. Once tea was poured, they sat back and just admired each other.

They sat at the kitchen table for their lunch. All the time Jane looked confused and intrigued. The lack of conversation was noticeable.

"I've got such a lot to ask you Emily. You know a lot about me but I know very little about you."

"What would you like to know?"

"You were about twenty-eight when you died, is that right?"

"Spot on, why?"

"So, what did you do, for work I mean?"

"Oh, I was a teacher. I worked in the village school. Ever since I left school, I was a teacher. I was good as well from what I can gather. If I had carried on, I think I would have ended up as the Head Mistress. I loved my job. But it wasn't to be. A stupid slip and that was that. In some ways I really regret it but in other ways I don't. It's one of those cases where either life would have been good. Given the choice between the two I really don't know which way I would go. I enjoy this life but it can get lonely when I don't have a companion. That's why I approached Beryl and now you. Don't get me wrong, it wasn't a selfish choice. I could genuinely see Beryl's torment and I knew I could do something about it."

"How did that come about?"

"Same as you Jane, I just appeared in her room, your room now. I even sat on that same chair. She was a bit shocked and, I think, slightly scared. She thought she had died. It took me ages to convince her that she hadn't and I was just a ghost. But once we had joined, she loved it. It was just for the company. She missed John so much and felt like she was rattling around in the house. I just filled a little hole in her life and we really did have a great time. We had so much fun. Did you know she cheated at cards?"

"No, laughed Jane. But that does explain why she always won. Anyway, why did you choose to join with me?"

"I must admit." said Emily. "That was a bit selfish. After the life I had with Beryl I really didn't want to give it up and I just wanted to help look after Chapwell, it's a massive part of my life and I wanted it to continue. And." she said hesitantly. "I really liked you, Jane. I liked you from your first visit and watched you every day you were here."

"Okay" said Jane, ending the conversation. "What else can we do then?"

"We can time travel" replied Emily, casually.

"No way!" exclaimed Jane.

"Yes way, we certainly can only it's a bit more complicated than that."

"How so?" asked Jane.

"Well, we can sort of view portions of time in any location but we cannot interact with anything because that would just be plain dangerous as it risks changing history and we just can't do that."

"What about the future?" asked Jane.

"Nope, that's out too, totally out, just cannot happen, which, to be honest is a good thing really. No, we are based in this time but we can see back into the past."

"I'm confused here Emily."

"Why?" came the response.

"Well, I am certainly not dead, not like you are but I can do stuff that you do as a ghost."

"Correct" said Emily.

"And, you are dead, not like me and you can do stuff that I can do."

"Right again," said Emily. "But. That will only work if we are joined as companions, like we are now though, to be honest, we have not yet got to our full potential."

"How do you mean?" enquired Jane.

"Well, we have only just begun our relationship. You see I, as you now know, can only be visible and in this solid state when I am attached to a person. My strength comes from you, my ability to take on living functions. And, for you it is the opposite. You get to take on some of the functions of a ghost. Eventually we become virtually the same."

"And by the same you mean what exactly?" asked Jane.

"We will be able to do the same sort of things independently but this will take training for you and a long time. I have been doing it for a while because I was attached to Beryl you see. And I've had the benefit of learning from other ghosts who have been around a while."

"How many are there?" asked Jane hesitantly, with an anxious look about her.

"Oh, quite a few in the area and there are a couple attached to this house, or at least to the grounds the house sits on. But don't worry about that right now, you will meet them in time."

"Right, so I can learn some of the things you can do. And I'll be able to do these things independently of you?"

"Eventually, yes. It may take years, though." replied Emily "But for now we must be in contact, like I said we are not fully connected yet. We need to be close to each other for a good while yet but if we need to do anything now, we can just hold hands. That will do. Eventually I will be able to let go of you and be farther away from you and you can continue being a ghost as it were and I can carry on being alive. Now, you remember you came over once and Beryl didn't know about it?"

"When you were in the garden?" asked Jane.

"Yes. You could see me because I was fully connected and could be visible anytime I wanted and anywhere. I didn't need to be close to Beryl at all. I remember you saw me in the bedroom when you first arrived here."

"Yes" said Jane. "But Beryl was gone then, ages gone and you could still be visible."

"I know, the effects last for ages, months in fact but they do fade eventually and that was really the last time I was visible like that. I needed you, which was why I came to you that very night. I didn't want to keep on scaring you because I was becoming useless at hiding myself in this house. I've been here for so long and after Beryl I was forgetting myself all the time. I needed you to understand and join me. You didn't mind, did you?" asked Emily.

"Of course, I don't mind" said Jane, smiling and reaching across the table to take Emily's hand. "I think, even for me it would be a bit lonely in this house on my own. Don't get me wrong, I absolutely love it here and can't think of a better place to live but it is quite big and will take a bit of looking after."

"There we are then." said Emily. "We live here together and can work together, I am sure."

"What about Sarah?" asked Jane "She's my best friend, well one of my best friends as I now have two." she smiled.

"That is entirely up to you Jane, well, and Sarah, I guess. She can come here whenever she likes or whenever you like and we can treat her however you would like her to be treated. She can join us in our double life or death, or she can remain as she is, it's entirely up to you and her. I'll do whatever you want."

"Do you mean she can join us?" asked Jane.

"No, not as such. We can only be joined to one living person at any time. Now, I know you read His Dark Materials"

"Yes, yes, I did, but what's that got to do with anything?"

"Well, you remember the Daemon that Lyra had?"

"Yes, Pantalaimon"

"Well think of me as your Daemon now, now that we are joined though there are differences. I can wander as far away from you as I like. I won't vanish if you die and I can't change shape but we work along the same sort of lines. Eventually, as time goes along, we will begin to understand each other more, what we are thinking and doing. We will be able to feel each other's presence. Even to the point where if one of us is threatened or frightened the other will be able to sense it.

"Wow, that's awesome," said Jane.

"Sarah won't be able to be part of us, though if we wish it and it is prudent, I can be visible to Sarah and we can interact, just not on the same level as you and I can, but there's no harm in her coming here to visit. No problem at all."

"Right." said Jane expectantly. "What about this time travel business then. How does that work?"

"For now," said Emily "You will need to be touching me, holding hands like we have been and then I can concentrate on a date in time and we can sit here and watch what was happening. We cannot interact, like I said but we can gain knowledge and knowledge is key. This only works for the time that I have been dead though, so we cannot travel any further back. We would need the help of the others."

"Others?" said Jane, a worried look on her face."

"Yes, I did say. There are others here as well, you saw the dog and the butterflies and things. There are other people as well. Leave that for now, we'll get onto that when you fully understand what we're doing now. Right, first expedition will be to my death birth."

"Eh?" enquired Jane, confused.

"My death birth, the day I died and was born, born as a ghost, that is."

"And you call it a death birth?" asked Jane with a wry smile.

"What would you call it then?" asked Emily.

Jane folded her arms across her chest and looked at the ceiling, thinking. "Dunno, I guess death birth is as good as anything, describes it well, doesn't it?"

"Exactly" came the response. "Come on, we'll go up onto the landing and I'll show you" said Emily grabbing Jane's hand as she walked around the table, dragging her out of the kitchen and up the stairs. "Right, lets stand right here by the balustrade, you can get the best view." They stood looking over the top at the stairs with a view right to the bottom. "Okay, now hold my hand again." said Emily. Jane gripped her hand. "Whoa, not quite so tight Jane, please."

"Sorry, I don't know how much I need to hold on."

"Not as much as that" said Emily, releasing her grip and shaking her hand to relieve the pain. "Try again, not so hard this time?" Jane held Emily's hand a little more gently and could immediately feel the energy moving through her body until she was totally engulfed by the warmth. "Okay" she said.

"Now what?"

"Be patient, let me sort my head out a bit and I'll get us back there." said Emily closing her eyes. Jane noticed things slowly changing. The décor slowly faded; the pictures moved around the walls; the mirror stayed exactly where it was. The stair runner disappeared to reveal the dark oak steps, polished to a shine. She looked around until everything stabilised. Emily, whose eyes were now open looked around expectantly. "Strange, normally I get us back to the exact moment I die but I'm not there at the bottom. Must have got something wrong somewhere, I'll try again." But before she got herself prepared, the bedroom door opened and Emily's live version came tumbling out of the door, took two quick steps onto the rug which rucked as it slid across the polished landing. Emily stumbled towards the stairs where she tripped on the rumpled rug, hit the wall, collapsed down the stairs, tumbled twice and crashed head first into the large, heavy urn on the bottom landing. She rolled onto her side totally still, not a movement at all. Slowly, a red pool appeared under her head and spread across the oak boards. They both stood totally transfixed by what they had just seen.

Unable to speak they just looked at each other with matching shock on their faces.

"I thought—" said Jane.

"Yes, so did I" replied Emily. "I have never seen that before. I have honestly never seen the bit of time right before I fell. It has always been at the point that I actually died which was a few seconds after the blood started pouring out of my head. Normally I can just see the pool of blood. They both looked over the balustrade, down at the lifeless body at the bottom. Emily's mother ran out of the kitchen and screamed, kneeling down, she lifted Emily's lifeless head, blood spreading over the floor, her hands and dress. "That's enough," said Emily, who was by now weeping quietly, covering her eyes. Jane felt a cold shock run through her and saw the landing returning to the present day, no body at the bottom of the stairs. No blood and no urn.

Emily wiped her eyes; tears had run down her face. Jane gave her a handkerchief. "Thank you, Jane," she said wiping the moisture from her face. "I can't stand any more of that episode. Not for me but for my mother, she was so heartbroken."

"I can understand." said Jane. "A simple slip on the rug and it was all over. But how come we could see you come out of the bedroom?"

"I don't know, that is so weird. We saw about 30 seconds before I actually died. It's never happened before. Unless it is something to do with you being attached to me?"

"Yeah, but you'd have seen it while you were attached to Aunt Beryl surely?" I never did the time thing with Beryl, never really did anything out of the ordinary with her, she didn't want any of that. Like I said, she just wanted a friend and companion and I was quite happy with that."

"Shall we get some fresh air?" asked Jane.

"Yes." replied Emily. "I think that's a great idea right now, fancy a walk down the village?"

"Okay," came the reply, as they walked back down the body free stairs, the image still lingering in Jane's mind. "It should cheer you up a bit."

"I'll show you what it's like to interact with others," said Emily, picking up her boots from the hallway floor, "and this is where a lot of discipline on your part is needed."

"Why?" asked Jane.

"Think about it Jane, come on. You are holding hands with me so you can be visible or invisible and that is something I control. I'll always tell you when you are visible and when not. But then you have to remember that you can always see me unless I decide to be invisible. You will always be able to hear me regardless of which state I am in so you have to listen. This is where the discipline comes in. You cannot speak to me, look at me, gesture at me or interact in any way with me when we are around other living people. They'll mark you down as mad otherwise. Beryl was not very good at that, there were a number of occasions that she made a mistake and spoke to me but I think folk in the village just thought she was perhaps losing it a bit after John died. They never suspected that she was talking to a ghost. Though perhaps they did, John's ghost maybe. Whatever, you cannot afford to let that slip as you are not old and haven't just lost your husband so you have no rational excuse."

"Yes, I see." said Jane deep in thought, tying her boot laces. "I guess we'll find out. I need to go to the shop anyway, get some ham and a lettuce for our dinner."

As Jane closed the little gate onto the road, Emily took a few steps forward and disappeared. "Where the hell have you gone now?" asked Jane exasperated.

"Don't panic I'm right here, right by your side." Just to confirm, Jane felt Emily's fingers touch her hand. "You'll need to get used to this now, this is training. We are going to walk down to the village, get the shopping and if anyone speaks to you, just act as your normal self. You won't be able to see me so I won't distract you and every now and then I will touch you just so that you know I am there."

"This is so weird." said Jane. "A bit difficult to get my head around it."

"Don't worry, you'll get used to it. The hard bit is going to be when I am visible to you and then, even harder is when we are both invisible. But as no one can see you they will not to interact but you do need to avoid them as they will feel you if you touch them and you always need to remember that you are invisible so no moving stuff, opening doors or picking stuff up or talking so we'll leave that lesson for now.

They reached the shop and Jane hesitated outside the door, not sure of what was going to happen as she walked in. "Go on, get in there, you're looking weird. And don't answer me, remember, just listen and feel. No talking." Jane was just about to speak as she turned her head. "Ah, ah" said Emily quietly as her wagging finger appeared in mid-air. "No talking and I mean no talking, not to me anyway."

Jane grabbed the door handle and turned it. Pushing it open, the little bell jingled. The same bell that was there when she was a child.

"Hello Jane!" she heard from the counter.

"Oh, hello Eileen." said Jane, recognising the voice of the bustling Eileen as she walked down the aisle to the end. "How are you?" asked Jane.

"I'm absolutely fine thank you Jane. Lovely to see you. How are you getting on at Chapwell? Is it a bit lonely down there?"

"No, not at all" said Jane turning around hoping she would catch Emily's invisible eye. "Obviously I miss Aunt Beryl."

"I know" said Eileen "We all miss her, well both of them. It was a terrible shock and they are missed terribly in the village, it is so sad." Eileen's eyes visibly saddened as she was reminded of the pair of them. Collecting herself she looked back up at Jane, placing her hands on the small counter, surrounded by newspapers, The lifeboats charity box prominent on top of the till "Now, what can I get for you?" she asked changing the subject as she could see how it affected Jane.

"Can I have a couple of slices of that lovely ham you always have, I'll go and get a lettuce."

"Take your time, take your time." said Eileen. Jane turned almost expecting to collide with Emily, but of course she wasn't there.

She felt a touch on her shoulder and before she could speak or look around, she heard Emily whisper. "Don't. Just keep on walking. Remember, I'm not here."

"Oh, Jane," shouted Eileen

"Yes" she replied.

"Mr Francis has just brought in some fresh bread if you need any."

"Oh, okay, thanks" said Jane picking up a basket and continuing around the shop.

"Ooo, look at those cakes Jane" said Emily drooling over the pastry counter. Jane turned to look and was just about to speak. "No, no. No talking, remember, but just put two of those custard slices in your basket, go on, go on, just do it." Jane placed two of said slices in a paper bag and carefully put them in her basket.

"No more." whispered Jane as she collected a fresh and noticeably warm cob loaf, placing it alongside the cakes. Provisions paid for and packed in her bag, Jane said goodbye and left the shop. Once out of the door she breathed a heavy sigh.

"Are you okay?" asked Emily.

Jane looked around her checking that there was no one else in sight and whispered. "Yeah, yeah, I'm okay but that was strange, just knowing that you were there by me all the time."

"Well, actually I wasn't by you all the time. I had a wander around by myself and you didn't even notice, did you?"

"No, I guess not but you weren't far away, were you? I could feel you somehow, particularly by the cake counter!"

"No but I just want you to get used to me being around you but not visible. The next thing we can do is try something with me visible. How about we pop in the pub. You can have a quick glass of wine and see what happens?"

"Okay, we can give it a go but if things start going a bit pear-shaped, you'll just need to disappear so I cannot see you, yes?"

"If you think it will help. One thing I will do is keep out of your way so you won't need to dodge around me if we are close. I'll just go in the door and sit down at a table. That way I won't distract you.

You won't need to open the door for me don't forget, I can pass right through them." Just try and imagine yourself on your own."

"Right, okay, with a ghost in tow." said Jane bewildered.

"If you like."

Jane picked up the pace a bit and walked along the road up to the pub. It was quiet. No traffic and only a few cars parked in the village. A ginger cat jumped down from a gate and wandered across the road, not in any rush, merely taking itself to its next place to snooze, it turned and looked at Jane briefly but quickly continued on its path, its tail twitching slightly. The pub, a black and white building was the in the centre of the village both physically and socially. It formed the heart of the community where folk from all around came to express their views, ponder over news and discuss the events that affected them. It also served the finest ale in the area and the food was renowned as being excellent, not pretentious, but, simple, wholesome fare.

The outer door of the Kings Arms was open but the door to the lounge was closed. Concentrating and fully aware that Emily was right there she just pushed the sprung loaded door open and let it go as she passed through. She just couldn't help thinking that the door had returned and smashed Emily right in the face, but no, a cautious look behind her saw Emily stepping straight through the now closed door. Emily flicked her hand towards the bar encouraging Jane to keep walking. The interior of the pub was an extension of the exterior. It was old and warm, comforting and calm, though, as Jane knew, the darts nights could get quite rowdy.

Jane walked up to the bar. Colin, the landlord was polishing glasses at the other end. He was chatting to one of the farmers Jane recognised. Both laughing at some joke no doubt. The farmer, in his overalls, looked across and seeing Jane, raised his huge gnarled hand in a small wave to her. He reached and touched his cap, oil and dust disguising its brand name. Colin, seeing Jane, placed the polished glass carefully in its rightful place amongst the other gleaming crystal and placing his drying towel down on the counter he absently picked up a different cloth, whereupon he wiped the bar as he walked down towards Jane, smiling as he went.

"Well, well, what a sight for sore eyes. How are you, Jane? So nice to see the lady of the manor frequenting our humble establishment." He bowed slightly in jest.

Jane smiled broadly. "Oh, stop it, Colin. You'll make me blush. I'm absolutely fine thank you. Are you all okay? Helen?"

"We're both fine thank you. All the better for seeing you. Helen isn't here right now; she's gone to see her mum for the afternoon. Anyway, what can I get you my dear?"

She ordered a half pint of ale, paid for it and turned to find Emily. She saw her sat alone at a table under the window, legs crossed with a look on her face which said, careful now, think about it. Jane sat down next to Emily, placed her shopping bag under the table and stared across at the bar.

"Get your phone out Jane," said Emily. "Make it look like you are doing something at least." Jane was about to speak but Emily's hand raised to stop her. "If you want to say something, you have a tool to do so right in front of you." Jane turned to Emily with a puzzled look. "Jane, come on use the notepad on there. You can type stuff on that and I can read it, easy, eh?"

Jane brought up the notepad on her phone and started typing. If anyone looked over to her it would appear that she was just texting or emailing. "How am I doing?" she typed.

Emily leaned over to read it. "You're doing fine, just don't tilt the phone towards me I'll lean over to read but you're doing fine so far. Who's that chap at the bar? He keeps looking over towards you. But before you look up remember I'm not here. Just take a glimpse casually."

Jane placed her phone on the table and nonchalantly looked around the bar tagging the chap stood there drinking. He looked right at her and before she could avert her eyes, he smiled at her. She smiled back but quickly picked up her phone and started typing. "I've seen him before in the village, don't know who he is but Aunt Beryl told me he was bad news."

"Bugger" said Emily. "He's coming over, just keep typing."

The chap came over and stood right in front of the table. "You're Jane, aren't you?" he asked, a not so pleasant smirk on his face.

"Yes, that's right." said Jane not looking up from her phone.

"Do you know who I am?" he asked. Jane looked up at the 50ish unshaven face, scruffy tee-shirt and grubby jeans. Unkempt hair that was obviously in need of a cut.

She placed her phone back on the table and replied, "Well, no, not really. I've seen you around but I can't say as I know who you are."

"Well," he said "I'm Rob, a mate of David's but I think we'll just leave it at that for now, shall we?" He quickly turned, spilling his drink on the table as he went and took his position back at the bar. The barman looked over towards Jane with a knowing look and picking up a towel he came across to Jane's table wiping the surface of the spilt beer.

"Don't worry about him Jane." he said quietly, mopping up. "We all just about tolerate him but we'll all make sure he doesn't cause any grief."

"Thanks Colin," said Jane. He finished wiping the table and returned to his place behind the bar giving a sharp, warning look at Rob as he passed.

Jane started typing. "What was that all about then?"

"I don't know." replied Emily. I don't know who he is but I do know who David is and it might not be good news that this Rob guy knows who you are."

"How do you mean?" asked Jane.

"I'll explain a bit more when we get home."

Jane was enjoying her beer, comfortable in the safe environment of the pub. She had spent many an entertaining evening here with Beryl and John in the past. John often walked up here and was always made welcome by everyone in attendance. He was a key member of the community, always helping with events in the village, joining in and organising some of the more historical village traditions. She wondered whether, she, too could be involved more and vowed to spend the odd evening in the pub. Though if this chap, Rob kept looking at her in the disturbing way he was right now, she thought she might need to ask for Colin's assistance in making her stay a little more pleasant.

Jane finished her beer and took her empty glass over to the bar, placing it on the mat. Rob turned his head to look at her. He didn't say anything but raised his glass to her in a mock salutation. With the nasty smirk still on his face he said, "See you around love, eh? Come back—"

"Leave it Rob." interrupted Colin, who had obviously been keeping an eye on his behaviour from the other end of the bar. "Don't take any notice Jane, we'll see you again sometime. Bring a friend if you like, you're always welcome."

"Oh, yeah." said Rob with another even more sinister smirk. "You're always welcome, and your 'friend'."

"Rob" said Colin sternly, bringing his hand down on the bar sharply. "Leave her alone now, she doesn't want anything to do with you, and be careful. Your ban is getting closer to being reinstated if you keep it up."

Jane smiled at Colin knowingly and turned to leave. Once out of the pub she breathed a heavy sigh. "C'mon Emily, let's get home. That was too much excitement for one afternoon."

Chapter Eight

David

They walked into the kitchen, Jane placing the shopping bag on the table, Emily putting the kettle on. "I'll make us some tea and I'll give you the low down on David, I guess it's time you knew it all."

"Now, hang on." said Jane. "It was not so long ago that I was told in no uncertain terms that David was not to be mentioned."

"Er, yeah, okay." said Emily. "But as his name was just brought up in the pub it may be time for you to know a bit more. Beryl did tell me that once we had settled down together, I should tell you everything about it."

"So" asked Jane "Aunt Beryl knew you would be attaching yourself to me?"

"Yes," came the reply "I promised her that I would become your friend, provided you wanted it of course, but yes, there was a sort of pact made between us. Because she knew me and she knew you and had an idea that we would get on, she hoped we could be joined. Also, with the knowledge I have, both from living, or existing would be a better word, in this house and what I have learned from Beryl, you would be better prepared for your future here."

"So, this was planned?" asked Jane slightly agitated.

"Sort of, not in a sinister way though. Beryl just wanted you to have the house and the money and be able to look after Chapwell and yourself for the rest of your life. Her priority was always you and the house. Nothing more, nothing less. But there are things that you don't yet know but really need to know and I'll help in all this. And after what happened in the pub, there's a chance that things may become apparent earlier than we would have liked."

"Sorry." said Jane shaking her head and still a bit fraught. "It almost seems to me that there is some kind of agenda here Emily and I'm not sure I approve to be honest."

"Please don't think of it like that Jane, Beryl loved you dearly and she always loved Chapwell. And, I hope she enjoyed my company as well. But she just wanted to ensure that your life here was going to be as delightful as hers was. The things that have been kept from you were kept from you for a reason. Christopher and Kate know all about it and as they said, they were not willing to bring it all up."

"How would you know about that?" asked Jane but suddenly, she realised. "You were here, weren't you? You've been here all the time. Watching and listening. How much have you heard and seen Emily?" Jane was becoming quite agitated now.

"Oh." said Emily sorrowful. "I know what it sounds like but it hasn't been like that at all, honestly Jane, my intentions, and Beryl's for that matter have always been for the best. For you in fact. Look, let me make the tea and we'll sit down and I can explain. It might take a while. Well," she said with a strained look on her face. "There's no might about it. It *will* take a while but please don't hate me Jane, I've known you all your life and during that time, yes, I have watched you, listened to you, followed you but from when you were a little girl, I knew that a life with you here at Chapwell would be an absolute dream. A dream for both of us. I wasn't being selfish. You see, our lives revolve around this house. It is a wonderful house that has a long, very long history. It has many secrets. It has seen total joy and of course it has seen sadness. But the house endured. Nothing can take the spirit from this house and now, it is for us to ensure that spirit lives on."

Emily made the tea and they sat in their usual places at the kitchen table. They looked at each other. Jane expectant and somewhat stern. Emily, hesitant and sorrowful. Sorrowful because Jane was upset.

"Firstly, Jane, I need to apologise, as I have lied to you." said Emily, her eyes turned down to the table.

"Lied? How do you mean lied?"

"Well." replied Emily looking up at Jane sheepishly. "Earlier I denied knowing anything about your Mum and her relationship with Beryl and John and, of course, Chapwell. This was a lie. I do know and I am going to explain but you'll soon see why I lied."

"Well, I guess we'll see now, won't we." said Jane sat in her chair, her arms folded in front of her, glowering at Emily.

"I think we need to get the David thing out in the open first Jane but there is one caveat."

"What's that?"

"It's this. Don't think any less of your mother as it involves her and will give you a better idea of how she is and why she is like she is, particularly with you."

"Intriguing" said Jane, leaning forwards and taking a sip of tea.

"Yes, I suppose it is and you'll realise eventually, exactly why things have been like they are and it all revolves around you."

"Me?"

"Yes" said Emily, "You. As you now know Beryl and John had another son, David."

"Yes, but that's all I know, they had a son and he was not liked and had been in prison."

"Yes, but there is a lot more to it than that though. It's easiest if I start at the beginning. David was the oldest child by a year or so and he was really naughty. He was a restless baby and this was followed by him being a naughty child. Both Beryl and John had difficulty with him. And, of course later on, as he grew up, it resulted in Christopher and Kate taking sides. Not because they wanted to. They both tried very hard to make David their brother. They always let him join in with their games but that usually ended in tears. David would just want his own way and to destroy everything. He was impossible. They sought help but even that didn't work. The school threatened to expel him on numerous occasions. He was, and I don't use this word lightly, a nasty child. He broke his toys and when he couldn't get his own way, he broke Christopher's toys as well. I watched him one day."

"How do you mean, watched him?" asked Jane.

"Jane, come on, I have seen most things and this whole episode with David was the most difficult. I haven't been spying as such, but I was worried for John, Beryl and the other children, it was so difficult to watch what was happening. Anyway, I was following him and he snuck into Kate's bedroom one afternoon. Everyone else was in the garden. John was cutting the grass, Christopher was clearing up the grass cuttings, Beryl was pricking out some seedlings in the greenhouse and Kate was just sat, as she often did, just watching the insects in the garden. But David was in Kate's room. He picked up every one of Kate's dolls, teddy bears and other soft animals and pulled their heads off."

"What!" exclaimed Jane.

"Yes, he pulled their heads off. And when he came across one of the teddy bears that he couldn't tear the head off, he went downstairs, got a knife and cut the head off."

"My god, that's awful. What on earth made him want to do that?

"No-one ever found out, and this is the real nasty part, where all the more serious problems started really. He was in the garden with everyone else to start with but he was just going around, catching insects and killing them. Totally indiscriminately. Stamping on the ones on the ground, swatting the ones on the flowers and catching as many as he could and pulling off their legs and wings, dropping them on the floor and watching them struggle. When he got bored, he would just stamp on them." Jane's face was showing increasing signs of disgust and revulsion. She pushed her tea away, no longer thirsty.

"How awful. What happened next, or don't I want to know?"

"Kate saw what he was doing and shouted at him to stop. This, of course alerted Beryl to yet another incident with David. Once Kate had shown Beryl what he had been doing, John obviously became aware that there was a fracas and came over to see what was going on. This turned to extreme anger in John. I had never seen him so angry. He went bright red. He just told David to go to his room and stay there. He didn't hit him, though I wouldn't have blamed him. I never saw John harm anyone or anything but this incident got him so close I was worried. David just said that he didn't want to be there anyway and stomped off."

"But what happened when Kate found her toys?"

"I was getting to that." said Emily. "It wasn't until later. After tea in fact, that Kate went upstairs to find the mess. She just wailed. Such painful cries came from her. All her favourite toys had been destroyed. It was such a sad thing to see, I felt terrible. Especially as I had seen what was happening but was powerless to do anything."

"What, you couldn't tell anyone?"

"No, I wasn't attached to anyone then, was I? I could only move about and see things, I had no way of materialising or communicating."

"So, you couldn't do the poltergeist thing then?"

"Stuff and nonsense that is, stuff and nonsense. Made up by people who think they believe in ghosts Jane. But as you can imagine things could only get worse. And they did, believe me."

"The destruction of things continued as he grew up and for some unknown reason these episodes went in short spells. One week he would be absolutely fine. Almost a normal child and then suddenly it was like Jekyll and Hyde. He turned into a monster. Eventually he was sent to a special school. A school that was set up to handle difficult children, and, for a while it did make a difference but it was short lived. The same things started happening there as well. He was violent and destructive and it even looked like the school couldn't handle it. They persevered and he did get some specialist help and that seemed to change him again. But as we now know, he was becoming clever; he was playing them. He knew that if he did what they wanted, he could get favours back and eventually he was allowed out on his own. Disaster, that's the only way I can describe it. A total disaster."

"How do you mean?" asked Jane. "How could it get any worse?"

"Well, it did. He was allowed out and, again, he played them. He knew exactly what he was doing. It caught up with him as he got older though, he came into the realms of adult crime. He was living in a hostel and that's where he started on drugs. Mild at first but as we all know it can only go downhill and it was like he was on a rollercoaster. Taking drugs was the start and that resulted in a few spells in a juvenile detention centre and, inevitably, as he got older this developed into dealing and that's where he ended up in prison the first time."

"I'm sorry Emily but I don't really see where this involves me."

"I'm getting to that." said Emily holding her hand up." While he was in prison he was, so called, rehabilitated. Rehabilitated to live in the outside world. He was clean and was no longer dealing, or so they thought, but he had bigger ideas. And this is where you come in. It's also the most difficult part of the whole story."

"Why?"

"You'll see." said Emily with a pause. "David came back into this area. He even came to see Beryl and John on the odd occasion but there was no love there, no affection, nothing, so the visits became more infrequent and eventually stopped altogether. He was only after money anyway. One day, he even went into the shop asking for money. Saying that he was John's son and was entitled to money out of the till. That got him another warning so he slunk off. But not for long. He then met your mother."

Emily stopped talking and looked at Jane. Jane was speechless. "How do you mean, met my mother?" she said, an exasperated look on her face.

"He met your mother. In the pub."

"Was mum married to dad then?"

"Yes, she was."

"And?"

"Jane, this is so difficult but please don't shoot the messenger. I have got to tell you this. I promised Beryl I would tell you if the need arose. She would have told you herself but knew it was going to hurt and she didn't want to destroy everything you had with her. She wasn't being selfish, honestly, quite the opposite in fact. She was protecting you."

"Protecting me from what exactly." said Jane getting quite frustrated and a little angry now.

"She was protecting you from what had happened and how it could affect you. You see your Mum was drunk. As far as we can tell, your mum had started going to the pub for company because your dad was away from home for so long. Your mum was having some kind of relationship with David while your dad was away and took David home with her one night. She didn't know him that well, and obviously didn't know anything about his history. The violence, the drugs and the prison spells." Emily took a deep breath and blurted out. "It ended in a rape case in court. David went to prison. Your father found out and left. That's it, I've said it now. Please don't be angry with me." Emily hung her head, tears dropping from her face onto the table. She sobbed. "I'm so sorry Jane but that's it, that is what was being kept from you."

Jane was stunned into silence. She started to shake. Her eyes glazed over. She blinked and the tears started. Just running down her face. Emily got up and went around the table, grabbed jane around the shoulders and hugged ger tight. "I'm so, so sorry Jane. I knew this was going to hurt and hurt a lot. Believe me I have had this knowledge for so many years and each time I looked at you I knew that one day I was going to destroy something in you. Your life would never be the same again. I'm so sorry."

"It's okay, Emily, honestly, it's okay. It's not your fault that this happened and I'm sorry you have had to carry this with you all these years."

"You don't hate me then?" Emily pleaded.

"No, no, of course not, of course not" said Jane looking straight ahead, the tears still making their mark down her cheeks.

Jane stood up and took Emily in her arms and hugged her so tight she never thought she could let go. "Oh, not so tight." came a strained whimper. "You'll kill me". They both let go and laughed. They laughed loud and long, the tears still coming. They hugged again.

"Oh, Emily. What can I possibly do without you now? You know all my secrets and secrets that even I don't know. It must be hard for you to keep all that?"

"Yes, it is, this secret, particularly. But it doesn't end there, Jane. There's one little bit that may be more devastating."

"How can anything be more devastating than finding out that your own mother had been raped by the son of someone you loved so dearly?"

"Well." said Emily. "Nine months later or there abouts. You were born."

Silence. Total silence between them. Jane looked right into Emily's eyes, pleading for her to be so wrong. "So, what you're saying is that this monster is my father?"

"Could be, Jane, could be." said Emily sorrowfully. "We don't know. No-one really knows. He was tried, convicted and sentenced. As you know, he's out now but living in Bristol from what we gather. The worst part of this whole thing is that your father left your mother because of this."

"Because he thought I was David's daughter?"

"No, we think it was just because Your father found out that your mother was having an affair with David. It had been going on for a few weeks before, well, you know, before what happened, happened."

"So, my mum thinks David is my father and that is why she treats me like she does?"

"Beryl and I talked a lot about this Jane. And, yes, we thought the same. Your mum blames Beryl and John for what happened. Or, at least she holds them partly responsible."

"So, me being left here so many times was payback?"

"Jane, look at it from your mum's point of view. She was raped by their son, and, as far as your mother is concerned you were the outcome, so she does, or did, hold Beryl and John at least partly responsible."

"My god" said Jane, shocked", so I was a burden to Aunt Beryl and Uncle John."

"No, no, Jane. They loved you from day one and with the situation with your mum, whether you were David's child or not you would have been treated exactly the same. It wouldn't matter what the circumstances were, given the opportunity to look after you and give you a life that you could enjoy was their priority and, as you now know, you have been given the house and a lot of money because they loved you. Not because they owed you anything, it was because they loved you so much. Just ask Christopher and Kate. They know how much you meant to Beryl and John. This was what they all wanted. Not through any kind of guilt, it was out of love and the way they trusted you as the person who would look after Chapwell for as long as you can. The thing is, your mum was good friends with Beryl and John before all that, well, your dad as well. David totally ruined that."

"But wasn't my mum at least partly responsible?"

"Look at it this way Jane. Your mum was not in a good place at that time. She was vulnerable and David, being David took total advantage. That is what he is like."

"I think I need to speak to my mum." said Jane deep in thought. "She has had this throughout her life and now I know. I think it is time that it was put to bed. I know about it now and I don't think it should be kept like that. It needs to be finished."

"Do you know, Jane?"

"What?"

"That's exactly what Beryl said you would say. It couldn't be brought out of the closet before she died because the animosity your mum bore towards Beryl and John would still be there. They are gone now so it can be cleared up. And, get this, Beryl wrote it all down for you and I was to give it to you if the need arose."

"Why didn't you give me this documented version then?"

"Because I wanted to tell you myself, because Beryl wanted me to tell you personally. It only seemed fair."

"I'm going to cook our dinner now; I think we've had enough drama for one day. Go and get us a bottle of wine and we can, perhaps relax a bit though it does seem a bit strange."

"What does?" asked Emily.

"Well. I don't actually know who my father is. And neither of the candidates are around. I know that it's not something I knew before. I mean, I have never known my father but this makes it far more complicated. Anyway, go on, walk through the door without opening it and get that bottle". They both laughed and Emily did just that. Walked through the door without opening it and promptly came back the same way, bottle included. "Wow" said Jane. "Didn't know you could do that."

"What?" asked Emily.

"Carry inanimate objects through doors as well."

"Anything I am touching goes with me Jane, if I could, I could drag the kitchen table through the wall if I wanted to."

"Awesome!" said Jane.

After dinner they settled in the living room. It was not often used but, in the evenings sometimes, it was a very comfy place to be and as Jane wanted to phone her mum, the landline was in there so she got comfortable on the sofa and dialled the number. There was a click and an abrupt "Hello".

Jane replied "Hello mum, it's me, Jane," she said hurriedly. "And before you say anything, please just listen for a moment. I just want you to know that I know everything now. I know all about David and what he did and really all I want is for us to be friends, like mother and daughter. I don't care what has happened in the past, it's gone and done. I think we need to have a chat and maybe get to know each other a bit better. I feel so sorry that this has happened but I don't want it to get in our way. I think we need to start again. Can we look to the future? Would you like to come over?" Jane could not hear anything, there was no response. "Hello. Mum, are you still there?" The silence continued.

"Yes." came a tearful reply eventually. "Yes, I'm here."

"Are you okay?" enquired Jane softly.

"Yes, I'm okay. I guessed this would have to rear its ugly head one day but I was scared of how you would react. Can I come over tomorrow, Jane, I'm not doing anything and I would like to see you and maybe explain."

"Mum, there's nothing to explain. Aunt Beryl has made it clear to me what happened and, like I said, it's in the past. Let's start again. From this point, right now, let's just start again." All Jane could hear were tears and sobbing.

"I'll be there first thing in the morning Jane. I'm just going to have a sit down for a while but I'll see you in the morning, is that okay?"

"Of course, mum. It's all fine, we're all fine. Bring some stuff with you and you can stay a while if you like."

A muffled tearful reply came back. "I'd love that Jane, I'd love that."

"How'd it go?" asked Emily when the phone was gently placed in the cradle, a look of concern on her face.

"Fine." replied Jane, a slightly bewildered look on her face. "Fine. Mum's coming over tomorrow morning" she said, looking up at Emily. "I asked her if she would like to stay for a few days. Is that okay?"

"Okay. Of course, it's okay Jane, you don't have to ask me, she's your mother after all."

"What about you Emily, how are we going to handle you being here?"

"Same as we did in the pub but if you like I'll stay out of the way, invisible, unless you need me."

"How will you know?" asked Jane.

"You'll love this Jane, it's all worked out. Beryl and I had a system. If you want me to appear, just get your hanky out."

"I don't carry a hanky." said Jane.

"Well, you'll need to carry one now. Get your hanky out if you want me to appear or disappear and if you want me to leave you alone just blow your nose. Easy, eh?"

"What happens if I want you to come back from wherever you've gone?"

"I'll always be in the same place Jane. On your bed, or my bed as it is now. You just need to come and get me. Now, Jurassic Park is on the tv tonight, let's just see if that can distract us from current events."

"Suits me." came the reply "But before we do, I'll just check that Christopher's room is ready for Mum to use."

"Oh, okay, I'll give you a hand." said Emily.

As they stood, Jane grabbed Emily's hand, preventing her from leaving the room. Emily turned, a surprised look on her face. Jane looked into her eyes and smiled. "Thank you, Emily." she said.

"What for?" came the reply.

"For everything. If it wasn't for you none of this would have happened and now it looks like my life is about to become more complete. I'll have my mum back." They embraced briefly, smiled at each other broadly and left the room.

Chapter Nine

Sandra

At breakfast the next morning, the atmosphere seemed a little tense but then it probably should. Jane was having her mother to stay with her in this big house. She really didn't know how her mother would react to it all but after hearing her crying on the phone last night she did think it might not be quite as fraught as she previously imagined it could be.

Emily and Jane sat facing each other at the kitchen table, silence dominating, mugs held tightly, cold and empty. Jane's phone buzzes and jumps across the table startling the pair of them. She grabs it, turns it over to read the text message that had just arrived. "What is it?" asks Emily impatiently trying to stretch over the table to see.

"Mum's just left home so she'll be here in about twenty minutes. Are we ready?"

"Well, I don't matter. She won't see me, will she?"

"No, but you know what I mean." said Jane sarcastically, carefully placing the phone back on the table.

"Yes, we're as ready as we possibly can be. Just make her comfortable and feel at home here, make her feel welcome. I know all this is obvious and I don't know how she'll react when she walks in the front door and sees you in that massive hallway, the stairs and the clock and all that. It could be a bit of a shock."

"Well," said Jane "It's not like she hasn't been here before, is it?"

"No, but think about it this way. Her daughter didn't own the place then, did she?"

"No, I didn't."

"Well then, it could be a bit overwhelming."

"I need another wee." said Jane getting up.

"You've only just been for goodness' sake."

"Well, I need to go again."

"Look," said Emily. "You go have a wee, and I'll get the kettle ready and put the cake out on the table. Everything is ready then, isn't it?"

"Yeah, yeah okay, whatever." A flustered Jane muttered as she went through the door.

Jane, having been pacing up and down the hallway for what seemed to Emily to be an eternity, jumped and looked up as the door knocker thudded against the thick oak, echoing around the house. She stood dead still, statue like as if the action had suddenly been stopped. She just stared at the door. "Oh, go on, open it, Jane." said Emily flapping her arms. "I'll just disappear for now but I'll be right by your side and remember the hanky."

Jane shook her head and blinked, walking towards the door she took a look back to see that Emily had indeed vanished. She grabbed the large knob confidently and turned it, slowly pulling the door towards her and peered through the new gap that appeared. There, stood quite quietly, was her mother, a bag by her side. Not a huge bag, but, equally not an overnight type of bag which Jane thought nice as just this small bit of information meant that her mum hadn't planned just a quick visit but she meant it to be a reconciliation, a making up, a new start. This made Jane smile. A genuine smile, not an 'I'm being polite' smile but a proper welcoming smile. She pushed the door fully open and looked at her mother. A nice dress and hair tidily done, straight, shoulder length, dark but showing signs of grey, she looked lovely. A hat would have finished the image completely. An image of a friend coming to stay. Her mother looked right back at her, right into her eyes and Jane noticed a softening in the expression, a smile forming and a warmth building. Sandra placed her bag on the floor and they stepped towards each other, slightly awkwardly, but embraced, cautiously at first and then more meaningfully, holding each other tightly. Not a word said, just a close embrace that felt to each of them like it could remove years of anguish and pain, wipe the slate clean, start anew. They both felt the other begin to shudder and they each heard the other begin to sob, slight at first but then more powerful.

"I'm sorry Jane," said Sandra.

"Don't be Mum. There's nothing to be sorry about, that's behind us, all of it. Come on in and we'll have a cup of tea." Jane bent down and picked up the bag and guided Sandra in through the door, into the hallway, the cool hallway, Sandra's breath caught as she looked around.

"Goodness Jane, I'd forgotten how beautiful this hallway was and how big it is. I know how much you love this house and I know how much you loved Beryl and John and they must have loved you so much to leave it all to you. It is amazing." Sandra was just stood turning round and round in the hallway taking it all in. Jane placed the bag at the bottom of the stairs and took her hand.

"Come on mum, there's tea to make." She gently pulled her into the kitchen and sat her down at one of the chairs. Jane went to the kettle only to find the tea already made. She turned and looked around the kitchen just hoping that one of her glances hit home on Emily's face knowing who was responsible for that. She took the teapot and placed it in the middle of the table alongside the milk jug and cake. Sandra was sat quite upright just looking around the kitchen, trying to take it all in. The large window, the immaculate woodwork, the pan stand, the Welsh dresser showing off all the best china.

"Well, what do you think Mum?"

"It's, well, it's amazing Jane. I didn't come in the house very often and never really took it all in but this all belongs to you now, doesn't it?"

"Yes mum, every brick, stone and piece of oak, it all belongs to me now. I'm still not quite sure why or how and I am still not quite used to the fact that this actually belongs to me. I still feel like I'm a visitor and I'll have to go back to my flat soon. But then Sarah is in my flat now, I rented it to her as she was in a right tatty place before."

"What do you intend to do with it then?"

"How do you mean?"

"Well, are you going to keep it as it is or update it?"

"Mum, no, of course not. I have always loved this place; you know that and as a historian I know quite a lot about this building and some of its history, not all but enough to know that any changes would be absolutely out of the question. In any case it's grade two listed so there is very little I could do anyway."

"Yes, I suppose," said Sandra, looking around the kitchen again.

"Here Mum, have some of this chocolate cake, I know you like chocolate cake and this is Aunt Beryl's recipe and I've got it down to a fine art now." Jane cut two large segments of the dark cake and placed them on the plates. For the next five minutes there was total silence. Jane watching her mum closely for that tell-tale smile that she knew the cake would bring out and it did. Sandra's eyes were wide with pure enjoyment. So much so, that she looked at the remaining cake on the table with a hint of greed in her eyes. "You can have another slice if you want." said Jane. "I made it for you because I knew you would like it and I just love this cake." Jane just hacked off another two slices and placed them on their crumb littered plates. These too, were demolished during a similar period of silence.

"That was delicious." said Sandra, "absolutely delicious, you were taught well Jane."

"I know. Aunt Beryl was an amazing cook and she could see that I enjoyed cooking and picked things up pretty quick so it was quite easy really. We had so much fun in this kitchen. Cooking from recipes or making stuff up as we went along, just using what was in the fridge or ready in the garden. I can't remember most of the things we did cook and the funny thing is we could never exactly reproduce a recipe we had used before but then we never measured anything or timed anything so it was often a surprise. Oh, God, Mum, that sounds terrible, I mean, I know we didn't do all that stuff when I was at home but, well, I'm sorry, I didn't mean it to sound like that."

"Don't." said Sandra, "It looks like you've had some excellent kitchen training, and, yes, you are a good cook"

"We'll see" said Jane, "wait till I cook dinner tonight, then you can judge. Do you want any more tea?"

"No thanks, that's fine."

"Okay, I'll show you to your room then." said Jane getting up from her chair with a flourish. "I think you'll like it, it used to be Christopher's. He's taken all his stuff so it doesn't look like a boy's room and Aunt Beryl re-furnished it as another guest room. I quite like it."

Jane left her mother to settle in and unpack and returned to the kitchen. Tidying up the tea things she looked around and whispered. "I know you are in here; I can just feel it." With that, Emily appeared. "Did you see and hear everything?" asked Jane.

"Yes, I was here the whole time and sorry about the tea being made but I couldn't not do it could I?"

"Forgiven" said Jane. "I think I'll take mum around the garden, that'll make the first few hours a bit easier."

"Good idea." said Emily disappearing.

Jane couldn't hear any noise from upstairs and using the excuse to herself that she was just going to get a cardigan, like she had loads of cardigans, she stole up the staircase quietly, intent on hearing any sound from her mum's room. "Everything okay mum?" she asked.

"Yes, yes." came the reply. "Come in Jane, come and see this." Jane walked in the room slightly confused as to what her mother could be looking at.

"What's the matter mum?" she asked.

"Oh, nothing but there's a squirrel running around the garden down there and there's a blackbird trying to shoo it off." Jane joined her mother at the window and looked down on the garden and sure enough, there was the squirrel, the same squirrel Jane had seen so many times, the one with the kink in its tail, running around the garden with a blackbird in close pursuit.

"The blackbird has a nest in that small conifer over there, mum, and is fiercely protective." said Jane, putting one hand on her mother's shoulder, the other pointing at the small tree towards the bottom of the garden.

"This garden is lovely Jane, it is so colourful, and big! It is so big."

"I know" said Jane, a look of total bliss on her face. "Come on mum, if you're finished unpacking, we'll go out there and I'll show you around. There's a lovely bench down there which has been sat on by everyone in the past, it's so well used and my favourite place in the garden. So many problems have been solved by people sat on that bench."

Jane spent nearly an hour wandering with her mother through the various parts of the garden, the greenhouse and shed, even the compost heaps were inspected. She walked her around the entire boundary fence and hedges ending up at the bench where they both sat down in the full sun. "Let me get you a hat, mum, I need one, this sun can be quite fierce sat here. I'll get us some ginger beer as well, if you like ginger beer that is."

"I'd love one Jane, and, yes I think a hat would be quite welcome, the sun is quite bright." Sandra sat back, relaxing in the warmth. Her eyes wandered around the garden, taking it all in and like anyone that witnessed it, quickly came to the conclusion that it would be impossible not to love it.

Jane trotted off to get the hats and ginger beer, entering the kitchen, there stood Emily looking out of the window. "All okay?" she enquired.

"Yes, fine" came the reply.

"Weren't you following us around?"

"No, Jane, I thought it best to leave you two alone. I don't want to interfere. That would be just rude now, wouldn't it?" Jane smiled at her companion knowing that she could trust her implicitly to always do the right thing.

Jane returned to the bench handing her mum a floral floppy hat and donning a quiet straw one herself. She placed the two bottles of ginger beer on the stone topped table and sat back. "I hope you don't mind mum but that hat was one I bought Aunt Beryl, only she never got a chance to wear it. It was so her, that one but it suits you perfectly, oh, and no glasses with the ginger beer, it tastes better out of the bottle."

"You are funny Jane" said her mum giggling. "Why, oh why haven't we been like this in the past?"

"We both know why mum, but, like we said it's in the past and does not affect the way we are going to be from now on, okay?"

"Okay" came the happy agreement.

They sat silently sipping the cool ginger beer from the bottle it's heat and chill reflecting a perfect summers day, sun shining and the slightest of breezes, just enough to waft the flower heads and send the bees dancing trying to catch the blooms.

"How long" they both said in unison.

"Sorry mum, you first."

"How long can I stay for?" her mum asked

"I was going to ask you the same thing," said Jane. "You can stay as long as you like as far as I am concerned, it's entirely up to you. After all, I don't exactly 'work' anymore, I can't bring myself to say that my hobby is now my work. The library makes use of me as and when and they let me use the library resources for some of my own work so it all suits me just fine. And even if I do have to go into work for a day, you can stay here, relax and just enjoy the garden."

"Don't you have a boyfriend or anything?" asked Sandra.

"Nope" Jane replied "I don't think I need that kind of complication in my life. I mean, how could I possibly find anyone who could be even vaguely interested in my life and the things that make me happy? I have everything I need here and now, and with you coming over it makes things quite complete. So, no, there is no boyfriend and as far as I can see there won't be one for the foreseeable future either. I'm quite content thank you." Jane looked at her mum and smiled, a genuine smile of contentment reiterating her message. "I have Sarah, she's a lovely friend and she'll come over now and then. And, I have this house and everything in it. There is nothing more I need."

"Blimey" said Sandra, jokingly, a shocked look on her face "I only asked."

"Oh, sorry mum."

"Don't be." said Sandra "I fully understand, I mean, look at all this, all this around us, it would be senseless to do anything to change it, particularly if you are happy with it."

"More than happy mum, more than happy."

"How do you manage all this garden, and the house Jane? I mean it's a lot to take care of, especially after only having a small flat before."

"It's not that difficult mum, Old Tom looks after all the grass for me, cutting the lawns and trimming the edges. I could do it myself but he enjoys it so much and makes a lovely job of it all it would be pointless doing it myself, I couldn't handle that mower anyway, it's a right beast of a thing. The borders are a pleasure to keep tidy and, like I said, I have plenty of time on my hands." What Jane failed to mention was all the assistance she got from Emily but then that would just make things even more complicated. All her mum needed to know was that she was happy with what she had inherited and could manage it all quite well.

"Jane?"

"Yes mum"

"Let's talk about what happened, shall we?"

"If you are ready for that mum, we can talk about it and we can both get a better understanding of where we both are. But this is on one condition."

"Oh, and what's that then?" asked Sandra.

"On the condition it does not jeopardise our future. I think I rather like what I have now and don't want our relationship to sour before it has started properly."

"Oh, absolutely." said Sandra "I'm totally with you on that. It's going to be easiest if I start at the beginning."

Sandra adjusted her seated position and placed her hands on her lap, brushing non-existent dust or crumbs from her dress. She briefly looked down, slowly building up the level of confidence required to describe this, the events that had changed her life and affected the lives of both her husband and her daughter.

"Your Dad, Mark, who you have never met, was a wonderful man, I always loved him and still do. There was a period of time where he was working away from home for long periods and somehow it just got to me. I didn't like being alone. Had things been slightly different, like I'd stuck it out for another few weeks, none of this would have happened." Jane was just about to speak but her mum stopped her. "Let me finish this Jane, it's needs to be gotten out and the sooner the better really."

"Okay" said Jane, sitting back, turning to look directly at her mother.

"See, your dad was earning good money working away and he was enjoying it. He was good at his job; he was well respected and successful. And, as I now know, he was doing it all for me because he knew it would come to an end eventually. He was to be promoted, well, he was promoted and the working away ended but it was too late. I made a mistake, a stupid, stupid mistake and ruined everything." Tears welled up in Sandra's eyes, she held her hands in her lap, nervously picking at her fingers, looking down at them, the gentle teardrops darkening the colours in her dress, she sobbed. Jane put her arms around her and hugged her.

"You don't need to do this mum if it upsets you, you know."

"Yes, I do." Sandra blubbed, "Yes I do." Looking up sternly and wiping her eyes with the tissue she retrieved from her pocket; rearranging herself on the bench and composing herself, she restarted. "Your dad had been away for two weeks, the longest he had spent away and the job meant that he was going to be away for longer before it was finished. The thing I didn't know then was that it would be the last time he went away and that will stick with me for ever. Anyway, I slipped into a spell of depression, not bad and more annoying than anything else so I, and I really don't like to admit this but I was starting to drink a bit. A bottle of wine a day turned to two and before I knew where I was, I was going through two a day and drinking wine rather than tea. Long story short I started going to the pub. We went there a lot in the past, me and your dad but this was for a different reason. I was in search of company. Just someone to talk to. David came along and he was nice, bought me drinks and chatted nicely. The alcohol was taking over and even though people warned me about him and his past, I didn't care. He was listening to me and doing all the things that I wanted right then. He didn't question my drinking and somehow or other even convinced me that it was okay. Little did I know at that time, that he was just grooming me and I couldn't see it. Or didn't want too more likely. This went on for a couple of weeks until that night."

"That night?" asked Jane but suddenly, she realised, took a deep breath and sighed. "Sorry mum, stupid question but you don't need to go into any detail if you don't want to. I know what happened."

"You need to know Jane; it'll help me as well. See, I had already had a bottle of wine, then I went to the pub and David was there of course. We chatted and got quite drunk. Well, I did anyway, he knew exactly what he was doing. He was barely drinking but I just didn't notice. He was acting like he cared and offered to take me home as I was 'a bit tipsy' and I was in no state to even comprehend what was happening let alone get home on my own. He took me to my door and I fumbled for my keys and dropped them on the floor. He picked them up and unlocked the door. He gently guided me into the front room and sat me down on the sofa. He closed the curtains and then it started and don't interrupt Jane please." Sandra held up her hand to her daughter, who, with a worried and concerned look on her face let her mother continue. "He started by calling me names and then slapped me. He gave me a hell of a beating and raped me." The tears were pouring down Sandra's face and the struggle to speak was obvious to Jane but she sat still, horrified at the pain she was seeing in her mother. "After that, he beat me again and raped me again. I was sobering up by then and realised what was happening and he saw this. He gave me another few slaps and called me some more names and left. He even left the door open as he went."

"Oh, god mum, I'm so sorry." said Jane, a look of abject sympathy on her face.

"What happened next? How did it all get to court?"

"Well, this is where you realise who real friends are. Luckily for me Colin at the pub, that's not the Colin there now, it was his dad. Anyway, he realised what had been going on for the past few weeks and, more importantly, he knew David and knew what he was like. He came to the house not long after David left, saw the door open and came in, found me and called an ambulance then called the Police. That was the end of that episode but it doesn't finish the entire story. There's your dad. He was called and came straight home and again, long story short, couldn't handle the 'affair' and the grief I had caused. He just up and left, there and then and I have barely seen him since. We got divorced and I was left alone to wallow in the mess of my own making. I can't blame your dad; he was doing everything he could for us and I chucked it back in his face. So, there you are. That is that torrid affair out in the open. But not finished." Said Sandra looking directly into Jane's eyes. "Then there is you, Jane. Not long afterwards I discovered I was pregnant. Nine months later or thereabouts, along came you. I put two and two together and got six, I think. As far as I was concerned at that time you were his child and I blamed Beryl and John for the whole thing. I really don't know why, and I really, really wish with all my heart I could go back and change that. They were such good people and they, like me at that time, were convinced that you were David's daughter which is why they took care of you. But, don't get me wrong here, they did it for the love of you and not through any kind of guilt. They could see that I was not going to be the mother to you that I should have been, so they took you on and cared for you, just as if you were their grandchild. I have no regrets as far as that is concerned, that could not have been better really. I am ashamed of myself for that, well, for the whole thing really. Thing is Jane, as far as we all know, you are his daughter. No-one actually knows who your father is in truth Jane. It is either David or Mark."

"What, so you really don't know?" asked Jane bewildered.

"No, Jane, I don't know. I guess the only way we will know is by a DNA test but neither Mark nor David are around and, in any case neither of them would consent to have a test done I wouldn't have thought."

"Okay, mum, let's leave that there for now. I think you have been through enough and just talking to me has been difficult, I can see. So, let's have some lunch. I need to get my head around it all. But, as far as we are concerned, right here and right now, nothing changes. We are as we are and that's that. I do have one question though."

"What's that?" asked Sandra.

"How did you come to know Beryl and John?"

"I used to work in the shop when I was a girl." replied Sandra. "I helped out there quite a lot and, of course we used the shop and we just got on really well. I'm really ashamed now, that I treated them so badly since you came along. They really did everything to make things right. I was just too stubborn to see it. As far as I was concerned, the Chapwell family had destroyed my life."

"Okay." said Jane. "That'll do, let's go and get that lunch. What would you like, a nice salad sandwich and some cake?"

Sandra laughed tearfully. "Oh, Jane, I can see this can only get better."

"Come on," she said, holding her mother's hand, rubbing it gently. "I'll put the kettle on."

It was as if nothing had ever happened. In twenty-eight years, Jane had barely known her mother for who she really was and she assumed the same was felt by her mother. Sat at the kitchen table, all mention of the past was avoided. Instead, they chatted lightly about the garden and the house. Both knew that there was more to explore about the past but it was obvious they wanted to keep the details to a minimum. A minimum necessary in order to maintain the relationship and forget the past. Little did they both know that the past was coming back to haunt them both.

"Mum?" asked Jane.

"What love?"

"Do you not know where my dad is? At least the Dad I have always thought of as Dad. The man you married?"

"No Jane, I really don't know where he is now. He left and cut me off completely and to be honest I don't blame him. Yes, I was angry at the time for various reasons but I don't blame him and I never will."

"Does he know about me Mum?"

"I think so." came the reply. "When I knew I was pregnant I told his mother as I couldn't get in touch with him myself but I still had contact with her."

"What. And he didn't get in touch?"

"No, no he didn't. Like me he must have put two and two together and got goodness knows what."

"We need to get in touch with him Mum, we need to have a test done for all our sakes, me, you and him."

Sandra looked at her daughter with sorrow in her eyes. She reached across the table and held her hand. "And what happens if the result is not what we want?"

Jane looked back at her mum, shocked, unable to answer, realising she had just discovered the mystery that was going to prove difficult if not impossible to resolve. Difficult for so many reasons and impossible because neither of the potential fathers were around. One because no-one wanted him to be available and the other because he didn't want to be available.

They sat in silence, hand in hand for some minutes until Jane realised the enormity of what she had just said. "I guess we'll just have to live with what we have" she said.

"Yes, love, I guess we will. But look, we've just found ourselves again. Would it be too difficult to live with what we have right now?"

Jane smiled. "No Mum, no it would not be difficult at all but if the opportunity does pop up, do you think we should seek the answer?"

"I don't know love, let's see if the opportunity does arise and handle it at the time, things might be different then. I don't think it's a question either of us can answer right now."

They spent the afternoon catching up on their lives, filling in the gaps and sharing their favourite things. Jane took Sandra on a full tour of the house from attic to cellar, showing her the earliest part of the building Jane had found which to her surprise was actually the remains of the original roman villa. A part of the wall in the cellar contained roman tiles. "There's so much history here Jane."

"That's an understatement Mum" said Jane excitedly, "this house goes back thousands of years, or at least the ground it was built on does. I would not be surprised if underneath all of this there is evidence of even earlier occupation, Iron age even."

"This house really suits you doesn't it love? I mean, even before you knew what you wanted to do with your life you always loved this house and, yes, I know how much you loved Beryl and John but the house was all part of that. There was never a time when you didn't want to come here was there? And look, Jane, I know what the past was and I know part of your love for this house was purely the love you felt here with Beryl and John and I can't blame you for that at all. That was partly my fault."

"Mum" interrupted Jane. "Don't think like that. We've agreed that the past is gone and yes, I do love this house, always have and, yes, Aunt Beryl and Uncle John did show me a lovely life but that didn't mean I didn't love you. I always came home, didn't I?"

"Yes love, yes you did but I could have done better."

"Whatever" said Jane. "It is what it is and I couldn't be happier with life right now. I live in the house I love and I can share it with my real Mum, the one I have missed for all these years. C'mon, I'll get the dinner started." said Jane standing up, ending the conversation which, she considered to be at a point where it could continue at a later date.

"Can I help?" asked Sandra.

"What are mum's for?" replied Jane seeing a smile grow on her mum's face.

Jane lay in bed, thinking about the day and how things had changed. How much she had learnt and how much the future could change for them both.

"Forgot about me then?" came a voice from nowhere making Jane jump.

"God, Emily don't do that. I nearly wet myself. And no, I hadn't forgotten about you, I could feel you around somewhere."

"Joking" said Emily, materialising at the foot of the bed.

"I see you're ready for bed then" said Jane noticing the pyjamas which in the past had lived in one of her drawers.

"Yep, and ready for your news" said Emily leaping in the bed next to her, sitting upright, arms folded in front of her expectantly looking at Jane.

"You mean you didn't hear any of what we talked about?"

"Nope, not a thing, I thought that would be just rude so I thought I would leave you to it. I did miss dinner though and it smelt delicious."

"Yeah, it was rather nice," said Jane "Beryl's infamous veg Bolognese with some lovely crusty Ciabatta"

"Oh, don't," said Emily "You're making me even more hungry."

"How can you be hungry? You're a blimmin ghost."

"I've explained this to you before Jane. I do not need to eat nor drink but I can, so why waste the experience? Hunger is just an uncomfortable side effect of this capability so don't go on about it please"

"Wooo, sorry" said Jane sarcastically.

"Anyway, the whole day went very well, my mum really is a lovely person and, as far as I can see, she always has been. It's just that David got between us and ruined the whole thing. My life has been totally marred by that man, well, mine and mum's to be honest. However, and this is the good part. We both agree that the past is the past and we should concentrate on making the future better and, I have a feeling that it is not going to be difficult. We've both missed so much and have so much to make up for. Only two things are outstanding really."

"Oh" said Emily, "What are they then?"

Jane, staring straight ahead just said "David and me."

"How do you mean?"

"Well, David is around as we know, he is out of prison and we've already met his mate, Rob. Then there is me, well not so much me but who I am and more importantly who is my dad." This she said whilst turning to look at Emily.

"Okay," said Emily "Are either of those going to cause a problem?"

"I really don't know Emily; I really don't know. I hope not for all our sakes."

Jane and Sandra spent the rest of the stay just getting to know each other better, relaxing in the garden, cooking in the kitchen and playing cards in the evening. A very idyllic scene for a mother and daughter but one they both understood and enjoyed. They both discovered that they were very well matched and quite quickly realised they were going to be good friends. All too soon it was time for Sandra to leave and, having packed her bag she stood in the hallway looking around the oak panelled walls, taking in the warmth of the wood and the comforting ticking of the great clock.

"Well mum, it's been so nice to have you here, I've loved it, it's been a lot of fun and please, please come again and make it soon. Any time you want to come just shout. The room upstairs is yours whenever you want it. We've got a lot of catching up to do."

"It really seems like I've been here for ages." said Sandra. "But I know it's only been a couple of days. We've crammed so much in and I've loved every minute. I've found my daughter and I've missed her terribly. I've been so selfish"

"Now, Mum." said Jane "We agreed, the past is the past, we only have the future now so we'll just go on from right here."

"Yes, I know" said Sandra "But I now know what I have missed and I'm looking forward to the future, it's going to be fun." They smiled warmly at each other and hugged tightly, tears forming in their eyes."

"Oh, stop it now," said Jane, "We can't keep blubbing every time we see each other"

"We'll get used to it Jane. Okay I had better get going and before you say it, yes, I'd love to come again, sooner rather than later. I'll ring you soon. Okay?"

"That'll be great mum, I look forward to our next holiday together, right here at Chapwell."

Reluctantly Jane opened the front door, feeling guilty, letting her mother go back to her life, but with the satisfaction that it had changed and will change further as time went on. Waving her off down the road, Jane felt happy and noticed her mother driving calmly down the lane now, hoping that in some small way her life was going to be different now.

Returning to the kitchen Jane noticed the teapot on the table and the chocolate cake sat in the middle, Emily, sat at the other side in anticipation of the chunk she was about to devour.

"Come on Jane, sit down, sit down, I want cake". Jane laughed as she sat, grabbed the knife and cut a huge piece of cake and placed it on one of the plates. She picked it up and placed it on the table mat in front of herself and just looked up at Emily. Seeing the seething look that confronted her she picked it back up and placed it in front of Emily laughing.

"I'll pour the tea then, shall I?"

"Go on then." came the cake muffled reply.

Chapter Ten

Threat

"Emily, Emily, where are you?" shouted Jane, standing in the hallway exasperated. "Oh, where on earth is she?" she said, looking up the stairs and for some reason back into the kitchen. She hadn't seen her for a good half hour now and was becoming slightly concerned. They were never apart these days and had become so close now that they both felt it when the other was not in the immediate vicinity. Jane had not felt Emily's presence for a while. Not that it mattered normally, they did occasionally do their own thing but generally a quick stomp around the house and a shout brought the other running. Jane slowly walked up the stairs and felt Emily's presence grow. As she walked towards Emily's room, she felt it even stronger. Tapping gently on the door, she quietly asked if she was okay. Nothing came back but Jane knew she was there, she could feel her very strongly now but noticed that the feeling was somewhat subdued and a little sad. She tapped on the door again. "Emily, are you okay?" she asked again.

"Yes, I'm fine, come in." Came the delayed and quiet response. Jane gently opened to door and peeped in. She saw Emily staring out over the garden, her wavy hair silhouetted against the mullioned window.

"Are you sure you're alright Emily?" Jane repeated.

"Yes, yes, I'm fine" said Emily turning to look at Jane. "Come here, you need to see this I think." Emily waved her over to the window and turned back to look out across the garden. Jane gingerly approached, not really knowing what to expect but stood beside Emily, placed her hands on the sill and followed her eyes to see what she could see. Sat on the bench was a man. A young man with blonde hair, neatly trimmed. He was just sat like so many people had, watching the bees and butterflies in the garden. Leaning slightly forward with his elbows on his knees as if deep in thought.

"Who is that, Emily?" asked Jane pointing towards the bench just as Emily was about to grab her hand. She stopped abruptly and turned to look at Jane.

"What, you mean you can see him?"

"Er, yes." replied Jane, confused. "Why?"

"You shouldn't be able to see him, he's a ghost, just like me. I was just about to hold your hand so that you could see him."

"Well, he is not as sharp and solid as you are, he's a bit sort of ghostly, but I can definitely see him. Who is he anyway?"

"That's Jan, Jane. He's lovely."

"Why is he here?"

"Same as the rest of us, obviously. He's dead and is stuck here, well, not stuck but like me he died here and has been here ever since."

"How did he die?" asked Jane.

"He's Polish, he was a bomber pilot and served at the aerodrome the other side of the village."

"Aerodrome?" questioned Jane.

"Yes, you know, the other side of the village where the farm is. It's not used now, obviously, it's derelict and part of the farm, well, it was a farm before they built it and now it's back to farmland. But it was built during the Second World War as a bomber base. Jan was a pilot on a Polish squadron based there. He was badly injured on a mission and was hospitalised when they returned but he managed to get their damaged aircraft back to the base and crash landed it. All the crew survived because of Jan's skill, though some were injured, Jan was the worst but after a spell in hospital he was sent here to convalesce, the house was used as a recovery centre for a few airmen at that time, they had beds in the attic. Sadly, Jan didn't recover, one night he died suddenly. But, as you can see, never moved on so he's here. Would you like to meet him?"

"Would he like to meet me do you think?" asked Jane.

"Yes, of course he would, I think he would like the company too, come on let's go and see."

"Could you stay back for a minute please Jane? I don't quite know how Jan will react." asked Emily as they came through the kitchen. Jane stood in the doorway, watching Emily tip-toe down the path towards the bench. She heard Emily call Jan's name and saw Jan turn towards her, smile and wave. Jane dodged back into the doorway just in case she was seen. She couldn't hear what was being said but it was obvious there was quite a conversation going on. She saw Emily kneel down in front of Jan and touch his hand. Emily pointed towards the house and Jan looked around. Emily stood and waved towards Jane beckoning for her to come over. As Jane walked down the path, she saw Jan stand and turn to greet her.

"Hello Jan," said Jane as she approached.

"Hello Jane" returned Jan very politely and in impeccable English, the slight Polish accent apparent. He raised his hand in order to shake Jane's. With trepidation she extended hers, not quite sure what she would feel. As they touched it felt quite normal, a firm hand, warm and soft though she did notice how vaguely transparent Jan seemed to be, not quite as solid as Emily.

"I'm very pleased to meet you Jan and I'm sorry for what has happened to you."

"It is okay Jane. I have got used to my predicament now and with the help of the other people around, particularly Emily, life, or death as it actually is, has been made more tolerable." Emily was fidgeting and obviously itching to get in on the conversation.

"What?" asked Jane, "What is the matter with you Emily?"

"I don't understand." said Emily. "You, Jane, you should not be able to see Jan unless I am holding you and even more mysterious, you should definitely not be able to feel him."

"I think that may be my fault." said Jan, sheepishly. "The other day I touched someone, only briefly, but I did touch someone, your mother as it happens Jane."

"JAN," shouted Emily, her hands now firmly placed on her hips. "You know that is forbidden, you just can't do that, certainly not without the permission of the person you are touching, do you realise what you could have done?"

"I know." came the forlorn reply. "But I..., I was lonely, more lonely than normal and she was sleeping so I touched her hand and felt the joining process start. I let go straight away but, as you can see, I became nearly visible. I'm sorry, it won't happen again. I hope your mother didn't feel any effects, Jane?"

"I don't think so. She enjoyed her stay here and I think she might have said something about a ghostly encounter."

"Okay, okay, forgiven" said Emily, "As long as that was as far as it went, we should be okay."

A chill breeze wafted across the garden and a darkness suddenly came over them. A large dark spot appeared on the stone table, then another. The darkness deepened, the breeze intensified and they, all three, looked up at the house, almost expecting some strange phenomenon but just saw a large black storm cloud edging its way over the roof. A massive flash shot across the sky, closely followed by a tremendous crash of thunder, the breeze suddenly blew up to a sharp cold wind fretting the flower heads in the garden. The table now being hammered by huge raindrops.

"Quick" shouted Jane, "Come on, let's get inside, we'll get soaked, not to mention struck by lightning." They all ran towards the house, Jan opening the door and letting the girls through. Following them in he closed it, leaving the storm to the garden. The rain pelting the kitchen window as if to complain at being left outside.

"Wow, that was close, I didn't see that creeping up on us," said Jane tidying her wind-swept hair. "Come on, sit down and I'll put the kettle on. Would you like tea Jan?"

"I would love a cup of tea." he said "only, as I am at the moment, I would only be able to look at it. I'm not joined so I can't drink anything or eat anything. I expect Emily has explained all this to you, hasn't she?"

"Oh, yes, sorry Jan. But you could touch me, I felt your hand in mine."

"That was only because you are joined and I was partly joined, it shouldn't have happened. You two go ahead, I'll just sit here and watch."

Jane made tea while the others sat at the table. Jan went through his life in England from when he volunteered to come over and fly with the RAF early in the war, escaping the Nazi's in Poland. He completed his training and was posted to the bomber squadron in the middle of the war. He flew over thirty missions into Germany with little in the way of drama until that last mission. He even considered himself becoming complacent about the job and seemed to blame himself for the incident resulting in him and his crew becoming injured and severely damaging an aircraft.

"But you gave your life Jan," said Jane, "never forget that, you were fighting for the freedom of Europe in a country foreign to you, not knowing what was happening in your own country, your own family. Dying here and ending up stuck here alone. I don't think you have any reason to blame yourself for anything."

"But I am lonely Jane, I have been here since 1944. Yes, I can see you and hear what is happening but I cannot interact with anyone, well, apart from the other ghosts that is."

"I keep hearing about these other ghosts. How many are there exactly? Hmm, Emily?"

"There are six, Jane, six in the immediate area but they keep themselves to themselves mostly, only Jan is like me and involves himself with the house."

"I love the house, Jane," said Jan, "I enjoyed my stay here when I was alive, it was comfortable and quiet, a lovely place to die. To a certain extent it was lucky that I died in a way."

"How do you mean?" asked Jane, confused.

"I learnt that my family were wiped out. I left Poland at the start of the war and came here but I was the only one of my family that actually made it. The rest were caught and died in the camps so there is nothing for me there, this house is my refuge. I just get so lonely sometimes."

"I'm so sorry Jan. But you have us now" she said with a growing smile", Emily is always here and I am here. Don't forget that Emily and I are joined so I can see you and talk to you, it's just a shame we cannot get you joined as well."

Jane and Emily looked at each other and both faces suddenly lit up as they had both thought of the same thing at the same time. "Sarah!" they both exclaimed. "Sarah would be perfect." said Emily.

"I don't know," said Jane, "I know she is a good friend but I don't know her *that* well really."

"Oh, come on Jane, she would be perfect, the little I know of her, the couple of times I have met her, well seen her, give me the idea that she would be right up for it. She doesn't have a partner or anything, she is a bit of a loner or, perhaps she just prefers her own company."

"I know," said Jane, "but that's exactly the point, she likes her own company. She likes living on her own."

"Can we give it a go anyway?" asked Emily.

"I suppose so, it wouldn't do any harm, she might surprise us, you never know. What do you think Jan?"

Jan sat with his hands in his lap, his head bowed. Looking up, he smiled. "Would you do that for me?"

"Of course, we would Jan," said Emily.

"But," said Jane, "this would only be on the condition that we explain everything to Sarah and she agrees totally. She needs to be fully aware of the complications, benefits and inconveniences."

"Absolutely" said Emily, "Absolutely."

Jane invited Sarah over for the weekend and Sarah, always loving a trip to see Jane, accepted with alacrity. She arrived on Friday night straight after work. The front door was opened almost as the knocker was lifted. "Sorry Sarah, I saw your car arrive. It's so nice to see you, come on in. We'll sort your room out in a minute, put your bag down there and I'll put the kettle on, dinner will be ready in a bit."

"Good grief Jane." said Sarah, "You seem a tad excited" looking at her, intrigued.

Well," said Jane "I'm just so happy to see you, I missed you recently and thought we need to catch up. Is the flat, okay?"

"Er yeah, why?"

"Oh, nothing just asking."

"You're not thinking of selling it are you?" asked Sarah, her smile disappearing.

"No, no," said Jane grabbing Sarahs hands, "No, of course not, I just wanted to make sure you are okay there, that's all."

"That's alright then, you got me worried for a second there."

"Come on let's have tea."

They went through to the kitchen, Sarah sat down, looking around the kitchen while Jane made the tea and stirred the pasta sauce she was cooking. "This place still amazes me Jane, it's a dream house, no wonder you love it so much."

"I know, I'm still not quite used to the fact that it's mine. It has so much more to it than I thought in the beginning."

"How do you mean?" asked Sarah.

"I'll get to that after we've had food, it won't be long, probably ready when we've finished our tea."

They ate quietly as usually happened. Jane happy that her food could bring silence just like Beryl's. "That was really nice Jane, pasta done just right and the sauce was delicious, you really are a great cook you know."

"I was taught by the best, Beryl was the best, her food was the best, it's as simple as that."

"Right," said Sarah, expectantly, resting her arms on the table. "So why exactly did you ask me to come over? You're obviously not upset about anything. In fact, quite the opposite I reckon. So, what's up?"

"Okay." said Jane. "This is not going to be easy and you may not believe me when I tell you what I now know but I do know that I can at least prove it."

"Prove what?" asked Sarah.

"Well," said Jane awkwardly, "the house is haunted."

"Ha! Exclaimed Sarah, stifling a giggle with her hand. "Come on Jane, you're a historian, I know, but haunted? That's taking things a bit far, don't you think?"

"See, I knew you might have a problem with what I'm saying."

"Okay, then, you said you could so off you go, prove it. Take me down the cellar and turn off the lights or take me upstairs so we can hear the creaky doors." Sarah sat back in her chair; arms folded almost defying Jane to prove her point, a sarcastic look upon her face.

"Okay, Emily, come on out." said Jane to no-one, looking straight back at Sarah, expecting a change in expression. What Sarah had not actually noticed or had noticed but disregarded, was the fact that one of the other chairs was pulled away from the table and within the confines of that chair, slowly, the form of Emily appeared. She was sat, leaning forwards, arms on the table, looking right at Sarah.

"Oh, my God!" said Sarah, leaning further back in her seat, a look of extreme fright on her face. "What the hell is that?" She scooted her chair backwards and stood up, the chair falling behind her. She grabbed the table to prevent herself falling and looked straight at Emily.

"Sarah, don't be frightened please. I'm Emily and, as you can see, I'm not like you, but it isn't quite how you see it."

"What do you mean?" asked an obviously shocked Sarah, still standing and now shaking slightly.

"Sit down Sarah." asked Jane, "sit down and we'll explain everything. Let me get you a glass of wine, it looks like you need it." Sarah slowly picked her toppled chair up and sat back down, all the colour drained from her face. Her eyes not leaving Emily.

"Whatever you are thinking," said Emily, "forget it, we'll explain what is going on and I'm sure you will understand."

By now, Emily had fully materialised and looked to all intents and purposes, just like anyone else, sat at the table picking up the wine glass that Jane had placed in front of her.

Sarah, absently picking up her glass, took a sip of her wine, her face still white, staring at Emily. Emily smiled back at her and reached across the table to hold Sarah's hand. Sarah immediately snatched her hand back across the table and put it on her lap. "I'm not going to hurt you Sarah, quite the opposite in fact. Look, just hold my hand and all will become clear." With trepidation Sarah slowly returned her hand to the table and reached to meet Emily's. They touched and Emily slowly stroked Sarah's fingers and the back of her hand, she turned it over and stroked her palm, then slipped her hand into Sarahs, gently holding it. Sarah could feel the warmth, the softness and even the life in Emily's hand. Sarah looked up and saw Emily's face, calm and soft, her dark hair curled down over her shoulders, falling to the table. A smile began to form on Sarah's warming face, the colour coming back.

"I can feel you." she said. "You feel warm and soft and tingly."

"Yes, Sarah, that's how I am. I am not like you as I am not alive but. Oh, how to explain this easily. I know. You've read *His Dark Materials*, haven't you?"

"Yes, yes I have. And I watched the TV series."

"Okay, the easiest way to describe it is to treat me as if I were Jane's Daemon. I am attached to Jane, we are joined, companions. This is how it works in the world of ghosts and spirits."

"So, you really are a ghost then?"

Between Jane and Emily, they went through the whole story. Explaining to Sarah how the existence of a ghost worked and what it meant for them both.

"Wow!" said Sarah "That's amazing. I don't know what to say. I mean, I had never even considered ghosts, as it were, never really thought about it. Certainly never experienced it, not until now that is, just assumed that it was a thing of stories and tales, films and the like."

"Well," said Jane "It's real Sarah, very real. I was shocked too but I enjoy it now, it's marvellous. Here, have a drop more wine. At least you don't look like you've just seen a ghost now." This procured a laugh from all three of them.

"There is a little bit more to it than we have told you so far." said Jane.

"How do you mean?" asked Sarah.

"How do you feel about becoming a part of this?"

"Sorry." said Sarah, shaking her head. "I don't quite understand what you are saying."

"How would you feel if you too, were joined to a ghost?"

"Er, sorry for seeming a bit thick Jane but I still don't get it."

"Okay, Emily is not the only ghost here."

"Oh, right, so there's loads of them then? How come I can't see them?"

"It's like we explained," said Emily. "You can only see the ghosts that are joined and only then when the particular ghost wants to be visible to you, so you won't see others unless you too are joined."

"But you just said that you can only be joined to one ghost."

"Exactly." said Jane exasperated. "But we have someone here who needs, or at least would like, to be joined. His name is Jan and he is a lonely soul who needs a friend."

"I don't know," said Sarah, "I don't even know this man, ghost, whatever."

"Okay, I think you should meet him."

"But you just said…"

"I know, I know, this one's a bit complicated but it doesn't matter. Would you like to meet him?"

"Okay, I think so but there's no commitment here, is there?"

"No," said Emily, "absolutely not. This is entirely up to you Sarah. You make your own mind up and we, and, indeed Jan, will honour your decision.

"How do I meet him?" asked Sarah.

"He's right here, in the kitchen." Sarah looked around and saw nothing but then, slowly she noticed a disturbance in the air beside the table. Gradually, the shape of a person became clearer until she could see that there, before her was a young man. He was smart, dressed in blue, sharply pressed trousers and a white roll neck jumper. In his hand, a forage cap, adorned with a Royal Air Force eagle and crown, the crown of King George indicating to her that the man before her was a second world war veteran. His hair was blonde and eyes were blue and soft, slightly sad but showed a brightness when they looked directly at her.

"Hello Sarah, I am Jan and please excuse my appearance, I'm not quite myself right now."

"Oh, well, hello Jan, I am pleased to meet you." Sarah stood and held out her hand towards Jan. He reached out and Sarah felt his soft hand in hers, vaguely transparent but still solid and firm. She could feel the warmth within the soft touch. Looking into his eyes and though, bright, they showed a sadness that was enduring.

Jane pulled out the chair at the other end of the table for Jan to sit. Sarah's eyes not leaving Jan's face. The next half hour was taken up with Jan explaining his history, why he was there and why he was lonely. All the time Sarah was enthralled, her chin resting in her hands. She asked few questions and listened intently to the story unfolding. When he had finished, he sat back and just looked forward at each of the girls in turn, all silent. Jane, waiting with patience to see how Sarah was going to react. Emily on the other hand was totally impatient, as was her nature and the fidgeting was quite apparent.

"Well?" asked Emily. "What do you think?"

"I don't know," came the reply, "I'm confused and a little overwhelmed if the truth be known. But I am warming to the idea of a companion, particularly one who is not quite your average acquaintance. I mean, you know, Jane, I'm not one for deep relationships which is why we get along so well and as this is not a commitment-based relationship then it might be rather nice. It would certainly help Jan I think, wouldn't it Jan?"

"Yes," came the reply, "yes it would. I would feel more complete. I know how Jane and Emily get along and how good it is for them both and that is all I want or need, just a friend, someone to talk to, share things with and perhaps even someone to think about."

"Is that a yes then?" asked Emily excitedly, a huge smile spreading across her face.

"I think so," said Sarah, hesitantly "let's give it a go."

"Don't forget," said Jane "if this doesn't work out for any reason, it is not permanent. Jan will need to re-charge himself every now and then, just like me and Emily. Only every couple of months or so but you'll find, like us, we are constantly touching which keeps things sweet. So, all that would happen is that you just don't come into contact with each other but, to be honest, if you two work out anything like me and Emily, you really won't want it to stop. There are way too many advantages."

"Are you absolutely sure?" asked Jan.

"Yes, Jan, I'm sure After all what can I lose?" came the more confident reply. "What do I need to do?"

"Just come and stand next to me and I'll just hold your hand."

"It might feel a bit weird Sarah," Emily interrupted. "Jan has not done this fully before so it might be a bit strange for him as well, and, you'll both feel really tired afterwards, but it doesn't hurt. It's quite pleasant really."

Sarah stood next to Jan and reached towards his hand again, a show of approval. Jan took Sarah's softly, looking into each other's eyes, the process started. They both relaxed and the pinpricks of light began to form around them, rotating and accelerating, expanding away from them. Jan stiffened; his eyes wide. There was a bright flash and the light spots exploded out of the room. Then, nothing, just the two of them holding hands, the whole process taking less than a minute. Jan was now fully solid, his outline sharp and clean. He released Sarah who was stood totally still, blinking and looking around her, not quite sure of what had happened.

"Are you both alright?" asked Jane, her eyes wide.

"Yes," came the simultaneous reply.

"But that was so strange," said Sarah, looking down at her hands, turning them over and over. "I've never felt anything like that before. It was like there was an energy flowing between us, I could feel it moving around my body, right down my arm and into Jan."

"Are you okay, Jan?" asked Emily "What do you think of your new body?" Jan was looking at his hands, touching his face and smiled.

Turning to Sarah he just said. "Thank you, Sarah, thank you, I hope this all works out, I feel just great. I haven't felt this good in years. Can I have a cup of tea now?"

They all laughed, Jane just turned and put the kettle on. "Want some cake as well?"

"Are you joking?" came the reply, "I've been watching cakes being baked and eaten here for a long time, I've got some catching up to do."

The scene was quite surreal in the kitchen. Two ghosts and two non-ghosts sat around the table, laughing and joking, eating cake and supping tea or wine. The evening slid past, accompanied by the chimes of the hall clock.

"My goodness." said Sarah, a huge yawn taking over. "I am so tired."

"Told you, you'd be tired." said Jane.

"I too am tired," said Jan, "I have not felt proper tiredness in years, I think I need to go to bed. But I have no-where to sleep."

"Don't worry Jan, Emily and I will get your bed ready in the attic. The little spare room is still there as you know, we just need to give it a quick tidy. We'll sort it properly tomorrow. You wouldn't mind sleeping there would you? After all that is where you died."

"That is not something that will bother me." he replied "I felt very comfortable up there and, to be honest, I have spent a lot of my time there since I died, it sort of felt like home."

Emily jumped up. "Come on then Jane, we'll go and sort the attic out while Jan and Sarah continue their life stories."

The attic room was in a reasonable order as Jane knew. They only needed to put fresh linen on the bed and tidy a few things and it was ready for use and in just a few minutes it was occupied by a very tired Jan who looked happy and content. Sarah was dispatched to Christopher's room who, too, looked happy and content and was also soon settled and asleep.

"Well." said Emily as they sat in the kitchen. "I think that went rather well, didn't it?"

"I guess so." replied Jane. "They both seem happy with the situation, but, like you said earlier, if anything goes wrong, things just revert to how they were. Provided they don't touch that is."

"And even then." added Emily, "Jan needs to induce the renewal process, like I do with you."

As expected, breakfast in the morning was going to be a first for two people; Sarah, who had not been in the presence of a ghost before, let alone being joined to one and Jan, who had not had a full English breakfast since the 1940's. With this in mind, Jane had prepared the finest breakfast ever, which, seemed to now be the way at Chapwell, it was consumed in virtual silence, barring the odd exclamation of pure pleasure.

"Oh, my god." said Sarah, "I just cannot believe how hungry I was. That really hit the spot Jane, thanks."

"You're very welcome. It's nice to see the food bin is still working well then." Jan looked up from his nearly cleared plate and stared. "Sorry Jan," said Jane, "you'll get used to Sarah's food disposal habits. I don't know where she puts it. She's as bad as Emily"

"Maybe." said Jan "But I do know why. This breakfast is very good, just like I remember when I was alive here. I shall never forget those breakfasts and having one for real now is a marvellous treat."

"You're quiet Emily." said Jane. Emily looked up from her now empty plate. Her face not the usual bright light in the house, had a worried shadow about it. "What's up? Breakfast not right?" Emily placed her cutlery on her plate tidily.

"I'm not sure. Well, no, the breakfast was fine" she said. "But last night I woke up and couldn't get back to sleep for some reason so I knew something was wrong somewhere and the feeling I had was centred on the house, so I got up and looked out of the window. I know it was dark but we can see things that live people cannot and I am absolutely sure I saw someone in the garden. Well, I certainly felt someone around the house and definitely outside. They were down at the bottom of the garden and I think, just the other side of the fence, just watching, stood there just looking at the house."

"Who was it?" asked Jane.

"Really couldn't see. Like I said, it was very dark but I could see their outline, or their shape. It's difficult to describe what I can actually see. I could feel someone like I said. They were there for a few minutes and then they just walked away to the left and went around the back of the oak tree in the corner. The feeling of them slowly diminished and finally left me altogether. I was awake for a good while afterwards but I didn't feel them again so I guess they went away." The four of them were silent, listening to this worrying event.

"Oh, it was just someone wandering around at night." said Jane. "You know Roger in the village is always out and about at night, looking for bats, foxes and badgers."

"No, it wasn't Roger." said Emily. "I know what Roger feels like when he's about. He feels like the earth and straw and mushrooms. This man, and I'm pretty sure it was a man, felt familiar. I just can't work out who it was. He was like stone and mud and angry dogs."

"I've never known you to describe people like that." said Jane.

"Well," replied Emily. "Everyone has a feeling about them, it's like the colour of their hair or eyes, just a feeling, you know, some people hear a sound and see a colour, I see a person and get a feeling which is a part of their persona for me."

"Do I have a feeling?" asked Jane.

"Oh, yes, you're chocolate and cotton and clouds." said Emily absently, her mind elsewhere.

"Did you feel as if this man was a threat?" asked Jan.

"Sort of, well, not a threat as such but certainly a bit creepy. Something to be aware of. I'm not sure. If he had stayed there, I could probably have got a better idea of who they might be and what they wanted."

"Did you feel anything Jan?" asked Sarah.

"No, I slept end to end, like a log as you say."

"But can you feel people like Emily can?"

"Yes, it's not something I've really thought about but yes and it was when Emily described Jane that I thought, yes, that's exactly Jane, just what I feel."

"What about me? What do I feel like?"

"Hmm, you are leather and pillow and bread."

"Weird." said Sarah.

"No, not weird." said Emily. "That's exactly what I feel. See, we don't have to actually see someone to know who they are if they are reasonably close to you. It's just another sense."

"It's like in a dream." said Jane. "I have had dreams where I know there is someone there, I haven't actually seen them but I know who they are in the dream, it's just a feeling."

"Same thing." said Emily "But we have a more enhanced version of that where we have a description of the feeling expressed in objects or materials. It's one of those senses that living humans have lost over the many years but we, as ghosts, have it and use it. Never thought much about it to be honest. I would still like to know who it was; it worries me a little bit."

"Well." said Jane getting up, collecting plates and cutlery. "We'll have a look down the bottom of the garden, see if there is any clue there. They might have left footprints or something. Anyone want any more tea?" All three responded in the negative and assisted the clearing of the table.

"Sarah?" asked Jan as Jane and Emily were tidying.

"Yes." came the reply

"Can I take you for a walk?"

"Yes, I'd like that. I don't know the area very well but I guess you do?"

"Yes, yes, I know the area very well. I've been walking around here for a few years." he smiled knowingly. "I'll take you along the old roman road. It goes across the field at the corner of the lane and ends up at the site of the roman fort. There are lovely views from up there."

"Okay, let me get some boots on and a jacket and we'll be off. Do you have anything to wear?"

"I have now. I can wear some of Christopher's stuff that's in the trunk in the attic. Is that okay Jane?

"Of course, it is Jan, you two go and enjoy yourselves and don't forget you are a ghost. The two of you need to act accordingly if there are others about."

"I'll wait for you in the hallway Jan." said Sarah.

Emily and Jane were both stood at the bottom of the garden leaning over the fence to see if there was any evidence left by last night's intruder. "The grass is a bit trampled down here Jane and this is roughly where he was stood." They both leaned further over, searching the grass and thistles for anything that would confirm the presence of a person in the field.

"There, there Emily." said Jane pointing down into the grass stems. "There's a fag end down there look."

"Hang on I'll go over there." said Emily who just walked straight through the fence to the other side."

"Almost forgot about that super power." said Jane sniggering." Emily bent down, parting the grass and, yes, there was a cigarette end there, together with a burn mark at the base of the grass stems. "Nearly started a fire as well." she said, picking it up carefully and holding it in the air, simultaneously walking back through the fence back into the garden. "I can feel him." she said. "I can feel him like I did last night, but stronger now and he's definitely not nice. And, definitely someone I have felt before, but I just cannot remember who. Oh, that's so annoying." She stared at the burnt relic almost expecting more from it but it didn't give anything else up.

"Keep it." said Jane, "Keep it and we'll let Jan have a look, or feel, or whatever you call it. He might know who it is. You never know."

"Good idea." said Emily.

"Got a surprise for you." said Jane when Sarah and Jan returned.

"For who?" asked Sarah.

"Oh, sorry, Jan. I, or we. Me and Emily, that is, have a surprise for you.

"This is turning into an exciting few days." he said.

"Come with me". She guided Jan upstairs and continued up the narrow stairs to the attic. The attic bedroom door was ajar where she led Jan through to see Emily sat on the bed. The room was transformed. All vacuumed, dusted and polished, the dormer window gleaming and bright.

"What do you think?" asked Emily smiling like a child and bouncing slightly on the bed. Jan looked around, mouth agape.

"It's lovely. Really nice, I love it, thanks both. Makes me feel properly at home, like I actually belong here. Not like I am only existing here. With that, he broke into tears, turning away to hide his emotion.

"Oh, Jan." said Jane. "Don't get upset. This is all yours. This is your room now; this is where you live."

"I know." he responded, barely containing himself. "You don't understand what this means. This weekend has changed my life, well death." he said with a stifled laugh. "I have a home and a family again; you are my friends and I can live and interact and be part of something. Oh, I have missed this feeling for so, so long you wouldn't believe."

"Know what you're saying." said Emily. "Been there, done that and I know how you feel."

"we'll leave you to it Jan," said Jane. "Come down when you're ready. Don't rush, but there is cake mind!!"

"Jan's upstairs admiring his new room." Jane said to Sarah as she came into the kitchen. "Have you had a good day?"

"Yes, brilliant." said Sarah. "Jan's been teaching me about the tricks you are all privy to. It's amazing what I can do now, well, with Jan's help that is. He disappeared and reappeared. I disappeared and reappeared, we walked through a stone wall. We also saw other ghosts while we were at the roman fort. There was a soldier and some animals and he explained how it all works, how these people and animals exist as ghosts. I understand a lot more now and have had my eyes fully opened to this other world. To be quite honest, I find it quite exciting and somewhat intriguing. I don't quite know where all this goes but I'm finding it endlessly interesting, and Jan is so nice. It's made me very happy to make him happy."

"Well." said Jane standing hands on hips. "I think everyone is happy now. What shall we have for dinner tonight? Have a think while I make some tea, I promised Jan some cake."

Later whilst they were all sat at the table, Emily presented Jan with the cigarette end, holding it up she just asked; "Do you feel anything from this Jan?" He took Emily's wrist and brought her hand closer, looking at the item and concentrating on it.

"Hmm, I don't like this person, it's a man, definitely. Rock and mud and a nasty dog are what I feel."

"Same as me." said Emily screwing her face up. "I just can't remember who it is though. Do you know, Jan?"

"No, I don't think so." He said, shaking his head. "Can't say as I've ever met them before."

Jane, who had been watching the expressions of the two ghosts felt mildly concerned as they had both been obviously disturbed by the event of last night and the fact that they could both detect an undesirable person who had invaded their privacy. "Tell you what we'll do." she said. "I'll do us an early dinner and we can all go down the pub afterwards, perhaps we can relax a bit. I fancy a beer. I know you two can't drink in the pub but we can at least bring Sarah into the world of people and ghosts, see how it feels."

"How do you mean?" asked Sarah confused.

"Think about it Sarah. We all go down the pub but two of our party are ghosts. Now, I know they can be invisible but they can also be visible to us. And, correct me if I'm wrong Emily but you can also become visible to all being as you're joined?"

"Correct." came the answer. "But, obviously, within our world that is definitively frowned on. We would only do that in very exceptional circumstances. It is avoided at all cost. There are those who do practice visibility, hence so-called hauntings. It shouldn't happen as there is no reason for it to happen."

Jane and Sarah walked into the pub together, Jane made sure she closed the door behind her. She still felt somewhat rude to close the door in the face of someone you absolutely know is behind you. They walked up to the bar where Sarah was introduced to Colin, hands were shaken and beer ordered. A quick look around the bar showed Jane that no-one appeared interested in them. As they turned, they both saw Jan and Emily sat at a table in the corner, under the window. Jane leaned towards Sarah and whispered as they walked "Now, this is where things get interesting and you do have to be very careful not to look like a mad woman. No-one else in here can see those two sat there, only us. As there are two of us, we can talk to each other but, unlike if you were on your own, we can also talk to the other two as well, but we just need to be looking at each other when we do it. We can hear them but no-one else can. Let's see how it goes."

They sat down, opposite each other with Jan and Emily between them. "Okay." said Jane, looking at Sarah. "Can you feel anyone in here you two?"

"Nothing offensive." said Emily. "Colin is nice, he's beer, grass and oak."

"That fits." said Jane with a smile "Jan, anything?"

"No." came the reply. "There are feelings but nothing strange or threatening, all quite nice really."

"Emily?" asked Jane.

"Yes."

"What were the feelings you got from Beryl and John?"

"Well." said Emily, "Beryl was lavender, pepper and hats. John was strong, chair and trains."

"Interesting." said Jane. "I can see the lavender and the chair but the rest, I don't know."

"We don't get to choose," said Jan "this is how people unconsciously present themselves to us. You recognise a face, clothes and perhaps how someone walks but we get this added identity and, like Emily said, we can get the feeling before we actually see someone. They can be quite a distance away. By the way, Sarah, keep looking at Jane, don't look at me, people will think you're weird." Sarah quickly diverted her look back to Jane smiling.

"Are you feeling that Jan?" asked Emily a few minutes later.

"Nasty dog." said Jan.

"Getting stronger." said Emily. A minute later the door to the pub opened and they all glanced across to see who had arrived. Who had this aura. "That explains it." said Emily.

"Rob." whispered Jane trying not to look. Rob walked across to the bar, all the time looking across to Jane, a sneer washing across his unshaven face. "I'm going to ask him." said Jane.

"Ask what?" asked Emily.

"If he was in the field last night."

"No, don't, don't make the problem worse. We don't want to wind him up."

"Okay, who is he?" asked Sarah.

"You don't want to know, suffice it to say, he's a friend of David's. You remember who David is?"

"Yes, yes, I do." While he was waiting for his drink Rob nonchalantly wandered across to their table, leaning on the back of Jan's chair. "You again." He said, looking at Jane. "And with a friend." glancing across at Sarah."

There was a shout from behind the bar. "Rob, leave them alone, they're nothing to do with you and right now you're walking on very thin ice."

Rob stood up, looked directly at Jane and, with clenched teeth said, "He knows, you know, David knows. And he's not happy."

"Rob" shouted Colin. "Get over here now if you want your drink. Otherwise, you'll be out the door."

"Yeah, whatever, I'm done here anyway." He turned with a humph and walked back to the bar.

"Come on." said Jane, "Drink up, I've seen and heard enough." Finishing their drinks, Jane took their empty glasses back to the bar and thanked Colin. Walking back down the lane, they were all silent. The evening sun was still warm but none of them noticed.

"What do you suppose he meant Jane?" asked Sarah.

"What, about David knowing and not being happy?"

"Hmm."

"I guess David knows that the house came to me and he got nothing, so he's probably not happy about that. But from what I gather he would never be happy about anything, unless it involved drugs and violence."

There was a feeling each of them independently had, that things were not quite as harmonious as they could be. The evening, what was left of it was somewhat subdued. Almost as if a cloud had formed over Chapwell with a prospect of rain coming. Sarah went back to her flat as she was working the next week. Sorry to leave Jan on his own, she opened the front door. "Don't worry Sarah, I'm not lonely any more, thanks to you. And I can survive quite happily in my current form for a few months so don't panic. I'm quite content. Though I will miss you terribly, I've got to know and like you very much and can't wait till you visit again."

"Me too." said Sarah. "Me too. I'll be back as soon as I can, if that's okay with you Jane?"

"Of course, it is. Just text me or just turn up, this house is your house. You are a part of it now whether you like it or not. Your room will always be available and ready for you."

"Thanks Jane and I'll see you all as soon as I can." They all stood in the doorway and waved Sarah off into the evening sunset.

With the recent events, there was a feeling of trepidation within the house. Almost as if it was expected that something was going to happen. But as the days passed, the feeling receded and things got more back to normal. The summer was coming to an end. The first leaves were just showing the signs of darkening, a few had already fallen. There were fewer bees and butterflies around. A lot of dead-heading was required to keep the garden tidy and the vegetables were at their most productive, some of which were put on a small table outside the front gate for anyone to take. Jane had placed a jar on the table for contributions which, to her surprise, filled each day, the money donated to charity. Which probably explained the amount of money received compared to the number of vegetables taken. This pleased Jane as it gave her the comfort that people in the village appreciated who she was and what her place in the village meant. That last link with Beryl and John. One that would be retained. The house remaining with Jane seemed to satisfy people, happy in the knowledge that Chapwell was safe in her hands and wouldn't change. That was not to say an attempt at change was not coming.

Chapter Eleven

Dead

The evening was quiet. Not so unusual at Chapwell. As far back as Jane could remember, the evenings were quiet. The radio was usually on now, the volume turned down but still there. Even if only to give the house the sound of days past when John would sit in the carver, reading the paper or doing a crossword. It always made Jane feel comfortable. The three of them played cards, Jan teaching them some new games which came from his younger family days back in Poland.

This evening was just one of those evenings until about nine o'clock. She knew it was nine o'clock as the news had just been on the radio. The three of them were staring down at their hands of cards, trying to work out the best play to increase the stack on the table. Both Emily and Jan looked up from the table and turned to each other mystified.

"Gate, key and fire." said Emily quietly. "I'm getting that too." said Jan.

"What are you two on about?" asked Jane, amused. "Is this some kind of cards cheat code?"

"No." said Emily quite sternly, absently laying down her hand of cards face down. "Nothing like that. There's someone around the house and it's not Rob. I'll go upstairs and have a look out the back."

"I'll go too." said Jan. "I'll Take a look out the front."

"I'll go and have a look as well." said Jane.

"No" came a sharp response from the other two. "You stay here Jane. Whoever it is will not be able to see us." said Emily.

"No, okay, that makes sense." acknowledged Jane.

Jan and Emily quietly made their way up the stairs leaving Jane in the kitchen, alone. It was getting quite dark outside, the sun having just dropped below the horizon and clouds building up meant the light was going earlier than would be normal for this time of year. She could hear the other two moving around in the bedrooms and on the landing but otherwise there was silence. Even the radio seemed to go quieter than it had been. Jane slowly got up and turned it off. Listening for anything now, her hand still on the volume control, wishing she could hold Emily's hand and experience the enhanced hearing she would get from it. But, nothing, total silence and, it seemed, total stillness. The only sound was the quiet, solid tick from the clock in the hall. The marking of time passing second by second.

For an instant she felt totally alone. Alone in the house, the silence enveloping her, crushing in. She stood completely still, uncomfortable but she dared not move in case there was something to hear, something to break the silence. Her anxiety increased with each tick of the clock; her breath slowed until it almost stopped. Eyes wide she looked around the kitchen. Nothing to see. Nothing to hear, but plenty to feel. The sensation of fright slowly crept into her, cooling her skin, catching in her throat, tightening her chest, paralysing her legs. A scrape, a shadow, a movement. There was something. She could feel it. Concentrating her senses even harder she tried to get some idea of what she was experiencing but there was nothing. The silence prevailed, the feeling passed and she felt the chill dissipate. She relaxed. But too soon. A crash. The front door. The door knocker crashed against the oak. Once, twice, three times, each getting louder, more aggressive and seemingly urgent.

Jane stalled but shook it off and walked into the hall, all the time trying hard to think who it could be at this time of night, knocking on her door. Habit took over and she turned the door knob. The door moved just as Emily frantically shouted from the landing. "Jane, don't, don't open the door." Too late, a gap had appeared. The next second was a blur. A painful blur as the door was forced open, smashing into Jane's head, knocking her sprawling to the floor, her head hitting the stone flags. The door thumped against the wall, bouncing back. All she could see through the pain and sparks was a man stood in the doorway, a silhouette against the outside light. He just stood still looking down at her. "Bitch." was all she heard. "You bitch. Just like your whore of a mother."

Her senses started to come back. With the shock and the speed her mind was now working, she very quickly realised what the circumstances were. Here was David. It could be no-one else. Someone she had never met, stood in front of her, his stance threatening, having injured her and now screaming at her. She tried to get up, moving onto her elbows, attempting to shuffle backwards form the door and from him. The pain seared through her forehead where the door hit her. She could feel a trickle of blood run down over one eye. Instinctively she ran her hand across her head, and, on looking at her palm saw blood, a lot of blood. The pain getting heavier, now the back of her head and neck joined in. She knew it was a serious injury. But then, there was a hand in front of her. Initially the thought was of assistance. A hand to help her up. But, no. The hand grabbed the top of her jumper and dragged her up. Not fully, just enough for him to bring his face close to hers. The stink of stale beer and cigarette smoke assaulted her senses and made her gag. She tried to turn away. "Get over here you bitch." he shouted. She didn't understand where here was, her mind was still numbed by the pain. Not working correctly. He dragged her across the floor, powerfully, the strength he unleashed astonished her. She felt like a rag doll being pulled along by a child. The door to the lounge was open and she could see this was her next destination. She tried to get up, her legs scrabbling on the floor, hands around his wrist trying to relax the grip he had. All in vain. He was too powerful, his arm as strong as a gorilla. She was powerless to resist. Almost giving up she dug in. Her thoughts suddenly coming into focus, knowing what this man had done in the past and knowing the damage he could do to her now. She started to fight back, screaming at him to release her. Grabbing his wrist, kicking at the lounge carpet, it gave her some grip. But still he was winning. He picked her up off the floor and threw her onto the sofa like a discarded cushion, her knee hitting the corner of the coffee table, added to the pain. He just stood there in front of her. The darkness of the room hiding his features, hiding the expression. All she could see from the light from the hallway was the strength he had, his massive arms and torso bulged with latent strength. "Sit there, bitch." he said as he walked over to the door and switched on the light. "See, I know where everything is in this house. MY house." he screamed. "The house you stole from me you little bitch." "It was left to me—" she started. "NO, It's mine. Mine by right. I am a Chapwell and this house is mine." "But, it's not. It's mine." stated Jane pushing herself up to a sitting position. Feeling clearer in her head though the pain still banging, she felt defiant. She couldn't have this animal taking anything from her. The thought of the house being taken from her gave her strength. "You were not part of this family, you were cast out, disinherited. And don't think I don't know what you did, you beast." she screamed. David just stood there, thick, hair covered arms folded across his massive chest, as if just content to listen to the ranting of an imbecile, letting her get it out, offload the anger before he... did what? He hadn't made his mind up yet. He looked nothing like his brother, he was bigger, much bigger, an untidy mountain of muscle. The legacy of many hours spent in the prison gym.

He laughed, false and loud, like a pirate before sending the convict to the end of the plank.

Jane blubbed, breaking down slowly. "You will never take this house from me. Everyone knows this house is mine. You would never get away with whatever it is you think you can get away with."

He leant down towards her, too close again, the stink of his breath covering her face. She turned away, trying not to breathe.

Closing her eyes, grimacing. Her head exploded with more pain. She was thrown across the sofa as he hit her hard on the side of her head. He picked her up and propped her upright again almost to make her an easier target. Her jaw was throbbing. She could feel the damage, her tongue exploring her mouth checking for missing teeth, tasting blood. She realised that he was going to beat her. How bad she didn't know but it seemed inevitable. What else he had planned scared her even more. She tried to think of what to do but with this powerful monster in front of her, with the power and evil he possessed made her think of compliance. An attempt to mitigate the damage that she was sure this man could inflict and would, given any reason to do so.

As things seemed to slow whether actually or due to her mind running at a much faster pace she thought of Emily and Jan. But quickly realised that they would be powerless to do anything barring trying to scare him by appearing. Even that would not work she thought. This man was ferocious, mean and determined to get what he wanted regardless of any other influence. Another lightning-fast punch smashed into her face, her nose taking the full impact. She bounced back into the sofa, pain totally taking control. She could feel nothing else. Her head screamed pain. Blanking everything around her. She had the growing realisation that this was more serious than she could possibly have imagined. It seemed like he really wanted to kill her and this scared her more. She felt totally vulnerable, just wondering how much pain she could take before consciousness left her. Her head swam and clouded, fogged. Sounds diminished. She felt herself drifting, waiting for the next blow. It didn't come. She slid down, consciousness leaving her. After how long she didn't know but she slowly tried to open her eyes, feeling the pain and unable to see from her right eye. Bruising and a cut had closed it completely, anticipating the monster in front of her waiting for her to move. Only to smash her back down again. But nothing. He was not there.

She reached down to prop herself up, defensively looking around her through the blood and tears, expecting him to reappear, ready to hit her again. She could not see him, but to one side there was someone. Smaller, slimmer. "Jan." she whispered.

"I'm here Jane. I'm here, oh, God what has he done to you?"

"Where is he?" she asked, barely able to speak. Her mouth swelling up.

"He's gone."

"Gone? Gone where?"

"Don't worry about him. He's gone."

"But how?"

"Emily removed him." he said.

"And how the hell did she do that, you saw how big he was."

"Never mind that right now." said Jan. "She escorted him from the premises."

"I really don't understand." said Jane laying her head back down on the cushion, closing her eyes.

"I'll get some water and a flannel, clean you up a bit but you need to call the Police Jane, and an ambulance. He really has beaten you. I'll be back in a second. Don't move."

"Like I can." she replied gasping.

Jane could see the blue lights flashing outside the front window. Dark now, it made the bright light painful to her eyes. Nothing like the pain firmly settled in her head. She was sat upright on the sofa. A Paramedic checking her face and head for obvious damage. A female Police Officer was sat beside her taking notes giving Jane a feeling of care. The officer was slim and appeared younger than Jane. Simple brown hair, short and tidy under her cap. Her smile was pleasing and soft. Jane explained the whole episode from the time the door knocker bashed the door to the point where she became aware that he had gone.

"I don't know why he left." she said. "He just went. I thought he was going to beat me to death. I don't know, perhaps he realised he would not get away with whatever he had planned and just left or this was just the beginning and he plans to come back. I don't care right now anyway, as long as he has gone."

"Okay, said the Officer. I think that will do for now. We may need to have a chat soon though. But I think the best thing is for you to get to Hospital and have these injuries checked over and treated. And don't forget. I'm Mandy and I'll be involved for as long as this takes."

"Okay, thanks Mandy. If I remember anything I'll get in touch."

Jane looked around. Jan was still there in the background. A concerned look on his face. Powerless to actually do anything but happy with the knowledge that Jane was being looked after. But she could not see Emily. She tried to attract Jan's attention. He looked at her and she just mouthed "Emily?"

"I don't know where she is Jane." he replied. "But, don't worry about her she'll be back."

The paramedic informed Jane that she did, indeed need to go to the hospital for some extra checks. Jane phoned her mum. The first time she had done so under such circumstances. Her mother, obviously upset, said she would meet her at the hospital. Jane had not felt this kind of care and affection from her mother in twenty-eight years.

"What happened?" asked her desperately worried mother. Holding her hand as she lay between the crisp sheets of the hospital bed.

"David mum, it was David. I didn't tell you the full story on the phone. I didn't want you to worry."

"Well, I'm certainly worried now. So, tell me exactly what happened."

Jane described the events of the evening up until the time the Police and Paramedics arrived. "What did he think he was going to get out of this?"

"I don't know mum; he was very drunk and absolutely mad."

"I know what that looks like." said Sandra.

"He just kept saying that Chapwell belonged to him."

"Well, he knows full well that it belongs to you and there's nothing he can do about that now."

"I'm a bit worried though, he just vanished. I thought he was going to beat me to death but he just stopped. I don't remember what happened after he punched me in the face, I lost consciousness, I think. But when I came round, he had gone. No sign of him. I'm a bit worried about you mum, you still live in the same house, he knows where you are."

"I don't think he'll come anywhere near me love, he knows what would happen if he broke the restraining order."

"Is that still in place?" asked Jane.

"Yes, love, it was made permanent because I live alone and haven't moved away from the area."

"Well, I hope the police find him and arrest him, I can't stand the thought of him coming back."

"Just make sure, until he is caught that you keep the doors and windows locked."

"Okay, mum, and, thanks for coming."

"That's what a mother is for." said Sandra leaning over to hug her daughter.

"Ouch, careful mum, my face is quite painful."

"Sorry love, sorry."

"Look, I'm okay mum, if you need to get home, I don't mind, I'm safe here and the damage is only cosmetic. I know you have to go to work."

"I don't like to leave you love but I am at work in the morning. Now," she said holding a wagging finger up, "if anything changes, just call me, okay?"

"Okay, mum. I think I'll just rest, I'm quite tired after all that, not to mention in pain."

Jane spent the night in hospital. Kept under observation for concussion and any other issues but was given the all clear later in the morning. She was very battered and the bruising on her face was ugly, but she was in one piece and allowed to return home. Sarah picked her up and drove her back to Chapwell. "Why didn't you call me Jane?" asked a frantic Sarah.

"Mum came straight to the hospital and after they said I was okay, just a bit bruised, I didn't want to bother you.

"You could have called me last night."

"I was okay, Sarah, they were looking after me but I don't know where Emily has gone."

"How do you mean?"

"Jan said that she had escorted David off the premises, how, I don't know but I'm pretty sure she saved my life."

When they arrived back at Chapwell, Emily was back, Jan was there and had looked after the house while she was away. Emily made a pot of tea and they sat in the comfort of the lounge. The experiences of the previous night still smarting but less so now the sun was out and the room tidy.

"Where on earth did you go Emily?" Jane asked.

"I removed David from the house." replied Emily, not offering to elaborate.

"I know, Jan said but how did you do that?"

"Occupied him." came the short response.

"Explain." said Jane curtly.

"Oh, okay. Something I haven't shown you because it is so uncomfortable and, in some cases, last night included, downright disgusting."

"How do you mean?"

"We can occupy the body of a living person. And, in doing so we can exert an element of control over them. This is what I did last night after David started pummelling you. Then I, well, persuaded him to leave. I also placed thoughts in his head so he will be unwilling to come back any time soon but I haven't finished just yet. I still have a bit of work to do, but you don't need to concern yourself about that."

"Where's he gone?" asked Jane.

"I don't actually know but I'm guessing he's at Rob's. I left him in the middle of the village. I have an idea that Rob is the only person around here that tolerates him. One of the other features of an occupation is that you can feel their thoughts, their memories and, believe me when I tell you that there was nothing pleasant in there at all."

Jane finished her tea and stretched, exercising her face, causing pain. "God, I must look a mess."

"Not surprising to be honest Jane." said Emily. "He really did give you a beating. We only saw the last punch but it was obvious he wasn't finished there."

"I think I'll go and have a bath and a lie down for a bit."

"You do that, looks like you could do with a good rest. I mean, you have been up pretty much all night."

"No, I *have* been up all night. I tried to rest after mum left the hospital but it was so noisy in there, the best I could manage was a slight doze. Even that was painful.

Two days later the house was again quiet. Jane felt much better. Her mum had been to see her and had been spoiling her with soup and toast. She still looked terrible but felt as if she was actually recovering. She settled herself in the lounge, on the same sofa that witnessed the beating. Not bothered with that she just curled up with a book, determined not to be disturbed by what had happened. She felt confident that the Police were going to handle things so she shouldn't bump into David again. Certainly not in the near future. Emily had also given her the reassurance that he would not be coming back to Chapwell.

Emily and Jan had given her space to recover. Not wanting to bring anything back, they kept themselves at a short distance. Jane knew they would be there if she needed them but the quiet was a blessing and the book a distraction.

There came a quiet knock at the front door and even though it was only a light knock Jane jumped, dropping her book. She felt the shock go through her but heard Emily in the hall. "It's just the Police Jane, it's okay." Relieved, Jane picked up her book and placed it on the table. Slowly she got up and walked into the hall. Emily smiled, comforting Jane. She opened the door. In front of her were three people. Two in plain clothes and one in uniform. The uniform she recognised as Mandy who was so nice to her the other night. Mandy introduced the other two as Detective Sargeant Philip Johnson and Detective Inspector Tony Davies who promptly showed her their identity cards. DS Johnson was a large man, quietly confident with slightly greying and thinning hair. DI Davies was shorter and would have looked very smart had it not been for the fact that he looked like he had slept in his raincoat. The stubble added to this impression. "May we come in Jane?" asked Mandy.

"Yes, yes, of course. Go through to the kitchen I can make tea. Would you like tea?"

"Maybe in a minute Miss Campbell." said the DI. "We have a few questions for you first. Can we go through?" DI Davies pointed towards the kitchen doorway. Jane, slightly confused and mildly concerned led them through.

They sat down. Mandy stood in the doorway as if guarding the exit. DI Davies produced a notebook, reached into his jacket and retrieved a pen with a flourish. "Do you want a better statement?" asked Jane. "I still haven't given a full statement of what happened the other night. I did make some notes to make sure I hadn't forgotten anything."

"We'll get to that Miss Campbell but I need to ask some questions first."

"So, you said." The Detective Sargeant was just sat, quietly looking around the room seemingly taking everything in.

"Okay." said DI Davies. "Can you tell me where you were yesterday afternoon between twelve pm and four pm?"

"I was right here, in the house. I've not been anywhere since the other night when, well, you know. Well, apart from going to hospital that is but, no, I haven't been anywhere. Why?"

"Can anyone confirm?"

"Yes." said Jane mistakenly thinking of Emily and Jan, who, incidentally, were stood in the corner of the kitchen. Emily grimaced noticeably.

"Well, no, no, I was here alone. There's no-one else in the house."

"Would you mind if we had a look around Miss Campbell?" asked DS Johnson.

"Why? Why would you want to look around the house. Am I in some sort of trouble?"

"It's just routine." said Mandy "This is just part of any investigation, especially when it involves domestic violence."

"Well, okay but everything happened in the hall and the lounge." said Jane.

"So, it's okay for us to take a look about?"

"Yes, yes, I guess so." said Jane worried.

"Are you ready for some questions?" asked DI Davies as Mandy and DS Johnson went through the door into the hallway. "How well do you know David Chapwell?"

"I don't. I never even met him till the other night. And, incidentally I don't want to see him again."

"Oh, and what makes you say that?"

"The bruises on my face should give you a clue."

"Is that 'don't' want to see him again. Or 'won't' see him again?"

"I don't understand. I just don't ever want to see that monster again." Jane was becoming a little agitated. "After what he did to me and my mother, and, indeed what he did to his own family and countless others during his drug fuelled rampage through life. I wouldn't care if no-one ever saw him again."

"Really." said DI Davies, his eyebrows noticeably raised. One hand cupping his chin whilst the other made notes. This prompted a whimper from Emily, her hand covering her face. Jane looked up trying not to change her expression, trying not to give anything away. "So" said DI Davies. "You have no-one to corroborate your movements yesterday and you seem totally unconcerned about the whereabouts of David Chapwell?"

"You've got that about right. That man is a monster, as you well know, or at least I hope you know. If he rots in Prison I wouldn't care."

DS Johnson and Mandy returned to the kitchen. DS Johnson held a bag in his hand. Jane could see it looked like an evidence bag and it contained, mysteriously, a pair of shoes. A pair of very muddy red shoes. "Found these, sir." said DS Johnson. "In a wardrobe upstairs."

"Hmm. Do you recognise these shoes, Miss Campbell?" asked DI Davies.

"Yes." came the reply. "They were Aunt Beryl's. But why are they muddy? They should be in her wardrobe in my bedroom. I never got rid of them."

"Jane Campbell." said DI Davies. "You are under arrest on suspicion of the murder of David Chapwell. You do not have to say anything, but it may harm your defence if you do not mention when questioned something which you later rely on in court. Anything you do say may be given in evidence. Do you understand?"

The room started to spin, Jane's mouth dropped open, her eyes widened. Unable to comprehend what had just been said. Speechless she looked up at Emily, a suspicion creeping into her head. Emily looked back compassionately and just said, "Don't worry Jane, everything will be fine, trust me."

"Murder!" Jane exclaimed. "I don't understand." she sounded frantic now, looking around the room, at each of the Police officers and towards Emily. "You're saying David is dead?"

"I suggest you leave any comments until we get to the station." said Mandy calmly.

Jane was now the subject of precisely the thing she had seen many times on the TV, an innocent victim sat in an interview room with Police Constable Mandy Beck stood by the door. A recording device on the table. The plain table. The room empty, stark and bright. "Mandy, what's happening? I haven't done anything, David left after he beat me and I haven't seen him since."

"Miss Campbell, Jane, wait until the DI comes, please, it'll be much better for you." The door opened and they both looked towards it, DI Davies and DS Johnson walked in and sat opposite her, arranged their jackets and placed files and notebooks on the table.

The formalities of the interview were carried out and the questioning started. DS Johnson asked first. "You say that you were at home during the times in question Miss Campbell?"

"Yes, yes, I was at home, I had just been beaten up and I was resting, trying to recover. Look, do I need a solicitor here?"

"If you think that would help your case then you are free to employ a solicitor. Do you have one in mind?"

"Yes. Jeremy Green of Jeremiah and Jeremiah is my solicitor."

"Okay." Said DI Davies, turning to the WPC. "Mandy, can you get in touch with Mr Green and we will continue this when he arrives. We don't want to be seen to be departing from procedure." Mandy nodded and left the room.

"Is that it?" asked Jane.

"For now, Miss Campbell, for now." replied DI Davies with a wry smile as he closed the file in front of him. DS Johnson stood and whilst the DI left the room, indicated to Jane that she should stand.

"What now?" she asked. A strained look on her face.

"I'll take you back to your cell Miss Campbell. While we wait for your solicitor." He took her arm gently but Jane could feel the strength in the grip, should she decide to run. He took Jane to a cell where she was confronted with sparseness. The door slammed shut and the small window cover closed. She couldn't quite believe what had happened. How could she have been put in this position? Whatever, she knew she was innocent of any crime, but with the absence of Emily, who, she knew had something to do with it, there was no evidence in her favour.

Jeremy was at the station within an hour and was presented to Jane as she sat in her cell. He was smart, as always and, as she had experienced in the past, exuded an air of confidence. Contrary to what she had always thought, the cell was sparse, yes, but it was warm and the mattress was reasonably comfortable. She was brought tea. Disgusting tea but tea nonetheless and welcome. She couldn't stop thinking about what could possibly have happened, together with the state of Emily as she was escorted from the house, who, incidentally, she had not seen since that time.

"Don't worry about this Jane." said Jeremy "You'll be home very soon. They have no reason to hold you here. They have no evidence and certainly no motive."

"But they have a pair of shoes, I don't know how they became involved. They are a pair of shoes that Aunt Beryl had, the red ones. They were in the wardrobe. But when I saw them, they were in an evidence bag covered in mud and I just don't understand."

"Like I say, don't worry, we'll go through this interview process and you'll be out of here. It will be interesting to see what they have to say."

The interview resumed, now in the presence of Jeremy which made Jane feel considerably more comfortable. "Now, Miss Campbell." started DS Johnson. "You say that you were at home on the afternoon in question?"

"Yes, like I said, recovering from a beating."

"So, you didn't visit the quarry?"

"The quarry?" asked Jane, confused.

"Yes, the quarry, the quarry where you pushed David Chapwell to his death."

"Don't answer that, Jane." said Jeremy, "You appear to be accusing my client of a crime? With no evidence and the clear statement my client made informing you that she spent the time in question in her home."

"But." said DI Davies. "Can you explain the fact that a pair of shoes, which you openly admit were in a wardrobe, in your home, and, were worn by someone at the precise point where David Chapwell was pushed to his death. The footprints in the mud match these shoes perfectly, absolutely no doubt. I think that it was you wearing those shoes as you pushed David Chapwell into the quarry."

"No." said Jane. Jeremy put his hand up to stop her further.

"Can we see these shoes? Just to confirm that they are indeed the shoes you think they are?"

WPC Beck was dispatched to fetch the shoes and returned with the evidence bag. "Are these the shoes you say they are Jane?" asked Jeremy.

"Yes." replied Jane hesitantly. "Yes, they are the shoes from the wardrobe. The wardrobe in my room. They were Aunt Beryl's."

"Okay, now tell me what size shoes you wear Jane."

"Size five." The reply came with a confused look.

"And what size are these shoes DS Johnson?" He turned the bag over, examining the shoes.

"I cannot see a size on them."

"Try harder." Jeremy insisted. Another inspection involved the donning of gloves and the removal of the shoes from the bag. "Size three." said DS Johnson, looking first at the DI and then towards Jane and Jeremy.

"There we are." said Jeremy turning towards Jane. "I think it's time we left."

"Whoa." said DI Davies. "Here is the evidence right in front of us."

"Yes." replied Jeremy. "It may be evidence but it does not involve my client. You see, Jane, here, has size five feet, as she said, so there is no way she could possibly have worn those shoes. Is there?" The three police officers looked at each other bewildered. "Well. Is there any reason why you will not release my client?"

"No, no I guess not stammered DI Davies."

"I'll give you a lift home." said Jeremy as they stood at the front desk, Jane's release being documented. Out in the fresh air Jane breathed a sigh of relief.

"That was traumatic." she said, running her hand through her hair, the bruises on her face still smarting. "But I don't understand. They have a pair of shoes from the house that, somehow were used by someone who they think killed David."

"It seems that way Jane, but as I have proven, this has nothing to do with you so I suggest you return home and relax. For two reasons. One, David is dead so he is no longer any threat to you. And, two, the perpetrator of his murder cannot be you so the police are no longer a threat either."

"But what about whoever did it? They were obviously in my house and..." the sentence faltered and ended.

"And what?" asked Jeremy.

"Nothing, never mind." stuttered Jane as she realised what was going on. "I'm just tired and a bit overwhelmed to be honest." Jeremy opened the car door for Jane and they travelled back to Chapwell in silence. "Thanks, Jeremy, for everything." said Jane as she opened the car door.

"No problem, and don't forget, if anything happens or the Police give you any grief, just call, okay?"

"Yeah, yeah, thanks. Oh, but Jeremy?"

"Yes."

"How did you know about the size of the shoes?"

"I didn't Jane, I didn't, I just observe things and take them in." Jane watched Jeremy drive off down the lane in his very expensive car, thankful that things appeared a little clearer. She did have a theory though and was about to check its validity.

"Emily!" she shouted as soon as she entered the hallway. "Where are you? I think you have some explaining to do." She stood impatiently at the bottom of the stairs and, looking up, saw a very sheepish looking Emily standing on the landing. "I'm going to put the kettle on and we are going to have a chat, aren't we?"

"I think we should." said Emily descending the stairs timidly.

"Okay." said Jane placing the mugs on the table. "I'm waiting for your side of the story. I saw, well think I saw you in the lounge when David punched me in the face. After that, I remember nothing apart from waking up and seeing Jan stood there. He told me you had taken David away. So, that is something I need to understand. Or, perhaps the first thing I need to know is, did you kill him?"

"Would you be desperately upset if I said yes." came the reply.

"Not particularly."

"Okay, yes I did, sort of. Look Jane, he has been a plague in this house ever since he was born." Emily leant on the table, her arms encircling her mug, fingers entwined, picking at her nails. "Think about it. I have had to live with the devastation that man, and, indeed, boy, has caused, not only from when he was a child in this house, but from when he met your mum and the total devastation that effected. I have watched your life from pretty much the day you were born, through your childhood and your growing into a woman carefully balanced between the love of Beryl and John, and, indeed your mother with the possibility that he could destroy it all. That has all ended now, finished and..." Emily's head dropped, her hair falling over her face, tumbling onto the table. She shook and Jane could see the tears dropping to the wooden surface. She sat up, leaning back into the chair, her hands covering her face. Jane just sat looking at the distraught soul in front of her and briefly attempted to think of just how much horror Emily had endured over the years. She remembered when she had told her about the day her mum was attacked and the mean acts against Christopher and Kate as children, the grief he caused his parents. Emily had seen it all, heard it all and kept it all for so many years. Jane was the centre of the whole tale now and only Jane could forgive.

She stood and walked around the table, placing her hands on Emily's shoulders. Smoothing her hair back to see her face. Emily turned to her and stood, immediately encircling Jane with her arms, burying her face in Jane's neck, crying uncontrollably. Jane stroked her hair, a small comforting gesture that always achieved its aim. "Don't worry Emily, it's over, all done. We are safe. He's gone and that history can be wiped away. We are both here now and it's due to you that we are." They just stood; no more words were needed. Jane just kept hold of Emily, wishing the pain would leave her. The physical injuries Jane had endured were nothing when compared with the untold agony Emily had soaked up over the years.

"Tell you what" "What?" snuffled Emily. "Sit back down and I'll put the kettle on. No, cancel that, I'll open a bottle of wine. I think we both deserve it. "Okay." came the quiet reply. "Let's go into the lounge and sit on the sofa. I rather like that sofa now. I think it saved me from some severe injuries. Come on." said Jane offering Emily her hand.

They sat at either end of the sofa, tears cleared and glasses in hand they just looked at each other. "We are inseparable, aren't we?" asked Jane, smiling."

"I hope so Jane." came the reply.

"I really don't know what I would do without you."

"Well, for a start you would just be a ghost." said Jane with a smirk on her face. This made Emily's face brighten. "And you wouldn't be able to eat or drink." the smile broadened. Emily leant back into the soft back of the sofa, her head against the cushion, seemingly relaxing.

"I cannot believe this is all over." said Emily with a heavy sigh.

"I didn't realise how much this has been affecting you over the years." said Jane. "But you have kept it to yourself all this time and I haven't actually known you for very long, in the grand scheme of things."

"Neither did I Jane, neither did I. But it has. I feel as if something heavy has been removed from inside of me. I feel lighter and cleaner." They both quietly sipped their wine, just enjoying each other's company. The bond between them growing perceptibly stronger.

"Are you ready to tell me exactly what happened?" asked Jane. "You don't have to if you don't want to. When you are ready." Emily's eyes dropped to her wine glass.

"No, it's okay. I'll tell you. You'll only be mithering about it if I don't, I know you Jane, I know you. Right, here goes"

"When I went upstairs, I went to my room first and looked out the window. The sense of him was less there so I knew he wasn't in the garden. Then I heard Jan, he went to the landing window first, then he called me so I went to him and looked down. We could both feel him really strong. That was when I realised exactly who it was. I should have known straight away. I saw him come around the corner and under the porch and my fears were confirmed. I heard the bang of the door knocker and I just froze Jane, just froze. We both heard you go into the hall. I ran back to the other landing and shouted to try and stop you opening the door but it was too late. You'd opened it. I couldn't move. I just watched as he dragged you into the lounge. Jan grabbed me and we both went down. By then you had taken a couple of blows and I could see that he was just going to keep battering you. He had smashed you in the face and you slumped sideways. He was just about to give you another punch when I took him over."

"Yes, you said that but I don't remember any of it, the next I knew was he had gone and Jan was there."

"The occupation of a living body is not nice Jane. I don't know what it is like for the recipient but for me it is quite uncomfortable. Well, saying that I have never actually done it before but this incident warranted a go at it. It's like, I don't know..." Emily looked up at the ceiling, folded her legs under her, thinking. "It's like climbing into a shell of a person but I can feel everything inside. I could feel his temperature, feel his breathing and I could smell him. He felt dirty, he stank, even from inside. Worse than this and I never want to experience it again."

"What?" asked Jane.

"I felt, absorbed or, I don't know, it's hard to describe. But I could see every memory he had, every thought, every action. And, let me tell you, it really was not nice. There was nothing in there but malicious intent. I immediately saw that his intention was to, well..." Tears welled up and fell down her face."

"What? Come on Emily, I need to know." Emily sniffed, took a sip of wine and settled herself.

"He wanted to rape you, Jane, he was thinking of your mum at the time and the evil in him was just out of control. Then he was going to beat you even more. I nearly lost control but I managed to sort myself out and got a hold of him. I got his thoughts and shut them down. He just stopped and so I just walked him out of the house and back into the village. I implanted new thoughts, removed the vindictiveness he felt towards you and let him on his way."

"So, he went home?"

"No, he hasn't a home, he was staying with that Rob bloke."

"But." said Jane. "It didn't finish there did it? David was murdered yesterday. Yesterday afternoon to be precise. And it involved Aunt Beryl's red shoes."

"I took the shoes, well I had them on anyway. I really didn't want anything else to happen and I didn't want David coming back. I knew what I needed to do, I'd had been thinking about it all the previous day, so I did it. I went to Rob's house. They were going down the pub for lunch when I arrived but I ignored that and took over David again. It was no better; he really was disgusting. I, from within David, told Rob that I had something to do and I would meet him at the pub in a while. Rob accepted that and, do you know what he said?"

"No."

"He asked David if he was going to give you a seeing to again. This made me quite angry and frightened. So, I just told Rob that I needed to see someone and I might be a while and just walked off. Rob went the way of the pub and I took David to the quarry. I got him right on the edge of the highest bit. I could see all the boulders and scrap down there so I just stepped back out of him and gave him the thought to take a step forward. He did, and down he went.

Right to the bottom, smashing into the metal and rocks. He didn't even scream." Emily was staring at the ceiling, a smile on her face. "I knew he was dead, the feeling of him stopped. Gate, key, fire. Gone, poof."

"So that's how the footprints appeared at the top of the quarry?" asked Jane.

"That's how the footprints appeared at the top of the quarry." repeated Emily.

"But." said Jane. "You didn't actually murder him, did you? Think about it. From what you just said you encouraged him to step off the top. I mean, you didn't actually push him, did you?"

"No. But I did influence his actions. Look, don't get me wrong here Jane. I don't regret what I did, I don't feel guilty about it. Is that so wrong?"

"No, no, it's not wrong. Not wrong at all. But what happens now?"

"Well, nothing." replied Emily. "It's finished, he's gone. But, and you are going to love this."

"What?"

"I have some of his DNA."

"And how did you get that?"

"Simple, I ripped a load of his hair out as he fell. It's in my drawer upstairs."

"You know what that means?" A brightness appearing on Jane's face.

"Yes." said Emily, a sneer arriving on her face. "We can find out who your father is. I mean. If it proves a match then we know David is your father, not the best news, but if, and I hope this is how it turns out. If it proves negative then we know that Mark is your father and that would change things for you."

"Yes, it would." thought Jane out loud, a spark of excitement running through her. "It most certainly would." This lightened the atmosphere in the room. Something positive had come from the event. Something they both welcomed.

"Where's Jan?" asked Jane suddenly.

"He's in his room." replied Emily. "He was a bit shocked. Well very shocked and upset actually, so he thought he would take a lie down. He was convinced, after having his life brought back, he was going to lose it again."

"Oh, no." said Jane, placing her glass on the table. "I'll go and get him and we can just reassure him that everything is okay now, it's all over.

Jane tapped on Jan's door. There was no answer. She gave another gentle tap and called his name. "Jan, are you okay, it's Jane, can I come in?"

"Yes." came a quiet reply. Jan was lying on his bed, ankles crossed and his hands behind his head.

"Hi," said Jane.

"Hi Jane." said Jan, turning his head.

"Look, Jan, everything is okay. It's all over. There's nothing to worry about now." Jane gently sat on the edge of the bed and looked Jan in the eye. His face sad, there was no smile, no emotion to take a hold of and work with.

"I'm sorry Jane, it's just that I was so worried that things were going to change. I had just found myself and found something to believe in. Something to live for and it just got angry and I didn't like that."

"Don't be sorry Jan. You are the very last person that has anything to be sorry for. You are respected here. You helped save our country which means we are constantly in your debt. So please never think you have anything to be sorry for."

"Okay, but I don't know, since I paired with Sarah I have begun to feel more and more. I have become aware of so much and the memories of the past have come back and I'm not sure I can cope with that. And, with what has just happened I felt very scared."

"Jan. You have nothing to be scared of. You have friends here. Friends who care about you and, I think Sarah, to a certain extent, depends on you. You wouldn't think it but Sarah is quite a vulnerable person emotionally. I don't know why. I wouldn't ask because she is such a nice person and I don't want her to be upset. She is okay, I know but underneath there is something hidden and when you came along you gave her hope. Hope that there are actually good things in the world. I think you can both benefit from each other's past trauma and build a better life for yourselves. So, do you want to come downstairs? We're having a glass of wine and winding down. You are safe Jan and we'll do all we can to help you in any way we can." Jane reached out and took Jan's hand, her thumb stroking it gently.

Jan sat up and smiled. "Thanks Jane. Thanks for everything."

"Don't be silly. Come on give me a hug."

The three of them ended the evening sat comfortably in the lounge, quiet in the knowledge that all was well at Chapwell. All relieved and all very tired.

Chapter Twelve

DNA

Sat around the breakfast table, Jane, Emily and Jan were casually reflecting on the drama of the previous days with relief that it was all over.

"The first thing I'm going to do," said Jane, placing her mug on the table, "is get this DNA test done. I can order a test kit online, send in the post and we'll know the result within a few days."

Are you going to tell your mum what you're doing?" asked Emily.

"I don't think so, not just yet anyway. I'll tell her what the result is when I get it, good or bad. I just don't want to stress her unnecessarily."

"Can you explain a 'DNA test'?" asked Jan, intrigued.

Jane pushed her empty mug to one side and turned to Jan. "A DNA test is like a fingerprint pattern, only more accurate. Each one of us has a biological identity that is totally unique to the individual and DNA is found in all the cells in our body. Modern science has found a way of extracting the DNA from our cells and producing a print which is, like I said, unique to each of us. So, I get a sample of my DNA from saliva, blood or even from the roots of my hair, we already have some of David's hair, thanks to Emily, so we can send these off to a lab and they will process them. The print that this test produces will determine whether David is my father or not. See, I have DNA from both my mother and my biological father so there will be a match with both. I know my mother is my biological mother but not my father and I really need to know who it is."

"Okay." said Jan. "And is this fool proof."

"Absolutely." said Jayne. "DNA testing is used commonly in crime solving. Oh, now there's a thing." A look of excitement appeared in her eyes.

"What?" asked Emily.

"Those shoes that the police still have."

"What about them?"

"Well, I'll suggest a DNA test to DI Davies. That way it will prove without a shadow of a doubt that I was not wearing them. Also, it would mean that the police would have a DNA sample from a ghost. If that's at all possible." she joked.

"Wouldn't have thought so." said Emily with a humph. "But wouldn't hurt anything to put an end to the mystery of the shoes."

"I'll get a test kit ordered then." said Jane picking up her phone as Emily stood and started clearing the breakfast things away. Moments later she placed it back on the table. "There. All done. Oh, but I might as well get in touch with DI Davies while I'm here." she said as she picking her phone up again.

"It's already been done." said the detective, responding to Jane's suggestion. "There was only one set detected and that, we are sure is from your Aunt Beryl. We know it couldn't be yours, though that could be confirmed if we can get a sample from your Aunt if at all possible. We know it is not yours as we had already tested for that."

DI Davies explained that the shoes had been removed from the investigation as there was no evidence to suggest that they had been involved in the death of David. He was still perplexed by the fact that they had obviously been at the scene but that was all he had.

"I can provide you with her hairbrush." said Jane. "It's in her dressing table. I kept all her bits and pieces and put them in one of the drawers. They haven't been disturbed so you are welcome to come over an collect it. I won't touch it. Hang on…, you said you had already tested for my DNA and you didn't find any. So why was I dragged in for questioning?"

"Because we hadn't sent the samples off at that time."

"So that means I am no longer a suspect then?"

"Correct. You are no longer a suspect. But, and I must stress this; the house is still within the scope of our investigation."

"Can I expect to see you soon, Detective?"

"I'll come over as soon as I can. It will, at least confirm or deny a line of enquiry which will help with cleaning up the investigation. I'll bring the shoes back as well. We have all the information we need as far as they are concerned."

The knock on the front door came within the hour and DI Davies was guided into the kitchen. He seemed, today, like the stereotypical detective, jacket and tie, the ubiquitous scruffy raincoat and signs of not having had a shave within the last twelve hours. His hair was distinctly tidy, cut short and neat. He wasn't old, around thirty-five thought Jane and not bad looking. "Would you like a cup of tea Detective?"

"Please Jane, call me Tony. You have no direct connection to the investigation now, so the formalities can be dropped. And, yes, I would love a cup of tea. Milk, no sugar, thanks."

"Sit down, sit down," said Jane pointing at the chair nearest the door. "If the formalities are now dropped you can be treated as a guest."

He removed his coat and placed it over the back of the chair. Smoothing his tie, he sat down, folding his arms on the table. "So" he said looking around the kitchen. "You inherited this from the Chapwell's? Nice."

"Yes, a long story but basically a result of the actions of David Chapwell."

"How do you mean?" enquired Tony.

"Like I say, a long story but I spent a lot of my childhood here as a result of his past actions, which I am now aware of. And due to my love of the house, I was left it in the will so that I could care for it."

"Ah, yes." said Tony tapping his index finger on his temple. "I Just remembered. Your mother is Sandra Campbell?"

"Didn't you realise that during your investigation."

"No, we knew who your mother is and the link with David, but missed the link with you. No need for it to pop up. I mean it would have done eventually but as you came out of the circle of suspicion no further action was taken on that line of enquiry."

"That explains a lot."

"Sorry Jane but sometimes detective work gets it wrong, not because it is wrong but just due to the procedure we have to follow. Often, like in this case we cannot see certain things until the procedure brings them to our attention." He thought momentarily. "So does that mean you didn't know about David Chapwell's crimes in relation to your mother?"

"Not until recently. The family obviously knew about it all. They kept it from me because my mother was being a bit awkward about it and Beryl and John never said anything because they didn't want to cause me any distress." She turned and looked at him pleadingly. "I don't particularly want to talk about that if you don't mind Tony. My mother and I have restarted our relationship with the agreement that the past stays exactly where it is. In the past."

"Oh, right, okay." came the response.

Jane put the kettle on and prepared the mugs. She also placed a cake on the table, two plates and a knife were added. "That looks nice cake Jane." he said politely but staring at it hungrily.

"Yep, it's nice cake and as you are a guest you are allowed some." she said, smiling wryly.

"Oh, thanks." he said with a snigger.

"Tell you what." She said whilst filling the teapot. While we are waiting for the tea to brew, I'll take you upstairs and you can collect the hairbrush."

"Good idea." he said, getting up from his chair. He followed Jane into the hallway and up the stairs, taking in the extensive wood panelling, the pictures, clock and staircase. Jane noticed him caress the acorn and slide his hand along the ample banister "This certainly is some house Jane."

"I know." She replied. "It has history going back to..., I haven't quite worked out exactly when yet but definitely pre-Roman and the family goes back to the sixteen hundreds."

"How do you know all this?" he asked.

"I'm a Historian."

"Oh, right, yes, sorry, I forgot." He stood on the landing looking around, seeing the mirror and adjusting his tie in the reflection, obviously a habit he had. Jane went into her bedroom, the door adjacent to the large landing window. Tony just stood at the mullioned expanse, totally impressed with the view both inside and out.

"Here." he heard from the bedroom.

"Sorry Jane, just admiring the view."

"you're welcome to look out of any of the windows. They all have equally wonderful vistas." she said opening the draw in the dresser. "There's your hairbrush." She added, pointing into the drawer at the decorative brush. "As I told you I haven't used it so there is none of my hair in it. I have touched the handle obviously but that is all." DI Davies put a glove on and took the brush from the drawer, dropping it into an evidence bag, zipping the top. "I will get it back, won't I?" asked Jane.

"Of course. As soon as we have finished with it, I'll get it back to you." He then wandered towards the rear of the room, glancing at the features of the room from the chair by the door to the huge wardrobe. He looked out of the rear window, over the garden. "How do you find time to care for all that garden?" he asked, leaning on the window sill.

"I spend a lot of time there Tony. I do have help though. A local gardener comes to do the heavy stuff for me but I have a rule to spend at least an hour a day in the garden to keep on top of it. But that turns into two, three, four hours or more during the busy times. I enjoy it though. I've been doing it almost all my life so I know my way around."

"Well, all I can say is that it's a testament to your skill Jane, it does look really nice."

"Well, thanks." said Jane, smiling. "That means a lot. If you are done, the tea will be ready."

Tony, turned but glanced back almost as if he didn't want to release the view he had over the flower beds.

"Well, Jane, you were absolutely right." said Tony wiping his hands on some kitchen towel.

"What about?"

"The cake, it's delicious. I'm guessing you made it yourself?"

"Then you guess right, my Aunt Beryl taught me and I have honed it to a fine art."

"You say your Aunt Beryl. I didn't realise that you were part of the family."

"Oh, I'm not, never have been. My mum was just a friend of the family and with the David incident, other things happened, but, like I said, it's a long story."

"Whatever, I'm not here to pry but I look forward to bringing the brush back if it might involve a slice of cake. Oh, by the way." he said, reaching down to the floor by his side. "Here are the shoes." He lifted the shoes, still in the evidence bag, up to the table."

"Whoa." said Jane. "You can't put shoes on the table it's bad luck."

He stopped, holding them, dangling in mid-air.

"Those, I think are mine." came a voice from nowhere.

"Oh, good grief." muttered Jane, putting her head in her hands. DI Davies turned around, fully expecting to see the owner of the voice stood behind him. Nothing.

"Who said that?" he asked, looking around the room, bewildered.

"Me." came the voice again. The chair at the end of the table now slid back across the floor.

"What the hell is going on?" he exclaimed, visually shocked at the impossible movement of the chair."

"Oh, good grief." repeated Jane looking up to see Emily materialising right in front of them both, stood, gripping the bag containing the shoes.

Emily wrestled the bag from DI Davies's hands though he released them instantly once he felt the pull. She sat down, now fully solid and placed the bag on the floor.

"I suppose you want tea as well?" asked Jane.

"What do you think?" said Emily smiling and looking across to the detective. DI Davies was paralysed, his hand still in mid-air having released the bag.

"Oh, god." said Jane exasperated, shaking her head. "I'm sorry Tony. This was not supposed to happen."

"I don't understand. I, what, how did that just happen." he stammered.

"Okay." said Jayne laying her hands on the table. This is not going to be easy to explain and even more difficult for you to understand but you have just met Emily."

"And who is Emily?

Emily was about to speak but Jane beat her to it having raised her hand.

"No, Emily, let me tell Tony what is going on and it'll be the entire truth, no bits missing and that will allow him to make his own mind up about everything."

"Okay." said Emily, sitting back in her chair after cutting a piece of cake and pouring herself a cup of tea.

"Tony." said Jane with a sigh.

"Yes."

"You need to listen to this carefully. It won't make sense but it will be the truth."

"What is she?" he said, pointing at Emily grimacing.

"Okay, we'll start right there. This is Emily Chapwell. She is an ancestor of the Chapwell family and she died in this house at the beginning of the last century. Don't worry, nothing sinister, she fell down the stairs and hit her head. Now, whether you believe or not, you have to accept that she is a ghost, or what we normally term as a ghost. It's far more complicated than that but for now, live with it. You know what David Chapwell did to my mother?"

"Yes, I remember that much."

"Right, well Emily, here, has had to live with that ever since it happened. She has been around this house all the while, she watched me grow up and we are now joined as companions. Okay, so far?"

"I don't understand but carry on, this is going to be good." he said, slightly sarcastically.

"Right. So, David Chapwell reappeared in the area and, having discovered that I had inherited the house and it's a possibly that he knew about the large trust fund I have control of, he was, perhaps a bit miffed. No doubt this information got to him from his good, and probably only friend, Rob Owens. I guess you know him as well?"

"I have had dealings with him, yes.

"The next thing that happened was when David came to the house and beat the hell out of me. This you know about in its entirety. What you don't know is what happened to David after that."

"And I would really like to know." he interrupted, "Being as this is my investigation and right now it has stalled due to a lack of evidence."

"Well, it might not have the solution you would like, unfortunately. Purely because Emily here was highly involved in his demise."

"Okay," he said "But first, I need to get to grips with what I have just witnessed here. Emily here, as I saw, just appeared in front of me." Emily vanished. "Oh, god, now she's disappeared." He said astonished. Emily promptly reappeared, leaving no doubt as to her capabilities.

"I'm just showing you," said Emily, "just in case you missed it. I am what you call a ghost. Here, take hold of my hand."

"Is this going to hurt?"

"No, I just want you to hold my hand, you may feel different about me." Tony held out his hand with a grimace. Emily reached out to grip it.

"There." she said. "Nothing wrong there.

"No, but it feels a bit weird."

"That, my dear Tony, is because I am a ghost."

"Look." he said, releasing Emily's hand. "I am a detective. I work on fact, solid fact. This is not solid fact."

"It is." said Emily. "How much more solid do you want? I am here, talking to you and interacting with you. What more do you want?"

"Oh, god, how the hell can I accept this. And more to the point how can this be explained to everyone else."

"Tony." said Jane jumping into the conversation. "We'll work that out in a bit. First let me finish telling you about the David incident. Okay?"

"Okay" he replied, subdued. A sideways glance aimed at Emily.

"Now, as David was giving me a thrashing, Emily intervened. That is, she, and don't interrupt." said Jane holding a finger up, wagging it, noticing Tony's desire to speak. "She occupied his body, stopping him beating me anymore. Then she removed him from the house and deposited him in the village and from what we can gather, he just went to Rob's house."

"That doesn't explain the murder though, does it?"

"I'm getting to that. The next day, Emily went to find him with the full intention of getting rid of him permanently."

"So, she killed him?"

"If you like. But listen. First, it's not quite as simple as that. See, Emily took over his body again. She simply walked him to the quarry and convinced him to jump off the top. She didn't push him, he fell off, or jumped, whatever. Either way, you do not have a suspect. Well, you do but." Jane pointed at Emily nonchalantly. "Try and arrest her." Emily looked at Tony, expectant, her eyebrows lifted and she held both hands in front of her, wrists touching, inviting a pair of handcuffs. She smiled and winked. Tony looked at Emily and then at Jane, exasperated.

"Exactly." stated Emily. "Now you know who was responsible, directly or indirectly for David's death. But you are totally powerless to do anything about it. Correct?" Tony didn't know what to say. He knew full well that this put him in a desperately precarious position. Here he had the perpetrator of the death he was investigating and he knew exactly how it came about but that was as far as it could go.

"Have you spoken to Rob Owens?" asked Jane.

"Yes, we interviewed him but nothing came of it. He didn't know where David went, he didn't go with him as he was in the pub all lunchtime, and most of the afternoon. Right around the time David was killed. And all that is backed up by the landlord."

"But did you ask him what state David was in?"

"Well, yes, he did say that David was acting weird but nothing else."

"Don't you think, maybe David was feeling guilty about what he had done and was just plain scared of going back to prison."

"I guess."

"So," said Jane "that looks to me like a suicide. He knew it was useless to do anything more as far as I was concerned as it would just result in his arrest. Which it would have done had you got to Rob's house before Emily did so, there you are, he topped himself.

"Here's a plan." said Emily who had been listening intently.

"What?" asked Tony.

"I will leave here in a minute and have a word with Rob. Once I've done that you can call him in for questioning again. Just see what he says.

"And what difference will that make?"

"Trust me." Emily said knowingly. "Trust me."

Later that afternoon the phone rang and Jane sat on the sofa to answer it. The call came from Tony Davies. It was short and to the point and included a request to visit Chapwell with the aim of returning the hairbrush.

"Emily, Guess what?"

"What."

"Tony Davies just called. Told me about Rob and David."

"And." said Emily.

"He said that Rob, when interviewed, opened up and told him that he knew what David had done that night and also, him acting weird was not the whole story. He told Tony that David was going to end it all and that was why he disappeared. He said that he didn't believe him and told him he'd see him down at the pub later. Obviously, that didn't happen but Rob said he didn't really care"

"How do you...oh, wait. I know how you know that. Because it was you who put those thoughts in his head."

"Hm, rumbled." said Emily with a grin. "Angry?"

"No, no, but I think you need to be careful how you use that particular skill, Emily."

"Don't worry, it won't happen often, if at all because it is just so disgusting. Solves his case though, doesn't it?"

"You do realise how powerful that skill is Emily?"

"I know. Now I've used it in anger I can see how dangerous it could be so I think it should only be used in exceptional circumstances. I've learnt a lot in the last few days and I didn't like it very much at all."

"It sort of means you can change history, doesn't it?"

"Yes." came the reply. "It is, but only from that point on. I couldn't do that from an earlier date. I couldn't go back in time to do it. It just wouldn't work."

Later in the evening Tony Davies arrived in order to return the hairbrush. They were, all three sat in the kitchen with tea and cake. "You don't quite realise how bizarre this whole thing is." said Tony. "I am sat here, in the company of you, Jane and a ghost."

"Two ghosts." said Jane, expressionless.

"What do you mean?"

"There're two ghosts in here." she replied. "Jan, show yourself." Jan materialised leaning against the sink, in front of the window.

"Okay, I really have seen it all now." said Tony. "How many more are there?"

"Well." said Emily. "There are at least six but you'll only encounter me and Jan." They sat drinking tea, eating cake and going through Jan's story. Tony, feeling totally defeated and confused sat quietly with his mug of tea clasped in both hands staring straight ahead.

"Whatever happens now, Tony," said Jane. "No-one is ever going to believe you and we won't show anyone else what goes on here, so we suggest you keep this to yourself. The only reason you know about it at all is because Emily here thought it the quickest and simplest way to end your investigation into David's death. Which it did, I believe?"

"Yes, I suppose it did."

"Right, so we'll leave that as it is. Now. Emily has a proposal she would like to put to you."

"Oh, god. What now?" said Tony, frustrated, his head lowered, hands covering his eyes.

"Explain Emily." said Jane.

"As a result of this David thing I had the pleasure of occupying Rob Owens' body."

"Okay." said Tony.

"Well, during that exquisite experience, that, incidentally, I never want to repeat, I learnt something that was quite distasteful and I think it involves you."

"How do you mean? I'm intrigued."

"Bobby Lewis." said Emily.

"Bobby Lewis, What about him?" Asked Tony, his interest suddenly sparked.

"Isn't he the boy who recently vanished?" asked Emily.

"Yes, why?"

"Well." Emily continued. "Was it not one of your cases?"

"Yes. Still is in fact. Never solved it. He just disappeared. No trace was ever found of him, apart from his bike that is. He is still classed as a missing person but as it stands the investigation is stalled pending further evidence coming to hand. What has this got to do with anything anyway?"

"While I was, ugh, the thought if it makes me gag, while I was inside Rob Owens' head, that name came up. He knows something about it. He was involved in the boy's disappearance."

"In what way?" asked Tony.

"Don't know, but it was there, clear as day, in amongst all the other nastiness floating around."

"Well, can't you go back in there and find out what happened?"

"No way, absolutely not. There is not a chance I'm going back in there. In any case, what good would anything in there do for you. He would deny it all and you can't change that."

"No, but you might be able to find evidence, or at least the location of evidence."

"We can do better than that Tony. We can go right back to the scene of the crime and see exactly what happened."

"Right, okay, and how does that work. Time travel?" he said, chuckling.

"Precisely." said Emily.

"Oh, come on." He said, sitting up and leaning back in his chair, hands on the table. "Now, I've accepted the fact that ghosts exist. Didn't have much choice there though did I. And now you want me to believe you can travel back in time?"

"That's just it, Tony, we can.

"Tosh!" he said. "Okay, okay, get me next week's lottery numbers and I'll buy a ticket." Tony was getting more exasperated with all that was being thrown at him.

"That's the thing. The key word there was *back* in time. Not forward." said Jane. "We can only go back."

"How do you mean *we*?"

"Me and Emily. We are paired, joined and she can take me with her."

"Can she take me?"

"No, sorry, it doesn't work like that, but look. We can get you the evidence you need."

"How?"

"Okay, Bobby disappeared how long ago?"

"It's around six months now, I suppose."

"Right, if you give us as much detail as you can about the day that he disappeared then we can go back there and see what happened, simple eh?"

"I can't believe this." said Tony, looking at each of the women in turn. He stood up and began to circumnavigate the kitchen, rubbing his forehead. "I just can't believe it." He leant against the sink, next to Jan. "I'm talking to ghosts and they're going to solve a crime for me. But, look, wouldn't it just be easier if you stopped it happening at all?"

"Forgot to tell you." said Emily. "We can only observe, we cannot act. Think about it. It would mean that we could change history and that just cannot happen."

"But it would sort this whole thing out and Bobby would be at home right now, as we speak."

"No, Tony, we literally cannot do anything in the past. We can only observe."

"Oh, that's so annoying."

"Sorry Tony but that's just how it is but, look, we can at least give this a go. If Bobby has been abducted and is still alive, there is a chance we can get him back."

The door knocker clattered against the front door and before Jane could get up there was a shout. "Only me." it was Sarah. She walked straight into the kitchen to see the four of them in there.

"Don't tell me." said Tony. "This is another one?" Sarah just stopped and looked around the room, confused.

"No." said Jane. "This is Sarah, a friend of mine and she's Jan's other half. Well not in that sense. She's Jan's companion. They're paired."

"This gets worse. How many more?"

"No, honestly." said Jane. "There are no more."

"What's going on here then?" asked Sarah, putting her bag on the floor and removing her coat. "What is he doing here." looking at Tony. "And why are you two visible?" looking at Emily and Jan.

"Complicated." said Jane. "I'll explain later. But, for now, we are going to help Tony here. Oh, you don't know Tony do you."

"I don't know him." said Sarah. "But I know who he is, he's the detective that is investigating David's death isn't he? Oh and he arrested you as well" Sarah's hand went to her mouth.

"Yep, and that's all cleared up now. David committed suicide so the case is closed. I'll tell you about that later as well."

"How are we going to help him if the case is closed?" asked Sarah.

"Not that case, we're going to help him with the disappearance of Bobby Lewis."

"Isn't he the teenager that vanished from the village?"

"The same. So, Tony is going to go away and go through the case and give us any relevant information so that we can go back and see what happened. Isn't that right Tony?"

"Oh, god, yes. I cannot believe what I have got myself into here. It goes against everything I stand for. Truth, rationality and not forgetting sanity."

"Yeah, but think about it." said Emily, leaning forwards, staring straight at Tony "How is it going to feel if you can solve the disappearance of young Bobby?"

"Okay, okay." said Tony putting up his hands in a gesture of surrender. "I need to get out of here before I go completely mad." He walked around the table and collected his coat. Slipping his arms into the rumpled sleeves he looked at each of them in turn, still not believing he had become involved in something he really could not rationalise. He reached into the inside pocket of his coat and retrieved a bag. "Oh, and here's the hairbrush back." Jane took it from him and placed it on the table.

"I'll see you out then." said Jane as she walked into the hallway. She opened the front door and stood to one side.

He stopped in front of her as he passed, looked right into her eyes. "You're trouble, you are Miss Campbell."

"Oh, I know." she replied, smiling cheekily with a slight squirm of her shoulders. "It's fun though, isn't it?"

"We'll see, we'll see." he said as he walked off down the path shaking his head.

Closing the door, Jane turned and saw the other three all stood in the kitchen doorway. "What?" she asked.

"Nothing, nothing." came the response as they turned back, returning to the kitchen table. They sat and explained to Sarah the events of the last few days bringing her fully up to date. "That's a hell of a result." she said. "I really have missed all the action."

"I know, sorry." said Jane. "I didn't want you to get involved in that. It sorted itself out rather well though."

"How long are you staying Sarah?" asked Jan.

"The weekend if that's okay with everyone." They all smiled, confirming that they were happy with having a full house for a few days.

"After all that's happened, I think I should cook us a nice dinner we can relax with a game of cards." said Jane. "All up for that?" The enthusiasm was obvious as they all got up and started preparing the table. Getting glasses and cutlery while Jane grabbed her favourite knife and placed it on the worktop.

The weekend was quiet and peaceful. Jan and Sarah went out walking while Emily and Jane tended to the garden, the workload was dropping off now as the year wore on. They were talking about the house, as they often did and Jane decided that she wanted to take a look at the cellar. "I don't know why but I have really not got into sorting the cellar." she said.

"It's tidy enough, isn't it?" asked Emily.

"I don't mean it like that. I mean sorting the history of it. I need to see what is down there to try and find out exactly how old this house really is. C'mon, we've finished out here now so let's go and have tea. Then we can take a look in the cellar."

"I don't quite see the excitement in that Jane to be honest." said Emily sipping her tea as they sat at the table.

"Well, we'll see won't we. Perhaps in the past you haven't seen it in the same way as I see it. I mean, I know this house goes back to at least Roman times. Maybe further but I would be satisfied with finding more evidence. I haven't had chance to actually inspect it. I've looked and I've gone through the paperwork exercise but to find tangible evidence beats anything."

"How about evidence that is not, as you say, tangible?"

"How do you mean?" asked Jane.

"How about we travel back in time to see what's going on."

"Yeah, but we can't can we? It was you who told me that."

"I know, but remember the time I showed you my death birth?"

"How can I forget."

"Don't you remember, when we went back, we actually appeared about 30 seconds before I actually died."

"Yeah."

"Well, I've been thinking about that and I reckon I should try that again sometime. Only, just think about a date and time that is before my death. And I mean significantly earlier"

"Do you think you made a mistake?"

"I don't know but we'll give it a go one day, see what happens."

Tea finished, they stood in the cellar and both looked around at the stone floor, the walls with different brick, tile and stone visible in differing layers. The cellar had always been kept tidy. It was dry and cool and had been a favoured storage for wine and beer. Two of the walls were lined with wooden racks with shelves containing a variety of wooden and carboard boxes together with the odd light fitting or obscure piece of machinery. "Any idea what that is Emily?" asked Jane pointing across the room.

"What?" she replied.

"In the corner there. There's a wooden floor."

"Yes, and it's covered by a variety of large, heavy looking chests Jane." said an exasperated Emily. "I suppose you want to have a look at it?"

"Of course, I do, it doesn't belong there. Whatever age this floor is there should not be a wooden floor in it. Have you seen it before?"

"Can't think Jane, I didn't come down here much to be honest, way too many spiders, and even when I did, I wasn't taking much notice."

"Well, time we did, I think. Give me a hand to shift these chests. What the hell is in them anyway?" said Jane struggling to get any sign of movement from the first box.

"Open one up and have a look."

Jane lifted the latch and opened the first. Lifting the lid, resting it against the wall they looked inside. There in the chest were tools, carpenter's tools. Old and showing the signs of age, rusty and worn. "Ah, said Emily."

"What."

"I know who those belonged to."

"Er who?"

"When I was young, well a little girl we had a man that came from the village and did bits and pieces in the house and the garden. In fact, I have an idea that he built the shed and the greenhouse. I can't remember his name but I know he kept some of his stuff down here. Weird how his stuff is still here though. Mind you, looking at them, they have been used quite recently."

"Maybe Tom knows they're here. I'll ask him next time he comes around. He might have been using them on the odd occasion. He does do a bit of handyman work in the garden."

With much grunting and straining they managed to shuffle the two chests off the wooden floor and onto the stone flags. Jane immediately knelt down and tapped the board. A hollow sound resonated through the wood. "Hmm, sounds hollow under there. Must be a void." she said looking up at Emily. "Can't understand why though. Hang on, there's a little ring set into the wood on that side, ah, and hinges on the other." Jane tried to flip up the ring which was recessed into the wood but it was just too stiff, indicating that the board had not been moved in a while. She opened up one of the chests and selected a large old screwdriver. The ring quickly flipped up with the slight pressure exerted. "What do you reckon Emily?"

"To what?"

"Well, what's under here?"

"I don't know do I? Just open it, that'll answer your question immediately."

"Yeah, but there's an element of mystery here isn't there. Think, a bit like Schrodinger's Cat."

"Sorry Jane, you've lost me now."

"Superposition."

"What on earth are you on about?"

"Well, in Philosophy there is the thought that there are multiple universes, where different conditions can occur at the same place at the same time. Whatever we imagine could be under here, may actually be there, but then it might not. We just don't know."

"Jane!" the exclamation came with a look. A look Jane now recognised immediately as Emily's impatience hitting the surface.

"Okay, here goes." Jane grabbed the ring and lifted; the door came away from its frame surprisingly easily, a slight creak from the hinges hinted at disuse. With the hatch vertical they both looked into the uncovered void. "Oh, my god." said Jane. "Oh, my actual god. That is the last thing I would have thought of."

"It's very pretty." said Emily nonchalantly.

"It's not just pretty Emily, it's absolutely beautiful."

"You're just saying that because you're a historian."

"Well, yes but even so it is quite fantastic. Made my day that has." They were both looking down at a perfectly preserved Roman mosaic. "I need a paintbrush." said Jane. She opened the hatch up fully to rest against the wall now, completely revealing the treasure beneath. A quick search around the cellar furnished Jane with the appropriate tool in order for her to clean away the dust covering the image. Very gently she cleared away the thin layer to reveal the full mosaic. "Now, if I'm not mistaken, that, Emily, is a depiction of a Roman god. I'm not sure which one but if I was just going to take a random guess, I would say it was Apollo. Wow! That is just so cool."

"Like I said Jane, it's quite pretty."

"Pretty. Pretty! It's absolutely priceless." said Jane, her excitement obvious.

"If you say so." said Emily, seeming to show the first signs of disinterest.

"This means, absolutely, without a shadow of doubt that this house was built smack bang on top of a roman villa. And, not just any roman villa. A very important one. This is totally in situ. The edge goes to the base of the wall perfectly and it is all in line. All the walls built above it, the roman wall, medieval wall and on up to the present Tudor wall are perfectly in context. I'm only going to guess here but I think this entire floor was originally a mosaic and has been carefully been preserved when the next floor was put on top of it. Someone knew what it was and preserved it quite deliberately and later this part was isolated and the hatch put over it. If they hadn't done that, it would remain hidden forever. I wonder whether Uncle John knew about it?"

"Well, Jane, I never knew about it and I've been here a bit longer than you."

"I know, that's what makes it even more mysterious. Why is this not public knowledge. Someone must know about it. Someone put the hatch there and that means they knew what it meant."

"Can we have a cup of tea now?" asked Emily.

"Go and put the kettle on then, I just want to clean the rest of this off and wipe it over. I need to take a photo of it."

Jane brushed off the remaining dust and gently washed the mosaic with a damp sponge, revealing the full beauty of her discovery. The colours of the individual tesserae were so vivid it looked as if they had only just been laid down. She took a number of photographs and was continuing to stare at the image when a shout came down the stairs. "Tea's ready Jane."

"Okay." replied Jane. "I'll be there now." She gently closed down the hatch, reluctantly covering the mosaic but happy in the knowledge that she could come down at any time to look at it.

They were sat at the table, steaming tea in mugs, cake on plates.

"I know you love this house, Emily."

"Goes without saying." Emily replied.

"But this makes such a difference."

"Why?"

"Well, it just confirms that this house and those before it have existed here for two thousand years or more. Right on this site and even, I think in the same orientation. Just think of all the people who have lived here in that time, all the lives that have been lived. Mind boggling."

"Some of them are still here though."

"What do you mean?"

"Like I said, some of them are still here. There are at least six ghosts here. Me and Jan are the latest ones but there are some from before."

"How far back?" asked Jane.

"I don't know Jane, they are not like us, they stay hidden. Don't ask me why but they do. I have seen some of them but very rarely and I got the impression that they were avoiding contact."

"Why would they do that?"

"Dunno. But it might just be that the situation they are in does not comply with their religious beliefs. They may think that they are being punished and that punishment consists of a life, well, death that is permanent. They probably don't understand the actual reason why they are still here. Well, there is one, a young lad who knows why he is here. He did a lot of exploring and travelled around learning about what being a ghost meant. He taught me a lot."

"Where is he?" asked Jane.

"Haven't seen him here for years, Jane. He might be here but, then, he could just be on one of his travels."

"What's his name?"

"Benjamin. Benjamin Carey. He got trampled by a horse."

"Ouch!" said Jane. "That's a very old name."

"What, Benjamin?"

"No, daft, Carey. Carey is a very old name, Celtic I think, and, if that's the case, his family may have been here even before the Romans. Any idea when he died?"

"I can't remember, sixteen hundred and something, I think."

"Wow! He'll know loads about this place. I bet he's seen everything."

"Only if he was here. Like I said, I haven't seen him for years."

"Can't you, sort of, call to him? Get him to come back?"

"I can try. I know we can sense each other. A bit like you and I can but in the ghost world it goes a lot further, provided, that is, they want to be called. I'll try when I'm in bed tonight, it'll be quiet then. Don't hold your hopes up though, I haven't felt his presence for a long time."

"I would so love to talk to him, he could teach me a lot."

Sarah, meanwhile had taken Jan for a walk around the village. Wandering the narrow tracks and lanes between some of the buildings, they found themselves facing the church. "I love churches, Jan. They are such majestic buildings and they are so old and strong. And the stained-glass windows are wonderful." Jan seemed to be quite subdued, stood in the lychgate. "What's the matter Jan?" asked Sarah.

"Nothing. I haven't been in here since just after I arrived in the country."

"Oh, why, Jan?"

"This is where I am buried Sarah. My body was put to rest right here."

"Where?"

"I don't know. I never knew where I was buried. A lot of us were repatriated to Poland but I had no family so I was buried here in the village."

"Shall we go and find your grave Jan?"

"I don't know, I don't know how I'll feel Sarah."

"Come on, hold my hand and we'll try and find it. But if you really don't want to, just say and we'll stop."

"Okay."

Sarah held out her hand and Jan took it. Sarah felt the warmth and tingling and the increased sensitivity that came with it. She could now see everything sharper, more colourful, louder and she could see more. There were other ghosts in the churchyard, some standing, some wandering around. "Who are they Jan?"

"They're just other ghosts Sarah. I think they come down here to find others, just for company. After all, this is where their bodies end up."

"How sad."

"Oh, I don't think they are sad Sarah, they just need a bit of company, somewhere to go. What you may not know is that when we are in this state, we don't get bored or anything like that but just a desire to be around our own kind."

"Why don't they find a living person to pair with, Like us?"

"They probably don't need it. Not like me and Emily, we're slightly different, I think. I did feel lonely. I don't know why but I was just plain lonely. And Emily, she had witnessed so much in the past and kept so much of it inside her, she just needed someone to share it with, take her mind off it. And, of course she's a bit wild."

Sarah laughed. "Yes, I suppose she is a bit, but she is lovely. A really nice genuine person, as are you Jan, as are you. Oh, look, Jan, look at this. These graves are all from the war, oh, and here's your grave Jan. And look, someone has been putting flowers on it. It's being cared for. How nice."

"It must be someone from the village I guess." said Jan.

"Perhaps we'll find out one day. How does it feel to be stood right in front of your own grave?"

"A bit strange I suppose but I cannot *feel* anything as such. It's just where my body is buried, nothing more."

"Shall we try and find Emily's grave?"

"Do you think it will be here?" asked Jan.

"I would think so, she's a Chapwell, after all."

They wandered further around the graveyard checking dates and names until they came across a whole row of Chapwell's. They went back years even to some of what appeared to be the oldest gravestones in the churchyard. "Here's Beryl and John, buried together. All tidy, I know Jane comes down here on her own sometimes and if she's not here Emily will come down. Oh, look, back there, there's Emily's grave. It seems weird being stood here by the grave of someone you are going to have dinner with later."

They spent a while looking through the gravestones, trying to build a family tree of the Chapwell's. Many stones could be identified but as they moved to the rear wall of the churchyard the stones were worn and crumbling, making identification difficult. Only small fragments of the original text visible in a few places, lichen making its home on the rough slabs. Sarah inspected each in turn and could identify some Chapwell graves going back as far as the late seventeenth century with other, older, illegible graves behind, giving her the thought that the Chapwell name had been a part of the village for centuries and with the house, these lives obviously revolved around the majestic Tudor house she was currently staying in. It was no wonder there were so many ghosts and secrets held there.

Sarah looked at Jan and could see that he was becoming a little melancholy. "Do you want to go back Jan?"

"Yes," he replied, "let's. Let's leave these ghosts to themselves."

They quietly walked back to Chapwell along the lane. The birds were flitting between the branches, keeping ahead of them, checking that no intrusion ensued.

When they entered the house, Jane and Emily were sat in the kitchen as usual. On their entering the room Jane immediately got up and put the kettle on. "I'm guessing you'll be wanting a cup of tea you two? Had a nice walk?"

"Yes, it's been interesting." said Sarah. "We ended up in the churchyard. We found Jan's grave. He'd never been there but we saw that someone has been looking after it. There were flowers on it, quite recent and the grass had been kept trimmed."

"There are folk in the village who recognise the sacrifice some people made during the war and try to keep the memory alive." said Emily

"We found your grave as well Emily. I said to Jan, it was weird stood there next to it knowing you were here. I had a look at all the Chapwell graves there. I couldn't believe how many there were. I found one really old one whose date was 1678. I don't know who it was as I couldn't read the name but there are others that go back even further. And, there were other ghosts there as well, we saw quite a few."

"I know." said Emily, "There are a few there. I think they find some comfort being with others."

"Here's your tea you two. We had an exciting afternoon as well." said Jane.

"Well, you did." said Emily.

"Oh, come on Emily, we found a roman mosaic."

"Where?" asked Sarah excited.

"Down in the cellar." replied Jane. "I'll take you down and show you after you've had your tea. It's amazing, just shows how old this house is, or, at least the foundations."

Jane showed Sarah down into the cellar and revealed the mosaic on opening the wooden floor hatch. "Oh, wow that's amazing Jane, I bet you're made up with that."

"Oh, definitely. If I had wished for something in the house to prove to me its age, I certainly would not have come up with that."

Jane kept staring at the newly found mosaic, totally mesmerised by not only its beauty but also its significance in relation to Chapwell.

A few days later the DNA kit arrived and between Emily and Jane they filled out the forms, took the samples required from Jane and carefully placed the hair samples that Emily had taken from David into the small receptacle. The package sealed, they took a walk down to the village and posted it. "Fingers crossed Emily."

"Yeah, fingers crossed. What will you do about your other father, I mean Mark, if it proves that he is your father?"

"I don't know, I guess I'll at least need to find him. If it turns out he is my father, he deserves to know the truth. I mean, it was because of this episode that he left mum. Not knowing whether I was his daughter or not. Well, as far as I know, he doesn't even know whether it was a girl or a boy. Whatever, if he is my father I'll try and find him. For my benefit as well as his, and my mum's for that matter. We'll see. We don't even know the result yet."

"Oh, hang on." said Jane, her phone ringing in her pocket. "It's Tony Davies" she whispered to Emily. Her hand held over the microphone "Hi Tony, what's happening?" she asked. The brief conversation ended with a 'see you later then'.

"What did he want?" asked Emily.

"He's coming over in a bit. He's got a load of information about the disappearance of Bobby Lewis."

"Better get the cake out then."

By the time they had walked back to Chapwell, Tony was sat in his car outside the gate. On seeing the two of them he got out. "I'll put the kettle on Tony and I made a chocolate cake. I'm guessing you would like a slice?" ask Jane rhetorically.

"Oh, yes, yes please." came the reply, with a smile. In the kitchen, Tony sat down and placed his briefcase on his lap, opened it up and retrieved a large wedge of papers. Placing them on the table he looked up at Jane. "I cannot let you have any of this stuff here Jane and really I shouldn't have it here and you shouldn't even be able to see it but if it solves this case then so be it. I couldn't absorb all this information so I brought it with me for reference."

"That's okay Tony. We can make a few notes if we need them but, to be honest we only really need to know about the dates, times and places from when he disappeared."

Jane poured the tea and cut cake for them all, silencing Emily as it always did.

Chapter Thirteen

Missing

"Okay," started Tony, "so Bobby Lewis vanished on the evening of fourteenth of May, this year. He left his house in Coopers Road at seven thirty and was going to his friend's house about half a mile away. He was seen last, on his bike, going down Chapel Lane at about twenty-five to eight. And that was the last sighting. His bike was found at the other end of the lane. Abandoned. It was found after midnight when local people were out looking for him. His parents called us but they started out with neighbours to find him and that was when they came across his bike. And that, is just about it. His bike was leant against the fence at the end of the lane which indicated to us that he had deliberately put it there. No-one saw anything else. No vehicles, nothing but, there isn't much traffic on the main road at that time of the evening. We reckon his bike was left at around a quarter to eight, going by how long it should have taken him to cycle along the lane. Nobody saw a thing. We are completely stuck with this. There was no evidence of a struggle, no tyre marks, apart from his bike and some bigger marks that we couldn't get anything from. We took photographs but there was no useful evidence there."

"Okay." said Emily. "I think we can help with that. We can travel back there and see what happened."

"I'm listening." said Tony, arms folded on the table, pushing his plate to one side, the crumbs on it evidence of the recently demolished slice of cake.

Emily began. "We'll do it in stages. First, we'll go to his house and see him leaving. Then we'll go to the top end of Chapel Lane to see him going down there. Finally, we'll go to the other end of the lane and see exactly what happened after he leant his bike against that fence. We'll work out what to do next when we have a better idea of what happened at that point."

"That." said Tony. "Sounds perfect but be careful yeah?"

"Don't worry Tony. No-one will be able to see us or hear us or interact with us. Thinking about it, Emily—." asked Jane, a questioning look on her face.

"What?"

"What would happen if we go back and I let go of you?

"You come straight back to the present time, or, at least, the point in time we left. I control the two of us and any break will result in you coming straight back and I will follow right behind you. Nothing to worry about."

"Oh, okay. So, if I come back, time in the present will not have moved?"

"No, it will be exactly as we left."

Jane seemed happy with this explanation, but a slightly confused looked remained on her face.

"Now, here's a thing." she said.

"What now?"

"Well, what do you reckon would happen if I took my phone with me and took pictures?"

"I really don't know."

"That would be brilliant." said Tony. "Having photographic evidence would be absolutely perfect. If it works that is."

"Well let's see if it works." said Emily. "Come on follow me."

They followed Emily up to the landing. Tony, again, viewed himself in the mirror and adjusted his tie, raising his chin. "Now,

Tony, this is where I died, well, I actually died at the bottom of the stairs but I fell from right here."

"Okay so what happens then?" he asked

"Well, for you." said Emily. "Nothing, you won't see a thing, quite literally, as we two are going to disappear for a minute or two. Ready?"

"Okay."

"Are you ready Jane?"

"Yep, let's give it a go, oh, hang on while I get my phone ready. If I'm holding on to you, I'll need to use the other hand." Jane prepared her phone and held it in front of her, ready. Emily took Jane's hand and they slowly disappeared. Tony took a step back, almost as if to avoid the area affected. He was about to look around the landing, but before he could take a step towards the large painting, they both reappeared.

"Well?" asked Tony. "That was just plain weird. And why were you only gone for a second or two? I still cannot quite believe what I am involved in here. Ghosts, time travel. Completely mad."

"Yeah." said Emily. "But useful, isn't it? And, to explain the time taken. It doesn't matter how long we are away for in the time we travel to, time here remains stationary. We could be gone for days, but, as far as you are concerned it is no time at all."

"Right, so, did you manage to get a photo?" he asked, still confused.

Jane prodded her phone and then smiled. "Yes!" she exclaimed. "It worked, here look." Both Tony and Emily moved closer as she showed them the image on her phone. It portrayed Emily, sprawled on the small landing at the bottom of the stairs, nice and clear.

"I bet you could even take a video." said Tony.

"No." said Emily, "Please don't. Having a picture is bad enough, a video would be a step way too far.

"Don't worry." said Jane putting the phone back in her pocket. It's deleted. It does prove a point though. We can record what happened. But you won't be able to use it as evidence Tony."

"No, I know. That really would be a problem if it got out. Okay, so whatever is recorded either stays on your phone or is deleted as soon as we get the information we need. Agreed?"

"Agreed." came the dual response.

"When do you suppose you could do this?" asked Tony.

"Anytime we like, it doesn't matter to us, well, as long as it's not raining." replied Jane. "No point in getting wet for the sake of it."

"Fair enough so, let's just go through a few events. The things we do know and then try and build up a sequence between that and what we are currently missing."

"Hmm." murmured Jane. "You seem to be missing an awful lot. I mean, did Bobby have a phone with him?"

"He had a phone, yes. At least when he left his house because we know he sent his friend Jack a text message when he left."

"So, where's his phone now?" asked Emily

"We really don't know. That text message was the last communication from his phone. We tried to find it as soon as we started the search but it was either dead or switched off."

"I thought you could find phones when they are turned off." said Jane.

"Tosh. If a phone is off, it is not visible to anything. That, I am afraid is a totally fallacy. The Police, nor anyone else for that matter can track a phone when it is switched off. In fact, if it has no signal then it is effectively invisible. Its last location was around about where his bike was found but we searched extensively and didn't find it, if it was even there, that is. We can only assume that he either still had it with him when he disappeared or whoever took him, also took his phone and disabled it. There is a monitor on his number so that if it is ever switched back on, we'll be notified. There is a slim chance that his phone was on but had no signal so it's location could not be ascertained but if he had any tracking software on it, that would still record the location. If that were the case and if the phone were found we might know where it had been. Slim chance but a chance."

"Okay." said Jane. "Tomorrow morning we'll start on our investigation. I can drive us down to the village and we'll walk to his house and see what happens. We'll do the three stages and come back, giving you anything we find, and any photos I get."

"Let's just hope you come back with something. Just coming back would be good right now." said Tony.

The next morning, suitably attired, Jane and Emily sat quiet at breakfast, both anxious of what they were going to experience. "I really hope we find something Jane. If we do, it means that the special skills I have can be put to some decent use. We'll both be learning something new anyway."

"I'm sort of looking forward to this Emily, I mean, think about it. If we can help solve this case for Tony, not to mention finding Bobby, it might mean a new occupation for us both. Could even be fun. The possibilities are virtually limitless. Have you finished your tea?" she asked, the excitement building.

They drove down to the village. It was early so there were not many people around. Jane parked in the small car park in the centre and they walked towards Coopers Road, where Bobby's house was. It was a tidy road, grass verges with an avenue of trees equally spaced along its length. Pre-war houses set back behind neatly trimmed hedges and driveways shut off by pairs of gates. A very smart neighbourhood that certainly did not look the part when it came to abductions. They found Bobby's house and stood directly opposite.

"Okay, I've got my phone and it's ready to go Emily" whispered Jane. "I'm trying not to look too conspicuous but it's a bit awkward, I mean, standing opposite his house is weird in itself. Just glad people can't see you as well."

"Are we going to do this Jane?" said Emily impatiently.

"Oh, right yes, as long as there's no-one around, I guess we can just go."

"Then we'll go, half past six on the fourteenth of May. Correct?"

"Correct." confirmed Jane but let's try a couple of minutes earlier. Just so we don't miss him. Okay, go."

Emily looked up and down the street. Once she was happy that there were no witnesses, she took Jane's hand and squeezed. They slowly disappeared from the present day where they could see the world change imperceptibly. The trees and hedges shrank very slightly. The recent growth being reversed. It all happened very quickly, even the day and night blurred together as six months were crammed into two or three seconds. As soon as things stabilised and they could see no further change Jane picked up her phone and checked the time. The phone showed the time as if they were there, six twenty-six. "Blimey, Emily, that's handy."

"What?"

"My phone is seeing the current time."

"Why wouldn't it?"

"Dunno, I suppose I was thinking it would still be in our time but, I suppose if it's got a signal, which it has, it'll just update to the current time. Whatever, it means any photos or videos I take will be stamped with the current time. That'll keep Tony happy."

A car went past them, occupied by a lone man who was pulling his seatbelt on as he accelerated along the road. Emily nudged Jane as she heard a door close and saw Bobby Lewis wheel his red mountain bike through the gate, carefully closing it behind him. He leant the bike against his hip and took his phone from his pocket. Jane held up her phone and started a video recording of the action she was seeing. "That's brilliant." she said. "I can record, with the time, exactly what Bobby is doing. I'm guessing he is sending his friend a text message, just like Tony said."

Bobby put his phone away, mounted his bike and cycled off down the road, his tail light flashing as it disappeared around the corner. There was no-one else in sight, no witnesses. Apart from the two stood opposite but invisible to anyone that may have been there.

"Ready for the next bit Jane?"

"Yeah, I guess so."

"Let's see which is the best way to do this. We can either remain invisible and walk to the top of Chapel Lane and then change the time or we can become visible and do it."

"Best stay invisible I reckon." said Jane.

They walked off, hand in hand, around the corner and down the road until they got to the end of Chapel Lane where they set themselves up opposite the entrance. "Right, I'll try and go back a bit now to six thirty-five, see what happens then."

"Lock em in." said Jane humorously.

"Sorry?" said Emily. "What are you on about?"

Nothing, nothing. Go on, just get us back there."

There was no visible change to their surroundings, not that they noticed anyway but right on time Bobby came flying around the corner, his jacket flapping around his back and red cycle helmet shining in the late sun. A short skid sent him slaloming around the lamppost and into Chapel Lane. Not so much a lane now, but more a footpath that had evolved from a lane as the undergrowth had encroached onto it.

"Did you get that Jane?"

"Yes, hang on let's wait here for a few minutes just in case anything else happened after he went down the lane. You never know, someone may have followed him."

They waited for five more minutes and there was still nothing. No-one out and about at that time. "Okay." said Jane. "That'll do. If there is anything else that may have happened after this we can always come back. We know the exact time now. Let's get down to the other end and see what happens there."

Ten minutes later they were at the end of the lane and immediately saw Bobby's bike leant against the fence. "Well." said Jane. "Whatever happened, happened in the time it took us to walk down here." They walked up to the abandoned bike and Jane reached out.

"Don't touch Jane."

"Oh, no, better not. My fingerprints might end up on it and that would take some explaining."

"Let me." said Emily. She touched the handlebar and then placed her hand around the grip gently. "My god." she exclaimed, looking directly at Jane, a smile forming. "He's alive Jane, he's alive."

"How do you know that?"

"Book, porridge, plastic. That's how I know Jane. I can feel him. This is his bike and I can feel him from his bike. It's faint but he's definitely alive. If he wasn't I wouldn't feel anything."

"I don't understand. I know you stop sensing people when they die but this is his bike, like you say. Doesn't it have some residual presence about it? If you get what I mean."

"Yeah, I understand what you're saying Jane but after Beryl died, I picked up her hairbrush and she wasn't there anymore. Bobby on the other hand is definitely still there. No doubt about it. And that's just brilliant."

"But doesn't that just mean he is still alive in this time? After all, he has only just been taken so there's a good chance he's still alive."

"No, I don't think so Jane. I think the sensation of someone is all pervading in the universe, it exists in all places at all times. If he was dead, I wouldn't be able to sense him. If you're not convinced, we'll check when we get back. If Tony has got anything of Bobby's that I can touch, it'll prove it beyond all doubt."

"Well, I certainly hope that's the case. Anyway, can we just go back ten minutes and see what happens here?"

Emily released the bikes handlebar grip and stood closer to Jane. "Ready?" she asked.

"Ready." came the reply.

The only thing they noticed was the bike suddenly disappearing. Jane readied her phone and started the video recorder. Within a few seconds they could hear Bobby coming down the lane on his bike, skidding to a halt at the end. He stood there, looking up and down the road; the bike balanced between his legs, almost as if he were waiting for something or someone. He reached into his pocket for his phone but as he brought it up to view, they heard a vehicle coming along the road. Bobby looked up and saw a grey van come around the corner. It slowed and then stopped in front of him. The passenger door window wound down and a face appeared.

"Hey, mate, can you tell us where the village hall is?"

"Yeah, yeah, hang on." came the reply. All the time, Jane was carefully recording all that was happening and trying to rid herself of the sensation of being visible.

Bobby put his phone back in his pocket and dismounted his bike, wheeling it across to the fence exactly as Tony had described. There was nothing sinister in what was happening at this moment, as he leant it against the fence.

"Jane. Get closer, we need to see who that is and what they're saying." They moved closer to the van, moving around Bobby to get a view of who was in the passenger seat and what they were saying. As Bobby got to the passenger door of the van and started to describe the route to the village hall, the rear doors of the van opened. Two men jumped out. They were darkly dressed with terrorist style balaclavas, only their eyes visible. Gloves on their hands. Heavy boots on their feet they quickly covered the ground to where Bobby stood. He froze, staring at them quite transfixed. Like a rabbit in headlights. They grabbed him roughly. One on either side. "Let go, let go. Let me go." Bobby shouted, struggling as they dragged him around to the rear of the van. He was roughly bundled into the back and the doors slammed shut. The tyres scrunched on the gravel, sending a shower of stones over the two witnesses. "Get the registration Jane, make sure you get that."

"Done." said Jane as the van sped off along the road. "Well, that explains that bit." she said. "He has definitely been abducted. But what do we do now?"

"I think we should get back to Tony and show him what we've got. Let's have a look anyway, see who's in the van." Jane started the video and they watched as the van turned up and she moved around to the passenger door. The angle turned upwards to reveal who was in the passenger seat.

"Who's that?" asked Emily.

"Not a clue. I don't recognise him, nor the driver.

"That's disappointing."

"Might be for us but I bet it won't be for Tony. Oh, hang on, look at this. The one in the passenger seat chucked a fag end out and he didn't have a mask on, so why did the other two? This is confusing now. Let's see if we can find the fag end."

They searched the ground in the area roughly where the cigarette end fell, a wisp of smoke giving its location away.

"I wish we could take this back with us Emily. They could get DNA evidence from that. I'll take some photographs of it and exactly where it is. You never know, it might still be there in six months' time. Come on, I think we've got enough, let's get back and show Tony." Jane squatted down and took photos of the still smoking cigarette end as well as a few of Bobby's bike.

Within seconds they were back in the present in the exact time and space they had left, walking back towards the car, the road still very quiet. "Wait a minute, Emily. Just had a thought. Let's walk back down to the end of the lane and see if we can find that fag end."

"Nice idea. If it is there, Tony could come down and pick it up."

They walked down the lane right to the end. The events that they had just witnessed, fresh in their minds but as they arrived the scene looked different. No tyre marks left and no bike. Jane got the photograph up on her phone that depicted the location of the cigarette end. Jane walked over to where it should have been, no longer tethered to Emily. She squatted down and picked up a stick and started moving some of the undergrowth and then she saw it. It was still there, intact but it had deteriorated. Fortunately, it had landed under a large wild plant and was sheltered from the worst of the weather. "I wonder why it wasn't found when they searched this area?"

"It isn't anywhere near where his bike was Jane. Perhaps they concentrated on that area. Anyway, give Tony a ring, I think he should get down here now."

Jane called Tony who was waiting patiently in his office for any news.

"I think you need to get down here Tony, down to the end of the lane where Bobby's bike was. We've found a fag end that was flicked from the van that Bobby was taken in." There was a pause in the conversation. "Yes, he was bundled into a van, right here. Whoa, hang on Tony, just get down here. I've got everything on video." Jane ended the call and put the phone back in her pocket. "Blimey, he wanted the full story there and then and there was me thinking you were impatient."

"I'm not impatient." said Emily

"Hah, you so are Emily Chapwell."

"Not."

They stood, looking up and down the road. Much like Bobby did, moments before he was so roughly taken and driven away. "This road really is quiet Emily."

"Mm, we've been stood here five minutes and nothing has gone past us." said Emily in agreement.

After what seemed like hours, Tony arrived and stopped a few yards away. Putting his hazard lights on he got out of his car. His long coat flailing as he had failed to do up any of the buttons. The only thing missing from this image, thought Jane, was a nice trilby so favoured by the stereotypical detective.

Immediately, Tony retrieved an evidence bag from his pocket and a convenient pair of tweezers. "I thought you picked everything up with a pen." said Jane, jokingly.

"Another fallacy made up by the film makers Jane. I don't go anywhere without my tweezers. Right, what did you find?"

Jane guided Tony to the location of the discarded cigarette end, lifting the leaves of the weed that covered it.

"And you're sure that was the one you saw?"

"As far as we can tell Tony. We saw him flick a fag end out and we found it from the video. It was still smoking. It was definitely there, right where it is now and I reckon this weed here has protected it from the weather."

Tony opened a new evidence bag, carefully picked up the cigarette end and dropped it in the bag, zipping it up carefully. "How come that hadn't been found when the search was carried out Tony? Surely they looked here as well."

"I don't know Jane, I thought they checked everywhere as well but I've got it now and I can send it off. See what comes back. Let's have another look at the video."

Tony was shown the complete video but nothing new became apparent. "Let's have a look at it at home, Tony, I can put it on my laptop, it's got a much bigger screen.

"Fine idea, got any cake?"

Jane laughed. "Course I've got cake. I've been having to make more since you've been visiting us."

CHAPWELL

Back at Chapwell, Jane set her laptop up once the tea and cake had been served and they all sat around the table while she transferred the images and videos. Tony got his notebook and pen out and lay them on the table, alongside his phone. He had rolled up his sleeves which gave the impression that he meant business and was absolutely determined to solve this case.

"Oh, Tony, one thing I didn't tell you on the phone and forgot when you arrived at the scene was the fact that Emily is certain Bobby is alive."

"How so?" he asked.

"I felt him." said Emily

"Are you sure?"

"As sure as I can be but if you have anything that belongs to Bobby, let me touch it and, I'll be one hundred percent sure. I touched his bike just after he left it and I sensed him and he was alive."

"That is really good news but who has him and why? There has never been any communication from whoever has him, no ransom demand, blackmail, nothing.

Jane played the videos in sequence, from when Bobby left his house until the van disappeared down the road.

"Looking at the videos, I, personally don't think he was a target. I think he was just in the wrong place at the wrong time. It was random. We are a step further though. We have the fag end for DNA and, more importantly, we have the van and its registration plate." He picked up his phone and dialled. "Hi Phil. Yes, yes, all okay. But can you do me a favour?... Can you check a vehicle for me, grey van? Tony gave him the registration number and ended the call. "He'll give me a ring back in a minute. Did either of you recognise the occupants of the van?"

"No." they both responded.

"Hm" said Tony rubbing his chin, "I don't know that guy but, I don't know, he just looks familiar. You know, when you get that niggling little feeling that tells you, you've crossed paths before, just can't put my finger on it right now. It'll come to me eventually, usually does. Okay, Jane, keep all that stuff on your laptop but don't show anyone, okay?"

"Yeah, that's fine, it'll never leave Chapwell. Where do we go from here?

"I'm not quite sure just yet, leave this with me, let me process it and get this fag end sent off. Then we can think about the next step. Oh, and I'll bring something of Bobby's over next time I come, probably tomorrow. Would that be okay?"

There was a tap at the front door, closely followed by the louder bang of the knocker.

"Postie." said Jane, who got up to go to the door. She returned with a thick, stiff envelope in her hand. Turning it over as she walked back, she paused in the kitchen doorway, looking at Emily and then Tony. "If this is what I think it is and I'm pretty certain it is, then in a couple of minutes I'll know who my real father is."

"Do you want me to leave?" asked Tony.

"No, no, you're involved in this just as much as I am. You know the history, so only fair you should know the outcome."

"If, you're sure?"

Jane turned the envelope over, without answering him, sliding her finger under the flap and gently running it across the top. She folded it over and reached in. The silence in the room was deafening. Emily was wide eyed, her impatience vanished.

Jane drew out the bundle of papers and turned it over, carefully reading the front page, then moving it to the back of the bundle she read the second page. Emily moved, shuffled on her chair, impatience returning.

The second page was then placed to the back of the bundle and Jane's expression changed. Her eyebrows raised and then lowered. She bit her bottom lip, a worried look moved across her face. She moved the third page to the back and read on. Then, a massive smile appeared and she jumped up, throwing all the papers in the air. "Yes." she shouted. "Yes, yes, yes. Oh, my god. Her hand covered her mouth and tears welled in her eyes. "Oh, my god." she spluttered. "Get a bottle of wine Emily, we're celebrating."

"Does that mean—."

"It damn well does."

"What?" asked a confused looking Tony.

"Mark is my real father. Oh my god, oh, wow, this is brilliant. Oh my god. I need to phone mum."

She scrabbled around on the floor, collecting up the sheets of paper. She tidied them up and put them in front of Tony. "Can you read through it please Tony? Just to be sure I read what I thought I read."

"No problem." he said picking up the bundle and reading the first page.

By the time Emily had returned with a bottle of red and some glasses Tony had got to the same point Jane had when she threw the papers up in the air. He continued reading till the end of the last page, looked up at Jane and smiled. "What you thought you read is exactly right Jane. Mark Campbell is your father. There was no match with David's DNA so that only leaves Mark, congratulations. I bet that's a relief, isn't it?"

"Oh, you wouldn't believe it Tony. How I have longed for that, ever since this started. As soon as I knew there was a possibility that David was my father, I just felt sick. "Do you want some wine?"

"Just a small drop, just to celebrate."

"I'm going to phone mum but I might just ask her to come over. I'd like to tell her face to face. I'll see if she would be okay with me finding my father. It would only be polite to ask her. I will phone Sarah though; she'll be well pleased."

"What's all the shouting about?" asked Jan, walking into the kitchen.

"Oh, Jan, go and get a glass. We're celebrating."

"Celebrating what?"

"I got the DNA results back and—."

"I guess from your general demeanour that David is not your father?" he interrupted

"You got it. Now go and get a glass.

Chapter Fourteen

Found

Jane's mum arrived the next morning. Slowly opening the little gate, looking up at the magnificent house she took a sharp breath, its beauty and strength had that effect on anyone who took the time to look. Walking slowly down the path she continued to take in the red brick and stone mullioned windows, a smile creeping embarrassingly across her face, almost to the point of laughing. She knocked on the door, still not quite believing that this beautiful house belonged to her daughter. "Hang on, I'll be there now." she heard Jane's muffled shout. With a few stony echoing steps, the heavy door swung open and Sandra could see her daughter with a huge smile dominating her face. It was bursting with pleasure. With her hair shining, eyes bright and sharp, it had an overwhelmingly pleasant effect on Sandra.

"What on earth has got into you?" she asked, feeling an equally big smile emerging. Seeing her daughter like this was something she had missed for so many years and now realised how much she liked it. She couldn't help but briefly consider the past and how much pain had been inflicted on the pair of them. The view she now had, swept that memory away like the tide on a beach washing away the footprints, leaving clean golden sand ready for the future.

"Oh, come in mum, come in. I'll put the kettle on" said Jane, almost beside herself with excitement. Mystified by this outburst Sandra followed Jane through to the kitchen, her shoes echoing in the hall, passing the clock's comforting tick.

"Are you going to tell me what's going on? What could possibly put a smile that big on your face? You haven't got a boyfriend stashed in here, have you?" she asked with a questioning gaze as Jane filled the kettle.

"Oh, mum, no." She said chuckling. "But I can't keep it in any longer. I had the DNA test results back yesterday."

"Oh, okay, and what DNA test was this then?" asked Sandra slightly taken aback, walking around the table and leaning on the worktop next to Jane.

"Mum, the opportunity came up and I just couldn't miss it. You see, I obtained some of David's DNA. And before you ask where I got it, don't." She said, holding her hand up in front of her, fending off any questions. "But the result came back yesterday and guess what it was?"

"Well." said Sandra. "That's pretty obvious isn't it, going by your excitement, David is not your father?"

"David is definitely, without doubt, not my father. So, that can only mean that Mark is my father. My biological father." Jane's smile faltered slightly. "I would be correct in assuming that, wouldn't I mum?"

"Oh, Jane, yes, yes, of course." Sandra hesitated, trying to process the consequences of this news. Realising that this event cleaned a lot of slates, she smiled broadly and looked deeply into Jane's dark eyes. "Oh, love, you don't know how much of a relief that is."

"Oh, mum, I do, I most definitely do." The smile returned to Jane's face and tears welled up.

They looked intently at each other, another connection had been made and solidified. The smiles softened and the tears came in floods. They hugged each other tightly. Both feeling the mutual warmth of the embrace, not only due to this news but the newly found companionship they had both been missing for the last twenty-eight years. This was the final piece in place for them both.

"Well, that's fantastic news. For both of us." said Sandra holding her daughter at arm's length, looking into her tearful eyes.

"Oh, come on, let's stop this blubbing mum. Sit down and I'll pour the tea. Want some cake?"

They sat at the table both full of smiles, from the good news and the equally good cake.

"Mum?"

"What?"

"Do you think" asked Jane hesitantly, picking at her cake. "Well, wouldn't it be a good idea if Dad knew I was his daughter. I mean, he doesn't know. Well, none of us knew but I've got it here in black and white. David is definitely not my father so Mark must be."

"Well, yes, Mark is definitely your father but I haven't seen him for years, nor, even, heard from him, certainly since the divorce. But yes, I think it would be nice if he did know. He should know really; he deserves to know. After all, part of the reason he left was because I was pregnant with you and it all went pear shaped then."

"Okay, thanks mum." Said Jane reaching across the table and taking her hand. "I'll see what I can do. Have you still got his mum's phone number?"

"Yes, I think so, somewhere."

"Can I have it and give her a call?"

"I don't see why not. I think it would be best coming from you as well."

"Alright, I'll do that. It would be so nice for all of us if we knew the truth about the whole thing. It's at an end now, the dark cloud that has been hovering over us has gone and it looks like the sun is coming out."

Sandra smiled. "So, you haven't got a boyfriend then?"

"Mum! No, of course not. I'd have told you if I had, wouldn't I? Although there is someone, I'd like you to meet. She's been a great friend and no end of help in all this. It wouldn't have happened if she wasn't here."

"She?"

"Yes, she, mum. Oh, no, it's not like that" she said startled. "Not that it would have mattered, would it?"

"No, oh no. If she makes you happy then that's all that matters. Do you mean Sarah? I met Sarah a while ago, nice girl."

"No, this is someone else, someone very special, not to say Sarah isn't special, she is. I'll go and get her." Jane jumped up and raced out of the kitchen, thumping up the stairs.

Emily's door was open. Jane slipped into the room, she could see Emily laid on her bed reading Mill on the Floss, the low autumn sun shining across the room back-lighting her hair. The smell of lavender pervading the room giving a dreamy ambiance.

"Emily?" whispered Jane guiltily, holding the door.

"What?" came the blunt reply, eyes not moving from the book.

"Two things. Firstly, why is it that when you are in this room, especially, I might add, the smell of lavender is so strong?"

"Because I am relaxing and enjoying my book, I love this story. And, when I am relaxed my, I don't know what you would call it but I suppose it would be my aromatic aura. Well, it becomes enhanced." Emily was still looking at her book, feigning reading.

"Okay, that figures. I guess that's why your hands are really warm as well." she said walking into the room, sitting beside Emily and reaching across to touch her hand.

"And two, what's two?" Emily said, eventually, looking at Jane, her book held to one side. "You've disturbed me now so out with it."

"I'm sorry Emily but do you think it would be okay if mum met you? I mean, not as a ghost but as you are now. And, we don't tell her you are a ghost?" Jane bit her lip and frowned, thinking that she may have taken one step too far. "Thing is, I've already told her you are my friend." She stood up, fidgeting, hands in front of her, like a little girl in trouble.

"Well." said Emily resting her book on her chest and turning to look as Jane. "There's no reason we can't do that but, and you need to think about this, it might get awkward if your mum ever mentions me outside of this house."

"I don't think that'll really be a problem. If it is, then, perhaps we will have to tell her the truth. I mean, after all we've been through, I don't think this would be a massive shock, would it?"

"We'll see." she said, thinking. "Okay, come on." Emily placed her lavender book mark between the pages and carefully placed the book on the nightstand as she sat up, swinging her legs off the bed and dropping her feet into her slippers.

Sandra turned to towards the kitchen door, her mug in both hands as Jane led Emily into the room.

"Mum, this is Emily." she said, smiling and looking at Emily as she politely presented her to her mother.

"Hello Emily." said Sandra as she placed her mug back on the table and stood up. Emily put her arms out, took two steps and hugged Sandra. Sandra, slightly surprised, reciprocated the attention and found a warmth and comfort in the embrace. A comfort that seemed somewhat different, deeper, softer and stronger than anything she had felt before. She instantly understood why Emily was special.

"You two are almost like sisters." said Sandra, standing back and looking at them stood shoulder to shoulder. "You are, you know, if I didn't know different, I would say you were sisters. And I love your lavender perfume Emily. It's so, well, lavender. Really nice."

"That's just it, mum, she is like a sister to me, well, what I imagine a sister would be. We are great friends and have a lot of fun together. Emily was a friend of Aunt Beryl, she used to help her in the garden you know."

"Where do you live Emily?" asked Sandra

Emily looked at Jane, a slight frown indicated her discomfort due to the rushed and unplanned attempt at deception.

"Oh, I live down in the village but I stay here a lot when we're busy."

"What do you do?"

The discomfort was becoming more apparent as Emily fidgeted, looking down at the floor and picking her fingernails. Jane had never seen Emily looking so uncomfortable. But her face suddenly lit up.

"I'm an archaeologist Sandra, that's what I do." The relief evident in her face, having dreamed up a convincing occupation. Though not delivering it in a very convincing manner.

"Well, because of what I do mum." said Jane, feeling the mild discomfort emanating from her friend. "Emily might even be moving in here soon. I mean, I have all these spare rooms and we are well matched in our jobs, so it would be great to have her here all the time. And it would save her rent and all that. Seems a waste to let all this space go unused, wouldn't it?"

Emily looked at Jane, her trepidation diminishing with each statement.

"Well." said Sandra. "Yes, I suppose it would. It would be company for you as well. Yes, a good idea love. You'd be like two peas in a pod. How did you two meet?"

Another awkward question, Jane thought. "We met here mum, right here at Chapwell, Emily was helping Aunt Beryl in the garden when I came over once and we've been friends ever since really."

"Yes." said Emily, trying to add to the story. "We met a while ago. It was after John died and a couple of years before Beryl died. I missed being with Beryl and when Jane took over the house, we just remained friends. Well, got closer I suppose. Didn't we Jane?"

"Yes, we always got on well and it just grew from there. We had both lost someone special when Aunt Beryl died so we found a lot of comfort in each other."

"But you've never mentioned her before Jane." said Sandra, slightly confused.

"Oh, well, with all that has been going on it never came to the surface really."

"Whatever." said Sandra "We've met now and I can see how much you like each other. I still can't get over how alike you are."

Later, once Sandra had left, the two girls were sat in the living room, relaxing with a glass of wine. "Oo, I've just had a text from Tony, Emily."

"What's he say?"

"He's coming over tomorrow at about ten."

"That's deliberate, isn't it? I mean ten o'clock is tea and cake time and he knows it." They both laughed.

"Do you think we are alike Emily?" Asked Jane looking at her friend softly.

"Yeah, I suppose. We're roughly the same height and build. We can wear each other's clothes, and do on the odd occasion. Our hair is similar in colour, mines darker than yours a bit but now, and I did notice this but never said anything, when you had your hair done last time you had it waved a bit more and you didn't have it cut which I thought nice as it matches mine. And, I suppose, if you put us side by side in the mirror we are quite alike really. We could certainly fool people into thinking we were sisters. But, and I'm not saying you will, but as you age our similarity will wane and that was one of the things I was worried about with your mum. I will never age. You will, and sure as eggs is eggs, she'll notice."

"Like I said, if it ever came to it, we would just have to tell her the truth." The clock ticked quietly in the hall. Each tick adding to Jane's age, unlike Emily, whose clock stopped back in 1903. They were both conscious of the implications of its effect on their lives and friendship. The effect on Emily would be more pronounced as she would continue as she was, meanwhile watching her friend age and hoping that the friendship would endure through the future years.

"Mum sent me my grandmothers phone number Emily. I'll call her in the morning, see how that goes. Oh, I hope it works out okay."

"So do I."

The morning was cool and bright. The garden was getting ready for winter, the few flowers left in the borders were warming the autumn light with their colour. In the kitchen, tea, toast and honey were consumed in relative silence as was usually the case. Both wondering what news Tony was going to bring them. And, of course what the outcome of the phone call to Jane's grandmother would be. Jane went into the living room and dialled the number for Mark's mother. An answer came within a couple of rings.

"Hello?" came a clipped but clear and quiet voice.

"Oh, hello." said Jane. "Is that Mrs Campbell?" The answer came back in the affirmative. "I don't quite know how to begin with this really but, and this might be a bit of a shock, I am Jane. Jane Campbell and I am your granddaughter." Jane grimaced, as the line went silent, looking up at Emily who was stood in the doorway. "Mrs Campbell?" enquired Jane. The phone was still quiet but she could hear the handset creaking at the other end.

"My granddaughter you say?" Even without seeing the person on the other end of the line, Jane could sense the confusion and mild shock in the voice.

"Yes, I'm Sandra's daughter and now I know for sure I am also Mark's daughter. I hope this isn't too much of a shock."

"I don't know what to say, it is a bit of a shock, yes. We knew Sandra had a child but we didn't know anything more than that."

"You say 'we' Mrs Campbell, do you mean Mark as well?"

"Yes."

"Oh, okay. Well, I thought, being as I now know that Mark is my father, he might like to know. I, I just thought it would be polite to tell him. I don't have any contact details for him but mum had your phone number so I thought I would call you first to see if it was possible." By now Jane was visibly shaking. Emily came right into the room and sat beside her, taking her free hand in hers.

"How do I know you are telling me the truth? You could be anyone."

"I know. But I wouldn't be phoning you otherwise. It's not something I would do. How about this. You know my mum. Do you still have her number?"

"Yes, I have somewhere."

"Give mum a ring and she'll confirm it for me and then, if you want to, you can ring me back. Would that be okay?"

"Yes, yes, I'll do that. Can you give me your number? Oh, wait, it's come up on my phone display. I'll phone you back."

The call ended and Jane looked at Emily, worried.

"How did it go?"

"Hard to tell. She did seem a bit shocked, but that's understandable really. I'll just have to wait for a call back. If she wants to that is."

It didn't take long for the call to come. Even though it seemed like an eternity to Jane. Her hands slightly damp, she grabbed the phone. "Hello."

"Hello Jane, this is your grandmother speaking." A smile warmed Jane's face. "I've spoken to your mother and she confirms what you have said. As you can probably understand, after so long, this is a bit of a shock. Mark left your mother because of you. Well because of what your mother did actually. But personally, I don't think you should be punished for that. I will call your father and see what he wants to do, it's up to him really. How old are you now?"

"Twenty-eight."

"Goodness, doesn't time fly. But you are well, are you?"

"Oh, yes, yes, I'm absolutely fine. A lot of things have happened recently which resulted in me finding out who my real father was and I just wanted to clear that part of my life up and only thought it polite and correct to tell my father, regardless of the outcome."

"Okay. Leave it with me Jane. One of us will get back to you but thank you for calling."

They said their goodbyes and Jane gently placed the handset back in its cradle. The girls looked at each other. The same emotions were felt between them. Another wait to see if the next step could be taken. But Jane felt a warmth, knowing that she knew who her father was and he was going to become aware that he has a daughter.

"Well." said Jane. That's as much as I can do. We'll just have to wait and see what happens."

As they sat in silence, there was a knock at the door. Jane sat up and looked at her watch. "Must be Tony. Oh, disappear for a minute Emily. You know, just in case he's brought someone with him." Emily vanished as Jane walked into the hall.

Tony was alone when Jane opened the door. His appearance the same as ever. A coat that could really do with being ironed, cleaned or just binned and a chin that could easily benefit from another strike of the razor or at least be a bit closer to it. He looked tired and his hair was a tad dishevelled which was a surprise for Jane.

"Hi Tony, how's things?"

"Tired Jane, very tired. I haven't actually been home yet. Did an all-nighter but all in hand now."

"I can get you some breakfast if you like, it'd be no trouble"

"Oh, that would be so nice, thanks." The relief obvious on Tony's face

"Okay, come on in and we'll get you a bacon banjo sorted."

"Bacon Banjo?" questioned Tony as they walked along the hallway.

"Bacon Bun with an egg in it." answered Jane over her shoulder. "A totally military invention. And a very nice one too."

They walked into the kitchen where Emily was already putting the kettle on and getting some bread out. Tony removed his coat, slung it over the back of the chair and sat down, placing his briefcase by his side. He yawned heavily, running his hands through his hair. "Oh, sorry you two, I'm just so tired. Anyway, I have, in my case a little notebook. And this little notebook belongs to Bobby." Tony reached down and removed an evidence bag containing a small blue notebook. He placed it carefully on the table, his hand placed firmly on top, guarding it. "Neither of us must touch this, Jane. Only Emily." He said seriously.

The smell of bacon pervaded the room overpowering even Emily's lavender. "Oh, that's torture." said Jane "Put another couple of rashers on. I'll have one as well."

"Well might as well finish it up then, I'll have one. Couldn't have you two sat there scoffing banjo's while I'm sat with nothing."

"While we're waiting. Did you get anything from the photos I gave you Tony?"

"Yes, we did, part of the reason I'm so knackered. We now know who owns the van and we also know who was in the passenger seat though, if you don't mind, I'll keep that to myself. At least for the time being. It has proved very useful but we have, unfortunately come to a stop again."

"Oh, why?" asked Jane.

"Only because I have to find a way or bringing this in as evidence. A bit difficult to say that a ghost gave me the information."

"Hmm, yeah, see what you mean. Wouldn't go down well, would it?"

"Here you are you two, bacon banjo's and tea. And kitchen roll Tony, you'll need it."

Silence descended on the room. The only noises were those of culinary pleasure. Well-cooked comfort food was something that had been enjoyed in the kitchen for many years. Tony now benefitting from this legacy.

"That was absolutely delicious." said Tony, wiping the runny egg yolk from around his mouth, the colour re-establishing itself on his face. A quick gulp of tea and he was ready. He looked refreshed. "You girls certainly know how to cook—And consume." he added. "Right, are you ready Emily? I don't want this book out of the bag for any longer than necessary."

"Okay, you only need to expose a corner Tony, I only need to touch it with a fingertip."

Tony reached into his case and snapped a glove onto each hand, he then reached in to retrieve the evidence bag which he carefully unzipped. Gently lifting the edges, he slid a corner out, being careful not to let it touch anything else. Emily reached over with just one finger extended and touched the exposed corner. Only gently but enough for her eyes to go wide and a smile appear on her face. "Okay, Tony, you can put it back now. Bobby is definitely alive. Nice and strong. No doubt at all."

"Excellent." said Tony, sliding the book back into the bag and zipping it up. "You don't know where he is though do you?"

"No. I can't tell you where he is but, mysteriously, he's not that far away. Certainly within ten miles I reckon."

"Interesting. But, how can we find him? I know who the van owner is. So, my next step would be to have a word with him."

"Wouldn't that put Bobby in danger though?" asked Jane. "If you start sniffing around these people, they might do something that we would regret."

"I've an idea." said Emily. "How about me and Jane getting in the van? We know the doors are going to be opened. We could just jump in and they'll take us to wherever they are holding him."

"I don't know." said Tony. "That sounds a bit dangerous to me."

"How so, me and Jane will be invisible. They won't be able to touch us, hear us or see us. And, if anything goes wrong, I'll release Jane and she'll be back here in a shot. Well, back to where we started from."

Jane shuffled in her chair. Her elbows on the table, holding her mug in front of her. "I think that's a good idea myself Tony. It would be a guaranteed way to find out where he is. Well, hopefully anyway. Whatever, it would give us more valuable information."

"Okay." said Tony reluctantly. "I don't like the idea of you two putting yourselves at any kind of risk."

"We won't be Tony. We'll be safe. And, like Emily said. If anything goes pear-shaped, we'll just come back. We've got to give it a go I think."

"When?" asked Tony.

"How about now? Nothing like the present." said Jane. "You up for that Emily?"

"Yeah, I don't see why not. Tell you what though. We could start from the end of the lane, go back to when the van arrived. Tony can wait for us right there. Well, he won't actually be waiting as it doesn't matter how long we are away, as far as he is concerned it'll be instantaneous. We'll disappear and then reappear."

"Can you spare that time Tony. After all, for you it won't take a few minutes."

"Yes, I was only going to go home and get some sleep. But this is important and I'd only be worrying about it. Every minute is another minute Bobby is unsafe."

"Okay, Emily, let's go get some scruff clothes on and we'll get going."

They left Tony to finish his tea. He was deep in thought. Worried that he was putting these two in danger, but also worried about how he could use any evidence that they did find. He convinced himself that it was worth the risk just to know where young Bobby Lewis was. He would work out what to do with the evidence later.

A thumping down the stairs told him that the two girls were ready. He walked into the hall to see the two of them in Jeans and thick jumpers. Big boots on their feet. Hair tied back and both looking like two excited children. "I can't believe you two."

"What?" came the stereo reply.

"Well, you look just like sisters."

"Funny you should say that Tony, mum said the same thing yesterday."

"Your mum has met Emily?"

"Well, yes but you must keep it to yourself. See, she doesn't know that Emily is a ghost."

"Not only that. You look like too very excited sisters. Almost as if you were just going out to play or something. This is quite serious you realise"

"I know, but this is exciting Tony." said Jane, a more serious look about her now. "If all goes well. You'll be able to pick Bobby up and take him to his parents."

"Let's hope so. Are we ready?"

"I'll drive Tony, just in case anyone sees your car in the village."

Collecting their coats and locking the front door, they started out. Within a few silent minutes they were parked up in the layby a few yards away from the end of the lane where Bobby was taken. They all exited the car and walked to the site of the abduction. All three of them looked around, almost expecting to see something significant. There was nothing. Nothing had changed. Nothing had appeared or disappeared.

"Ready?" said Jane as she got her phone from her pocket.

"Give me your hand." said Emily.

They joined hands and within a couple of seconds Tony watched them both disappear noticing a small spark, the last remnant of the two girls as they vanished.

"God, that's so weird." he thought out loud.

Jane and Emily saw the familiar changes around them, darkness descended, confirming the move back in time. They stood to one side nearer where the rear doors of the van would be when they opened. Then they waited. Waited for Bobby Lewis to come down the lane on his bike. "Will we see ourselves when we came back last time?" asked Jane.

"Er, no." replied Emily looking back at Jane as if she had lost her senses. "We move around totally autonomously and there can only be one instance of us in time. You can imagine what could happen if there were more than that. Total chaos."

"I guess. Oh, look here comes Bobby, let's get ready. We need to be in that van pretty quick. As I remember, they didn't hang about."

They heard the van coming down the road and watched, knowing what was going to happen but frustratingly powerless to do anything about it. They saw the van just as Bobby was stood astride his bike, retrieving his phone from his pocket. It appeared that the driver, having noticed Bobby, suddenly decided to stop, just as they would expect when someone was asking for directions. It was just a replay of what they had seen before. Both were looking for anything that they may have missed on the first visit but nothing made itself apparent. All too soon the rear doors opened and the two masked men jumped out. As they moved around to the side of the van Jane and Emily climbed into the back.

"God, look at this." said Jane. "It's lined with mattresses. This is no unplanned abduction—."

"Let's get up the front." Interrupted Emily "Try and keep out of their way. They can't sense us but I want to see everything that goes on." They made their way to the front where there was a pile of blankets in the corner. They heard the shouts of Bobby as he was grabbed. The next thing they saw was Bobby being roughly bundled into the back. He was jumped on by one of the assailants and held to the floor of the van. They could hear him trying to shout out but his face was pushed hard into the mattress which stifled the pitiful cries. The second man closed the rear doors and went to the front of the van, bashing his gloved fist against the front bulkhead. The engine revved and the van lurched forward unbalancing the girls as they held tight. They could hear the tyres skidding, sending stones against the metal sides almost like machinegun fire, all increasing the terror of the episode. Once on the road the forward movement slowed and became les erratic. The assumption being that the driver was attempting to avoid any unwanted attention. The second man opened a box at the side of the van, retrieving a bottle and rag. He removed the cap and tipped it into the cloth a chemical smell filling the fetid air. Handing the rag to the first man he replaced the bottle. Bobby, still struggling hard against the power of the man on his back had his head pulled back by his hair, making him scream in pain. The rag was roughly placed so as to smother his mouth and nose. He thrashed his head from side to side but all in vain, his struggles became less intense until he stopped moving altogether and was carelessly dropped, unconscious onto the mattress. His pockets were searched and his phone removed. A quick look from one of the men resulted in it being switched off, the back removed and the battery taken out. He put the useless phone back in Bobby's pocket.

Both men removed their hoods giving Jane and Emily a full view of their faces.

"I don't believe this Emily." said Jane, the shock on her face evident. She immediately lifted her phone and took photographs of the two men and Bobby as he lay on the floor. He was in an uncomfortable position just bouncing slightly, responding to the movement of the van.

"Now I know why Bobby's name came up when I occupied Rob Owens. But I didn't notice it when I was in David Chapwell's head and I should have done really. Unless he is able to just blank out those thoughts. But then I was fixated with getting him away from you and over that cliff. Being in Rob's head I was deliberately searching in there and planting thoughts. That was when Bobby's name came up."

"I know I said I don't believe this but, to be honest, I am not entirely surprised with those two."

Both Rob and David sat down against the rear doors of the van. Rob retrieved a packet of cigarettes from his pocket and handed one to David. A lighter appeared and the flame lit the back of the van with the flickering light enhancing the dim light from the bulbs struggling in the roof.

"That was too easy." said Rob.

"Was a bit, wasn't exactly planned but none of them are really. Kid was just there, ripe for the picking. And, a nice little earner for us. Call it a bonus." They both laughed cruelly at this comment, blowing smoke into the air.

"Once we get him to the farm and hand him over, we can go down the pub." said Rob

"That'll do for me." came the reply.

Nothing more was said between the pair of them throughout the remaining journey. They both smoked and flicked through their phones, jostling with the movement of the van. Jane took more photographs around the interior in an attempt to document any evidence that Tony could use.

The van slowed perceptibly and turned right making them both lurch towards the side, it became immediately apparent that they had entered a rough, potholed lane. The van shook and crashed with each depression. Bobby, bouncing more with the increased movement. Eventually, the van slowed and stopped. Someone got out from the front, Jane and Emily looked at each other wondering whether the journey was at its terminus. But they heard a rattle of a chain and a gate open, crashing against its stop. The man got back into the van after it had moved forward. The gate closed and rechained. The van continued on its tortuous journey, after what felt like a considerable distance, there was a final lurch and it came to a halt. It reversed, stopped and then the engine shut down. As soon as the van was stationary the doors were opened and Rob and David jumped out, walking towards the front of the vehicle. The doors, left open were a chance for the two girls to exit. They didn't hesitate.

"Where the hell is this?" asked Jane looking around.

"Not a clue." came the reply. "We'll find out soon, first we need to find out what they are going to do with Bobby." They both looked back into the van and noticed Bobby move. He was regaining consciousness. He groggily lifted his head. Not understanding what could possibly have happened.

There was a lot of loud conversation at the front of the van, laughing, joking and slapping of backs followed. Jane and Emily kept their eyes firmly on Bobby hoping he would escape but knowing that it was a very slim chance. He sat up and rubbed his eyes, looking around the van and noticing no-one was in it he stood up, groggily, leaning on the sidewall to steady himself. He stumbled towards the back, grabbing the door he reached into his pocket retrieving his phone. Realising immediately that it was now useless he flung it in frustration, landing in the rough bushes to the side.

"Get a photo of where he threw the phone Jane, that's evidence for Tony."

Jane was taking a lot of pictures around the area. The van appeared to be parked in a muddy yard next to a large steel barn. A double door dominated the front end, lit by a floodlight hanging above, sending a ring of light onto the ground, illuminating the mud that seemed to be everywhere.

On hearing the movement at the back of the van David ran to the rear, grabbing Bobby just as he was stepping down. "And where do you think you're going little man?"

"Let go of me, let go." shouted Bobby.

"You can shout as much as you like, no-one will hear you. We're in the middle of nowhere so save your breath. Keep it up and you'll get another dose. And struggling is useless as that will result in the same so I suggest you come quietly and you won't get hurt."

"Where are we?"

"Never you mind. No-one will find you; no-one will know where you are. You're here to help us."

"Help you what?" Bobby was, by now, clearly distressed. The girls watched in horror, knowing there was nothing they could do but observe.

"You'll find out soon enough, now come with me and no funny stuff, you'll save yourself a lot of pain."

He dragged Bobby around towards the front of the van. The girls followed as close as they could, squelching in the mud. "Glad we wore our boots, Emily; this place is stinking."

"What do you suppose this place is?" asked Emily

"It looks like a farm but it could be just an industrial unit." As they walked further, they could see that there was a significant stone building which had been a farmhouse, stone barns behind with numerous other outbuildings surrounding a yard. Some were in a reasonable condition; some were obviously derelict. The rooves missing tiles, exposing the timber structure underneath. Glassless windows and doors hanging from their hinges indicating that as a farm it hadn't seen any action for years. The yard contained neglected farm machinery and scrap cars, piles of rubble everywhere, overgrown with weeds and bushes growing wherever there was a space.

Bobby was walked roughly along the side of the steel building which stretched back into the gloom. It was in very good condition, obviously recently built with glossy steel outer walls studded with bolts holding the cladding in place. There were more flood lights along the side. No part of the surrounding area was devoid of the sombre yellow light illuminating the muddy ground.

David knocked on a door built into the side. This, too was illuminated by an overhead floodlight. A shout came from inside asking for his identity. He responded loudly and there was the sound of bolts being thrown, a loud metallic creak and the door opened outwards hiding the person operating it. Bobby was pushed inside followed by David. The door immediately closing behind them. There was a surprising silence. No sounds from the big building and no-one else around. "I guess the others went into the farmhouse. I must admit, I didn't see where they went." said Jane.

"No, I didn't see either." said Emily. "I was concentrating on what happened to Bobby."

"We need to get in there now, see what's going on. See what they are doing with him."

"That's easily done."

"Pardon."

"Oh, come on Jane, don't you remember what we can do? Come on, hold on tight."

Emily led Jane towards the door that had just closed and moved towards it, pushing her head into it and through it, she stood still. Her head came back outside. "All clear. Come on."

They graciously slid through the door to the other side. A corridor stretched in front of them, one door on either side. There was a muffled sound of movement to the left through the wall which appeared to be plain white plastic and with further inspection it was quite apparent that this plastic formed a large box inside the building much like a room within a room. On the right was a similar structure, also with a single door.

"Let's see what's making the noise Jane. I'll stick my head through the wall. See what's on the other side." Emily, again pushed her head through the wall on their left and after a short time pulled it back. "That is a really thick wall, Jane."

"I think that is built like a big cold store. They have them for storing food in warehouses."

"That'll be why we can't hear anything out here much, it's so well insulated. Come on, hold tight, we can get in here."

Again, they slid through the wall to leave the corridor empty. On the other side they could not believe what they were seeing. Stunned into paralysis they looked around them at what could only be described as a production facility. Stainless steel tables, drums, pallets, bagging machines and a lot of noise. The sides of the structure were lined with racking containing boxes and bags, the contents of which were not obvious. The one thing that stunned them the most was the fact that the production of what they didn't know, was being carried out by children. There were at least six working at various tables around the huge room. Once the shock diminished, Jane started taking photographs, all around the room. Taking images of everything that was going on. Emily walked her steadily through the space as she continued clicking, taking great care in getting a photograph of each of the young labourers.

"There's Bobby." said Emily, pulling her harder towards the other end of the building where there was a large open space. The two large doors adorned the end wall and were obviously securely locked. To one side there was a table behind which was sat a large, unshaven, dirty looking man, a cigarette hanging from his mouth, huge tattooed arms folded across his massive chest. The surface was littered with rubbish, empty cigarette packets lay scrunched into rough origami balls. David Chapwell stood in front of the table holding Bobby by the collar. As the girls moved closer, they could see the gun. The gun being worn by the scruffy man, in a holster strapped to his leg.

"That changes the perspective, doesn't it?" said Emily.

"Hmm, you've seen it too. Now, I'm going to jump to a conclusion here. But I think this is a drugs factory."

"I concur. Let's have a bit more of a look around, see what else is going on"

"What about Bobby?"

"Jane, there's nothing we can do. All we need is information. We can have no effect on this situation at all so best to ignore what's happening to Bobby and these other kids, get as much as we can from it and give it to Tony. After all, this happened six months ago."

They walked back through the main work area noting the children working at the tables. They all looked tired and very unhappy. Their clothes were ragged and dirty. Unwashed and unkempt, they were the epitome of slaves. Pouring fluids, mixing powders and packing boxes in a quietly efficient manner. A young girl looked up at the boy opposite her and whispered. "Are you okay Paul?"

"I feel really bad." came the answer. "But they won't give me anything and they won't let me go to my bed. My stomach hurts. I think it was that chicken they fed us last night, it was disgusting."

"Oy, shut up you lot and get on with your work." Came a rough shout from the gun man. "You haven't finished yet and if I hear another word, you're all going to get it. And you know what that means."

The two children quickly resumed their work, indicating the severity of punishment due if orders were not followed.

"Come on Jane. The sooner we get an idea of the rest of the place, the sooner we get back to Tony."

They went back through the wall into the corridor and continued through the door in the opposite wall. Here they were met by another corridor with numerous doors on each side, extending to an open area at the end.

The doors were all open and a look inside the first showed them with no doubt that this was a slave labour factory. The first room was little more than a cell with a pair of bunk beds to one side. The shiny, white walls, blank apart from dirty marks here and there. No window and a single fluorescent tube in a cage on the ceiling. Just the two beds with dirty blankets and pillows scattered across them. The smell confirmed that these children were being kept in appalling conditions. A mixture of sweat, sewage and a mysterious, rank, food smell. It was offensive to the pair of them. They continued along the corridor, peeking into the remaining rooms. All the same. Bunk beds adorned with dirty bed clothes. The two end rooms opposite each other were what could loosely be termed ablutions. Each had a wash basin and toilet with a shower that had obviously not been used in a long time. The overall impression was disgusting. The open area at the end was furnished with plain steel legged tables with plastic chairs randomly scattered around. At one end was a cooker and three microwaves. A large chest freezer hummed in the corner, obviously the primary source of food. A sink and drainer full of dirty plates and cutlery completed the picture of deprivation. This was the eating and resting area. Though the amount of rest these children seemed to be getting meant that as a rest room it was little used. Jane took photographs of the bedrooms, the toilets and the kitchen much to her disgust.

"I think we need to get back Jane. This is six months ago. Imagine what these children are like now. I'm guessing Bobby is just one more new recruit for these slave masters. Come on we'll take a look outside to see where we are."

They found themselves out in the yard. No-one around, the van still parked where it was left.

"Tell you what, before we go back, lets change the time to a few days ago and see what it's like now. I'll get us here in the daylight as well, might be able to see a bit more. We can take a look to see how Bobby and the others are getting along. Ready?"

"Ready."

Almost imperceptibly, the night fled, the mud dried and the sun was out. The yard was empty. The van not in sight. There was no-one around. The farmhouse looked empty but tyre tracks on the ground indicated that there had been recent movements.

"Let's go and have a look inside." said Emily

"Let's just hope they're all okay." replied Jane.

"Yes, let's hope."

They entered via the two large end doors straight into the production area. Standing in the middle of the open space they were surrounded by boxes and drums large and small. Obviously, the raw materials for the making of drugs. This was no small operation. It was huge. The massive building, the number of children they had working there confirmed this was no small-time business. They quickly counted eight now working at various locations around the room. The same scruffy monster was sat in his comfy chair behind his table, the now ubiquitous cigarette hanging from his mouth. The gun still in evidence. Very little appeared to have changed though it did look as if the number of workers had increased. Bobby the obvious addition. The clothes were more ragged and dirtier than previously, the children's hair had grown out of control. Matted and filthy.

"Okay, Jane they are all here, I think. Even the boy that was ill but they are not looking good. They've lost weight, I can see that and they are just so dirty. Okay, I've seen enough. Time to get back but we'll try and find out where this place is. Get some more photos and we'll get out of here."

They found themselves outside again in the sun, away from the mixture of chemicals and filthy bodies that had assaulted their senses.

"I'm going to release you now Jane. You'll get straight back to Tony. Meanwhile I'll take a walk down the lane to see if I can find out where we are."

"Oh, okay." said Jane slightly surprised.

"Don't panic, I'll be back there at the same time. I just want to do a bit more looking about, it'll be easier on my own. Here you go, see you soon."

Emily released Jane and she vanished. She looked around and took the opportunity to investigate the farmhouse. With her freedom of movement, she could wander wherever she wanted to. Passing through the front door of the house she found herself in a long hallway, a once proud stone floor was now filthy and scratched, plastered with dried mud. The walls once tidily decorated, were now adorned with strips of torn paper adding to the dilapidated appearance. To the left there was a large room, threadbare carpet on the floor and old tatty leather sofas facing a huge television. A coffee table no longer used for the traditional beverage was covered with empty and half empty beer bottles, an overflowing ash tray and piles of discarded food wrappers which had fallen to the floor. The mess was staggering and stereotypical of a drug house. The rubbish and stink dominated by the huge shiny flat screen television, under which was a games console and controllers. The image was now complete thought Emily. She grimaced and left the room, using the hall and doorways to move around. It seemed quiet which made her feel slightly more comfortable. Entering the room opposite she saw a large pine table. It was solid and surrounded by a number of matching chairs. A laptop sat in the centre with books and paperwork scattered around, almost as if this was the office of a busy industry. Tidier but still dilapidated, the room was never going to see a farming family sat around it for their meals.

She walked to the back of the house and entered what was the kitchen. The room did have a large kitchen table in it, the chairs, again, matching and this room was clean and tidy. No washing up in the sink, the work surfaces clean. She jumped as the back door opened and a young girl was pushed into the room. She was followed by a young man wearing a leather jacket over a white shirt and smart jeans, his hair cut short and his hands clean.

"I'm going to sit here and watch you cook our dinner but first you can make me a cup of coffee." He said to the young girl who appeared to be around sixteen. He pulled out a chair and sat at the end of the table, crossing his legs and leaning back in a dominating pose. She wore torn jeans and a thick Christmas jumper that was showing signs of wear and a lack of washing. Her hair was red and roughly tied in a pony tail, again, it was obvious that it was unwashed, her face an image of despair. She reluctantly walked over to the sink and began filling a kettle. There was an element of discipline in the way the girl moved around the kitchen. She knew where everything was and placed objects very deliberately and carefully in specific places, often surreptitiously looking towards the young man as if anticipating some form of punishment for things not being quite in the correct place.

Emily watched for some time as the girl continued in her chores, preparing food as competently as an expert under the constant watch of her captor. Emily could easily see how this whole facility was being operated. Young slaves were being kept in appalling conditions in order to manufacture drugs for a gang of thugs whose life consists mainly of abuse and the making of money. She had seen enough and left via the front door. The sorrow of leaving the young girl ate at her, that and the fact that she was unable to do anything about it.

She walked quickly down the lane between high hedges to see if there were any landmarks that would give her any idea of where she was. It must have been two miles before she came to anything. The gate they had come though on the journey in, stood chained and locked. Emily easily walked through it and there, on the left was a narrow turning between two walls. A track leading down a slight incline to a small farm. On the one side there was a fence with a post-box fixed, under which, a sign declared that this was Oak Tree Farm. At last, thought Emily, something that will locate this track. She walked onto the end of the main track to the tarmac road but saw nothing that would give her a better idea of where she was.

Without wasting more of her time and indeed, daylight, she jumped back to the present.

Tony, nearly fell over when they reappeared in front of him. "Back already?"

"Not really Tony." said Emily "I sent Jane back first and then I had a look around and tried to locate the place where Bobby is being held. I think we need to get back to Chapwell and hand over all this information. We need to sit down and go through it methodically but I will say this. Bobby is not the only one, right now there are at least eight kids being held."

"Held? For what reason?"

"Let's get back Tony and sit down with a cup of tea. I'm still buzzing with what we saw." Said Jane.

They drove in silence back to Chapwell and were, once again, sat around the kitchen table with mugs of hot tea.

Chapter Fifteen

Rescue

"Right." said Tony, purposely as he supped the last of his tea. "Let's hear what you know and let's take it right from the beginning. Right from the time I saw you both vanish. It's going to take a while for me to get used to that." he said shaking his head.

"You think?" said Jane, holding her hands up. "How about me, I'm the one going with her. Anyway, we got in the back of the van and travelled to where they're taking the children and basically, it's a drugs factory."

"Okay." said Tony rolling his eyes sarcastically. "I'll need a bit more detail than that."

"Don't worry, I'm getting to that. First though, did you find out where it was Emily?"

"It's near a place called Oak Tree Farm."

Tony shrugged. "Not a clue. Have you got a map?"

"I'll go get it." said Jane leaving the room.

On returning, the map was spread out on the table, mugs holding the corners down, and Chapwell quickly located.

"Hang on." said Jane. I've got an app on my phone which will show us where it is, I can search for the actual farm and then get it to set a route to Chapwell."

Jane picked her phone up and quickly got the app running and searched for the location. Out of the list of numerous 'Oak Tree Farms' she quickly identified the one nearest to Chapwell and got it up on the screen.

"There, there's Oak Tree Farm." said Jane pointing at it on her screen.

"Okay." said Emily. "Where the lane goes from the main road to the farm, it continues on past that for a couple of miles."

Jane moved the map across her screen with her finger, following the marked track until it came to a group of buildings which they quickly identified as the farm they had visited. Switching to satellite view they could see the layout of the area. The farmhouse, the large steel drug factory and the surrounding farm buildings.

"That's the place Tony, no doubt. It's well out in the sticks. It's surrounded by woods and rough land."

"What's it called?" asked Tony.

"Hang on." said Jane returning the app to map view. "Here it says it's Lower Bank Farm. Let's find it on the paper map." selecting 'new route' and set it to Home it plotted a route via the public footpaths to Chapwell House. "It'll give us a better idea of where it is in relation to Chapwell." She compared the digital map and new route with the paper one and quickly located the farm." Here we are." she said. "You were right Emily, certainly within ten miles. And it really is right in the middle of nowhere."

Tony was busily making notes while the girls were talking. "Okay, now we know where it is can you go through what you both saw, one at a time from the start. You first Jane."

Jane described what happened during their excursion, from the time they vanished to the time she reappeared after Emily released her. All the time she backed up her story with the photographs she had taken, Tony industriously making notes.

"Right, your turn Emily." he said "Same as Jane, just describe what happened and what you saw during the time you were away. The sooner I get all this down the quicker we can solve this case and get Bobby and the other children back with their families."

Emily, in turn described her view of events during her visit to the farm and, again, Tony was quietly taking copious notes as the story unfolded. Once Emily had completed her description of events he sat back and scratched his head, yawned and put his pen down on top of the notebook.

"Well, from what you two have described here and with the images I have seen, there is no doubt that this is, as you say, a drugs factory and if I didn't know any different, they are processing and packing Crystal Meth which is particularly nasty. Also, with what I have seen in the photographs, they are producing a staggering quantity of the stuff and it needs to be shut down. Snag is, I need to get this noticed and organise its closure. That's going to be a bit awkward, being as the only evidence I have is from you two. Not that it is not compelling but I need to convince my bosses that it exists and is in full production. Not to mention the fact that they are holding children as slaves."

"How about an anonymous tip off?" asked Jane.

"Probably the only way it could work, though I need the tip off to be convincing."

"Well," said Emily "you've already had the tip off, we gave it to you. You know who the van belongs to and now you know where it is being used and what for. You could use that as a start. Once you can convince your superiors that there may be a suspicion surrounding this van and its occupants you could just sneak in the location of the farm."

"It might work. Well, there's no might about it. It's got to work; we have no choice. There's nothing we can do that wouldn't endanger those kids. They were armed you say?"

"One of them, the fat guy in the factory, he had a gun. A handgun, strapped to his leg, I took a photo of it, look." Jane showed Tony an image showing the fat guy slouched in his chair, the gun very visible, cigarette hanging from his mouth, all the while looking over young Bobby Lewis as he was held by David Chapwell.

"Hah!" exclaimed Tony. "There we are, there's the link. David Chapwell. I interviewed him after he attacked you, Jane. I can easily say that he told me something regarding the drug factory but outside the interview room so there would be no evidence of him saying anything that was recorded. Let me think about it a while. But thanks, you two, what you have given me will end this, end all of it. Just hope it doesn't take too long." he said packing his notebook away. "I'll get going and drop this on the boss's desk. She'll be receptive and I think she trusts me." Tony stood and put on his coat. It was obvious from his worried expression; he was deep in thought.

"Keep us updated with what's happening Tony." said Jane. "We need to know that it's all going okay."

"I will. Thanks for the tea."

Tony collected his bag and with one arm not quite in his coat he left, trying to shrug it on. They both saw him race off down the road, leaving them stood in the front doorway. A feeling of anti-climax surrounded them both. After all they had witnessed over the last few days, being left outside of the current events gave them both an empty feeling.

"What now?" asked Jane.

"Nothing we can do." came the reply. "It's all on Tony now. We'll just need to sit and wait."

Tony knocked on his Chief Superintendent's door, clearly seeing that she was sat reading a document on her desk. She looked up and smiled, seeing Tony who was still in a somewhat bedraggled state, her look changed to one of concern. She quickly tidied the document she was reading and turned it face down on the desk. Standing, she waved him in. Tony opened the door and slid through, closing it carefully behind him. Standing there looking uncertain, he knew he was about to do something he genuinely didn't believe in, and that was lying. He knew the situation was very real and he trusted the two girls implicitly so he felt he could get it across in a simple manner, the overriding priority was to get Bobby and the other children released, with the bonus of shutting down what appeared to be a large drug production and distribution facility.

"What can I do for you Tony? Had a rough day?" asked his Boss, the look of concern becoming deeper.

"Sorry Ma'am I pulled an all-nighter. A couple of things have been bothering me and I have been thinking a lot about this and suddenly it all became clear. Plus, I've had a tip-off and it is all to do with the disappearance of young Bobby Lewis." He was looking at the floor as he hurriedly spilled this information out. Once finished he looked up.

"Okay." she said pointing at the chair opposite her desk indicating that Tony should sit. Without removing his coat, he slid the chair out and sat, dropping his bag on the floor beside him, he reached down, retrieving his notebook.

"Right." he said. "Now, Ma'am, you're going to have to trust me here as all the things I am going to tell you are either from uncorroborated sources, anecdotal evidence and hearsay. But; I have a hunch and it is backed by the information I have received from these sources and it does all stack up, no part of it has massive holes in it." He hesitated. "Put it this way, I am totally convinced." His look was serious which was noted by his boss who stood leaning forward, her hands steepled on her desk.

"You say the sources are, how shall we say not exactly solid?"

"Oh, they're solid all right." came the reply. "But I cannot produce them for you, which is where the trust comes into play Ma'am."

"Well, you know I trust you, Tony. I always have but I am intrigued by how my best detective who is normally dotting i's and crossing t's has come to me with this."

"I know." said Tony. "Let me give you what I have and you can make the decision. But I believe we need to act quite fast here."

"Because it involves Bobby Lewis?"

"Precisely Ma'am. Bobby Lewis is alive and he is not alone. He was abducted, alongside a number of other children and they are being used as slave labour in a drugs factory."

"Wow! That's some theory Tony, I think you'll need to elaborate a bit if you want my help, I'm afraid." She sat down in her high-backed chair, her eyes not leaving Tony.

"I was worried you would say that Ma'am. But, look, I've never let you down in the past and I really wouldn't be here now without my firm belief in what I now know. It started with two people we interviewed after the Jane Chapwell assault. David Chapwell and Rob Owens. David Chapwell let it slip to me after one of the interviews, so it was not recorded, that we were missing the biggest drugs bust we would ever see and it was right under our noses."

"Okay, I'm listening."

"Then there was a link between him and Rob Owens which we already know about. Now, I have had some anonymous tip-offs that Rob Owens had something to do with a van, the registration I have checked and it is owned by Stephen Watson, who we all know, and also that the van had been seen at a place called Lower Bank Farm. The next tip was that this farm was being used as a drugs factory and they were using kids to work there."

"How reliable are these tips, Tony?"

"One hundred percent, Ma'am, one hundred percent, solid, no doubt."

"You have my attention, Tony. So, what do you think we should do?"

"This is going to sound way outside of normal procedures Ma'am but I believe we need to raid this place as a matter of urgency. Two reasons. Firstly, we need to get these kids back to their parents and secondly, we need to shut this factory down."

"What have we got to go on, on the ground I mean?"

"I have the rough layout of the buildings, most of which is from good old Google Earth but I've had information about the interior of the building that is being used as the factory. So, we will know where to look when we get there. One thing though, and this makes it a tad more difficult. They are armed."

"Ah, okay." said the Chief Superintendent. "That changes things slightly. I take it we're going to need armed officers."

"Without a doubt Ma'am."

"Let me make a call."

She picked up the phone and with a few words she started the process. Within minutes there was a knock on the door.

"Hello Tony." said the officer as he came in through the door. "Good to see you." he held out his hand and they shook. "What's this all about then?" as he brought a chair over and sat next to Tony.

Tony went through the information again. Exactly as he had explained to his boss.

"And you're absolutely sure this is all solid and trustworthy information?"

"Absolutely Kev, absolutely."

"Well, that's okay then. Have you any detail on the building itself?"

Tony gave his colleague a sketch of the buildings plan as best he could with the information the girls had given him, together with the plans available online.

"What do we need now Ma'am?" asked Tony.

"I just need to convince upstairs but with me, you and Kevin involved I don't think anyone in their right mind will refuse the resources. Sit there you two, it shouldn't take a minute."

She again picked up the phone and again, with a few words which included the names of the two officers in close proximity she placed the phone back on its cradle.

"You've got a go Tony. You two are lead on this and use as many men as you need. I'm relying on your integrity here Tony, we all are."

"Thank you, Ma'am, thank you. You won't be sorry, I promise you."

"I really hope not Tony, you've never let me down in the past, don't let this be the first time." she said with a hint of a smile.

"Come with me Tony." said Kev as they left the room. "We'll go through the detail in my office. I'll get a team together and sort a briefing as soon as possible. First though, let's just go over it again and make a plan to get this done. It's good to work with you again by the way. Shame we went our different ways really."

"Well." said Tony. "You went down the armed route, I went down the detective route and to be honest I think that was the best for both of us, the force gets the best out of us in different formats. You're good at your job and I'm good at mine and that works just fine for me."

"Guess so." said Kev "But we did work well together didn't we."

"Yes." said Tony slowly. "But we still do when, like now, our paths cross."

By the next afternoon there was a call from Tony, the promised update was delivered.

"What did he say?" asked Emily.

"He did it." said Jane. "He convinced his boss that there was something worth looking into at that farm. They're sending someone to take a look, undercover so as not to raise suspicion. Just someone looking for their dog. He said, if they come back with anything, there will be a raid on the place. Everything is going to be put ready in case anything goes wrong but whatever happens it looks like this place will be shut down."

"When is this happening?" asked Emily.

"About now." said Jane.

"Come on then." said Emily, looking into Jane's eyes, a smile appearing.

"Come on what?" came the puzzled reply.

"Come on, let's go. We can watch this as it's happening."

"Is that a good idea? What happens if anyone sees us?"

"Oh, Jane, wake up, we'll be invisible."

"Okay, but we need to be really, really careful. These people look like they're dangerous. Well, it's obvious they're dangerous. We really, really don't want to mess things up. All those kids in there are relying on Tony and his team to get this sorted out. Let's go get our boots on." said Jane beaming with excitement.

It was a long walk along the lane towards the farm. Jane had parked well away from the area so they followed footpaths to get them in the right place. When they arrived at the steel building it seemed like all was quiet. No vehicles and no people good or bad were apparent. Hand in hand to maintain their invisibility they carefully manoeuvred around the farmhouse and the derelict yard. No-one to be seen.

"Listen." said Jane halting, as they were at the back of the steel building. "I can hear someone, sounds like it's coming from the front of the farm building."

They walked back to the front of the old farmhouse where they saw, at the front door, a man. Nothing special about him. He had walking boots on, a waterproof jacket and a dog's lead in his hand. He was talking to someone at the front door of the house. His face was hidden by the small porch sheltering the door. The conversation was short, the visitor raised his hand saying thanks and turned away towards the steel building and the entrance to the main yard. They could see the farmhouse man peering around the porch watching every step the dog walker was taking as he walked off, looking left and right and calling for his dog. As he walked towards the steel building, he got a shout. "Oy, keep away from there. That's nothing to do with you. Now sod off, your dog isn't here." Another wave from the dog walker and we went back down the lane.

"Let's just sneak a look in the steel building Jane, just to check."

"Just quick then, things might happen soon."

They walked across to the front of the building, Emily poked her head through the wall and quickly retrieved it.

"Something's happening Jane."

"What?"

"Have a look yourself, here."

Holding tightly to Emily, Jane too, pushed her head through the main door. On the other side she could see the same production area but there was a difference. The children were stacking a pallet with bags. To the side of these were two other pallets, both wrapped in plastic film. They just looked like any pallet stacked with non-descript bags, ready for dispatch. Jane listened to the conversation and the shouts.

"Come on, they'll be here in an hour, get that last pallet wrapped then go to your rooms." Was the gruff instruction coming from the gun man. There were others in the room watching and organising the packing of the pallets. Jane moved back through the door and looked at Emily.

"We've got to go. They're waiting for a vehicle. There are three pallets of the stuff ready to be loaded. The kids are just finishing the last pallet now. Once they've done that, they've been sent to their rooms. With a bit of luck, they'll be locked in. Come on, we need to tell Tony."

"What's the hurry?" asked Emily.

"Simple, If they raid the place when the vehicle is being loaded, the doors will be open and the kids will be in their rooms. Sounds like the perfect time to pounce. Or even after the vehicle has left."

They looked at each other, both coming up with the same idea.

"Run."

They ran down the lane as fast as they could, quickly catching up with the dog walker and overtaking him. Almost tripping in the potholes and getting splashed by the muddy puddles they continued, heavy breathing and hair everywhere were the most obvious effects of the run. Climbing over the gate they could see vehicles in the track to Oak Tree Farm, lots of vehicles and some were obviously Police vehicles. They could see Tony's car at the back and Tony within a group of officers, some armed in the regulation black uniform of an armed officer. They moved closer to Tony. Emily leant in and whispered in his ear.

"Tony."

He jumped and spilt the coffee from the paper cup he was holding. Shaking his now wet hand, he looked around. Nothing to be seen. Emily whispered again.

"Tony. Walk towards the barn. I'm following you and I have urgent information for you."

Tony knew what was happening and the look on his face showed to both girls that he was not entirely happy. He got his phone from his coat pocket feigning a phone call as he walked towards the barn.

"What are you two doing here? I'm assuming you are both here?" He whispered, the phone against his ear.

"We're both here Tony but listen. We've just been to the factory and they're waiting for a vehicle. They're sending three pallets of stuff out. They're ready to go. The vehicle will be here real soon. The kids are being sent to their rooms. If you're going to raid it, raid it when the vehicle has left. The kids will be safe and the rest of them will be distracted. But you'll need to get these police vehicles out of the way. They are visible from the road and that could cause a problem when the vehicle turns up."

"You two stay right here, and keep hidden." He stopped in his tracks and thought, looking back towards where he thought the two girls were. "Not that it matters." he said realising that they would remain invisible.

Tony ran up the track and confronted the group of armed officers.

The girls could hear the conversation from where they were, owing to the fact that Tony was being quite loud.

"Kev, I've just had a call from my source. There's a vehicle on its way to take a delivery. Get these vehicles hidden behind the barns and get off the track. Get the dog walker back here or tell him to hide."

A small discussion ensued whereupon the vehicles were duly removed from sight, hidden in the yard behind the barns. All the officers moved away and hid from sight, all the time watching the top of the lane. Within half an hour the dog walker came running down the track out of breath, briefly stopping to see that all Police evidence had gone. Standing bewildered he looked around until he heard a shout from the barns. Realising what was happening he joined the rest of the group. They all waited. A few short minutes passed and there was the sound of a vehicle. The large grey van appeared along the lane, passing the end of the track and stopping at the gate. The chain clanked as it was removed and the gate swung open. The van lurched through the gateway and stopped, picking up the passenger, the gate left open, anticipating a quick return.

"Someone needs to follow the van up there." said Tony. "Send the dog walker, he's still dressed in mufti." Tony could see the exasperated if not exhausted look on the officer's face. "Sorry, but it needs to be done." he continued. "Radio in with a sit rep when you arrive, we need to know when the van leaves. We'll apprehend it right here then we'll be on our way up to finish this."

The dog walker acknowledged the urgency and trotted off up the lane. Tony and Kevin came together to plan the next moves.

"This has moved quicker than we anticipated." said Tony. "But it is to our advantage. We need armed men at the factory to initiate the raid, or at least be there to secure the area where we can follow quickly, once the van, its contents and occupants are secure."

Agreement followed and the armed group came together for a briefing. Within minutes half the group ran up the track leaping over fences into adjacent fields starting their movement towards the factory, leaving the other half to secure the van when it arrived.

After what seemed a lifetime, the radios squawked. All was in place at the factory came the report. All armed officers were in position. The van was on its way back.

They could hear the crashing of the van as it clomped down the lane, reaching the gate, it slowed and stopped after passing through. The passenger leapt out to close the gate, or so he thought. As soon as he was at the rear of the van, he had an MP5 machine gun pointed in his face. Simultaneously, the driver was similarly exposed to a firearm. The shock was obvious. They were both very quickly apprehended, searched, disarmed, cuffed and brought down the track to the farm where they were handed over to uniformed officers, their heads hung down, lank hair hiding their faces. Their days of freedom rapidly coming to an end.

Once the two men were dispatched, the van was moved down to the farm and secured. The remaining armed officers leapt into their vehicles and roared off up the track. Tony was about to jump into his car when he heard a voice. "Not going without us are you, Tony?"

His car door open, he was stopped in his tracks and looking round he tried to see where the two girls were. Though gritted teeth he snarled. "You can't come, I don't want this to go wrong."

"We'll stay in the car Tony, promise." He heard Jane's voice. "Oh, go on then but do not get out. Okay?"

"Okay." came the muffled reply.

"Well, get in then."

"We're already in Tony, come on, let's go. Wouldn't miss this for the world."

They bounced up the lane, Tony trying hard to avoid the worst of the potholes but not being too successful. His radio in one hand on the steering wheel listening to the action up at the factory. As they approached, he slowed as he saw the armed response vehicles ahead of him. Stopping, he shut down the engine and slowly got out. He moved forward until he was in sight of the armed unit who were moving steadily along the lane, keeping to the hedgerows. The factory main building came into view. The doors were still open, no-one inside.

"Tony?" came a timid female voice.

"I told you to stay in the car you two." came the angry response.

"No, I know, but look, you know the layout of the building and it looks to us as if the thugs are in the farmhouse. Probably celebrating. This would be a good opportunity to get the kids out and safe, before anything goes bad."

"Leave it with me." said Tony. "And stay right where you are."

Even though Tony didn't know it, the girls could see the angry look on his face as he moved forwards towards the armed unit. A discussion took place whereupon fingers were pointed, heads nodded and the group split into two, half remaining at the entrance to the farm, the other moving closer to the large shed, keeping to the hedge side of the yard, weapons constantly scanning the area. Not a voice was heard, not even a footstep was apparent. They moved so quietly anyone watching would think they had been struck with total deafness. They slid around the open door and into the production area, moving around each side as they progressed towards the back wall and the door into the corridor. Now there was no movement, no sound, not even a breath as all present were waiting for any kind of result. The remaining armed team moved forward and positioned themselves to separate the factory building from the farmhouse, forming a firewall between the thugs and the children.

After what seemed like an eternity there was a movement in the factory building. An armed officer lead a group of children through the production area, towards the open doors. Following up were the rest of the team, surrounding the children in an armed protection blanket.

Once given the okay, they quickly and silently moved across the yard towards the waiting officers. They were guided past the group of vehicles to the rear where they were bundled into two of the cars and removed from the scene. The girls could see how scared, tired and dishevelled the children looked but it was obvious from their general demeanour that they were desperately relieved to be free.

As the two rescue vehicles reversed quietly back down the lane all hell broke loose. There were loud shouts and explosions, bright flashes and the front door of the farmhouse went down. Simultaneously windows were smashed and more flashes and shouts went up. The armed group moved, as one, into the building through the front door and a window. The shouting continued throughout the building and then there were shots. One pop and two quick retorts. Silence then descended. "All clear." came a crackled report through the radio. The remaining uniformed officers and Tony stood up, safe in the knowledge that all had been apprehended.

Tony walked forward to see the result of the raid. Armed officers were escorting four cable tied offenders from the farmhouse into the yard, weapons ensuring there was no resistance. Kevin approached Tony.

"All done. One dead, four in custody. No injuries to our team."

"Well, done." said Tony.

"It could have been better though."

"How do you mean?" asked Tony.

"Well, if that fat scumbag hadn't shot me, I wouldn't have needed to put two rounds in him."

"How do you mean 'shot you'."

"Cornered Tony, I got him cornered and he went for it. I was already there though. So, he got one round off which hit me in the chest. Nice shot but the Kevlar prevented any problems."

"But, you're okay?"

"Couldn't be better. The kids are free and we've shut down a drugs factory."

"I'll call in the forensics and the other investigative teams, they'll be here a while I reckon. The drugs boys are waiting to go in now."

After the short action they had both experienced everything became quite mundane. Groups of officers making plans on how best to wrap it up, Tony included.

"We'll get back down the lane to the other farm, the incident van is there now. Give them a debrief."

As Tony walked towards his car, he heard a whisper.

"Is everything okay Tony?"

He looked around, knowing that he wouldn't see anyone but just checking how far he was away from any witnesses. "That." he said. "Is so unnerving."

"Sorry." said Jane. "But we need to know. It all looked ok from what we saw."

"Everything went fine. Get in the car."

"Before we do, Tony, just over there is Bobby's phone, down in the bushes, I'll show you."

Jane guided Tony to the spot where Bobby had tossed his phone, whereupon, Tony retrieved it, placing it in an evidence bag.

They all jumped into the car and Tony started the engine.

"We saw everything as it happened. It was quite exciting really." said Emily squeakily.

"Where were you then?" he asked.

"In the middle of the yard." came the reply.

"Good grief." said Tony, exasperated, as he drove along the potholed lane.

Chapter Sixteen

A new life?

Jane and Emily were sat in the lounge, each cradling a glass of wine, a bowl of peanuts on the table which was slowly disappearing. The evening was quiet, only the standard lamp was on, giving a warm subdued glow to the room, enveloping them both in soft comfort.

"I think—"

"Emily...!" said Jane sternly.

Emily finished the mouthful of peanuts, swallowed and continued.

"Sorry, I think we did rather well there, don't you? I mean from very little, we managed to solve a number of crimes."

"Yes." replied Jane. "Yes, we did, but only because you are what you are."

"Well, yes. But even so, I think we did a good job. It all worked. Tony could act on the information he was given and produce a very pleasing result. I mean, the children are all back with their parents. Eight missing persons reunited with their families. A major drugs manufacturing facility shut down. And, from what Tony was saying earlier, that factory was the largest of its kind ever found. And that was all down to us really so I don't think we should understate ourselves."

"No, I agree but let's not make a habit of it eh?"

"Why not. It was fun. Guaranteed, if the opportunity came up again you wouldn't turn away from it would you?"

"Well, no. Of course, I wouldn't, but not right now. I think I need a holiday."

"A holiday!" said Emily excited. "I've never been on holiday before."

"Didn't you ever go on holiday when you were alive?"

"Not often. Father was always too busy. But think about it Jane. Why would anyone want to leave this place?"

"There are things out there to see and do Emily, it's not a case of going on holiday to get a break from your current life but to go on holiday to experience something new."

"Like what?" she asked.

"Well, like walking, you know I love walking Emily and I haven't been on a walking holiday for a long time."

"Where shall we go?" she asked as she placed her glass down on the table, folded her legs underneath herself and looked expectantly at Jane, eyes bright.

"I don't know, anywhere. I fancy some mountains and some history and fantasy."

"Okay, any particular mountains?"

"Snowdonia. How about that?"

"That's North Wales, isn't it?" replied Emily.

"Correct. And I know just the place. Beddgelert. It's a lovely village in the middle of the mountains. It ticks all the boxes. It has the mountains, yes, it has history with the slate and copper industries. It has lakes and rivers, waterfalls and loads of walking."

"Okay." said Emily. "What about the history and fantasy then?"

"Well, that's the thing. Not far away is a small hill called Dinas Emrys which holds more fantasy than you can shake a stick at. Then there's the legend of Gelert the dog."

"What's that about then Jane?"

"If you want to know that we'll need to go there and I can show you." she said. A smug expression appearing on her face. "I haven't been there for a good few years but the atmosphere there never fails to inspire me."

"In what way?"

"Well, it just gives me a good feeling. Just being in the same spot as some historical or legendary fact or fiction just gets the sparkle going. It's difficult to describe really. It makes me feel part of the landscape. The only thing that would make it better would be to be able to see exactly what actually happened in these places."

"Hmm." said Emily with a mischievous grin. "I might be able to help there."

"How so?"

"Oh, come on Jane, you do frustrate me sometimes." said Emily clapping her hands. "We can go back in time, see what actually went on."

"I know we can and that would be great but we can only go back so far, can't we?"

Emily sat, her eyes wandered around the room, thoughts coming into her head. "Not necessarily true Jane. Do you remember when I took you back to my death birth. Look, we spoke about this before." she remembered.

"Ah, yes." came the answer, a look of wonder on Jane's face. "And we went back a bit further than you had before?"

"That's what I'm thinking about. I wonder—." she said thinking deeply. "I wonder if we can go back further. I mean, thinking about it I have never actually tried to go back any further. That day I might have made a mistake with the timing or something. Perhaps I can go back further. And if I can, you can come with me."

"Dare we try?" asked Jane. A sinister look falling across her face.

"Don't see why not. But we'll need to be careful."

"Well." said Jane, we'll do it right here shall we? Right inside Chapwell. We know it's been here since Roman times, or at least there has been a building here so let's use the cellar as we know that has always been part of whatever building was here. At least we know we won't end up in the middle of a wall or something."

"Pick a date then." said Emily.

"Oh, okay." said Jane pursing her lips and looking towards the ceiling. "How about." there was a hesitation, her eyes narrowed. "How about Fifteenth of June 1536?"

"Blimey, that's a bit random."

"Not at all." said Jane. "Fifteenth of June is my birthday and 1536 was the year Anne Boleyn was executed. I will always remember that as a significant year. After all, I studied it for a long time."

"Okay, fifteenth June 1536 it is. Come on, it won't take a minute, just to prove the point." said Emily jumping up and leaving the room.

Jane placed her glass on the table, not quite sure what she had let herself in for. She slowly got up to follow Emily.

Standing in the middle of the cellar they looked at each other.

"What are we expecting to see?" Emily asked.

"I haven't a clue." answered Jane. "But if there is anyone here, we should be able to confirm the date by what they are wearing."

"Okay, hold on." said Emily as she took Jane's hand. A shimmer and a small spark and they were gone from the present day.

"Well. You were right Jane. The cellar was here back then. No lights." They stood in the darkness not quite sure of precisely when they were but knowing they were in the cellar or at least the site of it.

"But we don't know we are 'back then' do we?

"That's what we need to find out then, don't we. Come on, let's go upstairs, see what's going on."

From memory They tentatively felt their way to the stone steps leading from the dark cellar and made their way carefully to the top. The door was ajar, a faint light down the edge hinting that there was life above stairs. Slipping through the door in the usual ghostly manner so as not to attract attention, they stood in the hallway. Looking around they were both astonished and mesmerised.

"It's the same." said Jane. "Well, nearly. The clock isn't there but look at the dresser where the clock would be. That's medieval, absolutely no doubt about that. Oak, dark, chunky and absolutely beautiful. Can we take it back?"

"Don't be silly."

"Joking, but look, the staircase is just about the same, even the acorn is there."

They looked up at the staircase they both loved so much. Even though the same staircase brought about Emily's death, she still loved it for its strength and beauty. The front door was the only thing that appeared different in the structure of the hallway. Just as heavy looking but not as refined, large black iron hinges spread its full width. A large ring instead of a handle finished the doors furniture.

"It all looks quite new, doesn't it?" said Jane. "The oak panelling is very light and the staircase just looks so fresh, look, the acorn is not worn, the little nib on the top is quite intact. But then, I guess it would be relatively new in this year. I don't know exactly when this was built over or instead of the medieval building but we're probably not far out. Someone's coming." she said, her head turning towards the stairs, hearing a sound from the upper floor. They moved across the hall to get a better view.

A door closed on the landing and a young woman walked to the top of the staircase, paused and elegantly stepped down. The clothes she wore were astounding. A gown of red velvet with details sewn in of the finest silk, the entire gown embroidered with extraordinary detail in black and gold thread, the edges around the neck and arms were finished with fine white lace. Her head was adorned with a simple English hood, trimmed with lace and showing her dark hair parted tightly beneath. The finishing touch was a delicate and simple necklace of pearls and a large red ruby centring the attention of the eye.

"Oh, wow!" Jane whispered, stunned by the beauty confronting her. Her immediate thoughts were that it was precisely everything she could possibly imagine, in fact, everything she has actually imagined during her studies. She always thought it difficult to guess what the dress of the period was without seeing it first-hand. Museums and books were always a great resource but having the actual object in front of her in all its splendour, proved beyond doubt that there was opulence back in the Tudor period and not only for the very rich. This woman was in Chapwell House after all, and even though it was a magnificent house it was far from the large Tudor mansions favoured by the aristocracy.

Emily was shocked into silence, a rarity as far as Jane was concerned. As the woman walked slowly down the staircase their eyes did not leave her, looking her up and down, taking in the elegant beauty which almost seemed unreal. As she turned at the bottom of the stair, they could look her full in the face. Small, pale, but unblemished. Her eyes, almond shaped and dark with calm lashes gently moving with her eyes as they guided her feet down the steps. A small nose centred in her face above a pleasant mouth, her lips full, showing a hint of a smile. This woman appeared happy and comfortable.

The kitchen door opened with a slight creak, distracting them. The woman looked towards the opening where a maid stood, curtsied and said "Lady Margaret, I was about to come to get you from your room." The Lady Margaret replied quietly. "No need dear Agnes, I can walk freely from my room to the kitchen where I can join you for my lunch."

The Lady Margaret had a quiet, soothing voice. A slight French accent enhancing its elegance.

"But my Lady, you may have your lunch in the parlour." Said Agnes a slight look of concern on her face.

"I would prefer to join you in the kitchen Agnes, I may learn from you the art of preparing and cooking our food."

"I think you need to remember that you are the new Lady Margaret Chapwell and should be treated as such."

"Agnes, dear Agnes, we have known each other for many years have we not? My new life means a change from that which I have known and experienced. My past has not treated me well so to become more familiar with your life would make me happy. I will be content with a quiet life of comfort accompanied by the people I trust and love."

"Very well my Lady. It pleases me to be able to teach you the things that fill my life. A life I enjoy and now have the opportunity to continue without threat and danger."

"We are safe now Agnes, we need worry no more. I am wearing this gown for the last time. From today, I shall dress in a simpler manner, more suited to the status we now need to pursue, to be less conspicuous. So, let us have our last lunch as Mistress and servant and become more, well..., companions. We can learn from each other and enjoy our future, wherever it takes us. And I think it would be beneficial if you called me plain Margaret from now on."

The maid, Agnes looked a little shocked at this statement, but seeing the soft face of her mistress and the smile presented to her, she quickly realised that she was serious and relaxed. Agnes slowly turned and entered the kitchen.

The Lady Margaret followed Agnes, whereupon the door closed quietly behind them.

"Well, that was just amazing." said Jane looking at Emily with wide eyes, her mouth open. "History coming to life right in front of us. This is an incredible skill, Emily. I can see things that no-one else can see.

"Lady Margaret Chapwell." said Emily quietly transfixed. "The Lady Margaret Chapwell." she repeated. "Jane, if that is Lady

Margaret Chapwell then our family goes back to this point in time at least. But who is she?"

"I have no clue, Emily. But the impression I got was that they have only recently moved here. And the comments about being safe and the future and past are intriguing. Perhaps she was recently removed from the aristocracy for reasons we do not know. Perhaps her husband died and she was left with debts and had to 'down-size'. Whatever, we now know that in the year 1536 there was at least one Chapwell in the house."

Emily stood, still quite stunned, staring at the closed kitchen door. Her mind trying to take in this revelation and realising that what she had just witnessed meant that she had just met an ancestor of hers.

Jane suddenly found herself alone. Alone in the present-day cellar, the light illuminating what she now knew was a very old room. Emily was not at her side. A shock ran through her. The hairs on the back of her neck prickled and a feeling of dread fell through her body. "What have we done?" she queried herself, looking around the cellar, looking at the floor, her hands and up at the stone steps and the entrance door.

"Emily." she squeaked. Clearing her throat, she found her voice and shouted in panic, the desperate situation forming a look of horror on her face. "Emily, Emily." A tear formed in her eye, the dreadful feeling of loss overwhelming her."

"I'm here Jane, don't panic." came a frantic voice. Emily's face appeared around the door at the top of the steps. "I'm here." The door opened fully and Emily ran down the steps and fell into Jane's arms.

"Emily, oh my god, what happened? One second, I was with you back then, but suddenly I found myself here in the cellar on my own. You wouldn't believe how frightened I was." she held her companion tightly, her arms around Emily's neck.

"I'm sorry Jane, that was my fault. I let you go. It was an accident. You came straight back to where you started but I stayed there. I came back to the present but as I knew the hallway was always going to be there, I stayed where I was. Sorry, I didn't think."

"You're here now, thank goodness. I thought for a second that I had lost you and I couldn't bear that."

"It won't happen again Jane, I promise. I'll always come back to where we both started, though to be honest, I didn't actually know I could do that. I wasn't concentrating. I was so overwhelmed by what we saw"

"Okay, panic over, come on, let's go and finish our wine."

They sat in silence, pondering the events of the past few minutes. "You do realise Emily, that you have just seen one of your own ancestors, don't you?"

"I know, I thought that when we were there, I think that was what distracted me. I couldn't quite take it all in. She was a beautiful and elegant woman though, wasn't she? Where I get my good looks from, I suppose." she said, a smug smile fixed on her face as she looked at Jane, her chin lifted slightly in a superior manner.

Jane's narrow eyes met Emily's face. They both giggled childishly. "Yes, she was very elegant and I can see a resemblance between her and you even if it is over many generations. Whatever. We have learnt a lot in that few minutes. Not only can we travel back in time to goodness knows how long back and, this, I think is the most important part of the adventure, we know the house has been occupied by Chapwell's for longer than we perhaps thought. Oh, and there was you thinking history was boring."

"And." chipped in Emily. "As far as we could see, the house hasn't changed dramatically. All that panelling in the hallway was there then, oh, and the staircase. Each time I touch that acorn, I know it was touched by the Lady Margaret. It'll certainly change the way I'll look at things now."

"Now you know how I feel sometimes Emily, when I experience something that has a layer of history to it and try to imagine what it was 'really' like. Only now, we can confirm it is real. That feeling you'll get each time you touch that acorn is quite magical. Over five hundred years separates you and the Lady Margaret but each time you touch that acorn it will come right back to you. A connection between you and her has been formed. Something no-one else will experience. We are so fortunate Emily. We have found a way to bring the past, literally, to life and it's amazing, truly amazing."

Jane leant her head back on the sofa, holding her wine against her chest, a look of wonder on her face as she looked up at the ceiling.

"I'm beginning to see why you do what you do Jane. That short event has changed me. It gives me a strange feeling inside. I cannot stop thinking of her. But, for you, it must be so much more. I mean, you have studied history for all these years, trying to imagine what happened, when it happened and what it looked like. But now, you've have been there, seen it and, as they say, got the T shirt. It must have made all that study worth it."

"I know Emily, my head is spinning with the possibilities. I mean, imagine if we could go back and witness anything in history. Any documented account of any event can be seen by us, as it happened. It's mind blowing. The one thing at the centre of all this is the fact that we probably could not prove anything though. Imagine if, for example, I don't know, Admiral Nelson had been struck by a musket ball from one of his own troops. How would that change history? Well, I suppose it wouldn't as it could not be proven. But we would know. That's the thing, isn't it, only we would know. That is, unless we could find some evidence that still existed somewhere and exposed it. That would be the only way history as we know it would change." Jane felt exhausted with all the thoughts parading around her head, everything she had ever learnt could be corroborated or denied depending on what they could find.

"Jane?"

"What?"

"Don't you think you should calm down a bit." said Emily, concerned. "You nearly spilt your wine you know."

"Oh, Emily. This is the most amazing thing that has ever happened to me. And it's all down to you, I can't thank you enough for, well, just being you and what you are."

"It certainly changes the way our future is going to pan out, doesn't it?"

"Yes," said Jane quietly thinking, "yes, it will." She was still pondering the experiences they may have in the future. "What were we doing before we did this?"

"We were going on holiday Jane."

"Oh, yes. Okay. With all this excitement I'd forgotten briefly. Let's get a place booked and we can have a nice quite week or so walking and doing history and stuff and just being together, that'll be fun. Perhaps we can get to grips with this new part of our lives."

"Tomorrow, Jane, tomorrow, can we go to bed? I'm, well, a bit tired."

"I'll make us some tea." said Jane, emptying her glass and reaching across the table. "Finish your wine. Oh, you have."

The next morning, post breakfast, found Jane industriously searching for a place for them to stay in North Wales. She loved the experience of looking through so many exciting locations. She didn't like hotels much, and B&B's restricted what you could do to a certain extent and as they both loved cooking for themselves, she was aiming at a self-catering cottage which she eventually found in exactly the right place. Not in the village but not far away, an easy walk and with easy access to the places she wanted to wander. One click of the button and it was booked. Now she had to teach Emily how to pack for a holiday and prepare their clothing for a walking experience.

"Do you trust me?" asked Jane, walking into Emily's room as she was brushing her hair, sat in front of the dresser.

"Of course, I do. Why?" said Emily, spinning around on the stool, her hand holding a hank of hair as she pulled the brush through it.

"I've booked us a lovely little cottage near Beddgelert for us to stay for a week. Is that alright?"

"Well, it would be no good asking me, would it? I haven't a clue about how you would even do that so, yes, whatever you think best will be fine by me. What do I have to do?"

"All we need to do is pack a bag and put a few bits and pieces together to entertain us for a week. Now, let's see what you've got in your wardrobe and drawers that would be suitable for a walking holiday."

"Not much, I don't think." said Emily, placing her brush on the dressing table and pulling out a drawer, looking inside absently, without knowing what was required.

A few hours later, after a visit to town, Emily was provided with all she needed for an expedition to the mountains. New boots, waterproofs, socks and jumpers and a trendy fleece hat.

"There, I think that is all we need." said Jane, comparing her pile of clothes with Emily's to ensure there was nothing amiss. "We'll pack tomorrow and get on our way on Saturday. We were lucky to get a booking in the right place at short notice. Honestly Emily, you're going to love the experience."

"Well, I've never walked up a mountain before Jane, I don't really know what to expect. But what about Chapwell, Jan will be here on his own."

"I gave Sarah a ring, she jumped at the chance to stay here with Jan for a few days. She'll keep an eye on things and, let's face it, those two get along really well. They enjoy each other's company."

They sat at the dining table with a cup of tea brewed with soft mountain water looking out through the front window, a delightful view across the valley painting a picture in the glass. They both felt the soothing comfort the cottage afforded them, detached from everything they had experienced over the past weeks and months. Just a pleasant view over to the rocky mountain opposite.

"See." said Jane. "It gives a view right over to the Sygun copper mine. There's a lovely walk we can go on later which goes around the mountain. You can see a lot of the remains of the industry along the valley up there and the walk ends at the lake where it returns to the lane across the road. We can make a sandwich, get our boots on and go up there when we have unpacked if you would like to?"

"Yes, yes, of course Jane, it is lovely out there. I've never really thought about how beautiful mountains can be. I thought they were just rocky and impenetrable but they're not, certainly not from what I can see."

They were soon unpacked and on their way down through the village to walk alongside the river, past Gelert's Grave and along the side of the narrow-gauge railway. Jane told Emily the myth of Gelert, the wolfhound killed by his master Prince Llywelyn the Great who mistakenly thought the dog had killed his baby son, whereas in fact the hound had killed a wolf who had attacked the child.

"It is rumoured that the prince never smiled again." said Jane, pondering the story as she read from the metal plaque.

"Perhaps we can confirm the myth, Jane. I mean, go back in time to see what really happened."

"Well, to be honest Emily. I don't think that is a good idea. The myth is very sad and all that but it is the bedrock of this village. It is the reason the village is here. Beddgelert translates as Gelert's Grave. Even for me, being a historian, I just would not want to change that. It would take something away from the place. Some of the magic would disappear and I think that would spoil it. I mean, after all, we couldn't prove anything so it would just spoil what that this place has."

"You're right, we'll leave that where it is. A lesson for us that not all things need delving into."

They walked on along the riverside, watching the water joggling along the valley, over boulders and under trees, sometimes quiet and still, often loud and tumbling making its way inexorably towards the sea as all rivers did.

"The scenery here is wonderful Jane, I absolutely love it. I have only ever seen pictures and they really don't do it justice at all. Out here I can smell it, feel it and hear it. I'm going to stay visible while we're here I think, it'll be easier for you. And me, come to think of it. I don't think anyone will notice. Well, not unless they try and touch me that is."

"If you're happy with that Emily, then so am I. Come on, here's where we start climbing."

The route led them up through an Oak and Birch woodland, climbing steeply. The path flattened between the peaks either side, the valley opening out to a wide grassy path giving delightful views of the mountains either side. Littered along the route were rusty remains of industry, carts, wheels and a huge pulley.

"Was this something to do with the workings Jane?"

"This was where the copper ore was transported down the mountain to the railway at the bottom. They used an aerial cable system to carry the trucks down the valley. Hey, tell you what. Let's take a quick trip back in time to see what it looked like when it was all in action. That would be fascinating."

"Pick a date then Jane, I don't know when to go back to."

"Let's stick with June fifteenth as it's easy and in the warmer months, but the year, I'm guessing around 1870 would be good."

"I think it would be an idea for us to be somewhere out of the way Jane, you know, just in case it gets a bit busy down here."

They looked around the valley and chose a grassy bank higher up on the opposite side to the workings. They stood momentarily looking across at the quite mountainside. The bracken interspersed with the woollen backs of the grazing sheep. Rusty machinery scattered in a haphazard way, no indication of its original purpose.

"Ready?" asked Emily.

"Ready" came the reply.

They held hands and with the small spark and shimmer they vanished from the present day.

For some reason or other Jane closed her eyes and only opened them when the feeling of disturbance calmed down. They were both staring at an industrial landscape. After walking up the valley and seeing the remains of the workings, they could now see it in all its glory. The valley was unrecognisable in comparison to what they saw earlier. It was virtually stripped of any vegetation and the metal pylons stretched down the valley out of sight, the aerial steel ropeway moving slowly around the large horizontal pulley at the top of the incline. There were men everywhere, and noise, clanking and squealing, grinding and thumping. There were small rail tracks tracing a path from each of the adit's to the top of the ropeway where men manoeuvred the small trucks to frames hanging from the steel rope as it was moving. The trucks were picked up and started their journey down the valley. Simultaneously, empty trucks were unloaded on the uphill side of the ropeway to be returned to the tracks for more ore. The men were dressed in loose trousers and jackets, some wore waistcoats and all wore a hat of some sort. Most had beards and the age of these workers ranged from very young to, what appeared to be, very old. Though with the harsh environment that they were working, they were probably not as old as they looked. Jane was fully aware of how taxing this type of work was on the human body. Studies she had done on coal miners and quarrymen taught her how life expectancy was seriously reduced due to the conditions.

"My goodness Jane. This is almost nightmarish. It's around the same time as I was born, well just five years before. I knew that conditions for these manual workers were bad but this is beyond that."

"I see what you mean, it is quite horrific and nowhere near what I was expecting. Not romantic at all. You see what this is doing for us Emily?"

"What?" came the reply.

"It's allowing us to appreciate exactly how lucky we are with our modern life. Even your life at this time was far more comfortable. You lived at Chapwell. Far removed from the reality of the industry all around you."

"I know." said Emily quietly. Her face a picture of misery and sorrow. "There are young boys working Jane. I mean really working.

They can't be more than ten years old, look, over there. They're pushing the empty carts back up to the mine entrance. And everyone looks so sad and tired."

"This, unfortunately, is the reality of industry in those days." said Jane. "Yes, this country led the world in Iron, Steel and Coal. And from here Slate and Copper. But at what cost. We just have to accept that this is how it was. Well, we know this is how it was. It's well documented. But to see it with your own eyes is, well, quite traumatic really. Especially when, not far away the quarry and mine owners lived in huge mansions, a lavish lifestyle, maintained on the backs of these men here and the servants they employed.

The pair continued watching the labours of the men and boys, flabbergasted at the sheer scale of the industry in such a small area.

"Shall we return to the present? I think I've seen enough." asked Emily.

She released Jane and they returned to the pleasant, green and quiet valley. They looked at each other, their feelings subdued by what they had experienced.

"Hold my hand again Jane."

"Why."

"Something you should see."

Jane tentatively took Emily's hand in hers, not quite knowing what she was about to do. The atmosphere changed slightly; her senses began to grow more intense. She could see more, hear more and smell the heather heavily.

"Look, Jane, over there."

Jane looked at where Emily was pointing and she could see what had attracted her attention. At the top of the ropeway, on a small dilapidated wall, sat three men. Clothed as they had been in 1870.

"They're ghosts Emily."

"Yeah, I know. I saw them as we were about to go back in time. I know, I see other ghosts all the time but three together is a bit unusual. I just thought we would take a better look. They've seen us as well now, look."

Jane could see that the three men were indeed looking directly at them, one pointed towards where they were stood. It was obvious that they could see the two girls.

"Come on Jane, let's introduce ourselves."

"Can we?"

"Of course. I'm a ghost, you're attached to me so you can see everything I can, can't you?"

"Well, yes, I was forgetting myself a bit there. Would it be okay to talk to them?"

"Let's see." replied Emily, waving at the men whilst leading Jane down the side of the mountain towards them.

"Hello." said Emily as they got closer.

"Hello." said the man sat in the centre of the group. "Are you like us?" he asked.

"Yes." said Emily, "Well, I am but Jane here is attached to me. My companion, we're joined so she can see what I can as long as she's holding my hand."

"Ah, right." he said. "Only we don't see many of us up here, there's just the three of us." A heavy Welsh accent pleasing the air.

"But why are there three of you?" asked Emily. "That's very unusual. Did you all die at the same time?"

"We were caught in a collapse in the mine. Our bodies are still in there somewhere. They closed the adit right afterwards, left us in there."

"But." said Emily, confused. "Surely one of you would have moved on. I don't understand why all three of you became ghosts at exactly the same time."

"Something to do with the mountain." said a second miner. "We were deep in the mine when it happened. Our spirits couldn't get out, so we're here now."

"I'm sorry." said Jane.

"Oh." said the third man. "It's fine. We miss our families and all that but we are here in the land we love. We are still together. We've been together since we were children and best of all, we don't have to work." This got the three of them laughing with each other.

"Oh, how rude of us." said Jane. "I'm Jane and this is Emily. Emily is the real ghost here. I'm a fake one, but enjoying the experience. What are your names?"

"I'm Dafydd." said the man in the centre. "This," he said touching the man to his left "is Geraint, and this," he said, taking the other man's hat and throwing it to the ground, "is Tomos."

Tomos, reached down, collected his hat and slapped Dafydd across the face with it, laughing.

"And what brings you two here then?" asked Geraint.

"We're on holiday." said Jane. "Emily has never been on a proper holiday before and as I just love it here, I brought her along. I just had a thought. The last time I came here and walked up this valley, the three of you must have been here."

"Well." said Geraint. "We don't go far do we boys?" The other two nodded in agreement, Tomos placing the hat back on his head. "We wander around a bit but we enjoy our place right here, watching the world go by. We see all the changes going on. The mine closing, everything falling apart and rusting. But it was a hard place to be, the work was difficult and dangerous, as you can see. But it is now peaceful and pleasant, we have nothing to fear. We have each other and we can still sing, so we're happy."

"Well." said Jane. "It is so lovely to meet you all and to know that you are happy and safe now. We'll leave you to it. If we have some time later in the week, perhaps we can visit you again?"

"Yes, we'd like that." said Dafydd. The other two, again, nodded in agreement.

"Well, we'll maybe see you again then."

The three men stood and doffed their caps in a pleasant gesture as the girls moved on along the path, waving to the men as they walked on up the valley. As they continued on their way, there was a burst of song behind them where the three miners broke into *Hen Wlad Fy Nhadau* which echoed heartily across the valley.

"Well, that was nice Jane, but such a shame that these three men were killed due to the lack of safety in the mine."

"There's nothing we can do about it, Emily. That is history, we cannot change that. We just have to get used to the fact that we are going to experience some fantastic things and sometimes we are going to see things that upset us. But, and this I found in my studies, we can learn from these things. It makes us better people. We are better informed so really, what we should take from this is the hard work that these people did and admire them, respect them and, to a certain extent, pity them for what they had to endure. And, I know it is the case that they didn't know any different but they must have been aware of the lavish lifestyles led by their masters."

"You're right Jane. But it does make you feel very humble." The sadness evident in Emily's eyes.

"I know." said Jane. "Come on let's cheer ourselves up. There's a wonderful view of the lake from the top of this valley."

Emily released Jane's hand and they walked on up the valley, getting ever steeper and narrowing to a small col where the highest point of the walk heralded an open view of the mountains and lake ahead of them.

"Oh, wow!" exclaimed Emily. "That's breath-taking Jane. You can see for miles along the valley with the mountains beyond."

"I know." came the reply. "And we're not even very high here, you wait until we climb one of the bigger mountains and you'll see just how breath-taking it can be. Let's have a seat right here and have our lunch. We can just take in the view and relax before we continue on down."

They sat, comfortably on the grass, the sun in the cloudless sky bathing them in a pleasant warmth and the slight breeze wafting the smell of heather around them. Lambs bleated between the bracken, a Yellowhammer called mournfully from a hawthorn, making for an idyllic atmosphere, certainly a world away from the industry and toil they had just witnessed.

"I could quite happily sit here all afternoon you know Jane. It's so nice. It's like every bad thing, every nasty experience can be wiped away. At least temporarily."

"I know." said Jane. "And that's why I enjoy it so much. You always know that reality is not far away but at least for a few moments the experience of being here banishes it to the back of your mind. It's a real refresher. And, I might add, something we should do a lot more of. If you enjoy it that is." she added.

"Oh, I'd love to Jane. I'm sure I can cope with the harder mountain walking, but you can train me, show me how it's done. I know it is dangerous in the mountains and despite their beauty, they can bite. I've seen and heard of people who have been lost, injured and even killed in the mountains but I feel safe with you. You've done it before."

"Don't worry Emily. I'll keep you safe. I can navigate and weather watch and I know what to do in an emergency. But the rule I keep as number one is 'you can always turn back' There is never any point in putting yourself in unnecessary danger just for the sake of it. There is always another day."

They munched on their sandwiches, enjoying every morsel. Jane pointing out the mountains around them, Snowdon to their left and Moel Siabod in the distance. "Breath-taking." said Emily taking in the green and rocky beauty surrounding her.

"I know." said Jane as Emily leant towards her putting her arm around her neck. "It is truly wonderful."

They both laid back on the grass, eyes closed sensing everything around them and bathing in the comfort. Eventually Jane sat up and looked at her watch.

"Goodness Emily, it's time to go, I think. It won't take us long to get back, the path is easy now and walking downhill is always quicker than going up."

They packed their rucksacks and started the descent into the next valley, watching the lake get slowly closer as they walked.

"The water is like a mirror." said Emily.

"Amazing, isn't it?" replied Jane. "The reflection is absolutely perfect, the mountains at the other end are reflected in such detail. If you stood on your head, you wouldn't be able to tell the difference."

The path turned back towards the village, alongside the lake, dragonfly's stalking prey along the shoreline, darting and diving, their twin sets of wings reflecting in the sunlight, shining blues and greens. At the end of the lake the river exited and started its tumultuous journey down the valley, eventually to the sea.

Jane stopped abruptly and turned to look across the valley.

"What's the matter Jane? What have you seen?"

"That." said Jane pointing at a small wooded hill across the stream. "Is Dinas Emrys."

"Okay." said Emily, wondering why such an insignificant hill should attract her attention. "And?"

"You'll find out Emily." said Jane touching the side of her nose knowingly. "You'll find out."

They continued on along the river and found themselves back at the cottage, the sun just disappearing behind the mountains, a shadow slowly ascending the hillside across the valley. The higher areas turning orange as the sun lowered. The sky turning a darker blue.

Sitting in the cottage, watching the hills grow darker they looked at each other, the affection very obvious. There was a strong bond between them that was becoming unbreakable. They both felt this and embraced it. Neither had experienced this companionship before they met. Even Emily's bond with Beryl had not been this strong. For Jane, the feeling she had was indescribable. Not something she could easily explain. She merely put it down to the fact that Emily was a ghost. A ghost who was totally dependent on Jane for her wellbeing and, even, her existence in the living world.

They looked at each other, slightly mystified but both knowing what the other was thinking.

"Go on, you first." said Emily suddenly.

"Oh, I was just thinking how lucky I am. Lucky to have you as a friend and companion." said Jane. "I cannot think of anytime I have felt this kind of friendship. I know Sarah is a great friend, one you could only dream of really but what I feel between us is, well, I don't know. It's almost like there is a physical connection between us. It's like we are always holding hands, you are always there. Even when you're not. You know, when I appeared in the cellar the other day and you were still in the hall. I could still feel the connection. I knew you were there. I just panicked when I couldn't see you."

"Couldn't have described it better myself Jane. There is a bond or connection between us and it is almost physical. You can almost touch it. It's like having an elastic web joining us together. And, I like it."

"So, do I. More wine?"

They smiled broadly at each other while Jane topped up their glasses, a yawn escaping her. Reciprocated by Emily, they both laughed.

Chapter Seventeen

Dragon

Bacon, egg, tea and toast were the breakfast components required, which they prepared seamlessly between them. Little was said but it all came together and they sat at the table again, looking across the valley to see the first signs of the sun on the mountains. The sky was peppered with small white fluffy clouds heralding a fine day.

"What shall we do today, Jane?"

"A quieter day, I think. We'll just relax for a bit, sit in the garden and watch the world wake up and sort itself out. We'll pack our bags, make some lunch and I think we should take a walk to Dinas Emrys, it's not far away. Now, there's a place shrouded in mystery and legend, myth and magic." She said looking intently at Emily.

"Okay." said Emily, sitting back in her chair, holding her mug close. "And what do you think we'll see there?"

"I'm not quite sure." replied Jane. "I've never been there before. Always wanted to but never got around to it. It has a lot of myths attached to it, chiefly, it is supposed to be one of the places Merlin frequented. Legend has it that a King called Vortigern was fleeing the Anglo-Saxon invaders and chose Dinas Emrys to build a fortification. At each attempt to build the castle it had collapsed during the night. Merlin was chosen as a sacrifice to appease the force preventing the building. Merlin explained that the reason the building collapsed each night was due to the two dragons who occupied a hidden pool. One, the white dragon of the Saxon's was later defeated by the red dragon and peace returned. There are other stories, legends and myths but in reality, it is just that. There is evidence of a building on the top which, we know was inhabited after Roman times. I just want to go there to see if we can feel anything. I don't know, Emily, it may be nothing but it might give us a tingle."

"Well, I just love this walking thing." said Emily cleaning her plate with the last bit of toast. "So anywhere you want to go, I'll follow. What shall we put in our sandwiches today?"

They sat on the bench in the garden through the morning, watching the mountains wake up, the sheep wandering across the hillside, the odd bleat confirming the bond between ewe and lamb. The garden merged into the mountainside behind the house, rocky outcrops popping up between the trees and grass. It was as if the mountainside had flowed down to surround the house but had left a few more formal spots where a table and benches were placed for occupants to enjoy. The fluffy clouds thinned and eventually vanished, leaving another clear blue sky. The silence mesmeric, punctuated occasionally by the chatter of the birds. The odd territorial warning interspersed with the more pleasing songs of attraction to a potential mate.

"This is just so nice." said Jane squirming in her seat, enjoying the comfort of the sun's warmth, total peace and tranquillity. You couldn't make it any better."

"I know." said Emily, who was lying at full stretch on the other bench, her hands forming a pillow behind her head, eyes closed, a satisfied smile stretched across her face. "It's like the feeling I get when I'm sat in Chapwell's garden only there's mountains as well. I honestly never realised what holidays were for, but I see now and, personally I think we should make a habit of it."

"I was thinking the same thing." said Jane. "With my work, which, incidentally I need to get on with, we could spend a lot of time travelling about and just doing the history thing. Before I met you, I was planning on doing more travelling to historical sites and libraries for some of my research. And as our relationship has now established itself, we could make a start when we get back home. For now, though, let's just enjoy the week up here."

They both been lying in the sun for another half hour when Jane opened her eyes, squinted at the sun and yawned loudly, hearing the gentle snoring coming from the bench to her side.

"Come on Emily, wake up." she said standing with a long stretch and another yawn.

"Oh, really?" came the reply, as Emily lifted her head and swung herself upright. Running her hands through her tousled hair she yawned loudly and stood, turning to look at Jane, hands on hips, expectantly, smiling. "Okay, let's get our stuff ready and we'll take that walk. This place seems to hypnotise you into a very, very relaxed state."

They made a sandwich and packed their lunch, topped up their water bottles and checked their map. Jane made a point of showing Emily exactly where they were going to be walking so there should not be any surprises. A quick final check, boots on and they were walking down the steps and through the little metal gate, to the road. The path left the road and the walk started through the trees, oak and birch. Along a narrow but well-worn path traversing the side of the valley, eventually it turned uphill through more woods and across open hill fields, littered with grazing sheep. The odd ewe looking in their direction but quickly returning to the grass with a bleat to its lamb.

Eventually they came to the base of Dinas Emrys which loomed above them, where the path became rocky and steep as it went over a wall and into more woodland. They wound their way between huge boulders and knotted tree trunks. Birds giving loud warnings keeping them company. The path levelled slightly and they could see the sky through the higher trees as the top of the hill got closer.

Another wall, tumbling in places barred their way until Jane found a gap where the now indistinct path continued. Suddenly they were on the flat summit where they could see lumps and bumps where the ground had obviously been disturbed in the past.

"That was a bit of a climb." said Jane, blowing the hair out of her face, hands on hips feet apart and looking around herself.

"Yeah." came the out of breath reply as Emily staggered the last few steps to arrive by Jane's side.

"Blimey, you a bit puffed out?" Jane asked.

"hang on." came the stifled reply as Emily bent forward, placing her hands on her knees trying desperately to get her breath back.

Jane looked around while Emily recovered to see what they had walked to. A few trees surrounded them with grassy, open spaces between. To her left she could see the remains of a wall with more structures visible beyond.

"Okay, Jane." said Emily standing upright, a flush in her face. "I'm ready now, that was a bit of a struggle, especially the last bit."

"You haven't been doing it for as long as I have." said Jane turning to look at her companion. "You did well yesterday mind, that was quite a walk and to get up here as competently as you did it, is pretty good going really. I'm proud of you."

"Thanks." came the reply from a smiling Emily, shaking her hair back into place and tying it back tidily. "What have we got then?" she asked, looking at her surroundings.

"Well, not a vast amount to be honest Emily. It's not a huge area and the building up here doesn't look very big at all. The satellite image wasn't joking when it only showed a few walls. But we'll have a look around and see if there is anything of note here. It is quite amazing to be stood at a location where supposedly the mythical Merlin may have stood."

"Jane?" Asked Emily, looking around herself, an expression of confusion on her face.

"Yes. What is it?"

"There's something here, I can feel it. It's difficult to describe but I can feel a sort of, well, I can only think of it as something like a *buzzing* inside me. I can feel, I don't know, and a sort of *breathing*."

"Breathing?" enquired Jane, confused. "How do you mean, breathing."

"I don't know Jane. It just feels like the whole hill is breathing. I can't explain it but there is definitely something here. I don't suppose you can feel anything can you?"

"No, no, I can't feel anything. Only how quiet it is." Jane turned around trying to see something that wasn't there. "Let's have a look at the ruins over here." she said, pointing towards the structure at the end of the promontory. "See if the feeling changes."

They wandered across the clearing towards the stone structures that had tumbled upon themselves. The distinction of the original walls blurred by the collapsed stone. As they walked around the outside, they found what was a gateway or gap in the wall where they could penetrate the interior. The first room was quite large, the exterior walls, for the most part, rising to only a few feet above the bedrock. The rest of the wall, or significant amounts of it lay scattered on the ground, outlining the original structure. They exited this initial building and walked towards the southern side of the hill which was completely open, giving uninterrupted views along the valley over Llyn Dinas.

"That's some view Emily." said Jane marvelling at the vista she was presented with.

"Oh, wow, that's amazing. Oh." said Emily pointing down below them to the river. "That's where we walked yesterday. I can see the path as it joins the lake and comes back along the river. It looks so nice in the sun."

"I'll make a navigator out of you yet." said Jane, smiling. "There's not a lot here you know, only the evidence of buildings in the ground, not even much of the walls left over here. How do you feel now?"

"The same." came the reply. "Still just buzzing and the breathing is still there. They are huge breaths. Or, at least, that's what it feels like. Right under us, deep down. I can almost imagine the hill expanding and contracting with each breath. Perhaps it does Jane, maybe that was why the King's building kept falling down."

"Nice theory." said Jane, smiling as she looked at her friend. "I just can't get enough of this view you know; I could look at this for the rest of the day."

"Nothing to stop us and I don't know about you but I'm getting hungry."

"Thinking of your stomach again, I see." said Jane. "Here let's just sit here at the end, there's loads of suitable rocks to sit on."

They settled themselves comfortably on a large outcrop facing out across the valley, the lake surface shimmering with sparkling pinpricks in the sun. They sat with their sandwich box between them enjoying the enhanced flavours of the food, which always tasted better when consumed in a pleasant location.

"You know what we could do Jane?"

"What?"

"Jane!" exclaimed Emily turning to stare at Jane. "No talking and eating." she said laughing.

"Sorry." gulped an embarrassed Jane. "Anyway, what were you going to say?"

"We could just go back in time, see what this building was all about. That would be fun. We could try one thousand years, then two thousand and just move around in time until we find something."

"We could try." said Jane. "I don't know much about the exact dates that anything happened here. There is only what has been written due to the evidence of excavations. There is little if anything actually documented."

"There is no need." Came a deep, rumbling voice.

They turned in opposite directions in an attempt to find out where the voice had come from. But there was nothing. Just the silence. They simultaneously and absently placed their unfinished sandwiches back in the box. They looked at each other, both exhibiting a worried look.

"Who on earth was that?" asked Jane.

"I really don't know Jane, but I will say this. The buzzing inside me has stopped. I can still feel the breathing but no buzzing."

They sat in total silence, still, awaiting something, anything to happen.

"Jane! Look, over there." said Emily quietly, pointing towards the main part of the remaining structure. "Can you see that?"

"What? Where?"

"Just there look." said Emily, again pointing towards the ruined building her finger wagging as if to amplify the gesture.

"What is it?" asked Jane. "I can see something, or, oh, someone. There's someone stood on the wall. But they're not exactly clear. They look like one of you Emily, it's a ghost."

"I don't think that is any ordinary ghost, Jane. Firstly, you can see it and I'm not touching you. Secondly, I can't feel them. I can usually feel other ghosts."

"Perhaps they're paired with someone, like Jan was when I could see him after he touched my mum."

"No, this is different. This is something else Jane. I don't know what but it's no ghost."

They sat totally still, waiting for something to happen, staring intently at the apparition stood on the wall.

"Okay." said Emily standing. "You'll need to tell us who you are now. We can both see you and I know that you are no ghost so, who are you?"

The figure stepped down from the wall. Jane stood and got as close to Emily as she could, reaching down for her hand to obtain some feeling of security. The apparition walked confidently closer. They could see now it was a man, it walked like a man, a long staff in his right hand. He was clothed in a long cloak, his head hidden within a hood. The two girls stood, equally alert and aware of what they were seeing but feeling a little scared. He stopped a few yards from them, his outline becoming more distinct and with a slight disturbance in the air he became solid. He was not tall, only slightly taller than the two girls. He laid his staff on the ground beside him and removed his hood. His face, now revealed, was not what either were expecting though neither really knew what to expect. It was a quiet face, shoulder length hair, greying, surrounded warm skin, sharp blue eyes. A grey beard flowed down his chest. Nothing remarkable but equally magnificent. He exuded and air of confidence and calm. He sat, reaching out with a flat palm, inviting the girls to sit back on their rock. They obeyed in silence, their eyes not leaving this person.

"I expect you are wondering who I am Emily?" he asked.

"You know my name?" replied Emily, quite shocked.

"Yes." came the response as he took a seat. "I know the pair of you, Emily and Jane. And before you start getting frightened, don't worry, you are welcome here. I have been waiting for you."

"I'm sorry." said Emily. "Waiting for us? How do you mean, waiting for us?"

"As I said. I have been waiting for the pair of you. Let me explain."

Jane was silent, staring at this man in front of them, her imagination running totally wild, her mouth open. She breathed and spoke. "You're Merlin." she said quietly. "You're Merlin the magician, aren't you?"

He smiled. "Yes, Jane. I am Myrddin. We'll leave the magician bit for a moment though." His voice was warm and comforting, deep and mellow.

Jane smiled; her breath caught. She could not quite believe what she was experiencing. She just sat, staring at him, shocked.

"Please breathe Jane." said Merlin "Now I have met you I don't want to inadvertently hurt you, so please breathe."

Jane took a breath, her shock dispelled. Merlin smiled and placed his hands on his knees.

"Yes." he said. "I am Myrddin or as you say in English, Merlin. I welcome either. In answer to your question Emily. Yes, I have been waiting for you, the pair of you. I have been watching you over the years. Particularly you Emily. You endured a restricted childhood which had no effect on your outcome as a person and then you had an unfortunate accident. A disadvantage to you but an advantage to me. You have the virtues required for the work I may need you for in this world."

"And me?" questioned Jane.

"Ah, Jane, yes. I have been watching you as well, through your entire life. I noticed you were visiting Chapwell from a very early age. At the time you were not aware of Emily's existence but she was also there and, I might add, was also watching you. That is correct, isn't it Emily?

"Err, yes. Yes, I liked Jane a lot, I could not avoid knowing about her past but she was such a lovely girl and deserved a better life. She has that now, thanks to Beryl and John."

"Don't forget yourself Emily." said Merlin. "You have taken a big part in Jane's life. Everything that has happened to the pair of you was for a reason. Don't think for one minute that you have been moulded into something you were not. That is not the case. You have both grown into your personalities and developed into the people you are now. You have both proven your credentials over the years and now is the time to take the next step."

Jane felt a warmth in her that grew with every word that Merlin spoke. She felt a change in the atmosphere, as if something extraordinary was about to happen or be revealed. Emily, on the other hand felt a slight confusion. She was aware of the man sat in front of them and had no doubt that the truth was being told. It almost seemed as if her life had been planned up until her accident.

"I'm slightly confused." she said. "Are you saying that my life is part of some kind of plan?"

"Not quite." replied Merlin. He lowered his head thinking, bringing his hands together, he lifted them to his lips as if in prayer. After a few moments his hands returned to his lap and his head lifted. "You are a special person, Emily. You have, during your life given so much to those around you, your parents and brothers and then to Beryl whom you joined in order to make her life more bearable. When she departed, you were then left with a large space in your life which was filled by Jane. You have taken advantage of the special powers you have but have never abused them. You have only ever done good for those around you."

"But what about David Chapwell? I guess you know what happened there."

"Yes, I do Emily, but think about the harm that man had caused throughout his life. Not only to Jane and her mother but to countless people he came into contact with. The children at the farm are a good example of that surely?"

"But I led him to his death."

"I know. And that is a difficult thing to come to terms with but sometimes in this world there are things that are inevitable and his death was simply that. Had he been allowed to continue whether incarcerated or not he would have caused far more damage."

"How do you know that?" she asked.

"There are forces in this universe that are difficult to explain and even more difficult to control. Suffice it to say that his life would have caused misery and pain wherever it went. For him to die, in all honesty was the best thing to happen, for everyone's sake. You did what you thought best at that time. Unbeknown to you, the forces I have spoken about had an influence on exactly that. Do not think for one moment that you acted alone Emily. It is not the case."

"So... Oh, this is confusing." she said.

"Take your time Emily, take your time. We have all the time in the world but this is crucial to you understanding the future."

"Okay, so I was being influenced by someone else?"

"Not quite. The influence came from the universe around you. The forces that govern the way we live. All of us that is, not just those of us who are, how shall we say, not entirely alive."

"Is that why I can feel, see and hear so many things that others can't?"

"Correct, and, I know you are going to ask, Jane can experience some of this as well. Due to your joining, the power you possess is shared with Jane. Well, some of it anyway." He stopped for a moment and looked at Jane who was just sitting totally mesmerised by Merlin and his explanation of their existence. She was beginning to put things together in her head. "Can I help you with your thoughts Jane? You are looking a little confused."

"I am, totally, confused."

"You have a lot to learn and a lot to experience but I can tell you this. You will not be sorry for what will happen. Your lives, or, in

Emily's case, existence, will change slightly. You will be able to do more than you have, it will all become simpler to fulfil the tasks that will confront you.

"What tasks?" asked Jane. "Are we going to be given tasks to complete?"

"Not that you would know Jane. This is a difficult thing to explain but this world, and, indeed the universe it sits in responds to the vibrations of the entirety of existence. You are just a part of that and the things you do, are guided by, but not controlled by this overseeing fabric. The two of you have proven that you are able to take a situation and act on it in a manner that benefits the existence of the universe. Not all people are like that as we can see. It is a shame that there are not more like you but we keep looking."

"But isn't this going to make us more conscious of everything that happens around us?"

"Possibly." replied Merlin. "Take for example your walk yesterday. You did things that others cannot do. You visited the mine when it was active but acted accordingly. You were shocked at what you saw and you met Tomos, Dafydd and Geraint."

"You know them?" asked Emily.

"Yes, I do. I visit them on the odd occasion and we have a talk. They entertain me with their songs. But, like I say, you acted accordingly. Earlier though, you had the opportunity to confirm or deny a local myth. The myth of the hound, Gelert. You chose not to pursue this. Why? Because you acted accordingly. Not due to any influence from outside but from within yourselves. Consequently, for the two of you, the myth remains intact."

"Is it true though?" asked Jane mischievously.

Merlin laughed. A laugh that boomed around the remains of the castle. "Do you want me to tell you?"

Jane thought, and very quickly replied. "No, no, I don't want to know as I would be devastated if it were untrue."

"Well, there you are then, the myth remains a part of the magic you know and feel."

"Merlin?" asked Emily

"Yes Emily." he quietly replied, gazing into her eyes.

"You said that we would be able to do more than we can now. What does that mean exactly?"

The two girls sat in anticipation of what, they didn't quite know. They were both tingling and it seemed that even their surroundings were listening carefully to what was coming. The birds went quiet, the breeze dissipated and the air became still.

"It means that I can give you greater control of the things you can do. I can make the skills you have, more powerful and I can bestow them on you both equally." Emily was about to interrupt but Merlin held his hand up in front of him. "Let me explain. It will all become a little clearer but it would be beneficial if you just listen for now and ask questions after. Would that be agreeable?"

"Yes." they replied in unison. They leaned further forwards, totally engrossed in the conversation.

"The skills you currently have are limited in their effectiveness. For example, if Jane needs to see something whether it be another of your kind Emily or, you need to travel back in time, she needs to be holding your hand. I will change this so that you will be independent of each other. You will both have the same skills. For both of you the ability to witness the effects of changes in the past will become—."

"But we cannot change the past Merlin, only see it." interrupted Emily.

"I was about to say that you will have this skill and in addition you will be able to make changes in the past but only when you think it necessary. I am trusting you with this skill. It is a massive responsibility but you will be able to become visible to those you visit and you will be able to communicate with them." Jane was itching to say something. Merlin noticed her enthusiasm "I will explain Jane. You will also be able to touch and move objects. This, I know is unprecedented but as far as the universe is concerned there are some things that have not gone to plan for a variety of reasons. You will know when this is to be done. You will be able to see the effects it has and make the appropriate changes to ensure the result is the right one. Okay then, Jane, I can see how this is getting to you now. What would you like to say?"

"It's nothing really, but does that mean in simple terms, we can change things in the past that can have an effect on the future?"

"In simple terms, yes." came the reply.

"Isn't that a bit, well, dangerous, not to say unethical?" asked Jane.

"In the broad sense, yes. But for us, as we are special, no. We are able to put right the events that have gone wrong in the past. And, again I must emphasise the fact that you will know when to do this or not do it."

"Isn't that a bit like playing God?" asked Emily.

"Some will think so but you should not. Think of it more like making slight adjustments to the fabric of the universe."

"So, we could prevent two world wars?" asked Jane expectantly, looking at Emily.

"Some things are inevitable and as those two events are so huge in history and so devastating in their effect it would be almost impossible to make the right change in the right place at the right time and end up with a satisfactory outcome and, I think you both know this already. Inside you will know when a change is required and you will know when it is not."

"I'm not sure I'm ready for that kind of responsibility." said Jane.

"Don't think of it like that Jane. You will carry on with your lives as they are now, doing all the things you enjoy doing but on the rare occasion that a change is required, you will know. It is not something that you will think of constantly. You will not be aware of what you are able to do up until the time comes to do it. Then you will know and I am confident that you will both act accordingly."

"And you trust us to do this?" asked Jane

"As I have said. I have been watching you throughout your lives and they are lives that have been filled with challenges most people would not cope with. You have taken them in your stride and developed into excellent people. The sort of people the world needs. Yes, Emily, you had your accident and that was unfortunate but, it seems, necessary in order for you to be who you are. Everything happens for a reason; we just have to accept that but that is not to say the future whether from today on or from a point in the past, cannot be altered to benefit all. So, in answer to your question. Yes, I trust the pair of you."

"There are so many questions to ask." said Emily "Too many, really."

"Don't worry about that for now Emily. All your questions will be answered when the time comes. All your worries will be unfounded and you will find that your future will be rewarding. It already has been with your adventures at the farm. That would not have happened if you were not who you are and you had not taken the correct action at the correct time."

"I still cannot quite take this all in." said Jane "What you are saying is that Emily and myself will be endowed with skills that will enable us to change the past, present and future."

"Correct." replied Merlin, a smile warming his face.

"And where will these skills come from?" Asked Emily.

Merlin, opened his arms wide, the smile extending wider, his eyes brightening in the sun. His skin showed his age, craggy but soft, weathered but not beaten. "These skills will come from me. Well, I will enable these skills within you. The skills are already there, in all people but only I have the power to give you the ability to use them to their fullest. Initially, you will be given some powers but not all. That would be overwhelming for you so for now you will be given the ability to travel in time as you do now but you will be able to do this independently. And, now you have experienced the art of travelling back in time, wherever you have been, you can travel back to that location at any time you want to, from anywhere. For example, yesterday you travelled back in time to see the copper mines. So, now, from wherever you are you will be able to travel back to that location instantly. You will be able to interact with those you meet and you will be able to touch and manipulate objects. The last of these skills is the ability to see the future. Not to react with it but to see the consequences of your actions. This is something you should use but do not let it make you complacent with what you are doing in the past. You will know when something is right. There is one thing I have not told you about yet and it is very important. "

The two girls looked at each other, slightly worried.

"It involves you, Jane."

"Okay." came the cautious reply. "This is going to be interesting."

Merlin stood, collecting his staff as he did so.

"Is that a magic staff Merlin?" asked Jane, pointing at the object in his hand.

Merlin looked at Jane, then his staff. He tapped it on the ground and looked up and down its length, turned it around and tapped it on the ground again.

"I'm sorry to disappoint you Jane but it's just a staff, merely a piece of hazel that I use for walking."

"Oh, in all the books—."

"I know, I carry a powerful magic staff that projects forks of lightning and it has a special gem held in the top that glows. No, all myth, sorry but it is just a big stick, a nice stick but just a stick."

"Where does your power come from then?"

Merlin drew his arm around himself in an exaggerated arc to point to the centre of his beard covered chest. "From within. All my power comes from within. As it will with you soon. But, for you Jane, a lot has to change. It is entirely up to you as to whether want to continue with this. You can stay as you are and help the world in the way you have been or you can join us and become more powerful."

"How do you mean, join you?" she asked a concerned look creeping across her face.

"In order for this to happen you can become like us."

"What, like dead?" The concern had now grown to full blown fright as she stood up almost as if to confront Merlin.

"Not quite." came the reply as Merlin held his hand up. "You will, however become, like myself and like Emily here, immortal."

"Live forever you mean?"

"Yes, you will live forever. You will not age."

"Will I be able to cut my hair." she asked jokingly. "Emily can't, well she can but it won't grow back."

"Yes, you will be able to do that Jane, you will not be a ghost. But you will be a different being when compared to what you are now."

"What about the people that know me, they'll notice that I don't age won't they?"

"Perhaps they will but they will not think anything of it. You will still be Jane."

"So, no relationships?"

"Not in the normal sense but you will have the same sort of relationships that Emily has. With you and Jan. You will all be similar. Do you want time to think this through? It is a lot to take in and a massive step to take."

"Is it reversible?"

"It is and that can happen at any time you want it to."

"So, there's no harm and giving it a go. What do you think Emily?"

"It has its advantages and will make it easier for us to work together. It is up to you Jane; this is a big step for you."

"You would have to put up with me forever." said Jane smiling.

"Very true." said Emily. "But I'm willing to tolerate that I think. After all, you are my best friend and I really don't know what I would do without you now."

Merlin stood, watching to two girls deliberating over their dilemma. He knew that this was probably the biggest decision Jane would have to make in her entire life. After a few minutes of whispering, gesturing and smiles the girls looked back to him.

"Okay, Merlin. Let's do it." said Jane enthusiastically.

"Are you absolutely sure Jane?" he asked, leaning on his staff.

"Yes, I'm sure." came the reply.

"And you Emily. Are you sure? Because this is a big responsibility for you as well."

"Yes, Merlin. I'm sure." The girls looked at each other smiling broadly, eyes bright, anticipating their future.

"Very well." said Merlin. "This is the start of an exciting journey for you both. Not only will you be joined but you will find yourselves inseparable. Each will know of the others anguish, pleasure and pain. This journey, you take together. There is no other way. But you are the perfect people for this adventure. Everyone in my world, which will become your world, is depending on the pair of you being able to use your new skills to their best advantage."

Merlin carefully placed his staff against a tree and walked forward towards the girls. They stood close together protectively, not fully aware of what was about to happen. Trepidation and anxiety were etched on each of their faces. Merlin stopped an arm's length from them and smiled broadly. His ancient skin not giving away the years he had been on the earth. He held out both arms towards the girls, inviting them to take his hands in theirs.

"Stand apart and join hands." said Merlin. The girls separated and joined hands then, tentatively, they took Merlin's hands in theirs.

"Are you both ready?" he asked.

"Yes." came the simultaneous reply. "Ready."

Merlin closed his eyes and looked towards the sky. The girls felt a warmth flow through their bodies, much like the joining procedure. It became intense as if molten rock was forming under their skin. It flowed to all parts of their bodies and solidified. Fright was the initial feeling they experienced but almost as soon as it came, a calming coolness flooded through them as if the morning breeze was blowing over the sea enveloping them in its sweet saltiness. Their vision blurred, the trees and bushes, grass and bracken merging into a collection of greens, the sky darkened and clouds formed. The sun slipped behind a bank of slate grey cumulus and the mountains heaved. The heavy blackening sky closed in. Lightning flashed and the wind came up, a tremendous crash as thunder echoed all around them. They felt the vibration, the soul of the earth coming to life under them. All of nature's power was suddenly unleashed all around. Storms formed; rain smashed to the ground. The wind turned the sky into a tornado, twisting and turning, lifting the earth around them. They watched, terrified of the immense power being paraded around the small hill but they felt nothing, only the calm, cool liquid feeling moving through their bodies. Their hair was unruffled. Merlin's beard hung still and grey. Even his staff was unmoved by the storms swirling around them. Suddenly there was single beam of sunlight spearing through the clouds, enveloping the small group. Its brightness intensified to a blinding level. The girls squinted, closing their eyes against the light. Then, as quickly as it appeared, it vanished. The sounds of the storm quietened to a slight breeze. They opened their eyes to see everything was back to normal. The sun shining in an almost cloudless sky. The birds singing and the trees barely wafting in the breeze. They looked up at Merlin as his head turned down towards them. A look of peace adorned his face. His hands felt warm and soft, a slight tingling sensation filled the girls and moved around their bodies as if filling them with magic. Between the three of them a glowing, translucent sphere formed, rotating silently. The girls stared, transfixed as the universe formed inside the sphere. Stars and galaxies rotating within the dark blue orb which grew imperceptibly larger, quickly filling the space between them. It enveloped them, growing beyond of their perimeter. They were now standing in space, within the rapidly growing sphere as it engulfed everything around them until they were suspended in a black void, surrounded by stars and planets. Merlin smiled at them, reassuring them that all was well. The expansion slowed and stopped, then reversed, imploding, first slowly and then more rapidly. The sphere reduced in size until it, once again hovered between the three of them. It rotated slowly and decreased in size until it was the size of a pea whereupon it vanished with a slight pop and a brilliant flash of blue light.

They stood, looking at each other. Looking each other up and down, checking each had survived the experience. Merlin relaxed and their hands parted gently, a slight final tingle as they separated.

"Are you okay Jane?" asked Emily, concerned for her companion.

"I, I don't know, I think so." said Jane looking herself up and down, inspecting her hands. She brought them to her face. Brushing back her hair she could feel the sensation of tingling within her hands. "Yes, I'm okay. Are you alright?" she asked.

"I'm fine Jane. Absolutely fine. I feel complete, full and alive if you like."

"You have both done very well." said Merlin smiling at the girls in turn. "You might feel a bit strange Jane. For a while your body will need to get used to what has happened to it. It is not the same body that walked up this hill earlier. You will get used to it and become comfortable with it. Emily is now a fully formed Mage and is able to use all her skills to their fullest."

"A Mage? Are you saying I'm a Mage now Merlin?" asked Emily, a look of shock and awe on her face.

"Yes Emily. But don't think of it in the sense that you can perform magic. It is not magic. I am not a magician. I do not perform magic. Only living people consider our skills to be magic. We are just who we are. It is the nature of our being. And this answers your question, Jane. I am no magician. I am merely Merlin. I was born to a virgin many years ago and for reasons I have never fathomed, I was given these skills from birth as a living being. When I died, I became a ghost like Emily here but retained all the power I was born with. This also meant I could pass this power on to others, but only those who would benefit our cause. You can perform more than you previously could and you will learn those skills as you go, but be careful. I cannot teach you in detail how to use them. You will feel how they work, they are a part of you, like your senses, hearing and sight. This is just another sense and you will instinctively know how, when and where to use it. For you Jane, it is the same, though you have had less experience than Emily. Your learning and experimentation should take place together. Until you fully grasp how it all works, do not attempt things on your own."

"We will be careful Merlin, we promise that." Said Jane. The girls looked at one another searching in each other's eyes for any shred of concern. Non was found. They smiled in the knowledge that their relationship had just become much deeper. The reliance on each other was deafening. They felt equal, like sisters, totally bound to one another for eternity and any doubts were quickly dismissed.

"One thing you should both remember." said Merlin. He paused briefly ensuring he had their full attention. "If you feel uncomfortable at any time, in danger, lost or out of your depth, I will be there with you. If you need intervention, just call me."

"How do we call you?" asked Emily.

"Just think of me and this place, the message will get to me."

"I think it is my turn now Merlin." stated Jane

"How do you mean?" smiled Merlin, eagerly anticipating the next question.

"As you may know, I am a historian and thrive on our nation's history."

"Yes." said Merlin hesitantly.

"Well. You are in most people's eyes, a myth, a legend of our past. But, as I can see now, you exist and always have, so." She hesitated briefly. "What about King Arthur?"

"What would you like to know Jane?" asked Merlin intrigued. He collected his staff and sat, both hands gripping it and his head leant against his hands." His look was one of interest. He looked intently at Jane, expectant, as the girls too, sat down on their rock.

"Did Arthur exist?"

"Why, yes, of course he did. We was to be the greatest King this nation would ever know. He was the heart of this country and this country was his heart. He was betrayed by many including his best knight and of course his own son. When he returned to England his son had taken the throne for himself and thus a great battle ensued. The entire country was about to be put asunder but the result, as you probably know is that they both died. Ending their reign. This plunged Britain into an abyss of darkness and I too was betrayed by a woman. Her name was Nimue and she bewitched me, lured me into a cave and sealed me in with one of my own spells. There I died but with death comes freedom and so, here I am, still searching for her in order to punish her like she punished me."

"What of Arthur?" asked Jane. "And of course, Excalibur, his great sword."

"They are both right here in Wales Jane. Excalibur is down there, right below you in Llyn Dinas. Arthur is in a quiet place, on a hillside in the south west of the country. His grave is known to only a few who travel there. It is Arthur's Grave in the mountains of the blue stones. I go there myself, to sit in the solitude and to keep an eye on things. He will return if we need him."

"And Dinas Emrys, right here."

"I lived here for a while Jane. To keep an eye on the dragon."

"Dragon!" exclaimed Jane.

"Oh, you surely know the legend of the dragon?"

"But Dragon's don't exist...do they?"

"Come with me, the pair of you." Merlin stood and reached out his hands. "Hold my hand tightly, both of you." They gripped his hands and waited. The grass around them started to move, swirling in a vortex of green, lifting the few twigs and leaves to fly around their heads, tousling their hair. They began to move down as if in an elevator, down into the earth, a hole appearing and swallowing them. They fell for what seemed hundreds of feet until they came to a halt. The movement stopped and they found themselves standing on a rough beach. A glow warmed the air in a huge cave, small wavelets lapped at the pebbles as they looked across a lake. The light became brighter as Merlin moved his hands in a circle above his head, sprinkling light as it rotated.

"There, you see." said Merlin. "Across the lake to the centre, there is an island. And on that island is what Jane?"

"My goodness." said Jane totally transfixed by what she saw, or thought she saw. "Is that what I actually think it is?"

"That, my dear Jane is one of the greatest myth's this country of ours possesses. That is our beautiful dragon. His name is Tan Coch and he is one of many who live on this earth though few have been seen. He remains here asleep until he is needed. He guards Excalibur and the ladies of the lake. They hold all the power this country requires in times of need."

"This is amazing. Not only have I dreamt of there actually being dragons, I firmly believed it from a child. Something every child dreams of I suppose. But here he is, a living, breathing dragon. I am totally overwhelmed." She turned to Emily who had not said a single word since they left the surface. Her face was a picture of disbelief, mouth open and eyes wide. "Emily. Say something."

"What is there to say. We're stood here, underground, in a cave looking across the water to a dragon. Now I understand the breathing. I felt it as we came closer to the hill and now, I feel it deep inside me."

"Would you like to get closer to him?" asked Merlin quietly, his eyebrows noticeably raised.

"Can we?" asked Jane, her face lighting up in the warm glow.

"Of course, of course." replied Merlin.

"Won't we wake him?" asked Emily.

"Well, we'll see now, won't we?" boomed Merlin a rotund chuckle escaping him. "Come, follow me. You can release my hand now."

They tentatively let go of Merlin and followed him towards the water. He stood at its edge raising his hand he flattened it and moved it from his chest forwards as if to push the water away. But there in front of them a series of stepping stones appeared one by one, mapping a path to the island in the centre. Merlin stepped out, turned and waved the girls towards him. They followed, gingerly watching the water as it flowed around the stones.

"How deep is this water?" squeaked Jane.

"No-one knows." came the reply. "It is part of a massive underground labyrinth where only dragons dare go."

The girls continued, stepping carefully over the stone walkway, constantly looking down into the dark depths either side of them until they reached the island where they walked up a sandy beach towards the sleeping dragon.

"Oh my god." said Jane. "He is massive. His head is the size of a horse.

The dragon lay, curled around upon itself. Scales covered his body, with large plates running along his spine right to the tip of his tail. His head was covered in red armour. He breathed gently but they felt it right through their bodies. One foot was extended where huge black talons could be seen gripping the earth. An eye opened. The girls both jumped as they saw it.

"He's awake!" screamed Jane.

"No Jane." responded Merlin with a smile. "He is merely listening; he will not fully awaken until he is needed. He is just checking who is here."

The huge eye, now fully open, gave the impression of a deep fire within the animal's soul, burning brightly, the slit pupil as dark as the deepest black. Jane was transfixed, looking into the dragon's eye she could see her own reflection burning within. It felt comfortable and calm but did not hide the fact that this could quickly and easily change. His head gently lifted. The girls moved backwards astonished at the incredible size of this mythical beast. The dragon turned his attention to Merlin standing between Emily and Jane who were routed to the spot, staring in awe at the sheer size of his head and snout.

"Tan Coch, so nice to see you." said Merlin as he took a step forward, reaching out towards the animal. The dragon's head dipped gently towards the mage who placed his hand on the hard snout, rubbing it slowly. The dragons eye visibly softened; the eyelid dipped. The animal clearly enjoying the attention it was receiving. "All is well with the world my friend. Here are two people who are now our companions, they are now a part of us and very welcome they are too." The dragon lifted his head and breathed heavily. The vibration made the entire cavern shake, the water rippled over the underground pool.

"Merlin?" asked Jane.

"Yes, my dear?"

"This might be a silly question but, does he breathe fire?"

Merlin laughed loudly, the mirth echoed around the cave, bouncing back to them from all around, amplifying the sound. Even the dragon appeared surprised at the outburst. "I'm sorry Merlin, but did I say something funny?" asked Jane, somewhat annoyed.

"No, my dear, no." said Merlin, the laughter subsiding. "It is the biggest myth following the dragon. He does not breathe fire Jane. But he can generate a lot of heat if needed. He relies on his size and strength to achieve his aims when required. For most, just his mere presence is enough to quell any outbreak of a threat. People have the biggest respect for him, as he can appear very threatening himself, if he needs to."

"I can see that." said Jane looking along the full length of the read mass in front of them.

"It is time we left him to his slumbers I think." said Merlin, turning away from the beast and walking towards the edge of the water. The girls followed, keeping one eye on the dragon as he rested his massive head back on the ground, shifting his huge taloned foot as he did so. The scaled tail curling around to meet his snout and the fiery eye closed slowly, a last heavy breath escaping his mouth.

The girls followed Merlin as he retraced their steps back across the still, dark water to the beach on which they had arrived. The stepping stones returning to the depths as they passed. Bringing the three of them closer together he held out his hands. They took a hold and the swirling began, gently disturbing the smaller stones on the beach. As the vortex increased, they could see the dark void appearing in the roof of the cave, whereupon, they started on the journey upwards, through the very rock and soil of the hill to be deposited once more on the surface as the hole filled beneath them. Merlin released their hands. They stood totally still until the swirling breeze dissipated and the sun again bathed them in its warmth. The last disturbed leaves coming to rest on the ground around them

"You're very quiet Emily." said Jane turning towards her companion.

"Well," came the reply. "It's not every day you get to meet, not only one of the greatest mythical characters this country has ever known. But then you get to meet a huge red dragon and look right into its eye. I think that is enough to silence anyone."

"Even you." laughed Jane. "But, yes, this has been an amazing experience. My whole world has been changed dramatically today. Nothing is ever going to be the same."

Merlin smiled as he stood and watched the two while they recovered from the events of the past hours. He smiled, his inner self knowing without doubt that the choice of these two people to do only good was excellent. He was pleased with the result.

"I have a few questions, Merlin." said Jane.

"Let's sit." came the reply. "This may take a while."

The three took to their seats, facing each other. Jane picked up her rucksack and retrieved her water bottle whereupon she offered it to Merlin as an act of politeness. Merlin took the bottle and sniffed the contents.

"Hmm," he said. "Let's not drink that, it is water from the mountain but it is not as pure as it could be. Let me do something about that." He raised the bottle and upended it, emptying the contents onto the ground in front of them.

"Merlin!" exclaimed Jane. "That's my water."

"I know." came the response. "We can do better than that. Now, let me see." He brought the bottle down in front of him. One hand holding it and the other hovering above it. From nowhere, water began to flow from the very air around them. He guided the stream into the neck of the bottle. He moved his hand away and the flow stopped. He sniffed at the opening again. "There, that is so much better." He took a sip and then drank greedily from the contents. Once finished he handed the bottle back to Jane. Expecting it to be almost empty she grasped it, realising it was still full. Tentatively she sniffed the contents. The smell was clean and fresh, hard and cool. She took a sip and, like Merlin, took a long drink. She passed it on to Emily who looked into the bottle and, like Jane, saw it was still full. She too took a long drink with a smiling Jane looking intently at her with bright expectant eyes.

"That is absolutely amazing." said Jane. "What have you done?"

"The water is the purest water from deep within these mountains. The bottle will always be full. You will not be able to empty it and it will always be the fresh, clean water you have just tasted."

The girls looked at each other in amazement. "That." said Emily, "is pure magic."

"So," said Merlin. "what are these questions you have for me Jane?"

"You've just answered the first one Merlin. I was going to ask, if you are not a magician, what exactly are you."

"I don't really like that term, Jane." came the reply. "It is a word used to cover a plethora of actions that we use to change our environment. It is used to describe an illusionist as well. We are not illusionists. What we do is physical and uses the power of our environment and our mind to change our surroundings. The energy comes from the earth itself and manifests itself within us in our skills which we can control. In order to fill your bottle, I just used this energy to transfer water directly from the underground stream that feeds the lake below us, into your bottle and gave it a little bit extra so that it will always refill, wherever you are."

"So, are you a wizard or sorcerer?" asked Jane.

"There is no word that singly describes what we are Jane but if you need a word, use sorcerer as this best describes us. You two, on the other hand with your limited skills but equally, important skills, derived from your environment, may be termed Mage's as you will need to learn and hone your skills, whereas I have had my skills from birth."

"And where were you born?"

"I was born in Wales, in a small town called Caerfyddin. It wasn't called that when I was born as the town itself was named because of me. It means the place or fort of Merlin as I had a castle built for me once my skills had fully developed and I became a leader within Wales but politics took over and I was then used for advice and assistance in times of conflict." Merlin stretched and yawned long and loud. He picked up his staff and lifted himself to his feet using it to support him. He grimaced as he became upright. "I am not getting younger but I am not getting older. The joints ache now and then though." he said, rubbing his lower back. "I think it is time we all went home for a rest as I am feeling quite tired and I expect the two of you are as well. It has been an eventful day for you. Don't forget, if, at any time, you need me, you only need to ask. I can be with you in a trice."

"How do we call you?" asked Emily, needing a reminder.

"Just think of me." he said. "Just think of me and the situation you are in and I will be there to help. Never fear, there is no situation you will find yourselves in where I cannot assist if needed."

"Thank you." said Jane. "That is so reassuring but I hope the situation will not arise. I don't envisage us getting ourselves into situations we cannot manage ourselves."

"You never know." said Merlin wagging his finger. "You never know. Now, off you go. Finish your walk and enjoy your lives. Be careful and beware. Always beware. There are bad things in this world and bad people. You will go forwards now to put right the wrongs that have been inflicted on us all. As I said, you will know when something needs to be put right. It will come to you. You have been placed in the universe to do this and remember; you are not alone."

"Merlin?" asked Jane.

"Yes." came the reply as Merlin looked somewhat impatiently at Jane.

"One other thing. Were we brought here by you. I mean, I know I have always wanted to come here. I have always been fascinated by historic places. Especially if they involve some sort of mystery or myth or just a plain corroborated act. But we were coming for a walk to a place which is shrouded in mystery and, of course, the myth of yourself and here you are." Jane spread her hands in front of herself presenting them to Merlin. "This is no coincidence. I think we were brought here. But this must have started years ago, way back when I was studying. These events popped into my head. At the time I thought them merely casual interest but I'm not so sure now."

"What you have experienced is quite true." said Merlin, leaning on his staff. "For both of you. It is no coincidence that you are here in front of me. I would not say that you were brought here. More an act of guidance from the ether, the force that knits this universe together. Some people term it as fate, almost as if it happens for a reason and to be truthful, it does happen for a reason but it is a perfectly natural function of the universe we live in. Only a few of us have this sense and in some it is very powerful. I am an example of that power. I was brought into my world for a reason. Mainly to guide King Arthur through his life but, unfortunately control was taken away from me and the end was tragic, but that is another story. The two of you will be experiencing new adventures and challenges and these are part of your lives. They are already planned by the force for the benefit of others and, like I said, to put some features of history right. You cannot predict these challenges, nor can I but I know that you are here to do good. This you have already experienced and in both instances, you did what was right. Does that answer your last question?" There was an emphasis on the word 'last' and Merlin's eyebrows lowered perceptibly, a slight frown appearing.

Jane looked at Emily who for some reason was still very quiet, a questioning expression on her face.

"I understand Merlin." said Emily. "I have been thinking all through the events of today and, indeed the past. Everything makes sense now. Was that why I died?"

"That." said Merlin. "Is a very difficult question to answer and it would sound quite brutal if the answer was yes. But this force works in mysterious ways. Some events in history cannot be explained easily and sometimes there is a tragic loss of life. Examples of this are the great wars that have taken place through history. Totally unnecessary and terribly sad but in some instances the wars that have taken place prevented far, far worse. One of your recent wars resulted in the deaths of millions but, had it not taken place the world as you know it now would not exist. It would have been totally destroyed by the hideous developments that took place later on. Man has always been destined to destroy himself but we have to manage it in a way that protects this planet. It has a future that must be protected. And you two are now part of the force that does this. So, go now and start your work. Most of all, enjoy yourselves, have fun and never be parted. We are relying on the two of you as a single entity to do the work you are destined for. I will go now and rest. Goodbye Jane, goodbye Emily. And just remember this. Fate has a miraculous habit of putting the right people in the right place, precisely at the time they need to be there. You are two of those people"

"Goodbye." came the simultaneous reply from a pair of stunned girls.

Merlin faded as he placed his staff directly in front of himself and gripped it with both hands. His body became more transparent until, with a small spark he vanished altogether, leaving nothing but a few leaves wafting around on the ground where they settled quietly. No trace remaining of his existence. The girls stood totally still, the silence all around broken only by the gentle whispering of the breeze through the oak trees and the chatter of the birds.

"What have we done Emily?"

"We won't know. But it looks like we are going to have very different lives from now on."

Suddenly a face appeared in front of them. Just a face, not quite transparent but not quite solid. Merlin.

"One thing." came his booming voice. "Do not think too deeply about your new life, just do the things you want to do."

His face disappeared leaving them looking at each other quite shocked.

"I'm hungry Jane, suddenly very, very hungry."

They sat back down on their rock, finishing the lunch that had been interrupted. They sat in silence as the events of the day sank in. Both thinking about what their lives would bring.

"Do you know what?" asked Jane, holding her sandwich in her lap as she looked up at the blue sky.

"Er, what?" came the reply as Emily was about to take a bite.

"I think we are going to have a lot of fun Emily. This is right up our street. I mean, look, I own Chapwell, I am a historian, you are a ghost, we have powers that will allow us to travel back in time, we enjoy each other's company, what could go wrong?"

"Nothing, I hope." said Emily, taking a huge bite from her cheese sandwich.

"No, neither do I but what a future we have, it's going to be so intriguing. Not knowing when we will be doing something that needs us to put history right. It's like a dream come true."

"Are you going to eat that sandwich Jane? If not hand it over, I'll sort it out for you."

"No. You are such a pig sometimes Emily."

They sat, quiet now, enjoying their lunch. The sun streaming down through the trees, bathing them in warmth and light. The insects buzzed around them, much like in the garden at Chapwell. The background sounds filling the aromatic air with pure pleasure.

"It's weird you know."

"What?" enquired Emily.

"Well, here we are sitting on this rock. Both knowing that underneath us is a huge red dragon, sleeping. Quite surreal really."

"Well." said Emily with a smile. "Check out our new life!"

They both laughed, looking at each other. As the laughter subsided their look became more intense. They could see inside each other, feel the others senses. They both understood how close they had become. It was more than that, they had an overlap now. They were inseparable and they both realised it in the same instant, whereupon they embraced tightly, hanging on, feeling the mutual warmth and love passing between them. Their senses becoming joined. As they parted slowly, Emily could see the tears that had fallen down Jane's cheeks, her eyes reddening. Emily smiled at her companion, retrieved a hanky from her pocket and began gently wiping away the tears from Jane's face.

"It does feel special Jane. Very special. I am looking forward to our future."

They collected their belongings, repacking the rucksacks and checking the ground around them, looking for anything that they had left behind but also looking further around them, still not quite believing what they had experienced. They descended the hill and walked on back to the cottage. Sitting at the dining table looking out across the valley, a cup of tea steaming in front of each of them and a cake between them restored a more normal life. The late afternoon was quiet, the two of them still trying to come to terms with their new lives. Jane, particularly wondering how she was going to learn how to use her new powers. But she was confident that Emily would guide her and there was always Merlin if the need arose.

They spent the rest of their holiday wandering the mountains, enjoying food in the local hostelries and generally relaxing. All too soon, it was time to return to Chapwell. Neither of them found this saddening. In fact, they were secretly looking forward to it. New adventures awaited them; they were sure.

Chapter Eighteen

Dad

The front door opened and Jane burst in.

"Hello, hello you two, we're home." she shouted, her voice echoing around the oak panelled hallway.

Sarah came from the lounge, a huge smile of her face. Jan followed just behind. The pair welcoming the traveller's home.

"How was it?" Asked Sarah. "Have you had a good time?"

"Fantastic." said Jane. "Amazing." said Emily as they placed their bags on the stone floor, Jane closing the door.

"I'll put the kettle on." said Sarah as she turned towards the kitchen. "You can tell us all about it over tea and cake. Oh, and I have some news for you Jane."

"What's that?"

"Tea first." said Sarah as she disappeared into the kitchen.

"Are you okay Jan?" asked Emily.

"I'm fine." came the reply. "We've had a lovely week here, relaxing, walking and just getting to know each other more. We get along really well. Come on, let's have tea. Sarah even made a cake from your recipe. It's not bad either."

They settled at the great table in the kitchen. Tea and cake served. Emily shoved a large chunk into her mouth. A look of surprise sprang upon her face. She was just about to open her mouth but noticing the disapproving look from Jane she continued chewing quietly.

"I can't wait anymore." said Sarah excitedly.

"What?" asked Jane.

"Oh Jane, last night. Well, yesterday evening, actually, we had a phone call. It was your dad. He thought I was you to start with but I put him right and told him you were on holiday and we were just looking after the house for you."

"What did he say?" asked Jane, shocked and slightly frightened.

"Oh, don't worry Jane, he was absolutely fine. He sounds really nice and said he was so pleased about what had happened when you got the DNA result. He left his number and asked if you would give him a call. Oh, and he said call him this evening, after six as he'll be home then."

Jane placed her unfinished cake back on her plate, took a sip of her tea and placed the mug back on the table. "This has been such a week and this just tops it off. It couldn't have gone any better." she said, looking around the table at each of her companions.

"This cake's good Sarah, really good. Top marks." said Emily collecting the crumbs on her plate. "I don't want to appear greedy but I'm going to have another piece of that."

The other three just looked at her, amazed.

"What?" said Emily, looking up at the staring faces, seemingly oblivious to what Jane had just learned."

"Good grief." said Jane, shaking her head. "You are impossible."

The group sat in the kitchen and later in the garden. Sarah and Jan sharing the experiences of the past week. They described their quiet time walking in the locality and tending the garden and basically enjoying each other's company.

"I think we have grown closer this past week you know." said Sarah addressing her friends. We found that we have a lot in common. Neither of us has family that we can consider close. As you all know, I am an only child and my parents both died a few years ago. So having you three is a blessing for me and Jan has become a very close friend. I have something to look forward to now rather than the bland and sometimes lonely life I had been living before I met Jane. Things have changed so much over the last couple of years and I don't want that to end. I think we all get on rather well here and I enjoy it."

Jan smiled at his companion. Sarah smiled back. Both Emily and Jane could detect something a little stronger than friendship, more like the feelings they have between themselves and from that they knew the link between the two would only get stronger. Jane sat in the sun listening to the conversation and wondering to herself if this was one of those 'coincidences' Merlin spoke of, or one of those fateful occurrences that mould the world's future. Is it possible that her first encounter with Sarah all that time ago in the library was planned. It couldn't be though could it, she thought. It would be too obvious but, then Merlin did say that the events of the world all happen for a reason and this must just be one of them.

"Jane!" came a loud shout from Emily.

"Sorry, what?" asked Jane as she came back from her thoughts.

"I've been calling you for ages."

"I'm sorry Emily. What's the matter."

"Well, nothing really. You just seemed to be miles away."

"I suppose I was, just thinking about all the things that have happened to the four of us."

"I know what you are thinking Jane, probably not a good idea to think too deeply about it, like Merlin said."

"Merlin!" exclaimed Sarah. "What is that all about then?"

"Ah, well, I think we had better tell you about our week. You just wait till we get to the dragon."

"Dragon?" queried Sarah.

"Let us explain." said Jane.

Sarah and Jan sat totally transfixed as Jane and Emily took the two of them step by step through their experience during their holiday, in every red and scaly detail.

"I'm stunned." said Sarah. "I bet that was absolutely amazing. It's certainly changed my mind about myths and legends. We can't be sure of anything we see or hear anymore can we."

"Ah, but." said Emily. "We can now find out exactly what has happened in history, regardless of what we now think. And, we now have the capability of changing things."

"Hang on." said Sarah, a concerned look on her face. "Isn't that a bit dangerous? I mean changing the past can have some serious effects on history or could wipe it out altogether. Imagine if you changed something that meant you weren't born."

"That's just it." interrupted Jane. "All that is within our control. We can't change much and we have the capability of being able to see the effects of our actions. From what Merlin said, we will know how and when to change things, or intervene."

"I still think it's a bit dodgy." said Sarah.

"I must admit." said Emily. "I'm still a bit apprehensive about it but Merlin reassured us. We'll just have to wait and see what happens."

"What are you going to do first?" asked Jan.

"We don't know, Jan." said Jane, biting her lip. "Apparently, we will know what to do and when to do it. We're to continue with our lives exactly as they are. I don't think these things are pre-planned, they will just be a result of circumstance or, as it was explained to us, fate. Anyway, enough of this. Who's ready for lunch? And I'm not asking you Emily, you're always ready for food."

They giggled as they returned to the house.

Later, before the evening meal, Jane sat in the lounge with the phone in her hand. It was just past six o'clock and she was in a state. In the next few minutes, she was going to talk to her father.

She tentatively dialled the number. Only a few rings were heard before it was picked up. Perhaps a sign that her father was looking forward to the call. She imagined him pacing the room waiting for the call, or at least hoping that would be the situation at the other end.

"Hello." came a quiet voice.

"Hello, er dad." replied Jane.

"Hello Jane. How are you?"

"I'm fine, how are you?"

"Fine thank you."

Neither knew what to say. For Jane, she had waited her entire life for the moment when she would talk to her real father. But here she was, totally speechless. Unusual in itself but the need to speak was overwhelming.

"You don't mind me calling you Dad, do you?"

"Of course not Jane, I am your father, you've proved that and totally deserve to call me father, or Dad, or whatever you like. If you feel more comfortable with it you can call me Mark if you want to. I don't mind. All I care about is the fact that I have a daughter. A daughter I never knew I had. A daughter born from a disaster in my life and all I can say is that I am sorry."

"Oh, don't be sorry Dad. I'm so, so glad that I now know who my father is. Can we be like me and Mum? We agreed that the past is gone, done with, things have been put right and we can look forward to the future. A future without blame."

"I don't see why not." came the reply.

"Well, that's good, as I think that would be the best way to go. Yes, we need to understand the past but I don't think it would be constructive for us to dwell too much on it. Suffice it to say that the cause of the problem has gone."

"How do you mean?" asked Mark

"David Chapwell. He's dead, committed suicide. After all his offending it caught up with him so the threat to all of us has now gone."

"Oh." came the slightly shocked response. "Look, Jane, how about you come down to London to see me. You can stay here or in a hotel it you prefer. We could spend some time together, catch up on things. After all, it's twenty-eight years that have disappeared."

There was a silence between them

"Er, yes, yes." said Jane suddenly. That would be great. Can I bring my friend?"

"That would be fine. Do they have a name?"

"Emily, she's called Emily and she is a Chapwell. We'll stay in a hotel if that's okay, we can make a small holiday out of it. I have some stuff I can do in London. I'm a historian now and London is full of history so we can do some work while we're there."

"That would be fine Jane. Look, let me give you my email address so we can keep in touch. I'll work out when I have a good bit of spare time from work and we'll arrange a day, or few days. Or text me if you like, you've got my mobile number."

They exchanged contact details and the conversation came to an end. Jane gently placed the handset back in its cradle and just looked at it for a moment. A warm feeling engulfed her. She felt something inside that she had not experienced before. It was almost as if her life had a specific design and this latest event had straightened a kink in it. It felt right. Perhaps this was what Merlin was on about. She was here to do a job, without knowing what that job actually was but here was an example of the work being done. She heard a creak. The door moved slightly, the light from the hallway visible through the gap.

"Come in Emily." she said. "I know you're there. It's no good trying to sneak, I can feel you stronger than ever now."

The door opened fully and Emily walked straight in and flopped onto the sofa next to Jane. She sat back heavily and just looked at her companion. The expression needing no words.

"It was fine Emily," said Jane looking into Emily's eyes. "he sounded really nice. He's invited me down to see him."

Emily frowned slightly.

"Oh, don't worry, you're coming too. We'll stay in a hotel somewhere near where he lives. But I had a thought. It just popped into my head while I was talking to him. We can spend a few days down there and explore a bit if you like. It would be fun."

"Have you told him about me?" asked Emily.

"I told him you were my friend and I told him you were a Chapwell so your visibility would be useful again. Would that be, okay?"

"Yes, that'd be fine. I've never been to London before. What are we going to do there? I mean, apart from seeing your dad?"

"I had not made any plans. I mean, I haven't had time but I get this feeling that I am going to know exactly what we will be doing down there. I have this sense that a plan is forming within me. I don't know about you Emily, but, since the encounter with Merlin and what he did for me, I do get the impression that, like he said, I, and, indeed you, are here for a reason. I have a different outlook on life now. There is so much more to it. I have an idea that my pursuit of history was not by chance. There was a reason as to why I did all that studying. I feel it now, it's inside me."

"That puts my mind at rest Jane." said Emily "I thought it was just me. I feel so different now. I am not just a ghost anymore. I am a ghost with a mission. There are things that need putting right and we are here to do it. For example, that business with David Chapwell. Although, at the time I knew exactly what to do and how to do it. Now I feel that it was a correction, putting things right. How they should be. It's almost like there had been an error in the ether and David, for whatever reason should not have existed. We merely put that right. It was painful, yes, but then, I think a lot of things may need a bit of pain in order to put them in perspective."

They sat in silence, surreptitiously glancing at each other. Both knowing that they were thinking the same thing. They had a position in the universe, a place in time and space that was meaningful. They were where they were for a reason. They were no longer on some random path through life. They had guidance and meaning. Neither knew what these things meant for them but they knew they could rely in each other and the sense they both had that history can be put right.

"Come on Jane, let's have dinner. Your heads going to explode in a minute. Sarahs cooking and it smells delicious."

"I was wondering what that was." said Jane as she got up from the sofa, taking a quick look at the phone she left the room, sensing that her life had taken yet another turn.

At dinner they all discussed what had happened. How it might affect them, but they concluded that life would continue for Chapwell exactly as it had.

"I'll need to get off in the morning." said Sarah." I'm back at work in the afternoon."

"I've been thinking about that Sarah. Particularly while we were away in North Wales. How would it be if you lived here with us?"

"Wow." exclaimed Sarah. "That's a big step."

"Well, yes, I know but think about it. You are not far from work; you have been living here for the last week and I know how you and Jan get along. It sort of makes sense really. Have a think about it anyway."

"What would you do with the flat?"

"I'd probably sell it. Whatever, have a think about it Sarah. You know you are welcome here. How about you Jan, would that suit you?"

"It would suit me very well." came the reply. "I love it when Sarah is here. We get on well together and enjoy each other's company. I'm learning more about how to be a ghost and control my skills better."

"Where would I sleep?" asked Sarah.

"There's the spare room." said Jane. "Or, if you prefer, we can have another room set up in the attic. That wouldn't be difficult. Like I say, have a think about it and we'll sort out the details later but the spare room is not in use at the moment."

The next day, after Sarah had returned to her flat, Jane finalised the London visit to her father. A hotel was booked for herself and Emily. Now they just had to wait. During that time, they worked in the garden, keeping it in its perfect condition, the state of sanctuary whenever it was needed. It also provided them with a considerable amount of food. They were working on the vegetable patch when a thought came to Jane. Very suddenly and unplanned. As if it were an infant thought floating in the air until it entered Jane's head and popped open.

"That's weird." she said.

"What is?" asked Emily.

"Well, when we go down to London, I know what we are going to do. Or, at least, I know one of the things we can do while we're there."

"And what might that be?"

"You know how much I love the Tudor period in England."

"Yes."

"I think, or, this thought has just come to me but we should go to the Tower of London. I suddenly have this compulsion to go there.

We could explore the present building and even go back in time to see some things that happened there. My first thing to do there would be to see Anne Boleyn when she was incarcerated."

"You don't want to watch her being executed do you?" asked Emily, stabbing her trowel into the soil, a look of total disgust on her face.

"No, no. That would not be polite nor even pleasant. I certainly don't want to see that. I just want to see what she was like while she was imprisoned. There is a lot of speculation regarding her last days. Most people think she was dumped in some damp dungeon. Whereas in reality she was held in the very same apartments she enjoyed before she was convicted. There is a large part of the Tower of London that has disappeared. The Queens apartments, the great hall and various other buildings have been lost over time. But, with our skills, we can go back in time to the days before her execution. I just want to see her. There are also theories about her mental state at the time. Some say she was in a state of peace and coherence when she went to the scaffold. I'm curious to know what was going through her head in those last days. I've read so much about her life, how she got to where she got and then, how, in just a few weeks she went from being a queen, loved by the populace to convicted adulterer and traitor. She went through a most terrible experience, all because she couldn't bear a son and heir for her husband. It is a most fascinating story and, unfortunately, so much of her existence was destroyed and wiped out once Henry had got rid of her." Jane knelt there just looking up at the sky, her fork held in her hands, resting on her lap.

Emily remained silent while she listened. She, too, looked up at the sky, wondering whether this was one of those occasions they had been told about by Merlin. A point in history where a wrong needed to be put right. "That should be interesting Jane." Came a quiet and unconvincing response.

"Do you mean that Emily? It doesn't sound like it."

"Yes, yes, I do, I'm just thinking, that's all. Do you think this is one of those 'tasks' we have to carry out?"

"I don't know." replied Jane. "It could be, but we won't know until something is presented to us. "Let's not think about that. Let's just go to London, meet my dad and have some fun while we are there."

Chapter Nineteen

London

Not wanting to drive to the capital, they took the train and quite enjoyed the journey through the countryside. Watching it transform into the urban sprawl where, from the dirt-streaked window, they could see things that were not visible from the roads and pavements. Back gardens, the hidden structures, fences and walls, resplendent with the ubiquitous graffiti, made the journey intriguing. A small part of the world passing by but full of things happening, being what they are at that specific time, never to be seen again. Buildings flashed past, keeping their interior secrets. The odd glimpse of a person carrying out their normal day, oblivious to the two girls witnessing a snapshot of their lives. Lives they knew nothing of but they saw that one small part. In a flash, it was gone. On to the next view. The back of a vehicle repair shop where cars were stored, one being washed, the spray of the power washer building small rainbows as it scattered light through the drops of water as they flew into the air. Litter tumbling along the railway as the air is disturbed by the passing of a train on the opposite track. The carriage slowed and the smooth ride turned into a clunking, shaking experience as the train approached the station, passing over points, changing direction, nudging side to side in an attempt to reach the correct platform. A squeal and a jolt and the train came to a halt. The two girls stood up and reached up for their cases stored overhead. The noise from the city assaulted them as soon as they stepped onto the platform. Noticeably warmer and there was a smell. A smell of heat and pollution, oil and paper. Even Emily's lavender was overwhelmed. The platform turned into a racetrack, everyone rushing for the exit as they stood looking around them. As it quietened, they started on the next part of their journey, to find the hotel they were to stay in.

"It's not far." said Jane, retrieving her phone from her pocket. Quickly scrolling and clicking she was presented with a route to the hotel. Giving her various options as to how to get there, she chose to walk, as it was only ten minutes away and it would give them a chance to become familiar with their surroundings.

Their room, shared, gave them a view across the city. Jane deliberately chose a top floor room for the privilege of seeing the place they were visiting.

"This is not what I was expecting Jane." said Emily.

"In what way?"

"It's so much bigger, noisier and smellier than I ever thought. I mean, I knew it might be noisy but this is crazy." Emily opened the window, put her head out into the city air and was immediately assaulted directly by all the city could offer. Her senses hammered by everything going on. "Does it ever go quiet?" she asked.

"No." came the reply. "On every occasion I have been here whilst studying and working I have never known it to be quiet. It's a twenty-four-hour place Emily. Not like at Chapwell where everything stops for tea."

"But it means we can't have the window open."

"No, not a good idea. It's noisy, smelly and too warm to have it open. The room is quiet, air conditioned and quite fragrant with your lavender as well."

Reluctantly but happily excluding the smells, Emily closed the window, not really liking what was outside.

"I've never been to a big city before Jane, let alone London. It might be magnificent but I don't think a life here would suit me. I like the outdoors far too much."

"But it's nice to visit, don't you think?" asked Jane, unzipping her bag, removing her night clothes, e-book reader and alarm clock.

Emily turned away from the now closed window, welcoming the relative silence. She then did what all people, except Jane, did, when in a hotel room. She walked over and flopped onto her bed, hands behind her head, she looked across at Jane.

"I suppose you've never been in a hotel before either?" her friend asked.

"I have." said Emily. "Well, not so much a hotel, more a guest house down on the coast. Father took us there when we were children for a holiday. It was lovely. We went on the train then. It was not like the train we came here on though. It was pulled by a great steam engine, chuffing smoke and smuts into the air. We all loved the beach and the promenade. A cone of chips sat on a bench. It was delightful. But that was when there were three of us as children. Circumstances changed all that and we never went to the beach again and then, of course tragedy struck the family and that was that. Mother and Father didn't do holidays again. But, then, living at Chapwell is always like a holiday. I never get bored with it."

"I'm going to have a shower." said Jane. "I feel grimy all ready and we've only been here a while. Imagine living here all the time."

"I'll have a read and jump in after you." said Emily. "Then again, I might just have soak in a bath. Don't do that very often these days."

They both relaxed in anticipation of the evening ahead. They planned to take a walk in the park opposite the hotel and then meet Mark for an evening dinner at a restaurant around the corner. The park was lovely. Well-tended flower beds and nurtured trees, tidy paths and grass areas made it a very pleasurable and relaxing experience. A number of people out in the afternoon, walking, running or just sitting, enjoying the afternoon sun. Even the sound of the city seemed diminished in this small oasis.

Later, they walked into the restaurant and stood at the reception, waiting to be seen. On introducing themselves they were guided to a table. An empty table, where they sat down and gave the waitress a drinks order.

"Oh." said Jane. "Are we early or is my dad late?"

"I think you're being a bit harsh Jane; we are a bit early. Goodness, give the man a chance."

Within minutes a dark-haired man came to the table and looked at the pair of them. Jane stood, quickly followed by Emily. The man looked at both of them in turn. Appearing confused, his eyebrows knitted and his hand went to his chin. He, again looked at each of them in turn.

Finally, he said. "I give up. I'm sorry but I really cannot tell who is who here. You look so alike."

"Oh, sorry Dad." said Jane. Marks attention immediately concentrated on the face where the voice came from.

"Jane. Wow. I don't know what to say. Oh, and this must be Emily then." he said pointing at Jane's companion."

"That's me." said Emily.

They stood, embarrassingly staring at each other for what seemed like ages.

"Come on, let's sit down." said Jane breaking the silence.

They sat. Mark kept looking from one girl to the other, trying to understand how they could be so alike.

"This is weird." he said, still looking from one to the other. "You really are so alike." he repeated. "It's quite surreal."

"Everyone says that Dad. But then we do look a bit similar, I guess. We are about the same age and have a lot in common."

"Are you, like, a couple?" asked Mark, tentatively.

"No, no. Mum asked the same thing. No, we're just the very best of friends and companions. We do live together. At Chapwell I mean. Emily has her space and I have mine, though we spend the majority of our time together. We have both had our problems in the past but we put them all behind us and just concentrate on the future."

The two girls looked at each other and Mark could instantly see the strength of the bond between them. He wasn't aware of how much the last statement was ambiguous which was reflected in the knowing look they shared. The waitress came over to them and presented a menu to each. Mark ordered himself a drink absently, still overwhelmed by the two people he was with. It was almost intimidating. The friendship that was glowing within each of them was intense. He could tell that whatever their past had been filled with, they had both come through it unscathed and had developed an enviable relationship. They ordered food and shared their lives from the time Mark left Jane's mother.

"You are incredibly lucky Jane. Inheriting Chapwell, I mean. That is everyone's dream I suppose. But, from what you and Emily have told me, it was thoroughly deserved. It could not be in better hands. What, with your job and interests, I'm sure Chapwell will be looked after. I do remember Chapwell. I did go there once or twice when I was a boy. Always liked that house. It had something about it. It's difficult to describe but it had something."

"Home." said the two girls in unison. They sniggered.

"Yes." said Mark. "Home. That describes it perfectly. It looks like a home and it's been home to the Chapwell's all along. So, Emily, tell me. Why is it that you are a Chapwell, live at Chapwell but don't own it."

Both girls suddenly looked uncomfortable. There were always going to be awkward questions but this one was a good one.

"I am a Chapwell." said Emily, stammering slightly as she tried to find a convincing answer."

"If it upsets you Emily, I'm sorry for asking. We can leave it if you prefer." Said Mark, slightly embarrassed.

"No, it's okay." said Emily. "It's quite simple really. I descend from a different branch of the Chapwell family." she lied. "I came back to visit now and then, especially when John was ill and when Beryl was on her own. We got on well and helped each other. Jane and I just got to know each other and things went from there. I'm not jealous, if that's what you think."

"Oh, no, no." said Mark putting up his hands. "I was just curious, that's all."

"Emily is as much a part of Chapwell as its chimneys are." said Jane. "I might own it, well, I think of myself more as a custodian. I look after Chapwell and have been given the resources to do so. But it is Chapwell and should always have a Chapwell living there. I don't think it's anything either of us really thought about to be honest."

"Never entered my head." said Emily, smiling. "This pasta is to die for." she said, shoving another forkful in her mouth.

"Oh, by the way Dad. Emily is a food disposal unit. She'll eat anything and any quantity."

"Well, it doesn't show." said Mark, admiring Emily's slim figure. "That's a mystery though isn't it. I guess you don't eat as much as she does—"

"Certainly don't." Interrupted Jane sharply.

"And yet you both look the same." said Mark "I still can't get over that. How alike you are, almost as if you were sisters. But you can't be can you?"

"Like I said." replied Jane. "We do have an awful lot in common. Which is probably why we get on so well." They looked at each other, the secret obvious in their eyes. "You know a lot about us now Dad, what about you? Do you live near, what do you do now?"

"Yes, I live near here. I live alone. I didn't marry again. To be honest, two things. I've never met anyone like your Mum and I'm still totally devoted to my job, so the two things don't work together so I leave it like that. I have friends and now you two. I don't need anything else I don't think. I still work in the energy industry. More in a consultancy role now. My experience over the years has benefitted me and I like what I do. I get to travel a lot, all over the world as a consultant and can pursue my hobbies whenever I like."

"Ooh, and what does that entail?" asked Emily, interested.

"Well, I play golf with friends but I really enjoy paragliding and parachuting, skydiving in fact. I can't get enough of the adrenalin. My next move is to a wingsuit. Now that really does look exciting."

"Isn't it a bit dangerous though?" asked Jane.

"Yes, I guess it is but then anything is dangerous if you don't do it correctly and respect your kit and surroundings. I mean, you say you go walking a lot, the pair of you. We know that's dangerous.

Mountains are dangerous and need to be respected so it's the same thing really."

"I suppose it is if you put it like that."

The Dessert menu appeared, though after the large main course they had, Emily was the only one to partake.

The conversations they had were entertaining and casual. The three of them felt comfortable together and learned a lot about their past lives. Jane felt very happy that she had found her father and not only that, she discovered that he was a father she could respect and admire. She sat back watching and listening to Mark and Emily conversing and it made her smile. She quietly thought about her life up until now and how it had changed. From a young girl with only a mother to comfort her, to her relationship with Beryl and John, whom, she didn't doubt had contributed to her character in an immeasurable way. Her love of history and pursuit of her degree in history, resulting in her self-employment as a freelance historian. The biggest changes she experienced were the recent ones. Particularly her relationship with Emily. Just thinking about it made her smile, a warmth running through her veins, a soft comfort enveloping her. Emily meant the world to her and she felt it was reciprocated. They were as close to sisters as you could get. In fact, far closer if the joining was taken into consideration. They were permanently connected. They could sense each other's feelings. They knew when there was a problem with the other. Jane could not help noticing a gentle smile creeping across Emily's face as she was thinking this. She knew Emily could feel the comfort Jane was experiencing just by thinking about her companion. Now she had both renewed her relationship with her mother and had succeeded in identifying and meeting her father. Her life, as far as relationships were concerned was complete. Each of these relationships could develop now and she would do her very best to ensure they endured. She awoke from her thoughts noticing both Mark and Emily staring at her.

"What?" she asked.

"Where were you?" asked Mark

"Just thinking." She replied, a broad smile brightening her face. "Just thinking about my life really and how it has changed." She leant forwards resting her elbows on the table. Mark and Emily awaiting the explanation. "I feel so lucky now. I was just thinking that my life was complete. I have so many lovely people around me now, it makes me feel quite smug in a way."

Mark and Emily were both smiling. Mark because he had discovered he had a daughter. Not only that but she was clever and beautiful and for various reasons, highly successful. Emily purely because she could sense Jane's euphoria.

All too soon they were the only people left in the restaurant. All around them was quiet and waiters and waitresses were clearing tables and tidying the detritus of the evening.

"Ah." said Mark. "It looks as if we should be leaving. I'll get the bill. And before anyone says anything I am paying for this because it has been a great evening and you two deserve it for being such lovely people."

As they collected themselves and stood, it was obvious that a future was to be planned for the three of them. Ensuring that they had each other's email addresses and mobile numbers they made to leave.

"Don't you have a mobile Emily?" asked Mark.

"No, I haven't." said Emily. Aware of yet another innocuous but nevertheless uncomfortable question. "Mine died on me so I need to get a new one. I'll sort it out when we get home."

"Well." said Mark. "As soon as you get it sorted, give me your number. Always best to have two points of contact."

He turned to Jane and smiled.

"My daughter." He said simply. "My very own daughter. Well, I'd like to think of you as both daughters. You could easily be, you certainly look like it. He put his hands on Jane's shoulders. "Would a hug be out of place Jane?"

Jane's smile got bigger. "No, of course not 'Dad'." she emphasised the word 'Dad' as she pulled him closer. The embrace appeared slightly uncomfortable but then it was not surprising as they had only just met. Emily politely looked out of the window.

"How about my 'other' daughter?" asked Mark, releasing Jane and looking at Emily who turned towards him, her arms unfolded, welcoming his suggestion. The embrace was tentative as was appropriate for the occasion, but meaningful nonetheless.

"I would invite you back to my apartment" said Mark "but I don't feel it would be appropriate at this time and, to be honest I really need to rest tonight. I've had a busy few days and I've got an early flight in the morning. I hope you don't mind."

"No, of course not." replied Jane. "We have the rest of our lives to get to know each other. We have email, texts and we could even try video calls. You'll have to come to Chapwell for a visit. I think you would like that."

"Yes, definitely." he said. "Look, I need to get going, it's a lot later than I thought, are you two okay getting back to your hotel?"

"We'll be fine." said Emily knowingly. "It's only just around the corner, won't take a minute."

"Okay, just be careful though, yeah?" said Mark as he turned to leave. "we'll see each other again soon and it's been a delight to meet you both. I'm made up." His smile was obvious and the warmth it radiated instilled a feeling of sincerity. The girls both felt the comfort as he walked from the room.

Jane and Emily collected their jackets and put them on. Walking out of the restaurant Emily asked. "What do you think?"

"You know very well what I think." replied Jane. "And I know what you think as well." she said smiling surreptitiously at Emily. Now, I don't know whether this is one of my new skills but I constantly got this feeling or sense and I can only explain it as three words. Metal, Paper and sky. Is that the same thing that you feel when you meet people?"

"That is exactly it, Jane. I sensed exactly the same but it may be because we are so intricately connected now, you might be getting my sense as well. Like we are one."

"There is one thing that has been niggling at me for a while Emily."

"And what might that be then." came the reply.

"Well, you were born in what, 1876 or thereabouts, you died in 1903. So how do you know so much about modern technology. I mean, you certainly don't appear, on the surface as a nineteenth century woman, do you?"

"Well, that's a simple question to answer. I have been in this world, both alive and dead for well over one hundred years. I haven't had my eyes and ears shut in all that time, have I? I have learnt so much over those years. I have seen so much and experienced so much. Far more than anyone living. And that is, without a doubt, fact."

"Hmm." said Jane, putting her arm through Emily's, "I'd never thought of it like that but, I can see the logic."

They walked slowly back to the hotel. Both going over the evening. Neither sensing anything wrong. Quite the opposite really. They both felt happy that things had gone well and Jane had a father. They had a quiet drink in the hotel bar, retiring to their room both contented, which induced a deep sleep for the pair of them.

The morning arrived with the drone of the early traffic outside. No birds singing here. The awakening was a bit rude; car horns and emergency sirens were their alarm clock. Jane tried to ignore it and take advantage of time to attempt a further snooze but it was in vain, the noise won so she got up to go for a shower. She did note how, in the other bed, Emily was snoring quite tenderly, her hair flowing over the pillow hiding her face, her breath moving the dark waves imperceptibly. Jane smiled and walked into the bathroom. Emily was still fast asleep when she returned. She went over to her bed and gently stroked her hair, adjusting it carefully to reveal the face she now knew so well. Unblemished and fresh. She shook Emily tenderly but with no evidence of movement she shook a little harder. Nothing. She had to resort to a severe shaking and calling her name. Eventually an eye opened, slowly. The realisation moved across her face and she smiled. Turning to face Jane, Emily stretched the full length of the bed and yawned massively.

"Any biscuits over there?" she asked. "I'm hungry, put the kettle on."

"And what did your last slave die of?"

"Heh!" came the reply. "She's not dead yet." A giggle escaped her and she sat up. "Go on, put the kettle on and I'll have a shower. Then we can go and have a full English."

"Good grief." said Jane. "Had I only known what I was letting myself in for when I first saw you, I might have just gone back to sleep."

"You love it." said Emily. "Anyway, I'd have pestered you until you gave in." She jumped out of bed and made her way to the bathroom.

Jane put the kettle on and got dressed, listening to the singing from the bathroom. She had never thought about it before but Emily could sing very well. She had heard her in the past. On the odd occasion in the garden and sometimes in the bathroom. She also sang when she was cooking and it made Jane smile.

They sat and drank their tea. Emily consumed all the complimentary biscuits and then looked for more.

"Come on." said Jane. "I'll put you out of your misery. Let's go and have breakfast."

Jane sat and watched her companion eat a massive breakfast. Large enough to make a steel worker hesitate. With more tea they sat and looked at each other. They did a lot of that. It seemed to reinforce the bond between them. Each trying to see what the other was thinking. It seemed to be working as very often now they acted in unison, pre-empting the others next move.

"What is on the itinerary for today then Jane?" asked Emily, sitting back, putting her empty cup on its saucer.

"Today is the day we meet Anne Boleyn Emily. I have been thinking about it for a while, as you know. But, today is the day. We'll explore the Tower of London as it is now and then we'll sneak back in time. I really, really just want to see her. No-one else has this opportunity and I just feel drawn to it. Everything I have learnt, read and investigated has been centred around her. She has been the mystery that I, and indeed, most historians want to solve. The documentary evidence about her life is very sketchy. Henry VIII destroyed most of it and it is only the odd scrap that exists. Some in official documents as records of events but little or nothing remains of any personal stuff. It's heart-breaking to think of how her life could be pretty much wiped out. I want to see it for myself and this would be a good start. Right before she went to the scaffold."

Chapter Twenty

The Tower

They arrived at the Tower of London just like any other tourists and they enjoyed the spectacle of this majestic piece of masonry. Everything about it oozed history. Every nook and cranny had something to say about its own point in the past. Each stone that was used to build each part had been witness to some of the most significant events in the story of the country. Some spectacular, some gruesome. Some were even unforgivable. But now it was a tourist attraction, all the time maintaining an air of strength and confidence. Its history is now its key feature, there forever, for anyone in the world to enjoy. Jane was familiar with the tower as it now stands. She had visited in the past. First as a schoolchild where the kindling of her fascination with history first ignited. Today, she put that interest down to the enthusiasm of her history teacher at the time. Miss Turner. She was able to portray any event from any period in history with a flair that couldn't help but fire the imagination in a child's head. It wasn't wasted on Jane. She took every word, every expression and manufactured it into a real event taking place right in front of her. Her life, from that period on had been filled with dreams of the past. Everywhere she went, she needed to know, who lived there, what they did and how their surroundings had changed through time. She had the feeling that she wanted to see every part of history for real. Reading about it and imagining the reality of a point in time was one thing, but being able to actually see it with her own eyes was a dream come totally true. She now had that ability, thanks to Emily and Merlin. This was her opportunity to witness all those things that had, in the past, given her doubt, excitement or pain. She could witness anything now, both good and bad. How she was going to share this in the future she was unsure of but for now she just wanted to see it for herself.

"Probably best for us to join one of the guided tours from one of the Warders I think Emily. We will be shown around the tower and its buildings and you'll get to know some of the history. You've never been her before, have you?"

"No, I haven't." came the reply as Emily stared in awe at the buildings surrounding her.

The two followed the guided tour of the tower. Jane just enjoyed being there and learning a few new things but she felt humbled by the events of the past. Events that had changed the future and instilled a feeling of sorrow in her. Sorrow for the apparent abuse and deceit Anne Boleyn suffered. All at the hands of two very powerful men. King Henry Eighth himself and his ever-loyal servant Thomas Cromwell. She even wondered if she could intervene in the past, change things for the better. Having thought about it for a millisecond she realised it would be not only impractical but totally wrong to do. It would change the country to a massive degree. Even if it were possible, Merlin had already warned them about making significant changes to history. The thought left her and she continued enjoying the tour. She marvelled at Emily who was totally enthralled by the skill of the Yeoman Warder who was guiding them with his enthusiasm and skill. Portraying the events of the past in a way that children laughed and parents gaped. Each event was described in its truest form with additional dramatisation to enhance the experience. They had their lunch at a picnic bench on a quiet grassed area. A delightful cream tea was enjoyed as they sat in the sun, keeping an eye on the ever-watchful Ravens parading the grounds looking for titbits and exuding their status as the guardians of the tower.

"What do you think Emily?" asked Jane, about to take a bite of her raspberry jam and fresh cream scone.

"Oh, jam first Jane, definitely."

"No, no, what about the tower? What do you think of the tower?"

"Oh, sorry. It's amazing. I knew that there was a lot to learn here but how can you take in nearly a thousand years of history in a couple of hours? There is so much here, I never quite realised, and I can see your fascination for history when you come to a place like this. Mind you, the Warden was brilliant. Did you see the children? They were loving it."

Jane was in her element. Surrounded by some of the most important events in British history but there was one period she was most interested in and that was the imprisonment of Anne Boleyn who had, on second of May in 1536, been accused of adultery and treason. Anne and the five men she had purported to have contrived these crimes with, were imprisoned in the tower. The five men, Mark Smeaton, George Boleyn, who was Anne's own Brother, together with Henry Norris, Sir Francis Weston and William Brereton were held in the tower but Anne was confined to the Queens apartments where, ironically, she had spent her time prior to her coronation only three years before. All these things had been documented over the years. Speculation and rumour had, unfortunately tainted the truth which no-one actually knew for sure. For the most part the events leading up to Anne's demise were correct as these had taken place under strict supervision. This was mainly to ensure a conviction and sentence. All went through the trial procedure which was merely a formality as, in those days, offenders were guilty and innocence had to be proved. This, of course did not happen as the path to destruction had been laid by Thomas Cromwell, probably on the orders of his master. He also had his own agenda due to the disagreements they had had in the past. He did not like Anne, never had. They considered each other a mutual threat. Unfortunately, as Cromwell was acting on the King's wishes, his threat became reality for poor Anne. Jane desperately wanted to see the truth and she was determined to visit Anne whilst she was incarcerated. She now had the opportunity to corroborate every event in Anne's life and was feeling quite excited about what they had come to see. Emily sat back on the bench, wiping away the residual jam and cream from her face, smiling broadly.

"That was pretty good don't you think Jane?" she asked looking across the table at the catatonic figure sat opposite. "Jane!" she said more firmly, leaning closer to make herself heard, smacking her hand on the bench.

"Oh, sorry. What?" came the reply as Jane jumped.

"I said, these scones are pretty good."

"Oh, yes, yes." said Jane absently.

"Oh, come on, can we have a little more enthusiasm." said Emily, slightly frustrated.

"I'm sorry Emily. Yes, they really are nice." Jane was now giving Emily her full attention and looking down at her own unfinished morsel, all the time aware that Emily had greedy eyes on it. "Before you ask. You're not having it. I'm enjoying it thank you very much."

Emily looked despondent. Disappointed that she couldn't finish the scone and had to sit and watch Jane savour the last bites.

"Shall we start our own 'tour'?" asked Jane, a sinister smirk sneaking across her face.

"It's what we really came here for isn't it? Came the response bluntly. "Where exactly are we going?"

"Not far Emily. We are already in the inner ward. Or, at least what remains of it. We're sat just north of what was the Great Hall. This, in itself was an important building as it was where the trials of Anne and the five men took place. What we need to do now is find a quiet corner where we can disappear without anyone noticing."

They collected their bits and pieces and put all their rubbish in the bin, all the time looking around for a safe place to start their next adventure.

"Let's go down there Emily." Jane pointed towards the corner of the area. "Just behind the Raven's cages. It looks quite well hidden down there. As far as I can tell from all the diagrams I have seen it was an open area in the inner ward. That's not to say there wasn't anything there though. We'll just have to risk it. What happens if we do appear back in time right in the middle of a wall?" she queried.

"I'm not absolutely sure Jane." replied Emily screwing her face up. "If we do, the best thing to do would be to come straight back. We'll hold hands for this first go so that if anything goes wrong, I can bring us straight back. You'll feel what this is like and you can try it yourself. In fact, let's practice the time travel thing. You can have a go on your own then. Once you've got the hang of it, you'll find it easy. For now, though, let me do it so we know we're both going back to the same time. Come on, let's give it a try."

They walked down to an area near the Raven aviary and found a secluded spot where no-one could easily see them. They looked at each other excitedly.

"Ready?" asked Emily, holding out her hand. "Give me a time."

"Seventeenth of May 1536 at about twelve o'clock."

If anyone were watching them, they would see the two girls fade and, with a small spark they vanished.

They stood, holding hands and looking around them. They had, indeed appeared in a clear area within what could only be described as a castle. It looked like a castle. A considerable number of buildings had appeared where there were only ruins before.

"How was that?" asked Emily.

"Well, it worked." replied Jane. "I see what you mean about how it feels. Let's just go back to now and then return here. I just want to see if I can do it. Let go of me and I'll think myself back to the present."

Emily tentatively released Jane's hand and saw that she was still there. Jane smiled and vanished. Emily quickly followed where they reappeared in the ruined inner ward.

"Okay, that works, now let's both go back without the hand holding. See you there." said Jane as she disappeared.

Just as Jane was beginning to look around herself in the past, Emily materialised by her side.

"Hah!" she exclaimed. "That's not too difficult, is it?"

"Glad you find it easy." said Emily. It's difficult to describe how to do it. It's more of a feeling than an action. I think you've got the hang of it now though. Right. Now, where are we going?"

They both looked around them surreptitiously as they had not yet got used the fact that they were now both invisible. It was surprisingly quiet. The buildings around them were rugged and adorned with intricate stone carvings. The open area was mainly cobbled with paths constructed of large flags describing the circumference of the open space. Jane couldn't help seeing the resemblance to those in and around Chapwell, satisfying herself that the stones making up the floors and paths around the house were in fact laid in the Tudor period. From where they stood, the great hall was to their right with the elegant Queen's apartments in front of them. To the left they could see the dominating White Tower with the additional structure of the Jewel House and tower. The whole was enclosed by a wall with a walkway and the entrance made up by the Cold Harbour Gate, its massive doors firmly closed and, they now noticed, guarded by armed men, their main weapon being a long poleaxe which stood vertical in front of each of them. A sword and dagger visible at their side. As they continued their look around the area, they became aware of more men stood on the wall walkway, similarly armed. Within the courtyard there was very little movement. Each of the buildings exuded a column of smoke from the various chimneys, the still air permitting it to curl undisturbed into the cloudy sky making for a very peaceful atmosphere. Jane was aware that somewhere within these walls, Anne Boleyn was awaiting her fate. She needed to see this for herself. She felt frightened of what she may witness. It would be something that no-one else had the privilege of being able to do but inside she was humbled by the enormity of what she was capable of now. She took Emily's hand and with no words guided her towards the entrance to the Great Hall. This stood to their right. A grand entrance porchway suitably guarded by armed men. They carefully passed this initial hurdle and stood before the massive oak door. It, too was framed by a pair of guards. They quietly moved through the door to stand in the immense space that was the Great Hall. They both stood amazed at what they could see. Any thoughts of a lack of extravagance were quickly dispelled as they took in the elaborate decoration. From the intricately tiled floor with coloured patterns perfectly glazed, to the huge pillars holding up the delicately carved roof. The walls were adorned with colourful tapestries denoting stories and legends of the past. They walked forward, noting the huge trestle style tables lining the sides, bench seats awaiting the next person to sit for a feast. The right-hand wall was dominated by the biggest fireplace Jane had ever seen. It was enormous, fully twenty feet wide and ten feet tall. A pile of glowing logs sat crackling in the silence of the enormous open space. The windows, high up on each side allowed light to enter the hall, augmented by great candle stands placed strategically around the room, flickering shadows on the stonework and wood. At the end of the Hall was a table set high on a platform. It spread the entire width of the room with a pair of massive chairs at its centre. This was where the King and Queen took their food on occasions that demanded their presence. Each side of them, important officers of state, religious figures would sit, humble to their majesties. The two girls were stunned into complete silence, overawed at the extent of the lavish decoration.

"Where would the Queen be?" asked Emily, breaking the silence.

"She'll probably be in the Queens apartments. We need to find a way to get there. I know there is an entrance from the courtyard outside but there may be one from here. Let's try the door over there in the corner." she said, making her way to the left-hand corner where a doorway invited exploration. They moved through the door into a small hallway with a window to the left. To the right was a spiral staircase that disappeared into the vaulted ceiling and opposite was another doorway. This was the door they chose, each moving carefully through it into what appeared to be a storeroom of barrels and chests. Sacks were stacked in one corner. A desk sat to one side where documents sat. Some rolled, some held down by paperweights. A candlestick stood in the centre, its candle burnt down, the wax trail down its side and onto the wood indicated extended use.

"I would love to just sit and go through this stuff. Just to see what was here but we need to find our way to the Queen's apartments." said Jane, turning round but taking a quick look back as she did so.

They carefully climbed the spiral stairs to the next level where a small landing with a window to one end gave a view over the courtyard and another doorway. They could hear voices in the room behind the door. Emily slowly pushed her head through it and then disappeared. Jane followed. The room was quite large. About forty feet long and twenty feet wide. It was dominated by a large fireplace at the back and three windows on the courtyard side. In the centre was a huge, robust table. The surface was strewn with documents, pewter plates and goblets. Four men dressed as Jane expected, in classic Tudor clothing, surrounded the table, a heated discussion going on with a lot of finger-pointing and document shuffling. Jane could not understand what was being said. There were snippets that she did understand. She heard the word 'guards' and 'two hundred' which she immediately linked with what she had read during her studies where Anne Boleyn was escorted by two hundred guards on her last walk to the scaffold.

"This is amazing Emily. They are discussing the guarding of the route Anne will take in a few days' time. I am hearing and seeing history being made, right in front of my eyes. If I died now, I wouldn't mind. This is incredible."

"Remember Jane. You can't die now. You are immortal, just like me. Get used to it. This is your life now, embrace it, take advantage and enjoy it."

"Come on Emily, there's a door at the other end. I reckon that will go in the right direction for the Queen's apartments."

They reluctantly left the conversation and went through the end door. Now they found themselves on a large landing. To the courtyard side there was a large door which was attended by a guard on either side. Jane poked her head through the door and could see a wooden staircase leading back down to the cobbles. The base, of which was, too, guarded. The only option was to go through the only other door on the landing which led them closer to where Jane thought the Queen may be. The next room was lavishly decorated with painted ceilings and walls, tapestries telling stories of the past adorned the walls providing vivid colours. Again, a large fireplace sat at one end. Large oak dressers were positioned at each side and a table in the centre sat surrounded by elegant oak chairs with velvet seat cushions denoting the extravagance of the furnishings.

"What do you think this room is Jane?" asked Emily.

"Not really sure but it could be the dining chamber."

They continued through the next door where they were presented by even more lavish decoration. This room was totally dominated by a huge, heavy, oak four-poster bed.

"Wow!" exclaimed Emily walking towards the bed.

"I know what you are thinking Emily. Don't okay, just don't."

"Spoilsport."

I don't care, you are not jumping on what is obviously Anne Boleyn's royal bed. That would be plain rude."

A disappointed Emily wandered around the bed, gently touching its soft covers. Pressing her hand into it she felt how soft it was. To her it looked endlessly comfortable. She ran her hands around the massive oak uprights, touching the intricate carvings. Looking up, she could see how opulent the bed was with velvet side curtains lined with a darker material all swept up and tied to the uprights. At the base of the bed there was a huge chest. Emily was itching to see what was inside but Jane stopped her as she reached down.

"Emily. Will you stop it. We are here to observe. We mustn't touch stuff. Certainly not move anything. Who knows what effect it would have. Imagine if you lifted the lid on that and someone walked in while you were doing it. It would scare them to death and another legend would begin about Anne Boleyn's 'haunted bedchamber'."

"Okay." Came the response. "Sorry, I wasn't thinking. I've never been in this position before, it's as new to me as it is to you."

"All the more reason we need to be careful. Come on let's see what's next door."

The next room was slightly smaller and contained the now ubiquitous fireplace and a large number of stout chests with two heavy decorated wardrobes. Small tables were topped with carved boxes and under the window, a delicate dressing table which had on it a comb and brush and other unknown objects. A number of chairs were scattered around the room, with decorated tapestry rugs on the floor.

"Ah." said Jane. "This must be the closet or dressing room. This is where all her clothes were stored and where she was dressed by her ladies-in-waiting. That means she must be in the next room. Her privy chamber where she met officials and discussed business. Not that there will be anything discussed here, she's a prisoner. A convicted and sentenced one at that. Dare we go next door?"

"It's what you came here for Jane. It's your dream come true."

The door which was in the centre of the wall was approached tentatively. Jane pushed her head through and quickly walked on, Emily followed. What they saw was, again, a large fireplace dominating the room, a lively fire burning within its grate. In the centre a heavy table, surrounded by chairs, some under and some pushed back. Candle stands were arranged to best scatter the meagre light emitted by the numerous candles. Jane looked towards the window where there was a central, small table. A number of chairs around it. Stood facing out of the window was a woman. Slightly built, her hands in front of her, silhouetted by the glass, standing powerfully upright. Either side of her were her ladies-in-waiting. One facing towards the window, one hand on the woman's shoulder, her head turned slightly where tears could be seen, glinting in the light. The other sat in one of the chairs, her head bowed. Hands in her lap in a position of prayer. The whole formed an image of a Queen awaiting her fate with her loyal servants comforting and praying for their Queen.

Jane was stunned. She was like a child meeting her favourite superhero and finding they were real. Here she was staring at the back of Anne Boleyn. Her gown was simple but elegant, describing her slight build perfectly. It was in black velvet trimmed with lace around the collar and cuffs. A hood adorned her head in the traditional gable style. On her feet, small, pale coloured silk slippers supported her on the dark oak flooring.

Emily watched on, entranced by the view she had of history live in front of her.

Jane caught her breath. The Queen moved slightly, gently removing the hand of her servant. She produced a small handkerchief and tenderly touched the face of her companion, wiping the tears. Jane could now see Anne's profile which was tender and elegant. Then she turned to face into the room, still silhouetted by the window, her features hidden by the shadow. As she walked towards the central table the warm light from the candles lit her face.

Jane's hand leapt to her mouth. She took a sharp intake of breath. The shock of this sight engulfed her. Her hair felt as if it was struck by static electricity, goosebumps spread down her arms and her neck tingled. She felt her legs weaken and crumble. Falling to the floor she landed in a kneeling position. Looking up into the eyes of Anne Boleyn. The Queen loved by her subjects, but here, awaiting her execution. Jane was overwhelmed with emotion, tears formed in her eyes, her heart was beating so fast she thought everyone would hear it, even though she was invisible. The Queen's eyes lowered their gaze to the floor, right into Jane's eyes. Almost as if she was aware of Jane's presence. But the look was vacant. It shook Jane to the core, her mouth went dry, her skin flushed noticeably, a chill leapt down her back.

"Oh, my God." she eventually whispered, staring up at the figure in front of her."

Emily was stood by her side, a hand on Jane's shoulder, also looking straight into the face of this elegant woman."

"Emily." sputtered Jane

"I see." came the quietly whispered reply.

"We have to get back to Chapwell."

Chapter Twenty-One

The Lady Margaret

Jane felt quite nauseous once she was outside in the fresh air. She gulped and fought to breathe, still not quite coming to terms with what she had just experienced. Emily, who had guided the traumatised Jane from the Queen's Apartments, sat her down at the picnic bench having brought the pair of them back to the present day.

"Are you okay Jane? She asked, her hand massaging Jane's shoulder as she sat beside her.

"I, I don't know Emily. I really don't know. I cannot believe what I have just seen. My mind is swirling with thoughts. I cannot get that image out of my head. But you saw it as well, didn't you?" she said, turning towards her companion.

"Yes, I saw exactly what you saw. It didn't have the same effect on me as it has you but, equally, I am totally baffled by the experience."

"Let me try an rationalise this, for my own sake. What we saw was, we thought, Anne Boleyn, incarcerated."

"That is how I see it." confirmed Emily.

"But how can that be? The person we saw was the Lady Margaret Chapwell. I am absolutely certain of that."

"Again, I can confirm that."

"But." said Jane hesitantly, her mind trying to make sense of what she saw, or, thought she saw. "Then, where was Anne Boleyn?"

"I think you need to answer that one yourself Jane. You know the answer. I have the answer. You just need to say it."

They looked directly at each other, daring the other to state, what was now becoming more and more obvious, but difficult to believe.

"Well," said Jane, calming down, swallowing, even though her throat was dry. "It means that either we saw Anne Boleyn in her chamber a few days before her execution, or we saw the Lady Margaret Chapwell in that very same chamber."

"Come on Jane, there is another explanation and you know it."

"I know, Emily, I know, but that is ridiculous."

"But is it? Really?"

"If it is, then the Lady Margaret that we met at Chapwell is not who she says she is, but is really Anne Boleyn."

"There, that wasn't too difficult, was it?"

"No." replied Jane. "But impossible. It cannot be. How can it be? We just saw..." Jane's demeanour changed. Her face flushed; her eyes watered and she started to shake. "We just saw Anne Boleyn in her chamber, but we know that we also saw an identical person living at Chapwell, days, well, weeks after Anne Boleyn was executed."

"That is the conclusion I came to Jane. These two people, the Anne Boleyn we just saw and the Lady Margaret who we will see a few days from now at Chapwell, are the same person."

Jane was still shaking. "Let me get you a cup of tea, I won't be a minute." said Emily getting up. "See if you can calm down a bit, take a rest and try not to think about it for a minute. Wait there."

Emily shot off across the green towards the café.

Within a few minutes two paper cups were held between their hands, Jane's less stable than Emily's. A pack of biscuits sat in front of them which Emily tore open. "Here, have a biscuit Jane." she said, offering her the packet. Jane absently took one, her concentration still firmly embedded in the mystery she now needed to solve.

She nibbled at the edge of one, her expression constantly changing as she looked into the sky, her hand still clamped to the tea. She took a sip and then adjusted her position on the bench to face Emily directly.

"The only thing I can come up with is this." She hesitated, not quite believing in herself what she was about to say. "Anne Boleyn was not executed. How that can possibly be, I really don't know but with the evidence and facts we have, it is the only explanation. Either that or there are two of them and I am barking up the wrong tree."

"Well, that, my dear, dear Jane is what we need to find out. Isn't it?"

"But," said Jane, her face, again reflecting the intense concentration she was applying to the problem. "All the historical documentation, evidence, truth even and theory all point to the fact that she was executed. Right here, within the grounds of this very location. Actually, if you turn around you can see the exact spot where it happened." She pointed over towards the historical location of the scaffold where the execution took place. "Do you think Emily...?"

"What?"

"That this is one of those mysteries we have been given to solve?"

"Could be, it's hard to know really. If it is, then you have been tasked with this since you were a little girl."

"Exactly, Emily. This, I think, is how these tasks are going to manifest themselves." she said, hand gestures emphasising her thoughts. "I mean, we did not come here to the Tower for any reason, other than the fact that I always dreamed of meeting Anne Boleyn and, now, given the opportunity we have done exactly that. Well, sort of. It seems we have met two and I think we have a mystery to solve here."

"So, what now?" asked Emily.

"I'm not sure, but it would appear that our next task has just presented itself to us."

Acknowledgement

I must thank Angie at pro_ebookcovers for carrying out my instructions to the letter.

Marissa Lete at marissalete.com for her formatting magic.

Also my Wife, Diane for her support and extensive reading, to iron out the last niggles.

I put a lot of it down to the Coronavirus Pandemic that swept the world as it forced me to spend time at home which was very pleasant and also prepared me for retirement. The Pandemic hit hard and kept myself and my wife in the house for long periods where I decided that the many stories that I had in my head should go down on paper. This is the first.

Bibliography

In the Footsteps of Anne Boleyn Paperback – Illustrated, 15 April 2015.

by

Sarah Morris, Natalie Grueninger

Amberley Publishing; Illustrated edition (15 April 2015)

ISBN-10 : 1445639440

ISBN-13 : 978-1445639444

◆◆◆

The Lady In the Tower: The Fall of Anne Boleyn (Queen of England Series)

By

Alison Weir

Vintage; Reprint edition (3 Jun. 2010)

ISBN-10 : 0712640177 ISBN-13 : 978-0712640176

◆◆◆

This Sceptred Isle : 55BC-1901

by Christopher Lee

ISBN-10 : 0140261338

ISBN-13 : 978-0140261332

Printed in Great Britain
by Amazon